STEELE

13

ON THIN ICE

A
LAKESHORE U
STORY

ON THIN ICE

LAKESHORE U

L A COTTON

Published by Delesty Books

Edited by Kate Newman
Proofread by Sisters Get Lit.erary Author Services

LAKESHORE U

Bite the Ice
A Lakeshore U Prequel Story

Ice Burn
A Lakeshore U Story

Break the Ice
A Lakeshore U Story

On Thin Ice
A Lakeshore U Story

Beneath the Ice
A Lakeshore U Story

You alone are enough. You have nothing to prove to anybody.

MAYA ANGELOU

PROLOGUE

MASON

Hot Dog Tuesday was usually one of my favorite days of the week. Some of the guys from the team stayed in a house just off campus and grilled out. It wasn't a whole team thing. It was invite only—a few select players who were more like brothers than teammates.

I loved my team—the Lakeshore U Lakers—but I loved these guys the most.

Today was different, though.

Today Austin's little sister Aurora and her friend had joined us. *Crashed more like,* I quashed the thought as I glared over at Rory's friend Harper.

Blonde. Slim. Annoyingly pretty. She'd strolled into the yard like she fucking owned the place, sitting with us and talking hockey like she knew everything about it.

So her old man was a big deal back in the day. Didn't mean shit. She was a puck bunny through and through, all too happy to use her connections to bag a Laker.

And I was so over that shit.

"How was your day?" Austin asked his sister.

"It was fine."

"Don't be shy, Rory," Harper simpered. "Tell him about your big news."

"W-what?" Everyone stared at Rory as she turned firetruck red.

"Yeah, shortcake, why don't you tell us all your big news." Noah's eyes twinkled with interest. The guy was so fucking obvious despite insisting he wasn't interested.

"It was nothing," she said, ducking her head.

"Oh, come on," he teased, "don't be shy."

"Aurora has a date," Harper blurted. "Well, she will when we track the coffee shop cutie down and tell him she would love to go out with him." She clapped her hands together like a proud parent, and I had to refrain from groaning at her theatrics.

"Harper," Rory hissed. "It's not... it wasn't..."

"Big whoop," I mumbled. "Can we eat now?"

"You don't have to be so rude," blondie snapped at me, and my eyes narrowed.

"Sorry, who the fuck are you again?"

"I'm Aurora's friend, and you're an asshole, Mason Steele."

So she knew me—no big surprise there. The bunnies made a habit of learning all the important things. Name. Height. Hockey stats… Dick size.

"Friend, sure," I scoffed. "Because we all want a friend who sells us out to our brother and his friends. Way to go, blondie." I turned my attention to Austin. "Hit me up with one of those dogs. I'm starving."

Out of the corner of my eye, I noticed Harper smile sadly at Rory. "Aurora, I didn't— I have a habit of getting over-invested. I'm sorry if I made you feel uncomfortable."

"Relax, Rory's fine, right?" Austin slung his arm around his sister's shoulder. "You are okay, right?"

"I'm fine," she said.

"Good." He turned his attention back on Harper, and I saw the lust there. He wanted her.

Fucking dog.

"You hungry?"

"Always," she replied, but she wasn't looking at Austin… She was looking at Noah.

"I think I'm going to grab a sweater," Rory said, breaking the weird tension between the four of them.

And I went back to eating my drama-free hot dog.

"What are you two doing over there?" Austin called over to the girls.

After Harper had gone in search of Aurora, they had returned but kept their distance, choosing to sit as far away from us as possible—much to Austin's disappointment.

The two of them spent the last thirty minutes laughing and giggling at whatever they were looking at on Harper's phone. Noah hadn't taken his eyes off Rory since.

"You know, it's rude to share private jokes when you're not in private," Connor said with mild amusement, sipping his beer.

"If you must know, we're looking at Austen memes."

"Don't look at me," Austin grumbled. "It's Aus-ten, not Aus-tin."

"The author who wrote that Darcy dude chicks go ga-ga over?"

"Yep. We're both huge fans." Harper nudged Rory's shoulder, and she flushed.

"I'm not obsessed or anything."

"I don't get it." Austin sat back in his chair, running a hand through his hair. "What's so special about him?"

"Rich, handsome, and an avid lover of the written word. What's not to love?" Harper shrugged.

"It's more than that," Aurora said.

"Enlighten us, little Hart. Maybe these assholes will learn a thing or two." Connor winked at Noah, and I shook my head. He was so fucking whipped.

"Mr. Darcy is the epitome of a gentleman," she said quietly. "He didn't try to change Elizabeth or mold her into what he thought she should be. He treated people, even those outside his own social standing, with dignity and respect, but above all, he was open and honest, and he loved Elizabeth not for what she was, but who she was."

"Sounds like a snooze fest, if you ask me," I said around an exaggerated yawn.

"You would say that." Harper sneered, and I glowered at her, not liking her judgmental tone.

"What the fuck is that supposed to mean?" An icy chill went through the air.

"Come on," she scoffed, "you all walk around campus like God's gift to women."

"So, you haven't been batting your eyelashes at Holden for the last hour, throwing out major 'I want to ride your stick' vibes?"

Who the fuck did she think she was? She didn't know me or anything about my life.

"I... That is not the point," Harper stuttered, all flustered as she looked at Rory, who had gone as pale as a ghost.

Shit. I hadn't meant to make her feel bad, but her friend put me on edge. I didn't like it, or the way she made me feel.

Usually, I didn't let girls get to me. I was a steel fortress, and that was the way I liked it. But there was something about her—something that got under my skin.

"My stick is always available," Austin said in a lame-assed attempt to lighten the mood.

"That was gross and unnecessary." Aurora pinned him with a scathing look before turning back to Harper. "You ready to go?"

"Go? You can't go, little Hart, it's Hot Dog—"

"Sorry, Con. But Harper has to get back for her shift at Millers."

"Millers' Bar and Grill?" Connor asked, and Harper nodded.

"That's the one. I picked up some late shifts. I'm a night owl, and the extra money helps."

"Nice, but it doesn't mean you can't stay, Rory, baby," he pouted, laying it on thick.

"Another time. Come on," she said to Harper, who followed her up.

"Thanks for the hot dog." Harper smiled at him before turning her gaze in Noah's direction. "Hopefully, I'll see you around."

"Uh, sure," he murmured.

And something about their entire exchange bothered me.

The girls disappeared into the house, and Austin whistled under his breath. "Jesus, she's hot."

"She's fucking annoying," I said.

"You're just pissed she only had eyes for Holden." Connor smirked.

"Fuck that."

He was wrong.

So wrong.

"She's not my type," I said. "I like girls who are less... whatever the fuck that was."

I didn't like the way he was looking at me—all smug and secretive.

As if he knew something I didn't.

Didn't matter though. Whatever he thought he knew—he was wrong. Harper was the kind of girl you avoided, especially if you wanted a drama-free life.

And I didn't just want that; I needed it.

So I ate my hot dog, drank my beer, and pushed all thoughts of Rory's new friend out of my head.

I had no place in my life for a girl.

Especially one like Harper Dixon.

CHAPTER 1

MASON

"Good game, my man." Stu, the bartender, held out his hand, and I slapped my palm against his.

"Thanks."

"Looked a little hairy out there for a second."

No shit.

The puck hadn't even dropped, and some of our players were ready to throw down with the Fitton U Falcons.

But that's what happened when players lost their fucking minds over a girl.

Tempers flared, and tensions soared.

Despite a 6-2 win, Coach Tucker had almost blown a gasket after the game. Our goalie, Austin, was issued a one-game suspension, and Coach made it more than clear if we ever pulled that kind of shit again, it wouldn't only be the referee calling penalties.

My cell phone vibrated, and I dug it out of my pocket, smiling at the text.

> SB: Good game, Mason brother. Well done, although you did miss two assists. Bad luck. See you soon???

I chuckled to myself at his honesty.

> MB: Thanks, bud. I'll try harder next time. I'm not sure yet but I'll call tomorrow, okay?

> SB: Okay. Love you, MB.

> MB: Love you too, SB.

"Who is she?" Stu asked around a shit-eating grin.

"She?" I frowned.

"Yeah, the girl making you smile like the cat who got the cream." He smirked as he wiped down the bar.

The Penalty Box was the team's favorite hangout—it probably had something to do with the fact they didn't card players from the Lakers hockey team. The place was practically a shrine to the team's success over the years: jerseys, newspaper cuttings, and framed photographs of alumni players hung on the walls and littered the big glass display cabinet along the back wall.

But tonight, it was rowdy. A full house, all looking to celebrate with the team on their second win of the new season.

"Not a she," I said. "My little brother, Scottie."

"My bad, my man."

I waved him off, sliding ten dollars across the bar in exchange for my ice-cold bottle of Heineken. But I didn't go and join my friends right away. Instead, I leaned back against the bar, taking it all in.

Junior year.

Shit.

Sometimes, it felt like I'd blinked and missed the last two years. Between playing with the team, keeping my grades up, and traveling back and forth to Pittsburgh, it didn't leave much time for anything else.

I spotted my friend Noah and his girlfriend Rory across the room, lost in their own little world. She'd moved in with him, her brother Austin, and Connor at the beginning of the semester, and let's just say Noah wasn't fooling anyone when he'd said she wasn't his type.

I'd spotted the signs that he wanted her almost instantly. Almost a month later and they were already deep in the PDAs, and I love yous.

I didn't resent him. He'd found his girl, and she was a pretty fucking amazing one at that. I just didn't want him to suddenly think that I needed to meet someone and settle down.

Because I didn't.

Fuck that with sprinkles on top.

Deciding to head over to my friends and join the celebrations, I cut through the sea of bodies, only to be intercepted.

"Hey, Mason." The pretty brunette smiled up at me, all come-fuck-me eyes and legs for days.

"Uh, hey."

"I'm Tasmin. We met at the party the other weekend."

"I go to a lot of parties."

"I know. I've seen you around. I'm a sophomore." She batted her eyelashes, giving me that coy smile girls did whenever they wanted something.

And it didn't take a genius to figure out what she wanted—or was offering—tonight.

"Good for you, Tasmin," I said with a dismissive smirk. "I'm headed over to my friends, but maybe I'll see you around later." I went to move past her, but she grabbed my arm.

"Or we could get out of here? My roommate is away for the night, so my place is free."

Alarm bells started ringing in my head. I knew how this proposition ended, with me at her place, her trying to take a bunch of selfies for her socials with the hashtag 'Laid by a Laker.'

It was a thing some of the puck bunnies liked to do. But unlike a lot of the guys on the team, I had zero interest in being someone's claim to Laker fame.

"Not tonight, Tania."

"Tasmin." Her expression soured, but she quickly pasted on another soft smile. "I'll make it worth your while."

"I'm sure you will." My mouth twitched. "But my answer is still no."

I shoved past her and kept walking, thinking my beer wasn't going to cut it if I was going to survive the bunnies tonight.

"Mase—"

"Seriously," I whirled on the girl. "What part of no don't you— Harper?" My brows crinkled.

She was the last person I expected to see.

"Hey." Harper Dixon, the girl I'd tried really fucking hard to avoid ever since Rory introduced her to the guys at Hot Dog Tuesday a few weeks ago, smiled up at me. "Great game tonight."

"Thanks. If you're looking for Rory, she's over there." I motioned to where my best friend had his tongue shoved down her friend's throat.

"Actually, I was looking for you."

"Me?" My frown grew. I just wanted to have a drink with my friends and celebrate our win.

I didn't have time for this shit.

"Yeah. I... uh, so I was thinking we should hang out sometime."

"Sorry, what?" Strangled laughter spilled out of me because there was no fucking way. "Is this a joke? Did Holden put you up to this?"

"Why would Noah—"

"You're not joking?" I balked, trying to rack my brain for the part where she thought the two of us hanging out was a good idea.

We'd had very little interaction since our first meeting at Noah's house, where it was clear we rubbed each other the wrong way.

Her expression dropped, the air turning thick around us. "No, I just thought that maybe we could hang out since our best friends are together now."

"Why the fuck would we do that?"

Harper was... well, she was annoying as fuck. Easy on the eyes, sure, with all that long glossy blonde hair, baby blue eyes, and delicate features. But she was one of *those* girls. The ones who claimed to love hockey to impress guys. Add in her sharp tongue and over-the-top confidence, and she was everything I couldn't stand in the fairer sex.

"I thought it would be a nice thing to do." She gave a little shrug.

"Are you fucking delusional?"

"I... no, I just thought..."

"You thought wrong, blondie. Just because Holden is banging your friend doesn't mean I want anything to do with you. In fact, I think it would be better if you stay away from me."

Dejection glittered in her eyes as she tried to formulate a comeback. But I didn't give her the chance.

"What? Cat got your tongue?"

Her eyes narrowed with disappointment, but her

wrath barely touched the ice around my heart. "Well," she said. "I can see I made a mistake."

"Damn right, you did. Now run along. I'm sure you'll find one of the other guys willing to pity fuck you tonight."

The words were out before I could stop them, but I saw the second they landed. Harper sucked in a sharp breath, visibly wincing at my insinuation.

"Shit, Harper, I—"

"Forget it, *Steele*," she threw back at me. "I think I got the message. Don't worry. Consider this the last time I will ever speak a word to you."

She turned and melted into the crowd, leaving me with a bitter taste in my mouth.

I hadn't meant to be quite so cruel, but she was everything I didn't have the time or energy for. And the truth was, I had no desire to hang out or get to know her, even if she was my guy's girl's bestie.

Girls like Harper had headache written all over them.

And I had enough of those to last me a lifetime.

I ducked out of the bar before things got too messy. No one noticed. Not that I was surprised. Everyone was too high on the win. Of the season ahead. The possibilities. The chance to redeem ourselves after crashing out of the Frozen Four tournament last season.

The truth was, I was tired.

Bone-deep weary, and it was only two weeks into the season.

Fuck.

I inhaled a sharp breath, letting the frigid October air fill my lungs as I shoved my hands into my pockets and walked the short way home to Lakers House.

As it loomed up ahead, I remembered first arriving at LU. I'd been so fucking ready to move out and into a frat house full of hockey players. To finally have my own space and live my own life.

And it was good for a little while.

Until the guilt kicked in.

Until I realized I couldn't do it—I couldn't be here pretending that life back home in Pittsburgh was fine—that my mom and Scottie weren't struggling.

It's how I ended up spending seventy percent of my time here and thirty percent of my time there. They needed me, and I was determined to be there for them.

Even if my mom fought me on it.

The house was steeped in darkness as I walked up to the door, the rest of the team still at the bar celebrating. I let myself in and headed into the big open-plan kitchen, helping myself to a bottle of water from the refrigerator.

For a frat house, it was surprisingly clean and tidy, thanks to a couple of the guys who were neat freaks.

They got two of the best rooms in the house, and in return, we got a couple of in-house cleaners. Not that I was a slob; I wasn't.

I'd helped Mom around the house for as long as I could remember. It wasn't easy for her to raise Scottie alone, so I'd always tried to do what I could to lighten her load.

On the way up to my room, I checked my phone. It was too late to text Scottie, and I'd already checked in with Mom. I knew they watched my games when they could. If they weren't streamed live, Scottie would tune in to the radio to catch the updates.

His obsession with all things Lakers knew no bounds.

God, I fucking loved that kid, and I missed him something fierce.

My phone chimed, and I half-expected to see his name—it wasn't unusual for him to struggle to stay asleep, even with his medication.

But it wasn't Scottie.

It was Jenni Paulson.

> Jenni: Congrats on the win tonight—I heard you played a good game.

> Mase: You mean you didn't watch?

> Jenni: I was on the late shift. But I just got done. Where are you at?

> Mase: The house. Wasn't feeling it tonight.

> Jenni: Want some company? I can bring snacks.

My mouth twitched. A girl after my own heart.

> Mase: Think I'm going to hit the sack. Rain check?

> Jenni: Sure. You know where I am. xo

I didn't reply. Jenni wasn't needy like that. We hooked up occasionally. No strings. No promises. It was easy. Discreet. Zero drama.

Didn't hurt that she was a fucking stunner, either. All legs for days and feminine curves. And she had all this raven black hair that I could wrap my fist around and—

Shit.

Now I had a raging hard-on and only my right hand for company. But at least my hand didn't want to snuggle or talk, or any of that shit girls liked to do after sex.

Emptying my pockets, I stripped out of my sweater and jeans, and dropped my ass to the edge of the bed. Leaning over, I opened the bedside drawer and grabbed the bottle of lube I kept there, slicked up my hand, and wrapped it around my length, fisting myself slowly.

I hissed out a breath as I squeezed myself on the upstroke, conjuring up images of the last time I hooked up with Jenni. Her big hazel eyes staring up at me as she bobbed up and down on my dick.

But the mental image was all wrong.

Her hair wasn't as black as night; it was blonde like the sun. And her eyes weren't hazel; they were the bluest of blues.

An icy shudder ran through me because this fantasy was all wrong.

All fucking wrong.

Jenni was perfect—the perfect girl for me. Emotionally unavailable. Busy with school and work. With zero expectations of me or us.

So why the fuck was I imagining Harper Dixon on her knees, ready to suck the tension right out of me?

CHAPTER 2

HARPER

"Table's up, Dixie," Chad called from the service hatch.

"Better hurry, girl, or he'll be docking your tips." Jill, one of the other servers, smirked as we crossed paths.

"This is just the shift that keeps on giving," I murmured, making a beeline for the hatch.

So far tonight, I'd been cussed at, groped at, and almost puked on. And it was only nine-thirty.

Working a Sunday at Millers' Bar and Grill wasn't my usual shift, but Chad, the owner, had called me up asking if I could cover. I had no plans, and I'd heard weekend tips were usually triple a midweek shift, so here I was.

Service with a smile despite all the bullshit I had to endure.

"Dixie, let's go," Chad bellowed, making me flinch.

I hated that nickname, but it had stuck, and Chad Redford wasn't the kind of guy you argued with. He paid well. Provided good benefits. But if you screwed him over, you were out the door quicker than you could say, 'Table's up.'

My feet ached, desperate for a little reprieve as I stopped at the hatch and started checking off the order for table four.

"Things good out there?" he asked.

"Still a thirty-minute wait on tables."

"That's what I like to hear, Dixie." He grinned around the toothpick wedged in between his teeth. "Don't forget the steak knife."

"I got it," I said.

I might have only worked here a few weeks, but I'd bussed tables since I was fifteen.

Grabbing my towel, I lined the plates up on my arm, grabbed another in my free hand, and headed for the table. "Okay, we've got steak and fries, a Millers' special with extra pickles, and a chili dog, easy on the sauce." I placed the plates down. "Can I get you anything else?"

"Your number?" One of the guys smirked, making me bristle.

He'd been the same guy to *accidentally* grab my ass earlier.

"Drinks? Extra sauces?" I ignored his question and kept my smile locked in place.

"Come on, babe. Don't play coy. My friend asked you a question."

"And my answer is no," I said, taking a calming breath.

Just smile and walk away.

Smile and walk—

"What, you think you're too good for me?" Groper Guy leered at me, making no attempt to hide the fact he was gawking at my boobs in the ridiculously tight-fitting cropped black t-shirts Chad had us wear. The word *Millers* stamped right across the chest like a neon sign saying, 'here are my tits.'

"Okay, then. If you're all set, enjoy your food." I walked off before he could say anything else. When I reached the counter, Jill frowned. "Assholes at table four?"

"Assholes at table four."

"Why is it always the cute ones?" she mused.

"Because they're sexy, and they know it?"

We both burst out laughing, smothering the sounds with our hands. Chad shot us a disapproving glance from across the room. "Less talkin', more servin'," he grumbled.

"What time do you get off?" she asked.

"I'm on until close. You?"

"Ten. And then I have a hot date with Stefan."

"Ooh, Stefan. Sounds fun."

Jill gave her brows a little wiggle. "So fun. What about you? Got any big plans?"

"After surviving this shift? Hell no. I'll probably fall into bed and sleep until midday tomorrow."

"Freshman life," Jill chuckled, "I remember it well. Oh, my table calls." She gave me a warm smile and grabbed her notepad before heading off.

I watched the guys at table four. Thankfully, they'd moved onto a group of girls two tables over.

Usually, I liked the attention. I liked talking to new people, flirting, and being showered with compliments by a cute guy. But there was something about Groper Guy that weirded me out. And after working at a couple of places far seedier than Millers, I'd learned to listen to my gut over the years.

My mood got infinitely better when I saw a group of familiar faces enter the bar.

I bounced over to my friends. "Hey, what are you all doing here?"

"We thought we'd keep you company for an hour or so before we head to The Penalty Box to meet the guys," Aurora said.

"Come on. I'll get you a table next to the bar." I beckoned for the girls to follow.

Aurora was an English major like me, and we'd hit it off the first week of the semester. But I was surprised to see her here without her new beau, none other than Noah Holden, star right-winger for the Lakers hockey team.

"The guys are busy?" I asked them.

Ella and Dayna also dated hockey players. Aiden Dumfries and Connor Morgan, to be precise. The only three girls on campus to lockdown a Laker each, and I'd somehow managed to befriend them.

"Coach Tucker wanted to debrief after the weekend's games." Rory blushed.

"I would have paid to be a fly on that wall," Ella snickered.

"Are they in trouble?" I asked.

Noah and Rory's brother Austin had gotten into it with a few of the Fitton U's players on Friday, and I'd heard the second game was intense. Rory's ex, who was a cheating scumbag, played for the Falcons, so I didn't blame them for throwing down. I'd wanted to go down onto the ice and give him a piece of my mind too.

How anyone could ever hurt someone as quiet and inoffensive as Aurora Hart was beyond me.

"Austin wasn't happy being benched," Rory said. "But he did throw the first punch."

"Could have been worse." I shrugged.

"I still can't believe they did it."

"Seriously?" Ella chuckled. "Noah punched Abel Adams in the face after one week of knowing you, are you really surprised he—"

"What?" Aurora's eyes grew as wide as saucers.

"You didn't know?"

"No, I didn't." Her cheeks burned. "He really did that?"

"Yeah, after the costume party, remember? He told Connor that Abel said some things, and he just lost it."

"Oh my God."

"He knew, even then." Dayna smiled.

"Knew?"

"Yeah, that he wanted you."

The three of them began discussing Aurora and Noah's whirlwind relationship, and a pang of jealousy struck me in the chest.

It wasn't that I wanted Noah because I didn't. Okay, maybe I had at first. What girl on campus wouldn't? He was gorgeous and charming and, if the rumors were to be believed, dynamite between the sheets. But it wasn't about Noah.

I'd just never had *that*.

I had hookups—probably too many. But I'd never seriously dated a guy.

I was what guys called 'too much.'

Too talkative.

Too keen.

Too honest.

Too *everything*.

I tried to rein myself in. To be *less*. But when you'd spent most of your childhood having to fight for every scrap of attention you could get, it was hard to break the habit of a lifetime.

"What do you think, Harper?"

"Sorry, what?" I blinked over at Aurora.

"Are you okay?" she asked, and I forced a smile.

"I'm fine. Can I get you some drinks?"

"Uh, sure." She studied me, and I smiled wider.

Thankfully Ella and Dayna gave me their drink orders, oblivious to the strange tension between us, so she added, "Just a water, please."

"Coming right up."

I got their drink order and returned right as Aurora was whispering something to her friends.

"Oh my God," Ella said. "Good for you, babe. I'm so freaking happy for you."

"What's going on?"

"Rory was just telling us that Noah gave her multiple—"

"Ella!" Rory blushed, clapping her hand over Ella's face. "Oh look, the drinks are here. Thanks."

"Come on, babe." Ella peeled her fingers away, laughing. "We're all friends. And I'm sure Harper wouldn't mind living vicariously through you since she wanted to take Noah's stick for a spin."

I wanted the ground to open up and swallow me whole. My face must have said it all because Dayna offered me a sympathetic smile.

"Ignore her, Harper. Ella talks too much after a drink or two."

"What? I was joking." Ella's expression dropped. "It was a joke. You know that, right, babe?"

"Sure." I smiled. "It's all good. Rory knows how happy I am for her and Noah."

And I was.

She deserved nothing but good things.

I'd never wanted to date Noah; I'd wanted to sleep with him. There was a difference.

"I'd better go check on my tables," I said. "But if you need anything, just holler."

Aurora watched me carefully.

A little too carefully.

I gave her a small, forced smile and headed for one of my tables. She was my first friend at Lakeshore U— my only friend, really.

Now she was in love.

She'd found her person.

And I'd lost mine.

No, that wasn't true. Aurora wouldn't abandon me. She was good and kind and genuine. She wasn't the type of girl to drop her friends for a guy.

It didn't stop me from keeping myself busy, though —stealing glances at her and the girls as I found ways to fill my time. They tried to call me over to pull me into their conversation. But I couldn't do it.

I couldn't—

"Harper?"

I whirled around and came face-to-face with Aurora. "Hey," I stumbled over my surprise. "What's up?"

"Is everything okay? We've been here almost an hour, and you've barely had time to talk to us."

"We're short-staffed," I said. "Sorry, I—"

"It's fine. Maybe we should go and let you focus. I

thought it would be a nice surprise." She looked away, crestfallen, and I felt like an awful person.

"No, don't go. It's me. I'm sorry. It's been the shift from hell."

"You should have said... we didn't have to—"

"Rory?"

"Yeah?"

"I'm glad you came."

Her concern melted into a big smile. "You could always come with us, I'm sure—"

Just then, the door to the bar swung open, and a big group of guys ambled into the bar, and Aurora let out a little squeak.

"Rory, baby." Connor slung his arm over her shoulder. "Dixon." He winked at me.

"Hey, Connor," I chuckled because the guy was a big goofball who you couldn't help but warm to.

"I thought we were meeting you there," Aurora said.

"Change of plan. TPB was a little overcrowded if you catch my drift. So we thought we'd hang here instead."

"H-here?" I choked out. The hockey team didn't hang out at Millers' Bar and Grill. Not en masse, anyway.

"Dixie," Chad bellowed, and Connor grinned.

"Dixie?"

"Don't ask," I murmured, hoping he'd drop it. "I'd

better go and see what he wants." Hurrying over to the service hatch, I asked, "What?"

"Tell me I'm seeing what I think I'm seeing." Dollar signs danced across his eyes. "Did Connor Morgan and half of the Lakers hockey team just walk into my bar?"

Glancing over my shoulder, I confirmed that Connor had, in fact, brought some of the guys with him. Aiden Dumfries. Noah Holden. A couple of the rookie players. And... *him*.

Mason Steele.

My stomach dipped at the sight of the Lakers' arrogant, smug left-winger.

"You've been holding out on me, Dixie," Chad added, and I gawked at him.

"What?"

"You know them. You know them, and you didn't think to lure them away from The Penalty Box to my fine establishment."

"Chad, come on. They're not dogs. You can't offer them a bone and expect them to follow." He arched a brow at that, and I almost choked on the breath I inhaled. "You know what I mean."

"Give them anything they want. Give them the best seats in the house and keep the drinks rolling. Oh, and take them some snacks."

"Snacks?"

What the hell was happening right now?

"Chad, I don't think—"

"Don't screw this up for me, Dixie. I'm already pissed you didn't tell me you knew them."

"Don't you think—"

"Go. Help Kalvin behind the bar."

"But I'm a server."

"And now you're my new bartender." He flashed me a menacing smile that turned my blood cold.

Chad Redford wasn't a bad guy per se; he just wasn't a nice guy. As a ruthless business owner, he cared more about profit than anything else. But I needed the money, so I couldn't afford to piss him off.

"Dixie," Connor called with a knowing twinkle in his eyes. "Get your cute ass over here."

But I didn't beeline toward them. I slipped around the bar ignoring him and cast Kalvin a weak smile. "Need a hand?"

"This is new," he murmured, tipping his head toward the Lakers players gathered at the bar. "Friends of yours?"

I shrugged. "You could say that."

"I bet Chad is jerking off to—"

"Oh my God, don't say that. Now I'm thinking... ew. *Ew!*"

Laughter rumbled in his chest. "Come on. Let's serve them before they start growling and throwing things."

Kalvin was a senior at Lakeshore U, but he didn't run in the same circles as the athletes. He was an artist. A creative type. One of the few people I'd met here who didn't worship the ground the team walked on.

"Okay, guys, what can we get you?" I asked, flashing them my best 'Welcome to Millers' smile.

"Six bottles of Heineken and whatever the girls are having," Connor slapped some bills down on the counter.

"Actually, I'll have a Jack and Coke," Mason said.

"You sure that's a good idea?" Connor frowned, narrowing his eyes at his friend.

"Something tells me I'm going to need it." Mason's cool gaze flashed to mine, and everything turned to ice inside me.

I wanted to disappear. To turn around and leave. But I had a shift to finish.

"Am I sensing some tension here?" Connor glanced between us, his brow arching with amusement.

"Nope. No. I'll make a start on the girls' drinks," I hurried away, my heart fit to bursting out of my chest.

Mason Steele was... well, he was an asshole. Arrogant. Brooding. Aloof. He rarely cracked a smile, keeping his circle tight and his focus one hundred percent on hockey.

And I'd made the stupid mistake of trying to break the ice between us Friday night.

What the hell had I been thinking?

I took my anger and shame out on the shaker as I swung it back and forth to mix the apple juice, schnapps, and vodka for the girls.

"Who the hell pissed you off?" Jill asked, dropping her elbows on the counter and fisting her hands under her chin.

"I'm fine."

"Girl, shake that thing any harder, and you're going to give yourself whiplash."

She wasn't wrong.

I grabbed a strainer, popped the lid, and poured three Appletinis, adding a slice of apple to each one.

"Duty calls," I said to Jill, and she flashed me a knowing look.

"Which one has you all hot and bothered?"

"Excuse me?"

"Which guy?"

"None of them."

"Mm-hmm."

"Jill, I don't—"

"Dixie," Chad bellowed again, and I tipped my head back, closing my eyes and praying to the heavens that they would leave soon.

"Uh-oh," Jill muttered, and it was my turn to stare at her.

"Don't, okay? Just. Don't."

She held up her hands, amusement dancing in her eyes as I loaded a tray and headed back down the bar to my friends. "Three Appletinis."

"Yum. These look good," Ella said, helping herself. "Are you sure you can't come out with us? We've talked the guys into taking us dancing at Zest."

"No can do. I'm on until close."

"That's a shame."

"Sounds like fun."

"You could come after?" Rory added, but I said, "It'll be too late, and honestly, the only thing I want to do after this killer shift is soak my feet in an ice bath and crawl into bed."

"Another time, then."

"Sure." I smiled. "Do you need anything else?"

Connor slung his arm around Ella. "We got good beer, good company, and good bar snacks." He motioned to the little dishes of chips and nuts. "What more could we need?"

"Okay then." I gave him a tight smile. "I should probably get back to my tables. But Kalvin will take good care of you."

I didn't wait around to hear their protests, slipping out from behind the bar and making a beeline for the restrooms.

I didn't see the person coming out of the men's door.

Didn't see *him* until it was too late.

"Watch it," Mason growled, stepping back to put some space between us.

"Crap, sorry. I didn't see—"

He let out an exasperated breath and pinned me with a dark look that sent a shiver racing down my spine. "You should pay more attention next time."

"I didn't mean it. I didn't—"

"Not interested," he said, brushing past me.

His cold shoulder stung. But what did I really expect?

Mason had made no effort to hide his disdain for me. Ever since I started hanging out with Aurora, he'd made it clear that he didn't like me.

I could handle that. I wasn't everyone's cup of tea. What I couldn't handle, though, was the fact he looked at me like he had me all figured out.

Mason Steele thought I was a puck bunny. He thought I pretended to love hockey to get close to the team. To score with any hockey player I could.

But it wasn't like that.

Hockey was in my blood.

It was a part of me.

It was the thing I loved more than anything.

And also the thing I hated most.

CHAPTER 3

MASON

I NURSED MY DRINK, watching the flatscreen in the corner of the room.

"What are you doing all the way over here?" Noah asked.

"Just watching the highlights."

"Is everything okay?" His eyes dropped to the glass in my hand. "You seem tense."

"I'm always fucking tense."

"Okay." His mouth twitched. "You seem more tense than usual."

"I'm fine." I drained my glass and waved it toward the bartender. He gave me an understanding nod and brought me over a new drink.

"Is that a good idea? You know Coach's rule."

"I know my limits."

"Listen, did something happen with you and Harper—"

"The fuck?" I balked at the mention of her name.

"You keep looking at her, and I saw the two of you talking Friday night."

"Correction, she was talking *at* me."

"And?"

"And what?" My shoulders lifted in a half-shrug. "She talked. I told her to fuck off. Life resumed."

"Jesus, Mase. She's Rory's best friend. You couldn't have tried to let her down gently?"

"Just because you're with her friend doesn't mean I'm looking to dip my end there. She's annoying as fuck."

He choked back a laugh. "Say it how it is," he mumbled. "Harper is good people. And her old man is practically Lakers royalty."

"You're right. What a brilliant introduction. 'Nice to meet you, sir. I'm a big fan. And by the way, I'm pity-banging your daughter.'"

James Dixon was one of the best left-wingers the Lakers had ever seen. A legend. A myth around campus. But a chance at meeting him wasn't worth taking Harper up on her offer.

She had stage-five clinger written all over her.

Besides, Harper wasn't my type.

I preferred girls with some discretion. Girls with the ability to keep their mouths shut and my business off their socials, like Jenni.

Most of the guys had no issues hooking up with the endless flock of puck bunnies hovering wherever we went, and maybe I hadn't freshman year when it was all new and exciting and easy. But I quickly learned that most of them just wanted to tame a Laker, to be able to say they were the exception to the rule.

Seemed a little like double standards to me that guys got a bad rap for playing around. At least we were usually upfront and honest. It was sex. Nothing more. It wasn't a guy's problem if the girl he was fucking went and caught feelings.

Didn't mean we didn't enjoy the chase occasionally. We were red hot-blooded males, after all—males who thrived on adrenaline and competition.

The chase could be just as sweet as the win.

But the high soon wore off.

It sure as fuck had for me, anyway. Now I like to keep things simple, off the radar, and under wraps.

"Just... try and play nice." Noah leveled me with a serious look. "She's important to Rory."

"Yeah, yeah." I knocked back my drink. Two down. A fuck-ton more to go if I was going to survive a night out with my friends and their girls.

It wasn't that I didn't like Ella, Dayna, and Rory.

I did.

They were down-to-earth and didn't hang around with the puck bunnies. But too much PDA made me want to scratch my eyes out after a while.

"Zest is cool," Noah added. "And it isn't the usual crowd. You might meet—"

"I love you, bro. But do not fucking finish that sentence."

He chuckled. "I remember saying that once. Now, look at me." He searched out Aurora, something softening in his eyes.

Love.

He fucking loved the girl.

I never thought I'd see the day Noah Holden caught feelings. Yet here we were.

I couldn't resent him for it, though. Aurora Hart was the kind of girl you couldn't help but warm to.

Even if she was our teammate's little sister.

"You've got the look," he said.

"What look?" My brows furrowed.

"The 'what the fuck is he thinking' look."

"Nah, man. She's good for you."

"Yeah." He grinned. "She is. I hate to say it, Mase, but I'm happy. I thought love was for fools, but with Rory, it's like being in love with my best friend, you know?"

"Hey, fucker, I thought I was your best friend."

"You come a close second. Just don't tell Con or Austin."

"You're banging his sister. No way Austin still considers you his best friend." I smirked, and Noah flipped me off.

"Nah, I'm as good as family now." My expression

turned skeptical, and he flipped me off again. "You're a dick."

"And you're so pussy-whipped I'm beginning to wonder if your dick fell off, and you started growing a vagina."

"Pussy-whipped and proud." Connor appeared, hooking his arm around Noah's shoulder. "Isn't that right, Holden?"

"It's not an exclusive club, you know," I pointed out.

"No, but it could be."

"You're so fucking weird sometimes." I downed the rest of my drink and glanced over to the bar.

Only to find *her* again.

Harper cast me a shy smile, but it quickly melted away when I scowled.

"What's the deal with you two anyway?" Connor asked.

"What?"

"You and Dixie? What's the deal?"

Dixie?

What kind of fucking nickname was Dixie?

"There is no deal."

"Oh, there's a deal, alright. I can see it written all over your face. You want her."

The image of her on her knees, looking up at me with big willing eyes, filled my mind again.

Haunting me.

Why?

Why the fuck was this happening to me?

"Yeah, I want her to stay far, far away from me. She's annoying as fuck."

"She's James Dixon's daughter. You're telling me there's not even a shred of you that wants to—"

"No, and fuck no. She's not my type."

"Shit, my bad. I forgot you only hook up with girls who—"

"Who what?" Rory pressed herself into Noah's side, smiling up at Connor.

"Nothing for you to worry your pretty little head about, Rory, baby. Where's that gorgeous girlfriend of mine?"

"She and Dayna went to the restroom."

"What is it with girls peeing in pairs?" Noah asked.

"It's one of life's little mysteries." Rory gazed up at him like he hung the fucking moon. "What were you all talking about before I came over?"

"Nothing."

"Girls, then." Her brow went up, a knowing twinkle in her eye.

"Try girl, singular."

"And do I know this girl?"

"No," I said right as Connor drawled, "You're acquainted."

"Let me guess. Harper?" She pinned me with a narrowed look.

"Not doing this," I murmured, turning my attention back to the flatscreen while Connor's deep laugh filled the space around us.

Once he got something in his mind, the guy was worse than a dog with a bone. I think I liked him more before he persuaded Ella to give him a second chance. He'd been level-headed back then. Sturdy. Dependable. The sensible one, we'd called him.

Now he was jacked up on love juice calling everyone baby and trying to interfere in things he had no business interfering in.

Mainly other players' love lives.

My lips twitched. As annoying as he was, it was fucking impossible to dislike the guy. Connor Morgan was a goofball, but he was still one of the best damn guys I knew, on and off the ice.

"Something funny, Steele?" he asked, and I shook my head, keeping my gaze trained on the flatscreen.

"Nothing. Nothing at all. We heading to Zest or what?"

I needed to get out of here.

I didn't like the way Harper looked at me as if I was a nut to crack or a puzzle to solve.

I'd made it crystal clear the other night that I had zero interest in getting to know her better.

Because I didn't.

Even if her old man was a Lakers legend.

"We ready to get out of here?" I asked, downing the remnants of my drink.

"Already?" Rory pouted.

"We don't have to—"

"Yeah, Holden, we do. You guys promised me a night out," I pointed out. "I'm cashing in."

"Fine. Let me go say goodbye to Harper." She leaned up and kissed Noah's cheek before hurrying to find her friend.

"What?" I barked, noticing Noah watching me, a knowing glint I didn't like in his eye.

"Nothing, man. Nothing at all." He grinned.

"Whatever," I mumbled. "I'll wait outside."

I needed to call my mom and check in on Scottie.

Leaving the bar, I dug my cell out of my pocket and rang Mom.

"Hey, sweetheart," she answered. "How's your night?"

"Good, Mom. How is he?"

"We had a better day, although he's still upset we didn't make it to your game last night."

"Is he up? Let me speak to him."

"I don't know, Mason, I don't—"

"Mom, come on. It's me. Put him on."

There was a long pause then I heard her say, "Scottie, sweetheart, your brother is on the phone. Would you like to speak with him?"

"Mase? Mason?" My brother's voice filled the line.

"Hey buddy, how's it going?"

"I had to go to the store with Mom. You know I hate going to the store. It's too loud, and it smells funny." He made a fake-retching sound.

"Did you wear your ear defenders?"

"Mm-hmm, the ones with the Lakers logo.

"Atta boy. Listen, buddy. I'm not going to make it home tomorrow—"

"No. No, no, no, you promised. Mason brother promised me."

"I know, and I'm sorry, okay? I'll make it up to you. But Coach needs me for something tomorrow. And you know I can't say no to Coach Tucker."

"Coach Tucker needs you?"

I knew that would get his attention.

"Sure does."

"Maybe he wants you to be captain."

"Pretty sure that's not it," I chuckled. Damn this kid. "We have a captain."

"Yeah, number nineteen, Aiden Dumfries. Recruited from Monroe High School, Michigan. Most goals scored in a game, he has one of the—"

"Scottie?" I said firmly, trying to break through his hyper-focused thoughts.

"Yeah, Mase?"

"Do you understand what I'm saying? I won't be home tomorrow, but—"

"You'll make it up to me."

"That's right, kid."

"When?"

I smiled. Scottie liked to know everything. When? How? Why? His brain needed order. It needed things laid out for him.

But sometimes, I didn't have all the answers. "I'm

not sure yet." I went with honesty. "But as soon as I know, I'll tell you, okay?"

"Yep."

The line went dead, and for a second, I thought he'd hung up on me. It wouldn't be the first time. But then I heard him make a soft tsking sound. Over and over.

"What you doing, buddy?"

"Feels good," he said, the sound growing louder and louder.

"Scottie, give Mom the phone. I'll speak to you soon, okay?"

But he didn't answer, lost in his self-stimulating behavior.

"Mason?"

"Hey, Mom. Is he okay?"

"A little agitated. But he'll be fine."

"Dad?"

"Stopped by for ten minutes the other day. I swear Scottie's whole face lit up, and something inside me died, Mase. Gosh, sweetheart, I'm a horrible person—"

"No, Mom. Don't ever say that." Anger bubbled inside me, but I reined it in for her sake. "Scottie has always had a weird hero-worship bond with Dad."

"It hurts, Mase. I know it shouldn't." She let out a weary sigh. "But it does."

"I get it, Mom. I get it."

My old man had walked away a few years ago after Scottie was diagnosed with autism. We'd always known he was different. It had been apparent right from when he was a baby. But Dad didn't want to admit it—he didn't want to accept it. No son of his could possibly be autistic.

So I got it—I got how hard it was for Mom to watch Scottie idolize the man who had walked away when shit got too hard.

"I told him I can't stop by tomorrow, but I'll call as soon as I figure out when I can get there."

"Mason, it's okay to miss a week, sweetheart. You have so much going on with the team and practice and class."

"It's fine, Mom. I promised him—"

"I know you did, baby. And it's commendable. Truly. But Scottie is not your responsibility."

"Mom..." I swallowed over the giant fucking lump in my throat.

"Gosh, sweetheart, that came out all wrong. I just mean, I know how much you love your brother, but you're at college, baby. And you deserve to have the full college experience. I don't want you to keep worrying that I can't handle things here."

"Mom, stop. I'm ninety minutes away. I love spending time with Scottie. Besides, you deserve a break every now and again too."

She let out a soft sigh, but it was laced with pain. "You're a good boy, Mason. And you know your brother idolizes you."

"He's a good kid."

"He is…" Her voice trailed off because raising Scottie hadn't been easy on Mom. Which is why I went home as much as I could.

My father might have walked out on them, but I wouldn't.

Laughter filled the night as my friends spilled out of the bar.

"I've got to go, Mom."

"Okay, baby. You be good, and I'll talk to you soon. I love you, Mason."

"Love you too, Mom." I hung up and shoved my phone into my pocket.

"Everything good?" Noah asked, and I gave him a tight smile.

"Yeah."

"Want to talk about it?"

"Nope."

The corner of his mouth lifted. "You know, one of these days, I'm going to crack you wide open."

"In your dreams, Holden. I'm a closed book."

"Ain't that the truth." He grinned, grabbing Rory the second she filed out of the bar and pulled her in for a kiss.

With a little shake of my head, I slipped past them and joined the rookies—Leon and Ward—we'd brought along with us.

"Tell me again why we agreed to tag along?" Ward asked.

"Speak for yourself," Leon said. "I'll be glad for a change of scenery."

"Running out of fresh pussy already, Banks?" I smirked, and Ward chuckled.

"More like avoiding a certain bunny boiler."

"Let me guess, Madison Macintyre?"

"Bingo. She's taken quite a shine to our guy here." Ward could barely contain his laughter.

"Did you bang her?"

"No, I didn't bang her." He shook his head. "She has headache written all over her. She baked me protein cookies, for fuck's sake."

"Gotta get that protein." Ward was cracking up now.

"You're a fucking idiot." Leon elbowed him in the ribs.

"What about you, Mase? We never see you with the bunnies."

"It's called discretion, assholes," I tsked.

"Oh, it's like that, huh?" Ward chuckled, and I ran a hand through my hair.

"Yeah," I muttered. "It's exactly like that."

Like Millers, Zest wasn't a usual Lakers hangout, but Rory and the girls liked the vibe here.

I had to admit; I didn't mind it either.

Sure, there was something thrilling about walking into a bar where everyone knew your name, and where everyone wanted a piece of you. But it got old real quick, and after two years of Lakers' life, it made a refreshing change to go to a bar and not be hit on from all directions.

"Shit, no one even cares," Ward said as we walked toward the bar, and no one gave us a second glance.

Noah and I chuckled.

"You might have to rely on more than just your skills on the ice if you want to find a hookup tonight," Noah said.

"He's shit out of luck then," Leon grinned, "because we all know he's got zero game off the ice."

"Fuck you, asshole. I bet twenty dollars I can score with any chick in here."

Noah let out a low whistle between his teeth. "Fighting words for a rookie."

"You're on," Leon pulled a twenty out of his wallet and slapped it down on the bar. "But I get to pick the girl."

"What's going on?" Connor and Aiden put their girls down long enough to join us.

"Oh, nothing. Just Cutler thinking he's got game."

"I know I've got game, asshole." He smirked, casting his hungry gaze around the bar.

"Bunch of horn dogs," Connor muttered, leaning against the bar next to me. "Hey, about earlier, the stuff with Harper. I was only busting your balls."

"It's all good."

"You sure? Because I—"

"Con," I sighed, rubbing my jaw.

"Yeah?"

"It's all good."

"You know I just like to give you, Austin, and Noah shit. Although, I guess I can't include Holden now he's wifed up."

"Hey, speak for yourself," Noah glowered. "I'm not the one planning out my future and picking out the names of my kids."

"Fuck off. I was drunk and told you that in confidence."

"Connor Junior and Connie do have a nice ring—"

Connor lunged, clapping his big hand around Noah's mouth.

"Fucking idiots," I muttered to myself, wishing that I could be so easygoing. But I was always tense. Waiting for something to go wrong, worrying about Mom and Scottie, and what was happening back home while I was here.

Doing the college thing.

The hockey thing.

I knew she wanted me to pursue my dreams. To chase after the only thing I'd ever wanted. But I always felt pulled in two directions: one foot in the life back home and the other foot in Lakeshore.

Some days, it was an utter mindfuck.

Because going after hockey—dreams of going pro —meant turning my back on them.

On my brother.

He needed me. They both did.

So for as much as I loved it here, at LU, with my friends and the team, sometimes I couldn't help but feel like it was the wrong decision.

CHAPTER 4

HARPER

I WAVED at Aurora as she entered the coffee shop. When she'd texted this morning and asked to meet before class, I'd almost said no.

Even after a solid seven hours of sleep, I was still exhausted from my shift at the bar last night. But it was Rory, and we didn't hang out as much now she had Noah.

"Hi." She slipped off her over-the-shoulder purse and sat down. "Sorry, I'm late. I was, uh…" A deep blush dusted her cheeks. "Noah, he…"

"You can say the word," I whispered with a grin. "Sex. Rory. You and Noah were having—"

"*Harper*!" She spluttered, her cheeks burning ten shades darker.

"Oh, come on, babe. We're all doing it. Actually," I frowned, "I take that back because I am most definitely not doing it."

Much to my endless disappointment.

I'd been on a handful of dates since the start of the semester, and most of them had ended the same way, with me being friend-zoned or ghosted.

I tried not to take it personally, but it was hard when you knew you were the problem.

"You know," Aurora said, "I saw you and Mason talking the other night."

Everything went still inside me. "That was nothing."

Nothing I wanted to remember, anyway.

"Good. Because for a second, I thought you were doing something stupid like propositioning him."

"Mason Steele? Mr. Arrogance himself? Please, Rory, I have more self-respect than that." I rolled my eyes.

"Maybe you should set your sights a little further than the hockey or swim team?"

"Ha-ha." I poked my tongue out at her. "How is life with the one and only Noah Holden?"

"It's... God, Harper, he makes me so happy."

"You deserve it."

"But don't think I'm going to become one of those girls who dumps her friends for a guy because I'm not. And I'm going to need you, Harper." She dragged her bottom lip between her teeth, hesitating. "Once the team starts going on the road, I'm going to need you to keep me sane."

"You're worried?" I asked.

"Yes. No... A little. Noah is hot property; you know that. And I'm—" She stopped herself, and pride swelled inside me.

Aurora struggled with her body image and self-esteem. But since making their relationship official, she was positively glowing.

"I'd be lying if I said I wasn't a little nervous. But Noah loves me."

"Damn right he does." I grinned. "And girlfriend perks mean you get the best seats in the house."

"That's all I am to you now?" She feigned dejection. "A connection to get good seats?"

"I— Dad?" My brows furrowed as I watched my father join the line with another man I recognized. "Uh, Rory, what in the ever-loving hell is my father doing standing in line with Coach Tucker?"

"That's your dad?" she asked. "The infamous James Dixon?"

"Yep." I bristled, my heart sinking. "In the flesh."

What was he doing here?

Lakeshore U was his alma mater, but he rarely came back here. He rarely went anywhere these days.

A trickle of unease went through me as I sat there, paralyzed, unsure of what to do. Most students would rush over to greet their parents, but we weren't most people, and our relationship was deeply complicated.

"Aren't you going to say hello?"

I blinked over at Rory. "Sorry, what?"

"Your dad. Aren't you going to say hello?"

"I..."

"Harper, what is it? What's wrong?"

"Harper," *his* gruff voice made me flinch.

I turned slowly to be met with my father's cool gaze. In typical James Dixon fashion, he had the audacity to look at me like I was the one who didn't belong here.

"Hi, Dad." I fought a grimace. "This is a surprise. What are you doing here?"

"Came in to talk with Joe."

"Coach Tucker?" He nodded, and I asked, "What about?"

"Can't say too much yet. But it's nothing for you to worry about."

"Dad, come on. I go to school here. If something is—"

"One black coffee, no sugar." Coach Tucker appeared at his side, thrusting a coffee cup into my father's hands.

"Thanks, Joe."

"Ah, Miss Hart, and sorry"—his gaze flicks to mine —"I don't think we've met."

"Hi, Coach Tucker. I'm Harper. Harper Dixon."

"Well, I'll be damned. I see it now. Those Dixon eyes. James." He glanced at my father. "You didn't say your daughter was a student here."

Ouch.

I glanced away, trying to school my expression because I knew the hurt shone there.

Of course, he hadn't thought to tell Coach Tucker about me because I didn't warrant his time or energy.

God, I wanted to disappear into the seat. It was bad enough that I was here on the receiving end of this shit show without Rory sitting right there to witness it all.

An awkward silence followed. Coach Tucker looked expectantly at my father while he watched me with cool indifference. The three of us locked in some kind of painful stalemate.

Eventually, I managed to choke out, "I'm a freshman. English major."

Coach Tucker nodded. "Good choice."

My father tsked. Of course, he didn't like my choice of degree.

There wasn't much he did like about me.

"Well, we've got a meeting to get to, but it was good seeing you again, Miss Hart. Miss Dixon." Coach Tucker nodded, moving toward the door.

Dad lingered, his narrowed gaze making me shrink in my seat. "Harper," he said with little emotion. "I'll talk to you soon."

With that, he took off after Coach Tucker.

I noticed a group of people whispering and pointing. Of course, I wasn't surprised. He was James Dixon. Anyone who followed the Lakers hockey team knew that name and could recognize that face, all sharp angles and icy cold gaze.

"Harper?" The softness in Rory's voice almost killed me. But not as much as knowing she'd heard our exchange.

"I'm fine." I flashed her the brightest smile I could muster, forcing myself not to look out the window.

"So that's your dad?" Her smile was less enthused.

"Yep. James Dixon in the flesh." I glanced toward the door he'd walked out of, trying so hard to ignore the ache in my chest.

You'd think eighteen years would be enough time to get over the fact that your father treated you like a stranger, but that kind of pain never truly went away. Instead, it festered. Growing into something toxic and deadly. Something that poisoned your thoughts and actions and the person you became.

"He's... not what I expected."

"Sorry to disappoint." My lips thinned as I stared at my coffee.

"Do you want to talk about it? I know a thing or two about shitty parents."

"I'm fine, really."

Although, I couldn't shake the feeling I was missing something.

Something big.

Digging out my cell phone, I quickly texted Mom.

> Harper: Why is Dad at Lakeshore U?

> Mom: He is? He didn't tell me...

> Harper: He's meeting with Coach Tucker.

I didn't need to explain who Coach Tucker was. My father was a big Lakers fan. Still followed their progress, reliving his glory days from his favorite armchair.

> Mom: I don't know what to tell you sweetheart. I'm as in the dark as you are. But this is a good thing, Harper. It's been a while since he left the house.

I didn't know what to say to that, my stomach churning with guilt and other things I didn't want to think about.

Before I could figure out a reply, she texted again.

> Mom: Maybe you can spend some time together. I bet he'd like that.

Bitter laughter spilled off my lips. Was she for real?

I didn't know what was worse, having a father who didn't give a shit about you or a mother who refused to acknowledge it.

"Harper?"

I'd almost forgotten Rory was sitting there, watching me.

"Sorry," I murmured. "That was rude of me."

"It's okay." She gave me a soft, sympathetic smile. "I'm here for you. Always."

"Really, I'm fine. In fact, I've been thinking of doing some volunteer work. Something to keep me busy."

"Don't you already have a lot on your plate with classes and your job at Millers?"

"Yeah, but I have a couple of afternoons where I can make it work. And I volunteered back home." Anything to keep me out of the house and away from my father.

"What kinds of things are you interested in?"

"I don't know." I shrugged. "Something to do with kids, maybe."

"Kids? You have more patience than me," Rory chuckled.

"Well, if I want to be a teacher one day, it's kind of par for the course."

"You want to be a teacher?"

"You sound surprised."

"No, I mean... maybe, a little. I just assumed you were heading for a career in journalism or copyediting or something adventurous like that."

"I'm full of surprises." I smiled, and this time it felt lighter.

But I couldn't shake the surprise at seeing my father with Coach Tucker.

Maybe he was here for old time's sake. Or maybe LU was hosting some kind of alumni event, and they'd invited my dad.

Not that I'd ever hear it from his mouth.

"The guys mentioned the Halloween party they always do at Lakers House."

"Bite the Ice?" I asked.

"You've heard of it."

"I have." It was practically a campus legend. Every year the team turned Lakers House, the house on Greek Row where some of the team lived, into an epic scare house.

"It's where Connor made his move on Ella last year, isn't it?"

"Yeah." Rory nodded.

"What are you and Noah going as?"

"How did you—"

"Seriously, babe. There's no way in hell Noah is going to let you loose in a house full of drunken, horny hockey players and frat boys without making it clear as day that you belong to him. So come on, what costume ideas has he suggested so far?"

Her lips twisted in contemplation.

"Aurora..."

"Fine. But he's got another think coming if he thinks I'm going as Buffy the Vampire Slayer or Morticia Addams."

"Oh my God, now that I would pay to see." Laughter pealed out of me. "Morticia and Gomez, that is."

"I don't have the figure to pull off Morticia Addams, Harper. It's a stupid idea."

"Pfft. I always thought Morticia needed bigger boobs." I winked, earning a smile from her. "What about Jack Skellington and Sally? Or Little Red Riding Hood and the Big Bad Wolf. I can see you in a sexy little hooded red dress."

"Hmm, maybe. I'd rather not dress up, though."

"But it's Halloween, and you guys will look so cute together," I pouted.

"You'll come, right?"

"Hell, yes. You know me, any excuse for a party."

After seeing Dad, I was only sorry the party wasn't tonight because I could really use a drink.

"Great. Maybe we can all get ready at my place."

"Uh, Rory, I'm not sure Noah will want me encroaching on your—"

"Not Noah, silly. You, me, Dayna, and Ella."

"Oh, well, in that case. Count me in."

After a full day of classes, I headed back to my dorm room to study.

I'd been assigned one of the single rooms in

Hocking Hall. It was a nice block. Clean and modern with en suite rooms, which was a huge bonus. But I hadn't exactly had a warm reception my first week.

Things hadn't gotten much better as the semester went on.

I pulled out my key card and let myself in, hoping to make it to my room on the second floor without running into anyone.

It was quiet for a Monday afternoon, but I quickly learned that college life was busy. People had classes, study groups, work, or team commitments.

Keeping a quick pace, I hurried up the stairs. But I should have known it was too good to be true.

"Harper," someone called, the saccharine quality to her voice setting my teeth on edge.

"Natalie," I said, glancing over my shoulder. "What's up?"

"No need to sound so worried." Her smile was full of bite. "I just wanted to see if you're free. A few of us are hanging out in the common room, and you never come."

Because I don't make a habit of hanging around with mean girl bitches.

I pasted on the best smile I could. "Thanks for the invite, but I have a ton of studying to do. Maybe another time?"

"Yeah, of course."

With a small nod, I spun back around and marched

up the stairs, only to have her stop me in my tracks again.

"I heard about your date with Mathieu."

Everything inside me went still as I turned to face her again.

"You did?"

"He's in my Spanish class."

"That's... lovely."

Mathieu was a language arts major, and we'd hit it off in the coffee line. But one date and a French kiss later, and I'd already been given the 'it's not you, it's me' excuse.

"Too bad you weren't a good match. But don't worry, he's taking me out tonight, so I'm sure I'll help him get over you."

"Good for you." *Don't do it. Don't stoop to her level.* "I hope you have a nice time."

Her smile faltered, surprise simmering in her eyes.

Girls like Natalie Denham got off on being mean. On putting others down to feel better about themselves. She'd made that perfectly clear during freshman orientation when she'd caught me sneaking out a guy. But it was nothing I hadn't experienced a hundred times already.

Ever since I'd grown boobs and found the confidence to talk to boys, I'd been the target of girls like Natalie's spite. It had never bothered me when I was younger—a time when a girl could be friends with a guy without the whispers and stares and accusations. But by high school, things had changed.

A girl can't be just *friends with a boy,* they said.

I'd lost my best friend Todd first. He started going steady with a girl in our class, and she didn't like that he was friends with me. Then slowly, over time, the rest of our group found their own girlfriends or realized that having me hanging around all the time ruined their chances of scoring.

I didn't get it.

I didn't want to date, kiss, or be with any of them. I just found it easier to relate to them. I liked sports. I *loved* hockey. And I felt more at home talking about the latest NHL scores than hair and makeup and boys.

Somewhere over the last three years, my confidence, my smiles, and my flirtation became my armor. But I knew the deal. I was the girl other girls saw as a threat, and the girl guys liked to have some fun with before moving on to the girl that they might one day take home to meet their parents.

And it was all James Dixon's fault.

With a weary sigh, I climbed the rest of the stairs, ignoring Natalie's heavy stare as I went.

By the time I reached my room, my mood had plummeted—first, Dad, now Natalie.

Checking my cell phone, part of me—the little girl still desperate for her father's approval—hoped to see his name on the screen.

But it wasn't.

He wouldn't reach out. Not unless it concerned Mom. And even then, I wasn't sure he'd pick up the phone and call.

Because I was the daughter he never wanted.

The son he never got.

And I'd spent my life trying to win his approval and acceptance...

Only to know he'd never give it to me.

CHAPTER 5

MASON

I GLIDED down the left wing, ready to receive the pass from Aiden. The toe of my blade cradled the puck as I pushed off my inside leg to deke around one of the D-men.

"Nicely done, Mase," Assistant Coach Walsh yelled as I visualized the back of the net. "Take the shot. Take the—"

The puck soared right past Austin's glove, and the buzzer went off.

"Hell, yeah." Noah was on me in a second, clapping me on the shoulder. "That was as smooth as fuck. Think you can do that again this weekend?"

We had back-to-back away games in Houghton, Michigan. It meant I had to try and get home to see

Scottie before we left. But between class and practice, it didn't leave much time to make the trip.

"Only if you promise not to hog the puck." I smirked, and Noah shook his head, his eyes crinkling with amusement, even though we both knew he'd be the one lighting up the buzzer come game day.

"Where do you think Coach is?" he asked, glancing over to where Assistant Coach Walsh stood with the team's physio.

"Who knows. But maybe he—"

Coach Tucker appeared, and he wasn't alone.

A ripple of awareness went around the rink as a couple of the guys glanced my way as if they couldn't believe their eyes.

"Okay, ladies. Bring it in," Coach beckoned us over to the benches. "I'm sure some of you know who this is. James is a legend on campus, and I expect you to treat him as such."

"Now, now, Joe. There's no need for special treatment. I'm here for one thing and one thing only. To make this team the best it can possibly be."

"Holy shit," Noah hissed under his breath. "Does he mean—"

"I guess there's no use in beating around the bush," Coach added. "I'd like to give a warm welcome to our new assistant coach, two-time Frozen Four champ, and Lakers legend, James 'The Real Deal' Dixon."

"Holy shit," Noah muttered again as the guys began clapping. Abel Adams, the kiss ass, even whooped.

"Thank you. I appreciate the excitement." Coach Dixon stepped forward, his hands sliding over the top of the boards. "This team means a lot to me. Always has, always will. I'm excited for the chance to work with you."

I'd seen countless footage of James Dixon from back in the day with both the Lakers and his short time with the Pittsburgh Penguins. But he looked different up close. Older, sure. But it was something else—a shadow in his eyes.

"I wonder why Harper never told Rory about this," Noah whispered.

"Maybe she did, and Rory just didn't tell you." I smirked, and he scowled back.

"She was probably sworn to secrecy," he said.

"Yeah, keep telling yourself that," Austin added, earning him a hard look from Noah.

A few of the guys around us chuckled, well aware of the situation between the two of them. Austin loved Noah like a brother, and he'd given his blessing where Aurora was concerned, but he still liked to give Noah shit about it.

Couldn't say that I blamed him. If I had a sister, I wouldn't want to see her with my friend and teammate either. Some lines were never supposed to be crossed, and that was one of them.

"Okay, we'll wrap it up for now. But Coach Dixon would like to meet with you all individually. There's a sign-up on the noticeboard; choose a time that works and make sure you show up."

A rumble of "yes, sir" and "you got it" filled the arena.

"Good." Coach Tucker nodded. "Hit the showers and get out of here. I'll see you all bright and early tomorrow morning. Aiden, son, a word."

We all glanced over at Aiden and smirked. He mouthed "assholes" at us before shoving his way toward the coaching staff.

"Well, I didn't see that coming," Noah said as we headed off the ice and into the locker room.

"Harper never breathed a word of it Sunday night," Connor frowned.

"Maybe she didn't want things to be awkward," Leon suggested.

"Awkward?"

"Well, her dad is the new coach. She tried to bang Noah and then made a pass at you." He looked at me, and I pressed my lips together, teeth grinding.

As if I needed a fucking reminder that she'd wanted my best friend first.

I didn't think of myself as a jealous guy. I usually didn't care enough to feel territorial over things. Food. Hockey equipment. Girls. But there was something about our new coach's daughter that rubbed me the wrong way.

"She didn't try to bang me," Noah corrected as we hit the benches.

I already had my jersey and shoulder pads off when Leon said, "Okay, she *wanted* to bang you."

"Who doesn't," he shot back.

"What the fuck was that, Holden?" Austin stalked over.

"Jesus, it was a joke. I'm joking."

"You'd better be because I'm pretty sure Coach wouldn't be too happy if his star right-winger suddenly found himself injured."

"Hurt me, hurt Rory." Noah grinned.

Austin gawked at him, and the rest of us laughed.

"He's got you there, bro," Connor said.

"Whatever." Austin walked off toward the showers.

"She seriously worth all the shit he's going to give you this season?" Leon asked Noah.

"Dude could cut off my balls and string them up above the rink, and I'd still think she was worth it."

"There's the inside of a Hallmark card if ever I heard one. Dear Aurora, I'll love you today, tomorrow, and forever. Even if your brother cuts off my balls."

"Asshole." He flipped Leon off before stripping out of his underlayers and grabbing a towel.

"Jesus, he's whipped," Leon murmured when Noah was out of earshot.

"You guys are dropping like flies," Ward added. "Don't tell me you or Austin are going to catch the love bug next."

"Not fucking likely," I muttered.

I couldn't think of anything worse.

I barely had the energy to stay focused on hockey some days, let alone a girlfriend.

But Leon wasn't wrong—my friends were dropping like flies.

Connor had gotten with Ella last Halloween. And now Aiden and Noah were as good as shacked up with their girls.

But it wasn't in my plan.

The one where I was trying to get through college but spent every second of every day thinking it was a huge fucking mistake.

Scottie needed me.

Mom needed me.

And every day that passed and I didn't go home, the guilt in my chest only grew heavier. Until I was sure, I might snap under the pressure.

I took one of the first spots with Coach Dixon.

If I wanted to find time to drive home and see Scottie before leaving Friday for our back-to-back away games, I needed to clear my schedule.

Knocking on his office door, I waited for his signal to enter and slipped inside.

"Ah, Mason, son. Come in. Take a seat." He sat back in his chair, steepling his fingers. "I read your file. A top recruit from Riverview High School, Pittsburgh.

State record for most points scored by a left-winger. Nice."

I nodded, running a hand over my jaw.

"Modest, too, I see."

"I'm just here to play hockey," I said.

"You're a business major?" I nodded again, and he added, "Interesting choice for a full scholarship athlete."

"Wanted a solid backup plan, sir."

"You don't think you have what it takes to go all the way?" His brow arched as he scanned the papers on his desk again. "Because from what I can see here and what Coach Tucker has told me about your journey with the Lakers, you would have been a second-round pick, maybe even first-round."

"I need to graduate, sir."

"You couldn't do both? Enter the draft last year and graduate? Most NHL teams value college development. Unless hockey isn't what you really want?"

I wanted it.

Fuck, it was all I'd ever wanted.

But going pro meant a lot of unknowns. A lot of time on the road. A lot of time away from Mom and Scottie. I didn't know if I could do that to them, so I decided not to enter the draft.

Being a ninety-minute ride away was bad enough. If I turned pro, I'd be all over the country.

"Mason, son?"

"I love hockey, sir. And I want to win. I do—"

"But?"

"I have responsibilities back home. Obligations I can't just walk away from."

"You got a girl back home?"

"Fuck no. Shit, sorry."

"You're fine." He gave a hearty chuckle. "So, no girl. Family stuff?"

"My brother, sir. He's autistic. It's just him and my mom, so I try to go home and help out as much as I can."

"I can see why that might tug on your heartstrings." He leaned forward. "But this is hockey, Mason. The NHL. It doesn't get much better than that. And just think how much you'll be able to change their lives when you're cashing your first paycheck."

I didn't answer.

I didn't know what the fuck to say.

Hockey had always been it for me. From the second I put a stick in my hand and skates on my feet, it was all I'd ever wanted. But then Scottie started to grow up, and we realized he wasn't like other kids. Then our old man walked out, and I became the man of the house.

I became the one Scottie looked up to.

"I had it, Mason. I had it, and I lost it." Coach Dixon's expression clouded over with regret as he curled a fist against the desk. "We only get one life, son. Don't forget that."

There was something in his eyes, his voice. The

way he stared right through me as if he was looking into his past. A past that haunted him.

I shifted uncomfortably on my chair. "Is that all, Coach?"

"Yeah, get out of here. But Mason, think about what I said. You're good, kid. It would be a waste if you don't see this thing through."

I left his office with a heavy weight on my chest. He made it sound so fucking easy. But it wasn't. How was I supposed to choose between what I wanted and what my family needed?

Fuck, I needed a drink.

"Hey, man, how'd it go?" Austin lingered outside the long hall leading to the coaching staff offices and media room.

"It was okay."

"Okay?" He chuckled. "You just met James 'The Real Deal' Dixon. Tell me you didn't get a little bit starstruck."

"I... it was fine." I shrugged.

"Jesus, Steele, you're a tough nut to crack."

"You going in there now?"

"Yeah. Figured might as well get it over with. See you at the house later?"

"You're spending a lot of time there lately."

"Yeah, well, let's just say it's a little crowded lately."

"Noah and Rory—"

He grimaced, running a hand over his jaw. "Please don't finish that sentence."

"You know they're good for each other, right?"

"I know." His expression softened a fraction. "But I don't need to see them all over each other every second of every day."

"Fair point. Well, there's a spare room at the house still. You could always move in. Spend the rest of your senior year at Lakers House."

"Don't tempt me."

"Shit, you're thinking about it?"

"Yes. No. Fuck, I don't know." He ran a hand through his dark hair.

"Well, the room is as good as yours," I said. "Whenever you need it, you know that."

"Appreciate it, man. Senior year." He blew out a heavy breath. "When the fuck did that happen."

"I'm not thinking about it yet."

"It'll be here before you know it, Mase. And then you'll be making some hard fucking decisions."

If only he knew.

I kept my mouth shut, though. The guys knew about Scottie. They knew a little about my old man walking out. But they didn't *know*.

Even Noah didn't know everything, and we'd been tight since he started LU last year.

I wasn't good at opening up and letting people in because I'd seen too many times how people could disappoint you.

"What's the plan now?" Austin asked.

"Going to head back to the house. Get some food, and get some studying in."

"We should go out soon."

"You asking me out on a date, Hart?" I smirked.

"No, asshole. I'm just saying Connor, Aiden, and Noah are wifed up. Us bachelors have got to stick together."

"Sure. Count me in."

"Great. I'll set it up. We can invite Ward and Leon along too. Maybe a couple of the other guys."

"Keep it small. Less competition."

Joke.

It had been a joke. But Austin's eyes lit up. "Good point," he said. "Just the four of us then."

"Just let me know when and where." I wasn't against hanging out with the couples. But I didn't plan to spend the rest of the semester playing the spare part.

Austin flashed me a wolfish grin. "Catch you later."

"Good luck in there."

"Who said anything about luck? I intend on getting by with my sparkling humor and good looks."

"Let me know how that works out for you." I took off down the hall, unable to shake Coach Dixon's words.

We only get one life, son.

If only it were that easy.

If only I could say to hell with it and focus on my

future and not have to worry about my mom or Scottie. But I couldn't do that.

Because family meant something to me.

They meant something.

Playing hockey didn't mean anything if they weren't happy and taken care of.

And how the fuck was I supposed to take care of them when I was one hundred and ten miles away?

I managed precisely one hour of studying before the noise from downstairs became too much to ignore.

Closing my textbook, I threw my pen down and shoved back the chair, working the kinks out of my neck as I stood. Fuck, that felt good. After being hunched over the desk taking notes on purchasing strategy, my neck muscles were knotted. But it was nothing a little stretch wouldn't solve.

Grabbing my cell phone, I stuffed it in my pocket and left my room.

"Steele, get the fuck down here," one of the sophomores yelled. "We're doing dares."

Fucking idiots. My lips twitched as I hauled my ass downstairs.

"Seriously, you think that's a good idea." I arched a brow at the scene in front of me.

One of the rookies, a guy named Johnson, had a jar

of ghost chili peppers in his hand and a shit-eating smirk plastered on his face.

"Cutler said he can't taste spicy things, but I called bullshit. We're going to settle this the only way possible. He wins if he eats a whole chili pepper without needing a glass of water. If he loses, he owes me a hundred bucks."

"Come on, Mac. I didn't say—" The rest of the guys started jeering. "Fine, I'll do it. But you're going to look really fucking stupid when I smash one of those things without breaking so much as a sweat."

"Fighting words for a bullshitter." Johnson grinned, waving the jar of peppers at him. "Ready when you are."

"Okay." Cutler made his way over to the kitchen island, rolling his shoulders. "Let's do this."

"Fucking idiot." Leon came up beside me. "I knew a guy in high school who tried to do this. He ended up in the ER."

"You don't think you should tell him that?"

"Nah, let him do it." He shrugged.

"Better get a gallon of milk ready just in case," someone hollered.

"Fuck off, asshole," Ward grumbled. "I got this."

"Okay, here goes nothing." Johnson unscrewed the lid. "Oof, get a load of that." He wafted the jar in the air. "How do you want to do this?"

"Fish one out and—"

My cell phone started vibrating in my pocket, so I dug it out and checked the screen. "I need to take this."

"You're going to miss Cutler making a total ass of himself," Leon said.

"Video it or something."

"Hey, is everything okay?" His brows knitted together.

"Yeah, I'll be back."

I left them crowded around Ward and Johnson. As soon as I was out of earshot, I hit answer. "Mom, what's wrong?"

"Hey, Mase." She sounded weary. "Sorry to call you, but he's—" A loud bang echoed over the line, and she rushed out. "Scottie, sweetheart. Don't do that, please."

"Put him on the phone, Mom."

"He's not—"

"Put me on speaker."

"Okay."

"Scottie brother?" He didn't answer, but I could hear him grumbling to himself as he trashed his room. "Scottie, I need you to stop for a second and listen to me, okay?"

"Mason," Mom sighed, "I really think—"

"Scottie, it's me, bud. Mason. I need you to try really hard to calm down, okay? Do you think you can do that? Can you—"

"M-Mason?"

The frustration in his voice made my chest tighten.

"Come talk to me, buddy," I said softly. "I need your help with something."

"My help? What with?"

Relief settled inside me. I couldn't always distract him. But when he was in meltdown mode, he usually responded better to me.

"First, I need you to tell me what's going on, bud. Why'd you lose it just now?"

"Because I hate myself, Mase. I'm clumsy and stupid, and I'll never get a girlfriend."

"Don't tell me you're trashing your room over a girl," I teased.

Scottie had hit puberty, and it was playing havoc with his emotions. But it was heightened by the fact he couldn't always make sense of what was going on inside him.

"No," he grunted. "I told you. I'm too stupid for a—"

"Hey now, stop that. You're not stupid, Scottie. Not even close. What's her name?"

"Brianne."

"She pretty?"

"I like her hair."

"Her hair?"

"It's like the color of that squirrel we found. Remember? When I was seven? We put it in a shoebox and gave it nuts. I checked on him—"

"Every day for a week. Yeah, I remember, bud. So, your girl is a redhead."

"Carrot. Or maybe apricot. But not the skin, the inside bit. If a carrot and an apricot had a baby, it would be Brianne's hair."

Jesus. This kid.

"I hope you didn't tell her that?"

"What? Why? There's nothing wrong with—" He stopped himself and blew out another frustrated breath. "Mase?"

"Yeah, Scottie?"

"Brianne said she can't be my girlfriend."

And there it was.

His trigger.

The reason his room probably lay in disarray.

"Oh yeah? And why's that?" I forced myself to take a deep breath, preparing myself for whatever bullshit was about to come out of his mouth.

"She said I say and do weird things, and it freaks her out." He paused, his discomfort palpable. "She said I freak her out."

"Sounds like her loss to me, bud."

"Her loss? It's not a game, Mase. I want her to be my girlfriend, and she thinks I'm a freak."

"You're only twelve, buddy. There's plenty of time for girls."

"So you don't think I'm a freak?"

"No, Scottie, I don't think you're a freak."

"Okay," he said.

And that was that.

"Can you come home to see me tomorrow?"

"I'm going to come Wednesday, okay? I'm away this weekend, but I can come Wednesday and stay the night." It would mean an early drive back to campus, but I'd make it work.

"Can I come with you this weekend?"

"You know you can't."

"Fine," he snapped. "I gotta go. Mom is crying again. I don't like it when she cries."

Fuck.

"Okay. Help her tidy your room, okay? Now that I'm not there, I need you to help around the house. Do you think you can do that?"

"I hate chores."

"So do I. But I didn't clean my room or take out the trash because I liked doing it. I did it because I knew it made Mom happy."

"I guess I can help," he grumbled.

"Good kid. Wednesday, we can do whatever you want, okay?"

"Promise?"

"Pinky promise."

"Goodbye, Mason brother."

"Goodbye, Scottie brother."

Mom came back on the line, a slight quiver in her voice. "You're so good with him, Mase. When I try to soothe him, it just makes him worse. I hate to say it, but I don't know what I'd do without you."

Guilt snaked through me. Because she was without

me. Every day I was here was another day I wasn't with them.

"Crap, baby, I didn't mean... Listen to me, Mason, and listen good. I've got this, sweetheart. I swear."

"Yeah, Mom, I know."

If I argued, she'd only cry. And if there was one thing I couldn't stand, it was girl tears.

"I can handle things here. You go do whatever a college junior does these days. But not too much of it. I don't want to be made a grandma anytime soon."

"Mom!" I choked out.

Her soft laughter filled in some of the cracks inside me. "I love you, Mason. You and your brother are my whole world. I hope you know that."

"I know, Mom. I know."

Because they were mine, too.

CHAPTER 6

HARPER

"HEY." I slid into my seat beside Rory and grabbed my notebook and pen out of my bag. "What did I miss?"

"Not much; she's just getting started."

"Good. Sorry I missed your calls last night," I whispered.

Despite falling asleep early, I'd overslept. Then in all my haste to get ready for class, I had a toothpaste disaster and had to change my sweater. There hadn't been time to call or text Rory to see what was up. Besides, I knew I'd see her in my first class of the morning.

"That's okay. I just wanted to see if you were okay."

"Okay?" I frowned.

"Yeah, you know. The whole thing with your dad.

You seemed kind of confused to see him yesterday, so I figured it couldn't be easy finding out the news."

"News?" What the hell was she talking about? "What news?"

"Wait a minute," she whispered as a couple of girls sitting in the row in front glanced our way, disapproval shining in their eyes. "You haven't heard?"

"Rory, I swear to God, you're starting to freak me out."

Her expression dropped, and my heart right along with it. Whatever she was about to tell me was bad.

"Your dad... he, uh... he's the new assistant coach for the hockey team."

"*What*?" I shrieked, earning me a few more looks from the other students. "Sorry," I mouthed, clutching the edge of my seat. "He's the new assistant coach? That can't be right."

"Noah told me last night. He was introduced to the team yesterday at practice." She gave me a sympathetic smile. "Why didn't he tell you?"

"My relationship with my father is complicated."

Complicated enough it didn't even warrant a heads-up about this, apparently.

"He used to play for the Lakers, right?"

I nodded, still reeling from the news.

The new assistant coach.

My father was going to work here. With the team. On campus. And he hadn't breathed a word of it to me.

Or Mom, if her confusion yesterday was anything to go by.

"I... I don't know what to say."

"This will be a good thing, though, right? If he's going to be here on campus, you can spend time together."

"I'm not sure he'll want that." The words lodged in my throat.

"Harper," Rory laid her hand on my arm, but I shook my head.

"Please, don't. Not here. I need to stay focused."

"Of course. But if you ever want to talk..."

"Thanks, I appreciate it."

I just didn't know where I would start.

Rory's parents weren't going to win any parent-of-the-year awards either, but there was still something deeply shameful about admitting that my father hated me.

Like if I gave the words life by admitting them out loud, it would somehow immortalize them, and I'd finally have to accept that things were never going to be any different.

I'd have to part with the tiny seed of hope that one day, he would see me for me.

That he would be proud of his daughter.

"I love Professor MacMillan, but someone has got to remove the stick from up her ass," I murmured as we filed out of class.

"I don't know. I kind of agreed with what she was saying. Women have always had to fight to redefine their place in society."

"Yeah, but come on, Rory. It doesn't all have to be some big feminist movement. Maybe Austen wanted to explore her own sexuality through the characters she created."

She gave me a dubious look, and I snorted. "Look, I'm just saying maybe it isn't always about wanting to change the world or tearing down the patriarchy. Maybe sometimes it's about yourself, about filling a void. Or numbing some internal pain. Not everything is a social justice crusade."

"Are you okay?" Concern etched into her expression. "You seem a little tense?"

"I just found out my estranged father is going to be working here. At the college I came to so I could escape my messed-up family. Oh, I'm fine."

"Harper..." Sympathy glittered in her eyes.

"Relax, I am fine. At least, I will be." I mustered up the best smile I could. "Nothing much will change, I'm sure. But I have news."

"You do?"

"Yep. I'm visiting a community center out in Rushton later. They have some volunteer spots open, and it seems like a good fit."

"Rushton? Isn't that like an hour away?"

"Yeah, but I don't want to be too close to campus."

It was silly, but I didn't want to end up helping out somewhere where I might run into people I knew. A decision I was more than happy with, given the news about my father.

I still couldn't believe it. He hadn't held down a job for almost five years. And suddenly, out of the blue, he was the Lakers' new assistant coach?

It didn't make any sense.

We headed out of the English Department building taking the path toward my favorite coffee shop Roast 'n' Go.

"How's therapy going?" I changed the subject.

"Good. It's still the early days, but I like Marlene, and having Jordan to talk to helps."

Jordan was a mutual friend of Ella's. She had an eating disorder too and had been nothing but supportive of Aurora.

"I'm glad it's working out."

"Me too. You know, I dream about being able to eat out with my boyfriend and our friends. But I'm not there yet."

"Give yourself time. You'll get there."

It wasn't the same, but I knew all about feeling alienated when it came to social eating. Being celiac, I'd always found eating in public difficult. Gluten-free options were a lot better nowadays, but I'd had some awful experiences when I was younger. Being unable to eat at family gatherings because no one had catered for the awkward child who needed a special diet. Mom having to quiz the servers about gluten-free options whenever we were dining out. My father complaining constantly about what a nuisance my *condition* was.

Like I could help it.

Like I asked to be born with a serious auto-immune disease that significantly increased my chances of developing any number of serious health conditions.

His arrogance was as frustrating as it was hurtful. But a lot of people didn't get it. They didn't understand that even the smallest amount of gluten could wreak havoc on your body: diarrhea, constipation, reflux, fatigue, and insomnia. Being celiac was nothing if not glamorous, and the prospect of being *glutened* was every celiac's worst nightmare.

Rory opened the door to the coffee shop, and we filed inside. The rich aroma of coffee beans filled my senses. But I was here for the chai tea.

"I'll get these; you go find a table," she said.

I scanned the shop, making a beeline for a table near the back. I'd barely gotten situated when the door swung open, and Noah and some of the team piled inside.

Guess we weren't having girls' time after all.

I watched with that usual pang of jealousy as he slid his arms around her waist from behind and pressed a lingering kiss to her neck. I could practically hear the dreamy sighs of every girl in the vicinity.

Noah Holden was hot property on campus. At least, he had been before Aurora Hart barreled into his life and stole his heart.

He was with Ward Cutler, Leon Banks, and—

Mason Steele.

Ugh.

I hadn't noticed him behind Ward.

He caught me staring and narrowed his eyes, his arctic gaze turning everything inside me cold.

The guys waited in line with Rory, following behind with their drinks when she headed toward me.

"Do you mind?" she asked me sheepishly, and I shrugged.

What else could I do?

It wasn't like I could admit that I didn't want to be anywhere near Mason after he so cruelly dismissed me the other night.

"I got snacks." Noah threw a couple of bags of chips down on the table. "Dig in," he said to me.

"I'm okay, thanks."

"I got the sweet stuff too." He pulled out a bag of brownie bites and added them to the pile.

"Really, I'm fine." I gave him a tight smile, and he frowned.

"Why do I feel like I'm missing something?" He glanced between Rory and me.

"Harper is a celiac, remember?" she said. "She can't eat any of that stuff."

"Celiac? Like you shit yourself after eating pasta and stuff?"

"Seriously, Banks?" Noah grimaced, throwing me an apologetic look. "Sorry, he's not house-trained yet."

"It's fine. It's not a big deal."

"Celiac?" Ward added. "That's when you can't eat gluten, right?"

"Yeah."

"Man, I couldn't live without carbs." Leon rubbed his stomach. "They're my main food group."

"You get used to it," I murmured. "Besides, there are pretty good alternatives out there nowadays."

I peeked over at Mason, unsurprised to find him on his cell phone, completely ignoring our conversation. It was a mistake approaching him at the bar the other night. A bad idea fueled by vodka and false bravado.

The truth was, though, I didn't want to lose my friend. So I'd thought maybe if me and Mason—oh, who was I kidding? We weren't going to be friends. Let alone *more* than friends.

"What happens if you do eat gluten?" Noah asked, but he seemed genuinely interested.

"It isn't pretty. Even the smallest amount can put me out of action for a few days."

"Shit, that's crazy. No pun intended." His eyes crinkled with laughter. "I had no idea. Sorry about the snacks. I'll make sure I get something Harper-friendly next time."

My expression softened. He was a good guy. It was easy to see why Rory had fallen for him.

"Thanks." I smiled, risking a peek at Mason.

He still hadn't looked twice in my direction.

Asshole.

Maybe Rory was right; maybe I needed to leave athletes in my rearview. But usually, they were good for it—a quick tumble in the sheets with no promises of a next time. Most girls hated that. Not me. I liked to know where I stood. It was much easier not to be disappointed then.

"So are we going to talk about the elephant in the room," Leon said around a crooked smile.

He was cute. With a deadly combination of buzzed dark hair and piercing blue eyes, he reminded me of a younger Jesse Williams, staring at me with mild amusement.

"Leon," Noah clipped out.

"Come on, Holden. Surely, you're dying to know how her old man ended up our new assistant coach."

"I wish I could tell you," I said with a half-shrug.

"Ah, it's like that." He grinned. "They make you sign an NDA or something?"

"What? No. My father didn't think to mention it to me, so I'm as surprised as you are."

"Why wouldn't he tell you?"

I shrugged again, sipping my tea, trying to ignore the pit in my stomach. "Your guess is as good as mine."

"I'm sensing some father/daughter tension here,"

Noah said with a light chuckle. But his attempt at easing the tension was lost on me because he didn't know the half of it.

My father was going to work with these guys. Train and mold them. Every day, he was going to bond with them. Laugh and joke and get to know them. He was going to develop relationships with them. Earn their trust and respect. And he hadn't even respected me enough to give me a heads-up about the job.

Because he doesn't care. He never has, and he never will.

I checked my phone and let out a small sigh. "I need to get going."

"What? We just got here." Rory frowned.

"I'm sure the guys will keep you company."

"Sure we will." Noah grinned at her, squeezing her knee. He was always touching some part of her. I'd noticed it was his love language—to show her how much he loved her curves. Her body.

It was cute.

And I wasn't jealous. Not even a little bit.

Liar.

I drained my tea and placed the mug down on the table. "I'll text you later."

"Sure. Good luck with the thing."

"Thanks. See you guys." I gave Noah, Ward, and Leon a little wave.

Mason didn't look up.

And that was fine.

After the way he'd spoken to me the other night, the less we interacted, the better.

I arrived at the Rushton Community Center in good time. It was a cute little place with flower-lined windows and pristine sliding doors.

Since I was early, I stayed in the car and made the phone call I'd been dreading ever since I discovered my father's news.

"Harper," Mom answered on the second ring.

"Hi, Mom."

"Oh, Harper, baby. I'm so sorry. I swear I had no idea. He's been withdrawn lately. Inside his own head. You know how he gets."

"Yeah." I inhaled a sharp breath, trying my best *not* to remember. "So, he's the Lakers' new assistant coach. How does that even happen, Mom?"

"He and Joe were friends back in the day. I guess they must have reconnected."

"Aren't you angry he didn't tell you? I mean, how is it even going to work? It's almost a two-hour round trip."

Mom hesitated, and I braced myself for whatever she was about to say.

"They're giving him a room on campus."

"*What?*" I shrieked.

"It's not permanent, sweetheart. Just somewhere he can stay when he needs to."

"Did he give you a reason why he didn't tell you?"

I didn't add myself to the equation because we both knew I didn't factor into his decisions or actions.

"He didn't want to get my hopes up in case it didn't work out." Mom paused again, and I could sense her discomfort. She didn't like being in the middle, defending my father's constant dismissal of me and my life, and acting as a buffer during our strained interactions.

Deep down, I knew she was holding out for the day he realized that life was too short to live in the past, drowning in *what-ifs* and *could have beens* because he made her feel like she'd failed him too.

He'd wanted a son. Planned his entire life around the baby boy my mom was supposed to be growing inside. Only to be handed a baby girl in the delivery room. And with it, an eternal disappointment.

The disappointment he'd refused to let me forget for the last eighteen years.

Pain rolled through me. The kind of pain that lived inside you, festering in your soul, slowly eating its way into the very fiber of your being.

"Harper, baby?"

"I'm okay, Mom." Because my father's opinion of me didn't define me. I was a good person with hopes and dreams and aspirations.

"I wish things were different, sweetheart. You know

that. But your father is"—*an asshole,* I bit my lip, trapping the words—"a complicated man."

"Yeah. I've got to go. I'm starting some volunteer work today, and I need to head inside."

"I'm proud of you, Harper Rose. I hope you know that."

"Thanks, Mom. I'll call you soon, okay? Love you."

"Love you too, sweetheart."

We hung up, and I gave myself a second to compose myself.

When I was younger, it was easy to make excuses for her complicit behavior. James Dixon was the love of her life. Her husband and the father of her only child, the only child they would ever have. But as I grew, I realized that Mom didn't like to rock the boat. She liked a quiet life. An easy life. And as her excuses about my father's overt disappointment in me stacked up over time, so too did my frustration toward her.

I checked my reflection in the mirror and quickly pulled my hair into a loose ponytail over one shoulder. Then I climbed out of my car and made my way inside.

"Welcome to Rushton Community Center. How can I help you?" The receptionist smiled.

"I'm here to meet Jet about the volunteering opportunity."

"Ah yes, you must be Harper"—she scanned the clipboard on her desk—"I've got you down right here."

"That's me."

"Perfect, take a seat, and I'll let the boss know you're here."

"Thanks."

I moved to the row of chairs along the wall and picked up a leaflet about the center. A frisson of anticipation went through me as I scanned the photos of various groups and activities they provided here. My eye had snagged on a write-up on the inclusive access group for children and young people they ran, when an older man appeared through the double doors and made a beeline for me.

"Harper?" he said.

"That's me." I stood.

"It's good to meet you. Let's head to my office and get started, shall we?"

"Sounds good."

"Did you bring all the information we asked for?"

"ID and references? Yes."

"Excellent." He motioned for me to follow him down a long hall decorated with big noticeboard-style displays, each housing collages of photos. "Francine does an excellent job of regularly updating our displays. We're proud of what we do here and like to show it off as much as possible," Jet said. "You're a student at LU?"

"Freshman."

"How's that going for you?"

"It's okay." At least, it had been until my father showed up unannounced. "Classes are good."

"We don't get a lot of freshmen looking to volunteer. Too busy partying and soaking up their first year of college," he chuckled.

"I like to keep busy."

"I know that feeling. Right, I'm just in here. Come in." He opened the door and stepped aside to let me go first. "I have to admit, Harper. We don't get many inquiries from LU about working with our inclusive groups."

"I want to be an educator, sir."

"Please, no, sir." He gave me a warm smile, taking a seat behind the big desk. "You want to teach?" One of his bushy graying brows arched.

"I do. Middle school, I think. I haven't worked out the specifics."

"Well, we work with a lot of kids here, so you came to the right place. There are some forms to fill out. But once you're done, I'll give you the tour and take you to meet some of the staff."

"I'd like that very much."

"Great, welcome to the Rushton family, Harper. I think you're going to fit right in."

CHAPTER 7

MASON

"I MET A GIRL, MASON BROTHER."

"Brianne?" I frowned. "You already told me ab—"

"No, not Brianne. She's yesterday's news. This girl is older. Super hot. Like those girls in the magazines I found under your bed once."

Shit.

"Buddy, we talked about this. No snooping in my room."

"I didn't snoop, Mase." He tsked. "I was searching for my hockey card collection, and I found a box of stuff under there. I thought my collection might be in it. I didn't know it was full of titty—"

"Do *not* finish that sentence, Scottie. And for the love of God, don't let Mom hear you talk like that."

"What's wrong with saying titty? The boys at school

say it all the time. Fenton Jones said he touched a girl's titties. Said they felt all soft and squishy." He went quiet, and then asked, "Mase, what's a blow job?"

Fucking hell, it was too early for this shit.

I ran a hand down my face and let out a thin breath. "That is something we'll talk about when you're older, bud." *Much fucking older.* "Shouldn't you be getting ready for school?"

"I don't want to go."

"Scottie, we talked about this. You have to go, buddy. School's important."

"All the kids hate me."

"They do not hate you. They just don't always understand you, and that's okay. They can't all be as awesome as you."

"Can I tell you about the girl now? The not-Brianne girl. She had titties, Mason. Nice, round—"

"Scottie, I swear to God, kid. You've got to stop with this titty shit. You'll get into trouble saying stuff like that."

"I don't know what the big deal is." He huffed. "Fenton's dad said—"

"Okay, okay, bud. Time to move this conversation on. We don't talk about girls that way, okay?" Not until he was at least fifteen, anyway.

"Fine." He went silent, and although there were over one hundred miles between us, I could sense the tension emitting from him.

"Scottie, we talked about this. Sometimes, me or

Mom or your teachers have to point out when you're being inappropriate. It's not—"

"I said it's fine. Mom's calling me. I need to go."

"Scot—"

He hung up.

The little shit hung up on me, but I didn't take it personally. Puberty was hitting the kid hard. He didn't understand it for the most part. Just knew he had all these new and strange thoughts and feelings.

I tried to help where I could, but I didn't always get it right.

I'd read every book out there on autism when Scottie was younger. But none of the information could account for the fact that most people on the spectrum presented differently. There wasn't a one-size-fits-all approach, something I'd found frustrating in the early days when I didn't know how to deal with one of his meltdowns or his tendency to come into my room in the middle of the night and climb into bed with me.

As I'd gotten older, I'd realized I was his safe space. Scottie turned to me whenever he was stressed or overstimulated or anxious. It was a fucking honor to be his person. But now I was gone, and he was back in Pittsburgh, navigating his way through all these new and scary changes without me.

The guilt I tried hard to keep locked away rattled inside of me, making itself known.

There was no fucking time to dwell, though. Not

with someone hammering on my door loud enough to wake the dead.

"The fuck?" I muttered, stalking across my room and ripping the thing almost clean off its hinges.

"You're up." Ward looked confused.

"Yeah, I'm up, asshole. We have early practice."

"You didn't make it down for breakfast, I thought—"

"It's cute you care." I smirked. "But I was on the phone with my brother."

"Everything okay?"

"Yeah. Although, it won't be if we're late for practice."

Grabbing my bag, I followed Ward downstairs. Some of the guys had already left for the facility. But a few lingered, hoovering down their Coach Tucker-approved breakfasts of oatmeal and fruit or eggs and spinach. I opted to grab and go, snagging a protein bar out of the drawer and a bottle of water from the refrigerator.

We'd just reached the door when Tipper appeared with a petite blonde in tow. A couple of the guys wolf whistled, and he flipped them off, barging past us to walk her to the door.

"Call me," she said, leaning up to press a kiss to his cheek.

He slapped her on the ass and ran a hand through his mussed-up sex hair.

"Lucky bastard," Ward said. "Where the hell did you find her?"

"Stopped by the student center last night. It was yoga night." His brows waggled suggestively.

"Oh, shit," Ward laughed, holding out his hand for a high five.

"We should make a move," I said, too jaded to be swept up in the freshman's excitement. "Or we're going to be late."

"Yeah, yeah, Steele. Keep your hair on."

With a half-shrug, I slung my bag over my shoulder and headed out.

I needed to get on the ice and skate away some of this tension.

"Okay, here's how this morning is going to go," Coach Tucker said as we joined him on the ice. "I want my D-men working with Coach Carson. He knows the drill. Aiden, Noah, Ward, and the rest of the power forwards, you're with me. Mase, Coach Dixon wants to work one-on-one with you today."

"Okay," I said with mild confusion.

"Don't look so worried, kid," Coach Dixon chuckled. "Once I've put you through your paces, I'll move on to someone else." He winked, entering the rink and gliding off toward the far goal.

"We've got a hard couple of games ahead of us. The Huskies have started the season strong. So don't expect to get the win easily. Okay"—he clapped his gloves together—"get to it."

The team broke out into their various positions. The defensive men with Coach Carson, centers and wingers with Coach Tucker. While I followed Coach Dixon to the other side of the rink.

"I've been reviewing your game footage," he said, skating around me. "You create excellent chances for your teammates to score. Yet, you have a powerful shot, but you rarely go for the goal yourself. Why?"

"There's better guys on the team." I shrugged, not sure where he was going with this.

We all had our roles to play. I didn't shy away from taking the shot if the opportunity arose, but I was a playmaker. I wasn't a goal scorer. That was predominantly Noah's or Aiden's job.

"I don't accept that answer, son." He dropped a puck on the ice and slid his stick toward it.

It was a little surreal, watching James Dixon—a Lakers legend—skate toward the open goal, cutting down the left and picking up speed right before he faked a pass and took the shot instead.

"I played left wing, Mason. And with your speed and skill, you should be scoring more goals. That's what I want us to work on."

"I'm not sure—"

Coach Dixon drew up short, ice spraying up from

his perfectly executed stop. He might have retired early through injury, but clearly hadn't lost his knack on the ice.

"I watched that game footage, Mason, and do you know what I saw?"

I kept quiet, a little rocked by this whole encounter.

"I saw a guy withholding his potential. A guy on the verge of great things, but not if he doesn't master his full capabilities. Coach Tucker wants the Lakers to go all the way this season. You're an integral part of the team, but you're not working to your full potential."

"With all due respect, sir, I'm not sure—"

"You get one shot, Mason. One shot at making this happen. To make your future happen. Look me in the eye, and tell me you don't want it." His eyes narrowed, waiting, daring me to prove him wrong.

But I couldn't.

I couldn't do it. Because, of course, I fucking wanted it. I just didn't see a way to make it work. So yeah, I played in the background, letting my teammates skate into the spotlight.

"Thought so." A knowing smile tugged at the corner of his mouth, and for a second, I saw Harper smiling back at me.

Fuck.

Not a visual I *ever* needed to see.

Blinking away the intrusive and definitely unwanted thought, I cleared my throat. "What are we working on then, Coach?"

Another knowing grin. "Now there's the spirit, son. I want you to come at me and see how many you can get past the line."

If someone had told me that, one day, I'd be practicing with Lakers legend James Dixon, I would have laughed in their face. Though here I was, about to try and score against him because he saw something in me. If that didn't make my chest puff out a little, nothing would.

But now I'd caught a glimpse of Harper in him; I couldn't unsee it.

As I fired shot after shot at Coach Dixon, it got me thinking about what she'd said the other day about not knowing he'd gotten the job with the team. It was none of my business, but that seemed a little strange, especially since Rory mentioned that her parents were still together, living in Cleveland.

Why the fuck wouldn't he tell her he was about to start coaching hockey at her college?

He seemed like a good man. Eager to jump into the job—to offer a guiding hand to us players.

"Nice," he called as my sixth and seventh shots sailed right past him. "Again, but this time come at me from the straight."

I nodded, gliding toward the center line. Harper's business with her father was just that. Hers. I'd made it pretty clear where we stood, and I had no intentions about changing my stance.

We weren't friends.

That wasn't about to change.

So I shoved all thoughts of Coach's daughter out of my head and focused on a dream I knew would never be mine.

After my last class of the day, I headed for my car, hoping to beat the afternoon traffic. The plan was to get home, spend the evening with Scottie doing all his favorite things, and then crash early so I could head back to Lakeshore first thing.

I shoved my cell phone in the dash holster and fired up the engine. I didn't expect it to ring the second I got on the road. And I didn't expect to see *Mom* flashing across the screen.

I greeted her with, "I just left."

"Oh, good. Do you think you can pick up Scottie from his group? They had to move over to a center in Rushton."

"They did?"

"Yeah, I couldn't remember if I mentioned it. I'm so stressed lately; I'd lose my head if it weren't screwed on. Crap, Mase, I didn't mean—"

"It's fine, Mom." It wasn't, but whatever. "Text me the address, and I'll figure it out."

"Thank you. You're a lifesaver. Tony offered me

some extra hours, and you know I can't say no to extra hours."

Another bolt of guilt rolled through me.

"Sure thing, Mom. We'll see you later?"

"Of course. I wouldn't miss a visit from my eldest boy for anything. Maybe I can make us your favorite. Pierogies."

"Sure."

"Is everything okay, sweetheart? You sound a little deflated."

"I'm good. Just tired. Early morning practice kicked my ass."

"You can tell me all about it later. I'll call the group leader and let them know you'll be collecting Scottie instead of me."

"Don't forget to text me the address."

I fucking hated that she had to work extra hours just to make ends meet. Even with the alimony, Mom struggled. If I was home, I could get a job and help out. But she wouldn't hear of it.

Mom wanted me to go all the way. To chase my dreams and make something of myself.

But it wasn't that simple.

Mom's text came through, and I pulled over and quickly typed the address into my GPS. I knew she was between a rock and a hard place with work. She needed the money, but since she couldn't rely on my old man to take care of Scottie, she had to organize a bunch of activities to keep him occupied whenever she picked up an extra shift.

Coach Dixon had a point. If I turned pro, I could give them a better life. Pay off the mortgage and give her the means to reduce her hours so that she could be around more for Scottie. Our neighbor, Mrs. Hancock, helped where she could since she was one of the few people Scottie would stay with without too much hassle.

My brother didn't mind going to the occasional youth group or activity session, but in his black-and-white world, learning was for school. Downtime was for home. And nine times out of ten, if it was his downtime, he wanted to spend it at home, in his own safe space.

Twenty minutes later, I pulled up outside the center and cut the engine. I was ten minutes early, but I decided to go inside.

"Hello, dear. How can I help?"

"I'm here to pick up my brother. He's attending the Inclusion Group."

"Mason?" she asked, and I nodded.

"Your Mom called. You can go and wait outside if you'd like. You can't go into the session, but there's a window, so you'll be able to have a little peek of what they're up to. I believe it's baking and ball games today."

"Sounds good, thanks."

I headed for the double doors and made my way

down the long hall. The faint rumble of chatter and laughter grew louder as I reached a row of plastic seats and sat down.

Sure enough, there was a window giving me a glimpse inside the room. I spotted Scottie instantly, hyper-focused on the cookie he was decorating. The kid had a sweet tooth, but sugar didn't always agree with him. He seemed calm enough, though, nodding at someone across the counter. I couldn't see whoever it was, but they had my brother's undivided attention.

Until he spotted me, and his face split into a Scottie-sized smile.

"My brother is here," he mouthed, dropping his icing tube and bounding toward me.

"Shit," I got up, fully expecting him to burst through the door because rules and boundaries were another set of things he didn't always know quite how to navigate.

"Mason brother," I heard before the door swung open, and he appeared. "You're here."

"Hi, bud. How's it— You." I gawked at Harper, who stared back at me with utter confusion in her eyes.

"M-Mason, what—"

"Mase, Mase." Scottie grabbed my arm and yanked me down, bringing his mouth to my ear. "Don't tell her, but that's the girl I was telling you about," he said entirely too loudly. "The one with the great ti—"

I managed to slide my hand over his mouth before the word could form. "Okay, bud," I said calmly. "Why don't we save that for later. I'm sure Harper needs to get you back inside to finish up your session."

"There are only a few minutes left," she said, brows crinkled. "You're his brother?"

"Hold up." Scottie shoved me off him and glared up at me. "You know Harper?"

"Uh, yeah. We go to LU together."

"Are you friends?"

"I wouldn't say that," I murmured, running a hand down the back of my neck, aware of her heated stare.

My eyes flicked to hers, and she dipped her head a little.

"Scottie, bud, you should go back inside and help Harper clean up." I swear I saw a blush prickle across his cheeks.

"Yeah, okay," he mumbled, traipsing back into the room without so much as a second glance.

"Huh," I said.

"So I guess his name isn't really Sam."

"Shit, he told you that?" My stomach dropped.

"Yeah. I've been calling him it all afternoon."

"That's our dad's name."

"I see. Well, I really should get back inside." She went to double back, but I couldn't help but call after her.

"Harper?"

"Yeah?"

"What the fuck are you doing here?"

The blood drained from her face. "I had no idea

your brother would be attending a group here if that's what you're—"

"I'm not. Shit, you just threw me for a loop. You're here. Working with my brother. It's literally the last thing I expected to see."

"Sorry to disappoint you. I only started volunteering here this week."

What were the odds?

"Do you think you can get moved to a different group?"

Her expression dropped, the temperature turning subzero between us.

"Wow," she said. "I knew you were an asshole; I didn't realize—"

"Harper?" Scottie yelled. "I need help with—"

"Coming." She didn't hesitate, shooting me one last death glare before taking off to help my brother tidy his section.

Unease trickled through me as I watched them together. Scottie responded positively to her, following her directions and hanging on her every word.

It was obvious the kid had a crush on her.

Fuck my life.

But he'd get over it. Because there was no way in hell I could do this on the regular.

Fuck. That.

CHAPTER 8

HARPER

"*WHAT THE FUCK are you doing here?*"

I replayed Mason's words over in my head as I helped Scottie clean up.

It had sounded more like an accusation than a question. But it wouldn't surprise me if the arrogant asshole thought I'd manipulated my way into the volunteering gig at the center to insert myself into his life.

God, he really was something.

"So, you know my brother?" Scottie asked, not making eye contact as he meticulously wiped down the counter.

He was a sweet kid—a head of floppy brown hair that fell into his eyes.

Eyes I now realized belonged to his older brother.

When we'd met briefly yesterday, he'd told me his name was Sam. No one had questioned it, so neither had I.

Imagine my surprise when Mason called him Scottie and not Sam.

"We have some mutual friends, yeah."

"So, you're not friends with him?" He glanced up, a cute little frown etched into his expression.

"I... we don't hang around together if that's what you mean."

"Good." He nodded and went on with his cleaning.

I didn't ask him to expand. I wasn't quite sure how to handle the revelation that he was Mason Steele's little brother.

Clearly, Mason wasn't happy about me being here, working with his brother. But I didn't want to switch groups. This one worked around my class and work schedule, and I liked the kids and the other volunteers.

Besides, Mason wasn't the boss of me.

Just because he wanted me to switch groups didn't mean I had to.

Although, it will mean fewer awkward interactions with him.

"Are you and your brother close?" The words slipped out before I could stop them.

Dammit, this wasn't appropriate, was it?

Although we'd talked about other stuff: Scottie's likes and dislikes, his friends at school, and the kids who teased him because he was different, I wasn't sure

I should be asking him questions about Mason. But before I could pivot, Scottie replied.

"Mason is the best," he said definitively. "He's going to be a professional hockey player one day like Alex Ovechkin and Brendan Shanahan."

"I heard he's good." I smiled.

"He's better than good. In high school, he had the record for most goals and assists in a season."

"He did, huh?"

Scottie looked up again, a small hint of a smile playing on his lips. "Yeah. He was the best player the Riverview Rockets had. He always wanted to be a Laker."

"And what about you? Do you like hockey?"

"I do." His gaze dropped, a wall going up between us. "But I get scared, so I can't skate."

"Oh. What scares you? Is it the ice or—"

"Falling. Getting hurt. Cutting my fingers off with the blades. Someone else skating over me and cutting me in half."

"Did you have an accident?"

He peeked up at me, shaking his head a little. "But I can't stop the bad thoughts. I watch Mase a lot though. I like watching him. Sometimes, I wish I was more like him."

"What do you—"

"Okay, everyone," Linda, the group leader, called. "That's it for today. Parents and caretakers are out in the hall. We'll sign you out one at a time, so everyone, go grab your belongings and line up at the door."

"Bye, Harper," Scottie said.

"Wait, don't forget your cookies." I handed him the container. "You worked hard on those. Enjoy. I'll see you next week, okay?"

He nodded before moving toward the line forming at the door.

"You did great with him today." Linda came up beside me.

"Thanks. Did you know his name isn't Sam?"

"Ah, yes. His mom did mention that he was going through a phase. She didn't go into much detail, but there's some tension between her and Scottie's father, I believe."

"Oh, I didn't know."

"Why would you?"

"I go to college with Scottie's older brother Mason."

"I see."

"That isn't going to be a problem, is it?"

"Of course not. You're not the first student from LU we've had here."

"Oh, okay." I was about to tell her how much I'd enjoyed the session when I heard my name.

"Harper. I want to say goodbye to Harper." Scottie refused to budge when one of the other volunteers tried to sign him out.

"Buddy, let's not make a scene," Mason said as I

approached them. "I'm sure Harper has other things—"

"Hey, Scottie. What's up?" I said, joining them.

"I wanted to say goodbye and give you a cookie."

"That's really sweet of you, but you worked hard on them, so you take them home to share with your mom and Mason, okay?"

"But I want you to have one."

"I—" I glanced at Mason, silently asking for some help, but he said nothing.

"You should have one. You helped bake them. It's only fair, and Mom said I need to try and share more."

"Just take the damn cookie," Mason murmured.

I looked at him incredulously. He knew I couldn't eat it. But I couldn't exactly tell Scottie no now.

"I'll take one for the ride home. How about that?" I said, hoping it would appease him. Scottie flipped the lid and offered me the container. "Thanks." I took a small one. "I'll see you next week, okay?"

Scottie didn't seem appeased though, fidgeting with his container, rocking back and forth on the balls of his feet, clearly agitated.

"Scottie?"

"I'm sorry I told you my name was Sam," he mumbled, refusing to meet my gaze.

"That's okay. I know your real name now, so it's all good."

"You're sure?"

"I am." I smiled. "Now you should probably go. Mason is waiting."

"He's staying the night with me." He finally looked at me, and I saw the flicker of love and adoration for his big brother in his expression. "You could come over and—"

"Harper has to get back to Lakeshore, bud," Mason jumped in.

"Another time, then?"

I looked to Mason for an out. I didn't want to lie to Scottie. I knew how literally he could take things. He might never let me off the hook if I told him yes. But I couldn't exactly tell him the truth either.

"Mason's right," I said. "I need to get back to Lakeshore. But I'll see you next week."

"Scottie, we need to go now." Mason laid a gentle hand on his brother's shoulder.

"Yeah, okay." Scottie gave me the smallest smile.

I gave him a little wave in return, ignoring his big brother's eyes drilling holes into the side of my face.

"Bye, Harper."

"Bye, Scottie."

I watched them leave, hardly surprised that Mason didn't say goodbye or give me a second glance.

Even if it did sting a little.

"Someone has a crush," the volunteer—an older woman named Mary—said.

"Sorry, what?" I gawked at her. Because surely she didn't think that Mason—

"Scottie. That boy looked at you with stars in his eyes."

She was talking about Scottie.

Oh, God.

How embarrassing.

"I'm sure that's not—"

"Been working here long enough to see it over and over again."

"He's just a kid," I scoffed.

"A kid with all kinds of hormones raging inside him," she chuckled. "A beautiful young girl like you, and I'm sure all the boys are looking in your direction."

The conversation made me super uncomfortable. I was here to help. Not be a poster girl for teenage boy fantasies.

Thankfully, when she signed the next kid out, their parents had a bunch of questions, which meant I could slip away. I headed straight for the staff room to grab my purse and jacket. I didn't expect to walk out of the center and find Mason trying to coax Scottie into his car.

He glanced up, his jaw clenching at the sight of me. I had two choices, and his tense expression told me which one to take, so I hurried to my car and climbed inside. But I couldn't resist glancing at him in the rearview mirror.

Mason had crouched down to look Scottie in the eye as he spoke. It was hard to imagine someone like Mason handling a boy like Scottie with the patience and compassion he required. He always seemed so cold and rough around the edges. Whatever he said worked though, and Scottie climbed into his brother's car, and Mason went around the driver's side.

I'd been staring long enough, so I jammed the key in the ignition, the car rumbling to life beneath me.

After my disastrous conversation with Mason the other night, I'd promised myself to stay out of his way. But I wasn't volunteering here to piss him off. It was great experience for my future, and it beat working in Lakeshore, where I would run into too many people I knew from college.

I didn't want to give it up or swap groups; I didn't.

But could I really survive seeing him here, knowing that he didn't want me working with his little brother because he disliked me that much?

Mason Steele's opinion of you does not define you.

Screw him.

I wanted to work with Scottie's group.

Mason Steele was just going to have to get over himself.

By the time I got back to my dorm building, I was tired, hungry, and cranky.

I couldn't eat the cookie Scottie had insisted on giving me, so I decided to brave the communal kitchen to make myself a quick snack. But I regretted it the second Natalie and a couple of her friends appeared.

"Harper, didn't expect to see you in here."

"I'll be out of your hair soon enough." I grabbed my gluten-free bagels and a clean baking tray for the grill.

"You know, you could just use the toaster."

Actually, I couldn't. But I wasn't about to try and educate someone like her on the issues of cross-contamination.

"It's fine," I said, hoping she'd drop it.

"It's just a toaster, Harper. Don't you think you're overreacting a little?"

Smothering a groan, I focused on putting my bagel on the grill. This was one of the reasons I tried to avoid the kitchen. Or the common room. Or any dorm parties.

Natalie didn't like me, and since she was popular, everyone had taken her side.

Ignoring the three of them, I went to the refrigerator to grab my Nutella, but their conversation caught my attention.

"Need to look hot for the Bite the Ice party this weekend. Maybe I'll finally get Mason to notice me."

"Don't hold your breath, girl. You know how discreet Mason likes to be."

"I can be discreet," Natalie snorted.

"You can also be a vain bitch."

"Rude, but true."

They all laughed. But all I could think about was the way Mason had acted earlier when he'd realized I was volunteering at the center.

I pulled out the grill rack and offloaded my bagel onto a plate. After smearing Nutella all over it, I grabbed a piece of kitchen towel and headed for the door.

"You're not staying?" Natalie called.

"Nope," I murmured under my breath, walking out of there without so much as a backward glance.

If she ever found out about my failed attempt to befriend Mason, she would never let me forget about it. And she had already made my life at Hocking Hall difficult enough.

But her voice stopped me in my tracks before I could escape. "You know, I heard an interesting rumor today," she said.

Great. Just what I didn't need.

"You did?" I played dumb, barely glancing back at her.

"I heard that your dad is the Lakers' new assistant coach."

"So what if he is?"

"Well, that's got to kind of suck. I mean, the guys won't touch you now. You're the coach's daughter."

"Or they'll want to touch her *because* she's the coach's daughter." One of the other girls laughed, but it wasn't a kind sound. It was bitter and full of thorns.

"Makes no difference to me." I shrugged, trying to ignore their mean girl comments.

"You say that, but it's got to suck being friends with the only three girls lucky enough to be dating Lakers."

"Are you getting to your point?" A weary sigh rolled through me. "Because it's late, and I'm tired."

And I didn't want her to burrow under my skin any more than she already had.

"Are you close? You and your dad? Because I heard something else interesting."

And there it was—her point.

Crap.

"I heard that you didn't even know he'd applied for the job. Ouch." Her eyes were crinkled with phony sympathy. "That's got to hurt."

You have no idea. But instead of letting the words out, I pasted on the brightest smile I could and said, "My personal life is none of your business."

With that, I walked out of there wondering which was worse.

Living in the dorms and tolerating the likes of Natalie and her mean girlfriends.

Or living at home and trying to get my father to *see* me.

It was impossible to decide at this point.

Because both made me feel like absolute crap.

The next day, I waited for Aurora to get our pre-class coffee, but she never showed. I rechecked my cell phone, but there was nothing.

If I didn't make a move soon, I was going to be late. So I got my coffee to go and headed for the English Department.

When I rounded the corner, I ground to a halt at the sight of Aurora wrapped in Noah's arms, the two of them lost in their own little world as students came and went around them. For a second, I contemplated retracing my steps to avoid any awkwardness, but Noah spotted me, waving.

"Hey," I said, approaching them with a hesitant smile.

"Harper, I am so sorry. I overslept, and my phone battery died. I'll make it up to you at lunch?"

"It's fine; don't sweat it."

"You're sure? I feel just awful."

"Honestly," I chuckled. Sharp and strangled. "It's all good. But we should probably head inside if we want to avoid being singled out by MacMillan. I'll just..." I thumbed toward the door and slipped around them. But I stopped last second and glanced back. "Good luck tomorrow."

The Lakers had their first two away games.

"Thanks." Noah gave me a small nod before ducking his head and whispering something to Aurora.

They were sickeningly cute. The way he towered over her, gazing down at her as if she was his entire world.

With a soft sigh, I slipped into class and took a seat, waiting for Aurora. She came in a minute later, cheeks flushed and eyes twinkling with desire. "Sorry." She slipped into the seat next to me.

"It's fine."

"No, Harper, it's not. I don't want to be that girl. The girl who starts standing up her friends for her boyfriend. It was a mistake. It won't happen again."

"Relax, Rory. I get it." I smiled, hoping it didn't deceive me. "You're in the honeymoon phase."

"It's not an excuse for being a shitty friend."

"I know you would never be that girl."

"You sure?" She gave me big puppy-dog eyes.

"Yes, now stop worrying."

"How did your session at the center go?"

"So... uh, you know I told you about the sweet kid named Sam."

"Yeah..."

"Well, it turns out his name isn't Sam. It's Scottie." Everything went tight inside me. "And he's Mason Steele's little brother."

CHAPTER 9

MASON

"How's Scottie?" Noah asked me as we hit the free weights.

"You won't believe it. Mom asked me to pick him up from his group, and guess who's there volunteering... Harper."

"Harper." His brows pinched. "As in Rory's Harper? As in Coach Dixon's daughter, Harper?"

"Yep."

"Holy fuck, this is the best thing I've heard all week." I glowered at him, and he chuckled. "Why the hell is she volunteering in Rushton?"

"Beats me." I shrugged, grabbing two barbells and starting some bicep curls.

"She wasn't just volunteering with Scottie's group," I added. "She was working with him. Spent all afternoon helping him bake fucking cookies. The little shit didn't shut up about her."

"He's got a crush... on Harper." His eyes crinkled with amusement.

"Yep."

Fuck my life.

"I talked to him the other day, and he told me all about the new girl he liked. Got talking about her titties—"

"He said that? Way to go, Scottie."

"Seriously, Holden. He's twelve. I do not need to hear my twelve-year-old little brother saying the word titties."

Especially when he was talking about Harper's tits.

"He's going through puberty." Noah switched arms and started a new set of reps. "It's a confusing time. I'm sure you can remember being twelve."

Of course, I fucking could. I'd spent most nights beating off to porn I found on the internet. But it was Scottie. He didn't understand stuff like that was for private.

I let out a huff of frustration, remembering how good she'd been with him. How easily they'd talked. Scottie was weary of new people—choosy about who he let into his life. But he'd made an exception for the one girl I'd been dead set on keeping out of *my* life.

Talk about bad fucking luck.

"You know it's some strange fucking karma that

Harper just happens to be volunteering at the center your brother attends."

"What are you saying?" I narrowed my eyes, not liking the insinuation in his voice or the hint of amusement there.

"I'm saying: maybe it's a sign."

"A sign?"

"Well, yeah. You and Scottie are a package deal. Whoever decides to take on your cranky ass also has to take on Scottie. Harper's—"

"Do not finish that sentence," I warned. "Harper isn't my ty—"

"Type. Yeah, yeah, so you keep saying. But has it ever occurred to you that maybe your type is all wrong? I mean, look at Jenni. She barely has time to see you."

"Which is the major plus side of keeping her around."

I liked that it was no strings. No pretenses. No promises.

Noah laughed. "So you're telling me it's never even crossed your mind that maybe Aiden, Connor, and I are onto a good thing? That maybe, finding a girl to put up with all our baggage and bullshit isn't—"

"Not interested."

He chuckled again, swapping his barbells for the dumbbells. "I get it. You think you don't have time. You think a girl will complicate shit. I would have said the same thing before I met Rory. But now look at me."

"Oh, I'm looking alright. I'm just not sure I like what I see."

He flipped me off. "I'm not *that* bad."

"You're worse than Morgan when he first got with Ella, and that's saying something," I said.

"No way I'm worse than Morgan. He was like a lovesick puppy."

"You really need to take a long hard look in the mirror, Holden."

"She makes me happy."

"And I'm happy for you; I am. But seriously, man, you've got to leave the rest of us in peace."

"Fine. I won't say another word. Harper who?" He smirked, and I shook my head.

I didn't need his encouragement. She was ingrained in my mind. It was unsettling, to say the least.

Scottie had dissected their entire time together. Replaying their conversations over and over. My kid brother was a huge Harper fan, by all accounts. There was no way I could ask her to stop working with him now. Which meant I had to apologize for even suggesting it.

Fuck.

"You think we can win tomorrow?"

I appreciated his change of subject.

"I think we stand a good chance."

"I noticed Coach Dixon has taken a shine to you." His mouth twitched, and I rolled my eyes.

"He has not taken a shine to me."

"He didn't spend an hour working one-on-one with anyone else," Noah pointed out. "He wants you to take more shots, am I right?"

"Something like that," I murmured, not entirely comfortable with this line of conversation.

"I don't disagree. You're great on the assist, but you shy away from taking the shot."

"Because I know my strengths, and I play to them."

"Or you're scared."

"The fuck?" A bolt of defensiveness went through me.

"Relax. I'm not being a dick. I'm just saying that maybe you're scared to play to your full potential because it might mean you have to make some difficult decisions down the line. Decisions you're not ready to make."

"It's complicated."

"It's rarely straightforward. You're a good hockey player, Mase. You wouldn't be wearing a Lakers jersey if you weren't. But good doesn't earn you a call-up to the pros. You've got to be great. You've got to want it more than anything."

"Anything?" I threw the question back at him.

"Oh, come on, asshole. Give me a break. I can have hockey *and* the girl."

"Your heart might belong to Rory, but your ass belongs to Coach for at least another sixteen weeks."

He flipped me off again, but it was accompanied by

a deep rumble of laughter. Noah knew I was only half-serious. Being with Rory was his decision, and he was right. He could have hockey and the girl.

But one day, something might have to give.

"Rory, wait up," I jogged up to Aurora, falling into step beside her.

"Hey," she said a little warily.

"Don't look so worried. I just wondered if you know where I might find Harper."

"Harper?" Her expression turned downright suspicious, and I didn't blame her.

Girls talked.

They talked a lot, and Harper and Rory were good friends. She'd probably spilled the details of our little altercation the other night and again at the center.

"Yeah, I need to talk to her."

"About what?"

"Come on, Rory. It isn't like that. She's volunteering with my brother, and I need to clear something up."

"She's a good person, you know."

"I'm sure she is." I rubbed the back of my neck, feeling all kinds of awkward and wondering when life had gotten so fucking complicated.

"I'm supposed to be meeting her at Roast 'n' Go."

"Great, I'll walk with you."

"Is everything okay... with your brother, I mean?" she asked.

"Yeah. Everything's fine."

"Okay."

This was awkward as fuck. Even though I liked Rory, I hadn't really gotten to know her beyond the surface-level stuff. It was just my MO. I found it difficult to nurture relationships when I was already pulled in so many different directions.

"How's life with our star player treating you?"

"It's good. Noah makes me very happy."

"Yeah, he's a good guy. And you're good for him too, you know."

Aurora peeked up at me and smiled. "Thank you. So you and Harper—"

"There is no me and Harper. I just want to talk to her." Apologize and move on with life.

She could volunteer at the center, and I could handle seeing her with Scottie on the odd occasion. It was a small price to pay to see him happy.

Besides, it wasn't like anything had actually happened between us. Harper hadn't actually gotten on her knees for me. It was nothing more than a fantasy. My brain's fucked up way of telling me that despite everything that annoyed the fuck out of me about her, maybe I did find her attractive.

Okay, maybe I found her a whole lot more than just attractive, but it didn't change anything.

"Sure, okay..."

"I mean it, Rory. Don't go getting any ideas. I'm not looking to get involved with anyone."

Especially someone like Harper Dixon.

"What is it with you athletes thinking that being in a relationship is such a curse?"

"I can't speak for anyone else on the team, but I have too much on my shoulders to date."

"With your brother?" she asked.

"He's a part of it, yeah."

"Sorry, I didn't mean to get pushy."

"You're fine." We reached the coffee shop, and Aurora hesitated.

"You go on ahead," she said. "I'll wait until you're done."

My brows pinched. She was turning this into something it wasn't. But I needed to get it over with.

Pushing the door open, I scanned the shop and immediately found Harper sitting over in the corner. She sucked in a sharp breath at the sight of me, shifting uncomfortably on her worn-leather chair as I made my way toward her.

"What do you want?" she bit out.

"Can we talk?"

"If you came to tell me to switch groups, you can—"

"I didn't." I raked a hand through my hair. "Actually, I came to apologize."

"Apologize?" She snorted. "I find it hard to believe that Mason Steele apologizes."

"When he's an ass, he does. My brother likes you." I dropped into the seat opposite her.

"He's a sweet kid."

"He'll be gutted if you aren't at the group next week."

"But you said—"

"I know what I said, but this isn't about me. It's about Scottie. I had no right telling you to switch groups."

"You can say it."

"What?"

She gave me a withering look. "You can't say it, can you?"

Fuck, this girl.

"Look, I... I'm sorry, okay?"

"That wasn't so hard, was it?" Her lips twitched, and that unwanted image filled my head again. All that long blonde hair wrapped around my fist as I guided her head—*her mouth*—down on my aching cock.

Jesus. Harper Dixon was under my skin, and I didn't like it.

I didn't like it one bit.

"You know my little brother has a big crush on you."

Fuck, why had I said that?

"He clearly has good taste." Harper's eyes grew wide as if she couldn't believe she'd said that out loud. But she didn't retract it or try to excuse it. She just held my stare waiting for me to say something, anything.

I didn't, though.

At least nothing she wanted to hear.

"Okay then. I should probably go."

"You don't have to. You could stay and get a drink. We could—"

"No."

"No?" She flinched at my harsh tone. "But I thought we could—"

"Look." A weary sigh rolled through me. "This wasn't me giving you the green light to try and do whatever it is you're trying to do."

"Drink coffee? I was suggesting we drink coffee and talk, Mason. It might help to know a little more about Scottie if I'm going to be working with him." Defiance shone in her eyes, but I saw the hurt there—the dejection.

And maybe I was a dick for making her feel that way, but I didn't come here to talk over coffee. I came here for Scottie. To appease my guilt and apologize.

That was it.

"Why do you dislike me so much?" she asked— brazen and bold.

Or plain stupid.

Because I wouldn't back down, and I wouldn't be forced into saying something I didn't want to say.

"You really want to know?"

"I asked, didn't I?"

"I know girls like you, Harper. Needy. Clingy.

Willing to fuck their way through an entire team if it means they get a prize at the end of it."

Her breath caught, anger and disbelief swirling in her eyes. "I can't believe you just said that to me."

"The truth hurts, blondie," I sneered, pissed that she'd put me in this position.

"You know, I feel sorry for you, Mason."

The fuck?

"To be so wary of everyone's intentions. To be so... so cold."

"I'm perfectly happy with my life, thanks very much. But do me a favor and stay out of my way."

"Fine."

"Fine."

The air crackled between us like a live wire, sparking and snapping. Threatening to set us alight.

What was it about this girl that affected me so much?

I refused to go there.

With her.

With anyone.

I liked my life without any added extra complications. And this girl had major fucking complications written all over her.

Where the fuck did that come from?

Get out of here. Just walk away and be done with her.

"Mas—"

"I need to go," I cut her off before she could bewitch me anymore.

Because that was the only explanation for my weird fixation on her. Those pouty lips and big blue eyes. Eyes I wanted to tumble headfirst into, lips I wanted to be wrapped around my aching—

No.

Fuck. No.

I hurried out of the coffee shop with my stomach in knots. Harper Dixon wasn't the girl for me. Even if she was, it would never work. I had the team. I had class. And Mom and Scottie. I had responsibilities.

Jesus.

I blamed Noah for this.

He was so fucking gone for Aurora, and I'd caught it like a fucking rash or a sneeze. He'd infected me, and now my subconscious was all mixed up.

I didn't need a girl.

I didn't.

And I sure as fuck didn't need a girl like Harper Dixon.

"You're quiet," Noah said as we changed in the visiting team's locker room.

The game was a sellout, the Huskies fans eager to come out and support their team.

Too bad we planned on winning.

"I'm fine." I pulled on my shoulder pads and then yanked my jersey over the top.

"Wouldn't have anything to do with a certain coach's daughter, would it?"

My head snapped up, and Noah smirked. "Say that a little louder, why don't you."

"Relax, Coach D didn't hear me." His smirk only grew. Asshole. "He's too busy kissing Coach Tucker's ass."

He wasn't wrong.

Coach Dixon had been in fine form since we piled onto the bus and left for Houghton, following Coach Tucker around like a little lap dog.

It was kind of embarrassing. But I guess he was excited about his first game with the team.

"You know Rory told me you went to meet her yesterday."

"I didn't go to meet her. I went to clear the air."

"Clear the air. Okay, *Dr. Phil*," Noah snorted, and I flipped him off.

"You're an asshole."

"And you're in denial. You"—he jabbed his finger at me—"want her. And I'd put money on her being in your bed by the end of the month."

Considering the end of the month was Monday, I felt pretty confident when I said, "Never going to happen. She's not my—"

"Type, yeah. You know, I remember saying exactly

the same thing once. Now, look at me." He pulled out his cell phone and thrust it in my face.

"What the fuck is that?"

"We got matching hoodies."

"You got…" I stared at the selfie of him and Rory grinning at the camera in their ridiculously matching outfits. "The Bertram to her Price. What the fuck is a Bertram?"

"Rory's favorite Austen character."

"You're reading Austen now?" I snorted.

"Don't knock it until you've tried it." Noah dropped his cell back in his bag and sat down to lace up his skates. "We could all learn a thing or two from Austen's top-tier fictional men."

"Have you heard this shit?" I asked Austin and Connor.

"It's a phase," Austin grumbled. "It'll pass."

"You're just—"

"Okay, ladies, look alive." Coach Tucker stepped into the fray. "We need to be out on the ice in five. Aiden, son, you ready?"

"Damn straight, Coach."

"Glad to hear it. I want you to go out there and play the game I know you all can without inciting a brawl before the puck drops." He pinned Noah and Austin with a dark look.

"Don't look at me," Austin said. "I learned my lesson when I had to sit on the bench last game."

"Not the point, Hart, and you know it." Coach

Tucker glowered. "The Huskies lost a lot of senior players last season, so we should have the upper hand. But don't take anything for granted out there. Now get in here. Lakers on three."

We all joined Coach in the huddle, standing shoulder to shoulder with our teammates as *Lakers* echoed through the locker room like a battle cry. He wasn't one for big motivational speeches; he trusted us to know our roles and get the job done. But Coach Dixon seemingly had other ideas.

"Mind if I say a few words, Joe?"

"Go for it." Coach Tucker stepped back, giving Coach D the floor.

"It's only the beginning of the season," he said. "But if you want to be the best, you have to go out there and play your best... Every. Damn. Time. Mason, son."

"Yes, sir?"

"Don't be afraid to go after the shot. Remember what we worked on this week. As for the rest of you, use him. He's an untapped resource on the ice."

Noah caught my eye and arched his brow, barely containing his shit-eating grin. Asshole. He would never let me hear the end of this.

"Okay, James, thank you for that." Coach Tucker clapped him on the shoulder. "We should let the guys get out on the ice."

"Use him," Connor mimicked, grinning over at me.

"He's an untapped resource." Ward smirked.

"Oh, fuck off. I didn't ask him to take me under his wing."

"But he did, hotshot. And now he wants you to take all the glory."

"Worried I might steal your thunder, Holden?" I quipped.

"Nah. You hold our assist record for a reason. We've got a good thing going, Mase." He gave me a cocky smile. "Don't fuck it up."

CHAPTER 10

HARPER

"I CAN'T BELIEVE Chad is making us watch that," Kalvin flicked his head towards the flatscreen where the Lakers game was being aired.

"It's all part of his plan to turn Millers into the next Lakers hangout." Jill rolled her eyes. "I guess we can thank you for that," she snickered.

"I didn't know they'd show up. You can't blame me."

"What are we blaming Harper for?" One of the other servers, Janelle, joined us.

"Turning this place into The Penalty Box 2.0," Kalvin grumbled.

"Nah, you'll never lure them away from TPB."

"Don't be so sure; half the team turned up last weekend to see Harper."

"They did?" Janelle frowned.

"I'm friends with some of the girlfriends. Not the guys."

"Huh, I didn't know that." Janelle was new, like me. Her schedule was flexible, so she tended to cover wherever Chad needed her.

"You a hockey fan, Jan?"

"I prefer football. But the guy I'm seeing is a huge fan."

"Unlucky for you."

"Yeah." She gave a small, strangled laugh. "I should get back out there before Chad loses his shit."

"We should all get back to work," Jill suggested.

But as I moved from table to table, taking orders and delivering food and drinks, my eyes kept wandering to the TV screen. The Lakers were winning, but it was a close game. Number 13 had the puck flying down the left wing. He faked the pass, ducking around a defender, and sent it flying toward the goal. The buzzer went off, and the Lakers moved another goal ahead of the Huskies.

The rest of the team piled on Mason, celebrating his goal. The camera panned to the Lakers bench, and I caught a glimpse of my father, fist-pumping the air and cheering alongside the rest of the team. He beckoned Mason over, grabbing him by the shoulder and smiling.

Damn, that one little interaction hurt more than any of the cruel words Mason had spat at me.

My father had *never* looked at me like that.

All I got was disappointment and indifference, but there he was, grinning at Mason like he was the proudest man in the arena.

Dejection trickled through me, turning my blood to ice. All he'd ever wanted was a son to continue his legacy. To bond over hockey with.

Instead, he had gotten me.

Emotion clawed up my throat, but I swallowed it down.

"I'm taking five," I said to Kalvin, dropping my pad and towel on the counter.

"Hey, you okay?" he asked, but I waved him off.

I needed to get out of here for a minute.

Bursting through the door leading into the small staff room, I pressed the heels of my palms against my eyes.

"Don't cry, Harper, don't you dare fucking cry," I murmured.

But it was easier said than done.

My father hadn't played an active role in my life for a long time. He didn't care. And over and over, I told myself that it didn't matter.

But it mattered.

Deep down, in my heart, it mattered, and having him here, in my space, in what was supposed to be *my* fresh start, was the final straw.

I came to Lakeshore U to escape him and a life's worth of disappointment and heartache. But now he was here, ruining everything. And from the looks of it, winning the hearts of the team and the fans, too.

They didn't know James Dixon, though. Not the way I did. They didn't know that this was all an act.

A ruse.

Nothing but smoke and mirrors.

But I guess when you were a hockey legend, none of that mattered.

Being a good person didn't matter.

Something I knew all too well.

The Lakers won both their games. Aurora called me last night, inviting me over to her place to celebrate, but I wasn't feeling it.

Something about watching my father on the television with Mason had bummed me out.

It was silly.

It wasn't like Mason was choosing him over me—he'd made it perfectly clear he had no interest in getting to know me.

But it still stung.

Instead of sitting around and dwelling on the fact I would never earn my father's approval or love, I decided to torture myself some more and headed to the rink just outside of Rushton. I sometimes went when I was feeling particularly self-sabotaging.

Dropping onto the bench, I took my skates out of their bag and pulled them on. I'd had the same pair of Bauer's since my feet stopped growing when I was about fourteen.

They'd been a present. One I'd thought was from my father but turned out to be from my mother. She'd signed the card from both of them, letting me think that he'd finally wanted to share his lifelong passion with me.

Of course, he'd reveled in telling me the truth after one too many whiskeys.

I could vividly remember the crushing pain I'd felt when he'd sneered at what a waste of money it was buying me—*a girl*—a pair of Bauer Vapor Hyperlite skates.

I'd refused to wear them for a month. Had even asked Mom to return them, but she'd admitted to getting them on sale, so she couldn't get a refund. Eventually, I'd decided to put them to good use.

Tightening the laces, I secured the ends and zipped up my hoodie before making my way out onto the ice.

It is such a strange thing to love something so much and also hate it. I loved skating, the ice, feeling the cold smart my lungs. I loved the feel of the air whooshing around my face, the adrenaline coursing through my veins as I glided up and down the rink.

And I was good.

Really damn good.

But I couldn't do it. I couldn't chase a dream that

was so tangled up with my deep desire for my father to accept me.

There had been a time when I'd dreamed of being the second woman ever to play for an NHL team, but I knew it still wouldn't be enough for him.

Pushing the disheartening and painful thoughts out of my head, I got on the ice and let myself fly.

There was nothing quite like it, gliding around the rink, zigzagging in and out of the beginners. A small group of kids all stopped to watch me, pointing and giggling when I gave them a small wave as I passed them.

"She's good," I heard someone say.

"Too good for this session," another one said with slight annoyance.

A smile tugged at my mouth, that needy, affection-starved part of my soul lighting up at their compliments. I knew it wasn't healthy to crave strangers' attention, but it made me happy.

It made me feel worth something.

Playing up to the small crowd now watching me, I did a couple of fancy moves, earning a small round of applause. God, I loved this. The rush of endorphins, the joy spreading through me like sunshine.

Until I came to an impressive stop, spraying ice into the air, and looked across the rink to find Mason watching me. And my good mood evaporated just like the ice melting beneath my skates.

Mason was here, and he wasn't alone.

"Harper. Harper's here," Scottie yelled across the rink, flapping his hands excitedly.

Even from a distance between us, I could see the way Mason's jaw tightened, his eyes cold and hard.

Great.

Just what I didn't need.

"Harper, Harper," Scottie waved stiffly, and I noticed he wasn't wearing skates, unlike his big brother.

Deciding to be the bigger person, I headed their way, stopping at the boards. "Well, this is a surprise." I smiled, refusing to meet Mason's confused and slightly irritated gaze. "What are you doing here?"

"Mason is going to let me watch him skate."

"He is, huh?" My eyes finally flicked to his. "That's nice."

And it was, dammit.

He was so good with Scottie; it really didn't help my case, remembering he was an arrogant, cruel asshole.

"Those were some fancy moves out there. Where'd you learn to do that?" he asked, surprising me.

"I skate a little." I shrugged, still butt-hurt after our conversation Thursday. "Maybe I can hang out with you while you watch Mason?"

Scottie's eyes got big with wonder. "For real?"

"Sure. If Mason says it's okay?"

No way I wanted to be on the ice with him.

"Yeah"—he scratched his jaw—"whatever."

We switched places, and I directed Scottie over to one of the benches along the side of the rink.

"You didn't say you could skate," Scottie said as he watched Mason do a few warmup laps. I knew because I'd seen him play, and he wasn't going anywhere near his usual speed.

"I learned when I was a little girl."

"I wish I could learn. I wish... I wasn't afraid."

"Maybe we could try one day together. I heard the group does a visit to the rink sometimes."

He peeked up at me, barely meeting my gaze, and said, "Maybe."

No preamble. No explanation. Just a straight, simple answer.

I smiled. It was impossible not to. There was something so endearing about this kid.

"Go Mason brother," he vigorously clapped as Mason began showing off.

I refrained from rolling my eyes as he whizzed past us, winking at his brother.

At least, I assumed he was.

God, he was gorgeous, with so much power and speed in his legs and arms as he circled the rink again and again. My audience was nothing compared to the one Mason drew. Girls watched him with that dreamy expression while fathers and their sons watched on in awe.

"Doesn't it scare you when Mason is on the ice?" I asked Scottie.

"He's very good. Strong too. If he hurts himself, the doctor will fix him."

"The doctor would fix you too, you know."

He gave a nervous shake of his head. "I don't like going to the doctor."

"Yeah, me neither."

"Really?"

Another peek. Another curious glance.

"Really. I don't like the smell or those plastic chairs in the waiting room. And I really hate needles."

"I hate needles, too."

Just then, a succession of loud bangs filled the arena, startling us, and Scottie went deathly still. His fingers curled around the edge of the bench as he closed his eyes and began rocking back and forth, murmuring softly to himself.

"Hey, bud, you okay over there?" Mason rushed over, leaning his forearms on the boards. "Scottie, look at me. It was just a loud noise, buddy. Nothing to worry about."

But Scottie didn't respond. The repetitive noises coming from him grew louder and louder until people started to look.

A sense of protectiveness swelled inside me, and I shot them a scathing look. Mason raised a brow, and I shrugged. "They should mind their own business."

He frowned, coming off the ice to sit on Scottie's

other side. Reaching down, he grabbed the backpack at his brother's feet and dug out some ear defenders and a fiddle toy. He fitted the defenders onto Scottie's head and gently pressed the fiddle toy into his hands.

A minute passed, and another, and slowly, Scottie settled.

"Better?" Mason asked, and he nodded. "What do you want to do, buddy? We can stay or go? It's your choice."

"I'm hungry for pancakes."

"Pancakes it is, then."

Scottie nodded again and then said five little words that made Mason bristle.

"I want Harper to come."

"Uh, I'm not sure—"

"Harper?" Scottie looked at me with big expectant eyes, and I couldn't say it.

I couldn't tell him no.

Even if I could *feel* Mason silently telling me to.

"If Mason says it's okay."

The guy in question sucked in a sharp breath but managed a curt nod as he murmured, "Fine. We can go to the diner next door."

We headed back into the locker room and traded our skates for sneakers. Mason didn't say a word to me, and he didn't need to.

Hostility rolled off him in angry waves.

He was pissed.

Again.

Sometimes, I wished I wasn't like this. I wished I could just say no and refrain from overstepping, from inserting myself where I wasn't wanted. But you couldn't change your heart. And mine was broken, bruised, and starved for affection. Constantly searching for a quick fix.

I liked making people happy. I liked feeling like I was a part of something. Craved it even if I didn't always know how to handle it.

I followed Mason and Scottie out of the rink, both of them deep in conversation about the Lakers games against the Huskies. Neither of them tried to include me, and, for a second, I wondered what the hell I was doing, encroaching on their brother-bonding time.

Until Scottie glanced back and said, "Do you like pancakes, Harper?"

"I… who doesn't like pancakes." The words spilled out before I could stop them.

Crap, I hoped they did a gluten-free option. But when I spotted the little diner on the street corner, my hopes were dashed.

"It's a bit rough around the edges," Mason said as if he sensed my thoughts. "But the food is good."

"I'm sure it is." I pressed my lips together, mentally drumming up a list of excuses as to why I wouldn't eat more than some granola and fruit.

"We can share a stack," Scottie said, ducking into the diner.

Mason turned to me and said, "You didn't have to

come," but it sounded a lot like, *'I didn't want you to come.'*

"Don't worry. I'm only here for Scottie." I slipped around him and joined the younger Steele brother.

"Table for three?" A woman called from behind the counter.

"Yes, please."

"Grab a booth, and I'll be over to take your order."

Scottie chose a booth by the window, giving us a front-row seat to the street and beyond. I picked up a menu and scanned it, hardly surprised there was no mention of any gluten-free options.

Ugh.

"Problem?" Mason asked, noticing my frown.

"Nope." I dropped it onto the table. "I think I'll have the fruit salad and some granola."

"But we have to get the giant pancake stack," Scottie said. "We always get it."

"You can still get it, buddy. I'm not that hungry, is all."

"But it's pancake Sunday."

"Scottie, bud, leave it."

"But—"

"If Harper wants a boring fruit salad, then that's her loss. More pancakes for me and you." He winked, and it seemed to pacify Scottie.

"Welcome to The Stack"—the woman appeared —"what can I get y'all?"

Mason scanned the menu. "We'll take a mega stack with bacon and two Oreo milkshakes, please."

"And for you, doll?"

"I'll take the granola and fruit salad, please, and a water."

"Don't get many requests for granola and fruit salad around these parts," she chuckled as she noted it down. "I'll be right back with your drinks."

"I hate granola," Scottie said with disgust.

"Oh, I don't know. It's not so bad with a little yogurt."

He made a hacking sound, and Mason laughed. "Scottie has an aversion to most dairy-based products."

"Chocolate?" I arched a brow.

"Except chocolate. But milk, cream, butter, it's all a big no-no. Something to do with the texture."

"But the filling in Oreos—"

"Is delicious," Scottie chimed.

"Right. Got it."

"You couldn't have the eggs?" Mason asked.

"I could have, but places like this don't tend to worry about cross-contamination. It isn't worth the risk."

"Must suck. I couldn't live without carbs."

"You get used to it."

"What's cross-tamination?"

"Cross-contamination is when things are exposed to each other when they shouldn't be. So like a vegetarian being served a meal that was prepared around meat. That would be cross-contamination."

"Why does it matter?"

I looked at Mason, and he shrugged.

Well, okay then.

"Because for some people, they might not be able to eat certain things, or it could make them sick."

"Like what?"

"Some people can't eat peanuts or shellfish or dairy."

"Will it kill them?"

Jesus.

"I... in some instances, it could make them really sick, yes."

"Will I get sick if I eat peanuts?"

"You eat peanuts all the time, buddy."

"Sorry," I said, feeling like I'd overstepped. "I didn't mean—"

"It's fine. Scottie knows he has no allergies. But he does have some strong aversions to things. Isn't that right, bud?"

"Yep. Are you allergic to pancakes, Harper? Can they kill you?"

"I..."

Thankfully the server returned with our drinks, and Scottie was too engrossed in his milkshake to ask any more awkward questions.

"Good?" Mason asked, and Scottie grinned, ice cream and cookie crumbs smeared all over his mouth. "You're supposed to eat it, bud. Not wear it."

Mason handed him a napkin, and Scottie ducked his head, blushing.

Just then, the server returned with our food order. "One mega stack with bacon. And granola and a fruit salad for you." She slid two dishes in front of me, and I frowned.

"Problem, doll?"

"Is this natural granola?"

"It's Dirk's special recipe. He throws in a bit of this and that. Never had any complaints." She glowered, and I shrank into my seat.

"Okay, thanks." I smiled.

"You need anything else, just holler."

"Is the granola cross-taminated?" Scottie asked, already digging into his pancakes.

"It might be," I said, pushing the bowl away.

I should have just stuck to the fruit salad.

"It's only a bit of granola," Mason said. "Surely, it can't be that bad."

Great, even he thought I was overreacting.

"It's fine. I'm not hungry, anyway," I snapped, a tad defensive. But it was frustrating always having to justify my choices or scrutinize the menu or question the servers about their food preparation habits.

Even in restaurants that were more allergen-friendly, it could be awkward. But experiences like this one made eating out barely worth the hassle.

Scottie was oblivious to the tension, wolfing down his pancakes like they might disappear at any second. When he finally came up for air, he wiped his mouth with the back of his hand and looked at me.

"It's a shame pancakes can kill you, Harper," he deadpanned, "because you don't know what you're missing."

CHAPTER 11

MASON

All I'd wanted was a nice calm morning out with my brother.

Instead, I got the most random brunch I'd ever experienced.

Scottie watched Harper poke and prod her less-than-appealing fruit salad as he inhaled pancake after pancake. At least he'd stopped talking about death because that had been hella awkward.

That was Scottie, though. Once he got something in his mind, he fixated on that shit until the next thing came along to steal his attention.

As I tucked into my third pancake, adding an extra dollop of syrup for good measure, part of me felt a little bad for Harper. The fruit salad didn't look very appetizing, and she couldn't touch the granola due to cross-contamination. I'd known a gluten-free diet could be tricky, but I hadn't quite realized how serious it was.

"How are those pancakes, Scottie?" she asked.

She'd barely looked at me. Her restraint was impressive. That or she really didn't give a shit.

Me on the other hand, I'd barely been able to look away.

Seeing her out on the ice had floored me. When I'd finally picked up my jaw and told my heart rate to calm the fuck down, I noticed everyone else watching her too. The way she zipped around the rink, her long legs skating lap after perfect fucking lap. It had almost short-circuited my brain, especially when she pulled off some fancy ass moves before Scottie started shouting at her.

Harper Dixon surprised me at every fucking turn, and I didn't like it.

I didn't like that every time I tried to shut her out of my life; she found a way to creep back in.

Watching her with Scottie had been something but watching her own the ice had made me see her in a whole new light. Which was a real fucking problem because: a) something told me Harper Dixon wasn't the kind of girl who fooled around without catching feelings, and b) she was the new coach's daughter.

I needed to get all the dirty thoughts currently running through my mind out because Harper and I could never happen. No matter how much I wanted to see just what else she could do on the ice or in the locker room or in my bed.

Fuck.

How had this happened?

How had I become such a fucking cliché?

"Mason?"

I blinked at her, trying to figure out what she'd asked me.

"Don't you think it's a good idea?"

"Uh, yeah," I said, confused as fuck.

"Great." She flashed me a megawatt smile. One that had my chest tightening. "I think we can do it. What do you say, Scottie?"

"Maybe." He shrugged, going back to his pancake stack. Sometimes I wondered if the kid had hollow legs the way he devoured food. But only food he could tolerate.

"Okay, what are we talking about?"

"Haha, gotcha." Harper grinned, jabbing her fork toward me. "I knew you weren't listening."

"I'm tired, alright. Cut a guy some slack, blondie. Playing back-to-back games will do that to a guy."

"Fair point. But it's a dangerous game agreeing when you don't know what you're agreeing to."

"Okay, you got me." I held up my hands. Surprised —and fucking unnerved—at how easily the banter flowed between us when she wasn't annoying the shit out of me.

Maybe I'd been too quick to judge her.

Not that it matters now, asshole. I mentally reeled off the list. *Volunteer at Scottie's group. Coach Dixon's daughter. Your best friend's girl's friend.*

She was a walking-talking red flag. One I needed to stay the fuck away from.

"I was telling Scottie that I think we should try and get him out on the ice sometime."

"Yeah, that's not going to happen."

"But there's an inclusive session at the rink. I was thinking—"

"Harper," I snapped, side-eyeing my brother," I said leave it."

Her expression dropped right along with my good mood. "Sorry, I just thought—"

"Yeah, well, don't. It's getting late. We should probably wrap things up here."

"Oh, okay."

She stared at me, but I couldn't look at her. Who the fuck did she think she was waltzing into our lives and acting like she knew what was best for Scottie? He couldn't go out on the ice; he was terrified. I knew because I'd witnessed the fallout more than once.

"You done, buddy?" I asked him, and he nodded.

Harper got up and pulled ten dollars out of her purse. "For my food." She laid it down on the table. "It was nice seeing you again, Scottie. I'll see you at the center next week."

"Okay, bye, Harper." He was more interested in his fiddle toy than her. If she knew him better, she'd know that he tended to get like that after a big meal—especially one full of sugar.

"Bye." She hesitated, probably waiting for me to apologize. But that wasn't going to happen. Scottie was my number one priority, always.

But Harper didn't back down; she locked her blue eyes right on me, daring me to do it. To concede.

"See ya." I gave her a dismissive nod.

Disappointment glittered in her eyes as she shook her head softly and walked out of the diner with her head held high.

"Do you think she'll die?" Scottie said, a rare flicker of concern in his eyes.

"What?"

"Harper. Do you think she'll die from the cross-tamination?"

"Nah, I don't think she'll die, bud." I ruffled his hair, unable to resist watching her out of the window.

Hopefully, she'd finally gotten the message and would give up trying to be my friend.

Fuck knows it would make my life a hell of a lot easier.

After I dropped Scottie home, I headed back to Lakeshore to help the guys get ready for the Bite the Ice party.

It was a big deal on campus, one of the highlights of the student social calendar. Every year, the team turned Lakers House into a living, breathing scare house. And every year, the team tried to outdo the efforts from the previous year.

I'd heard the guys throwing around talk of animatronics, pigs' blood, and taxidermy. Thankfully, Scottie-duty had gotten me out of the heavy lifting this morning, but I'd promised to make it back in time to help with drinks and snacks.

"About fucking time," Ward said as I fought my way through the webbing strung up outside the front of the house.

"How's it going?"

"Dumfries is supervising." He arched his brow. "Not going to lie, it's a shit show."

"Out here is looking good."

"Because yours truly is working this area." He grabbed another handful of webbing and started stringing it up, stretching out the web to cover more of the house.

"I hope you didn't have plans to take a girl to your room tonight. Tipper and Johnson have completely fucked up the staircase."

"The fuck?"

"See for yourself." He tipped his head toward the house.

"I'll see you later."

"I'll be the one bleeding out."

That was a visual I didn't need. But along with the expectation we all pitched in for the party was the expectation we all made an effort with our costumes.

Last year, I'd gone as Michael Myers. This year, I had a pretty dope Wolverine costume picked out.

Costume parties weren't my first choice of fun, but I'd do it for the team.

I found Aiden inside, barking orders at some of the guys. "Hey, about time." He tipped his head in greeting. "How was Scottie?"

"Good. Is Noah—"

"Over here, asshole." Noah peeked up from behind the counter, stacks of red Solo cups in hand.

"I'll be on drink duty," I volunteered, heading for Noah before Aiden could say otherwise. "Remind me why we have to do this every year?" I murmured, and he chuckled.

"It's good fun. You never know. You might pull a Connor and find the girl of your dreams—"

"Seriously, still at it with that shit? I don't have the time or the energy for regular pussy."

"How was little bro?"

"Good, yeah," I hesitated. If I told him about Harper, it would only be more ammunition for his cause. I wouldn't hear the end of it. But if I didn't tell him, I feared it would eat me up inside.

"Harper was there," I blurted out.

"Harper was where?"

"At the ice rink just outside of Rushton. Surprised the shit out of me."

"You know if she's stalking you—"

"She isn't stalking me, asshole. She was already there, out on the ice." Looking like every guy's wet dream.

"She skates?"

I nodded. "Fucking incredible too."

"Well, shit."

Yeah, shit. I rubbed my jaw. "Scottie saw her, called her over, and then invited her to brunch."

"Oh, shit. How did that go down?"

"We had brunch." I shrugged.

"Then what happened? Because I feel like I'm not getting the whole story."

"I panicked and called time on the whole thing."

Not entirely true, but he didn't need to know the specifics.

Noah regarded me for a second, a slow smirk spreading over his face. "She's under your skin."

"No."

Yes.

"I think you're lying."

"I think you're an asshole."

"Takes one to know one." His smile grew. "For a girl you claim to dislike so much, you sure do end up spending a lot of time with her. I mean, as one of your best friends, I feel a little jealous."

"Will you stop? Harper is annoying, and I'd prefer

not to spend any time with her. But Scottie loves her, and she's good with him."

At least, she was until she suggested we take him skating.

"Yeah, okay."

"Okay?" My eyes narrowed, wondering what his angle was.

He wasn't usually so... agreeable.

"Yeah, I said okay." His mouth twitched.

"What?" I groaned.

"Nothing. Nothing at all."

And then it hit me.

"She's coming to the party, isn't she?"

"Yep," he chuckled, clapping me on the back. "But you don't care. So watching a bunch of horn dog hockey players paw all over her won't matter, right?"

Right.

My lips thinned, jealousy coursing through my veins. Not that I'd ever let Noah know that.

Denial was king, and I was going to wear that crown for as long as possible.

Lakers House was at full capacity. People filled every room, hall, and yard. I'd heard there was even a line out front of half-dressed freshman girls all looking to get in.

I didn't go check it out like Leon and Cutler, though. I was too busy avoiding a certain assistant coach's daughter.

I'd seen Harper arrive. Damn near blew a load in my jeans at her outfit. The Ringmaster costume clung to her curves like a second skin, showcasing her perfect ass and perfect fucking tits.

Jesus, her tits looked incredible. Small and perky, and just enough to fill my hands.

Noah had taken one look at me and roared with laughter before mouthing, "Good luck with that," and I'd skulked off to get something stronger to drink.

"Who are we hiding from?" Connor asked as he joined me in the yard where I'd spent the last forty minutes watching some of the rookies play a game of giant yard pong.

"No one," I said, refusing to meet his inquisitive gaze.

"No one, right. So you being out here all alone wouldn't have anything to do with a certain sexy Ringmaster, would it?"

"Nope."

"Didn't think so." Laughter rumbled through him. "Good thing, too, because I think Adams is going to make his move."

"The fuck?" My head whipped around, and Connor's eyes lit up with victory.

"Asshole," I muttered.

"It's okay to want her."

"No, it really fucking isn't." I ran a hand through my hair and down the back of my neck. "There are so many reasons why it's not a good idea."

"Nobody said you had to marry the girl. Just enjoy it, and have some fun."

"With our new assistant coach's daughter?" My brow lifted.

"Yeah, you have a point. But if you don't do something about your little problem, it's only going to drive you to the brink of madness. You know that, right?"

I pleaded the fifth.

I didn't want to admit I wanted her. Because I didn't fucking want her.

"I know you think I'm girl-obsessed—"

"Don't think it, Morgan. I know it." I smirked, and he flipped me off.

"Ella is the one, man. She's the girl I'm going to marry and settle down with. When you find that girl, it's worth it. It's all so fucking worth it."

"How drunk are you right now?"

"Pretty damn wasted. But don't tell my girl." He leaned in, whispering, "I promised her multiple orgasms tonight."

"You might want to lay off the shots, or the only thing getting up will be Ella to pass you a bowl to puke in."

"Hey, Mase?"

"Yeah?"

"I love you, man. You know that, right? I know you live at the house still, and we don't hang out as much as the other guys, but you're still my brother from another mother." He slung his arm around my neck and hugged the air from my lungs.

"Fucking big bastard," I grumbled. "If you don't let me up, I'll have to scream for—"

"Connor Morgan, why are you feeling up Mason?" Ella looked over at us, her fists planted on her hips.

"Ella, my kitten. El. Love of my life. Light of me—"

"Oh Jesus, how many shots did you let Cutler feed you?"

"Too many, babe. Too fucking many."

"Okay, party boy. Let's go."

"To have the smexy sexy time?" He staggered to his feet, swaying all over the damn place. "Because I'm ready to rock my girl's world."

"A little help?" She glared at me, and I held up my hands, barely containing my laughter.

"Oh, he's all yours."

"Ella, what's— oh my God, Connor!" Aurora joined us with Noah hot on her tail.

"You good there, Con?"

"Does it look like he's good?" Ella snapped. "He can barely stand. What the hell did Cutler put in those shots?"

"Zombie brains," Connor slurred. "With extra brains."

"So much for rocking my world tonight." Ella rolled her eyes.

"Give me ten minutes and a gallon of water, and we'll be good to go." He grabbed his junk.

"Okay, mister, party's over. I'm taking you home."

"Stay here," I said. "You can take the spare room."

"The sex pit?" Her face wrinkled with disgust. "No thanks, I know what goes on in—"

"Relax. It's off-limits for... that. I swear. There are fresh sheets on the bed and everything. You'll be fine in there."

"Beats carrying his big ass all the way home," Noah added.

"Fine. But if anyone tries to get in, I will cut a bitch."

"Jesus, you're scary when you're pissed."

"And while you're at it, tell Cutler he should watch his back for getting my boyfriend wasted before eleven."

"Come on, let's get him upstairs," Noah took Connor's weight, earning himself a Connor bear hug.

"Good luck," I said, lifting my beer to them.

"Asshole," Noah shook his head, but I saw the humor there.

After they'd wrangled Connor inside, I stayed behind. I wasn't feeling it tonight. Knowing she was in there somewhere really put a dampener on my mood.

I didn't ever get stuck on a girl, not like this. I liked

to keep things simple. Complication-free. But I couldn't stop thinking about her.

Maybe Connor had a point.

Maybe the only way to get over this weird infatuation was to fuck her out of my system.

One night. No strings. A chance to break whatever spell she'd put on me. To put it to bed—*literally*—and move the fuck on.

But Harper wouldn't be down for that.

She wouldn't—

"Oh, sorry." That voice drifted over me, electrifying every nerve ending in my body. "I didn't realize you were out here."

Fuck, she looked incredible.

My eyes ate up every inch of her. The dip of her hips and the soft curve of her waist are accentuated by the tight red and black corset-style jacket. I could imagine spanning my hands around her body, laying her out, and—

"I'll just go," she rushed out, turning to get away from me.

"Wait." I stood. Drawn to her. Unable to fight the tug I felt deep in my stomach.

"Mason?" Her eyes grew big as I stalked closer, the air thinning around us with every step, my heart in my fucking throat. "What are you—"

"Shh." I pressed a finger to her pouty lips, something strange and unfamiliar swelling in my chest as she gazed up at me with lust-drunk eyes. "One night."

"W-what?"

"This... whatever is between us. We give ourselves one night to get it out of our system. Then we move on with our lives."

"One night..." The words rolled off her tongue as if she was testing them out.

"It'll be our little secret."

"Why?" she asked, surprising the fuck out of me.

"Because I want you even though I shouldn't, and I'm not sure I'll be able to stop wanting you until I've had you."

"So you basically want to fuck me out of your system."

"Something like that." I winced.

It sounded much worse coming from her mouth than it did in my head.

"One night. No strings. No promises."

Shit. Was she really considering it?

I hadn't gotten that far when I'd decided to lay it out for her. All I knew was Noah and Connor were right. I couldn't keep doing whatever the fuck we were doing without doing *something*.

"Yeah..." I waited, watching her as she considered my words—my offer.

"And you'll stop being an asshole to me afterward?"

"Yeah, I think I can do that." My mouth twitched.

Who knew, maybe we could even be friends. It

would sure as shit make life a little easier, especially if she was going to be around Scottie.

"Okay." She nodded.

"Jeez, blondie. Don't sound too excited about it."

"Well, you've given me nothing to get excited about yet." She leaned in, her expression turning expectant, the air heavy and thick around us.

"Well, then." I moved closer, dipping my eyes to her stark red lips. "I guess we should—"

"Steele," someone yelled, and I jerked away, putting a safe distance between us. "Get the fuck in here. We're celebrating."

"Celebrating?" I murmured, straining to see whoever the fuck was standing in the doorway. Tipper, I think.

"Put the blonde down and come hang with us."

I muttered something under my breath, and Harper chuckled. "Go," she said. "We can pick this back up later."

"You're sure I can—"

"Later." She nodded.

"How are we going to do this?" I asked, not sure I could wait. But the party was still in full swing, and if we both dipped out now, people would notice.

"Come find me." Harper didn't give me a chance to ask how the fuck I was supposed to do that as she slipped away and hurried back inside the house.

Leaving me staring after her.

CHAPTER 12

HARPER

I WAS DRUNK. Not enough that I didn't know what I was doing, but enough that I had some liquid courage flowing through my veins.

Mason wanted to have sex with me. He wanted to exorcise the strange chemistry between us.

He wanted to fuck me out of his system.

And I was going to let him.

It was a dumb move. I knew that. Just like I knew that in the harsh light of day, I would probably regret it. But the minute the words left his mouth, I had only two thoughts. Number one: I wanted to discover if the rumors about Mason Steele's monster dick were true. And number two: If I slept with him, I would own a piece of him my father never would.

It was petty. Downright pathetic even. But a jealous

beast had stirred to life inside me ever since finding out Dad was coaching the team. And to think he was working particularly close with Mason was too much to bear.

So I had daddy issues.

What girl wouldn't after being ignored by her own father for the best part of eighteen years?

Mason didn't want a relationship, and I wasn't sure he even liked me, not really. Especially after the way he'd talked to me earlier at the diner.

But he *wanted* me.

And I was so desperate to feel desired that there was only one answer in my mind.

"Maybe you should slow down," Rory yelled over the music, motioning to the drink in my hand.

"I'm fine," I shouted, draining the rest of my vodka orange.

We'd been dancing among vampires and zombies and slutty angels for the last hour. It was hot and sticky in the Lakers' living room, a constant trickle of smoke pouring out of a machine in the corner of the room, giving the whole place an eerie vibe.

"It's getting late," she said. "I'm tired."

"You're leaving already?"

Mason hadn't come to find me yet, but then, the party was still in full swing.

Maybe he changed his mind or found a better offer. I shoved down the little voice of doubt and danced some more, rolling and popping my hips to the sultry beat. A couple of guys dressed as zombie hockey players over by the door watched me, hunger blazing in their eyes as I danced for them. My skin hummed with awareness, my stomach fluttering with anticipation.

I didn't want to be like this.

Starved of love and desperate for attention, but it was ingrained in me. No matter how much I tried to tell myself I didn't need a guy to validate me, I always ended up right back at square one.

I wasn't girlfriend material. Past experience suggested I wasn't even second-date material. I was the girl guys turned to for one night of no-strings sex.

Time and time again, I told myself I was okay with that. Because being wanted for sex was better than being wanted for nothing.

But the truth was, it wasn't okay, and I was waiting for the day that somehow someone saw past my flaws and saw *me*.

Suddenly, I didn't feel much like partying.

"I need some air," I said to Rory.

"You want me to come?"

"No." I waved her off. "I'll be fine."

I weaved through the sea of bodies and out of the room, heading for the kitchen and the yard beyond it.

The frigid fall air smarted my lungs the second I stepped outside, but it felt nice against my skin, and I tilted my head back to the stars, inhaling a sharp breath.

I was a good person.

A kind and loyal, and compassionate person.

But it wasn't enough.

I was never enough.

Because you let yourself get too invested, Harper. You need to slow down, go with the flow... you need to rein it in.

Tears pricked my eyes as a life's worth of pain and heartache swelled inside me.

I hated it.

Hated that after all this time, I still cared what my father thought about me. But it wasn't just him. It was the impact his indifference—and downright rejection —had on me growing up and how it had shaped and molded me.

Broken me.

"Ugh, get a grip, Harper." *Mason wants you; he wants you. Maybe it'll be different this time. Maybe he won't—*

"I've been looking for you."

The rasp of his voice sent a violent shiver running down my spine. I turned slowly, my eyes clashing with Mason's. He crooked a smile, and my heart exploded in my chest.

God, he was beautiful. All hard angles and sharp lines. His eyes were an arctic storm I wanted to get swept away in.

"Well, you found me."

I don't know why, but I stepped backward, letting the shadows envelop me. Mason came willingly, stalking toward me like a predator. When he finally reached me, my back hit the wall, a big tree concealing us from view. Not that many people were out here now. The party was winding down. People had paired off and gone home or moved onto a bar or club with their friends. It was mostly just the team and their inner circle left.

Mason stared down at me, but I felt his eyes everywhere, my skin vibrating at the intensity there. "I didn't like watching you dance for Adams and Heller."

"W-who?"

"It doesn't matter because you're not theirs tonight." He reached out, snagging a stray curl between his fingers. "You're mine." His hand slipped to my jaw and buried his fingers in my hair, tilting my face up.

"Mas—"

He kissed me. Sliding his lips over mine and slipping his tongue into my mouth. He tasted good, like mint and the slightest hint of whiskey. I liked it.

I wanted more.

I wanted the rush of serotonin I knew would come. The burst of adrenaline.

Curling my fingers into his white tank, I pulled him closer, kissing him deeper. His free hand dropped to the curve of my ass, pressing me closer until I felt him at my stomach. Hard and ready.

Jesus. He was big and thick, and the words *monster dick* sprang into my head. Dayna had said she'd heard rumors... but hearing it and *feeling* it were two very different things.

A nervous laugh slipped out of me, and Mason pulled back, frowning.

"Sorry, I... it doesn't matter." His brow arched, and I sheepishly added, "I guess the rumors are true."

"The rumors?"

"About your monster dick."

"Jesus," he breathed. "Maybe this is a bad idea."

Panic slammed into me, and I grabbed his tank again. "No, I want this. I want you."

"Meet me upstairs in ten minutes." He slid his hand around the back of my neck, holding me there. "Last door on the left."

"What if someone notices me?"

"I'm sure you'll think of something." Mason gave me a rare smile before kissing me hard again, leaving me there breathless and flushed while he walked back into the house.

Oh. My. God.

My heart crashed so violently in my chest, I thought it might burst right out of my rib cage. *Breathe, Harper. Just. Freaking. Breathe.* This was happening—Mason and me.

One night only.

A frisson of excitement zipped up my spine, making me shiver. He'd kissed me with such need. Such possession and hunger. I touched a finger to my mouth, tracing the seam of my lips, replaying the kiss over in my mind.

I knew Aurora would warn me this was a bad idea.

A really freaking bad idea. But I wasn't the kind of girl who was going to get her fairy-tale happy ending. I wasn't the girl guys took home to meet their parents. Hell, I'd never even made it to a third date before I got let down gently or ghosted or, worse, passed over for another girl.

I was the girl who got scraps—cookie crumbs of attention.

A bolt of anguish went through me, but I shoved it away.

I didn't come to the party dressed as a sexy Ringmaster to wallow in self-pity. I came to have fun. To prove to myself that I could have fun and be content with being young and free and single.

Liar.

I ignored the little voice in my head, refusing to give her attention.

After a few minutes, I made my way into the house, searching for Rory. But I couldn't find her.

"Dayna," I said, tapping her on the shoulder. She was wrapped in Aiden's arms, the two of them so freaking cute in their coordinating *Ghostbusters* outfits.

"Hey, what's up?"

"Have you seen Rory?"

"Last I saw, she was heading upstairs with Noah. Ella's got her hands full with Connor, I think."

"I'll try upstairs."

"Take a right at the top of the stairs and head all

the way to the end. The spare room is back there," Aiden said.

"Thanks." I smiled. "Enjoy the rest of the party."

Making my way through the house, I reached the staircase and slipped upstairs, my heart racing in my chest. It was quiet. The music from downstairs drowned out whatever noises were coming from beyond the row of doors that greeted me.

I glanced down the hall, but there was no sign of Rory or Noah. While the coast was clear, I took a left and hurried down the hall.

God, I couldn't believe I was doing this. But there was something exhilarating about it.

Something addictive.

When I reached the last door on the left, I didn't get a chance to knock. It swung open, and Mason grabbed me, pulling me inside.

"W-wait," I rushed out. His brows drew together. "I need to text Rory, or she'll wonder where I am."

Quickly, I dug my cell out of my purse and texted her.

> Harper: Came to find you but there was no sign of you so I'm heading home.

> Aurora: Sorry, Connor puked all over himself. Had to help Noah and Ella clean him up. You're okay getting back?

Harper: I'll be fine. Text tomorrow. xo

Aurora: Okay. xo

"All good?" Mason asked, still watching me.

"I think so." Guilt swarmed in my chest, but it was nothing compared to the sheer lust coursing through my veins.

"So, this is Mason Steele's room," I said as I went to his desk and placed down my purse, his gaze following me the whole time.

It was dark, a desk lamp casting a dim amber glow off the walls.

"Didn't ask you up here to discuss the décor, blondie." He crooked his finger at me. "Come here."

I went to him, sucking in a sharp breath when his hand went to my throat, his fingers curving there. Holding me. "Did you turn up here tonight looking like this just to drive me wild?" Hunger sparked in his eyes.

"I..." The words died on my tongue because Mason was looking at me like he was starved, and I was the only thing on the menu.

His thumbs stroked along my skin, sending tiny shocks through me, making my stomach tighten. "One night," he said. Repeating the words as if he needed to remind me.

Or maybe he needed to remind himself.

"Promise me you won't tell anyone about this," he added.

"I promise."

"Good, because something tells me Coach Dixon wouldn't be too happy if he knew I was ten seconds away from ruining his daughter."

Coach Dixon wouldn't care; I swallowed back the retort, gasping as Mason captured my mouth in a bruising kiss, pushing me up against his bedroom wall.

His hands were everywhere. In my hair, tracing my curves, squeezing my ass. He wasn't soft or gentle or careful. He didn't handle me like glass. He took what he wanted, controlling the kiss—my body—with his sheer dominance.

"Fuck, you taste good." His hand stayed around my throat as he licked the corner of my mouth, staring down at me with a feral kind of hunger.

"Touch me," I whispered, my body wound so tight I could hardly stand it.

"You going to beg, blondie?"

"Please." I sagged against the wall, my eyelashes fluttering.

"How drunk are you?" he asked with a frown.

"Not drunk enough that I'm not fully aware of what you're doing, but drunk enough that I don't care that this is a really bad idea."

Crap. Did I say that aloud?

His mouth twitched. "Bad ideas are the best kind."

I couldn't argue with that because having Mason's

hands on me, his lips on mine was the best kind of bad there was.

He roughly grabbed the back of my knee, hitching my leg around his waist so he could grind against me, and a moan vibrated in my chest.

"Think you can take it?"

"God, I hope so."

He chuckled. Mason Steele buried his face in the curve of my neck and laughed.

What was this life?

The roll of his hips was enough to make me pant for him. He was so big, he felt incredible, and he hadn't even gotten me naked yet.

Jesus, I was in trouble.

So much trouble.

"Time to get you naked," he said, lifting me up and carrying me over to his bed.

He dropped me like a sack of bricks, and I landed with a little huff. But he only smirked, dragging a thumb over his bottom lip as he loomed over me.

I felt like a poor helpless lamb being stalked by a predator. Only, my first instinct wasn't to run because I wanted to be caught.

Mason leaned over me, flicking open the buttons on my corset, moving through them until the material fell away from my body, bearing my black satin underwear to him.

Heat burned in his eyes as he ran his eyes over me. "Fuck," he choked out.

"Like what you see, Steele?"

"Yeah, although I'd like it even more if you were completely naked." He pulled me into a seated position, pushing the dress off my arms before unclasping my bra. Leaning down, he flicked his tongue over my nipple before sucking it into his mouth.

"God, that feels... ah," I cried as he lightly grazed the sensitive bud with his teeth. My fingers stroked through his hair, mussing up the Wolverine ducktail style as he worked my body with his teeth and tongue and lips.

"Lie back," he urged, and I fell against the pillows.

Mason stood, pulling off his leather jacket and tank before unbuttoning his jeans. He grabbed a condom from his wallet and discarded that and his jeans.

I didn't know where to look first. His chest was sculpted and hard from hours upon hours spent in the gym working out; or his thighs, strong and muscular; or the huge bulge in his tight black boxer briefs.

Jesus. Despite the gush I felt between my legs, there was no way that thing was going to fit.

As if he heard my thoughts, Mason smirked. "Don't worry. You'll take me."

"So cocky." I rolled my eyes, fighting a smile.

"Oh, I'm definitely cock-y."

Soft laughter pealed out of me. God, I liked him like this. Playful and naked. Definitely naked.

Slowly, almost teasingly, he pushed his hands into

the waistband of his briefs and shoved them down his hips.

"Oh my God," I breathed, feasting my eyes on the most beautiful dick I'd ever seen.

Long and thick and hard with a slight curve in the tip.

"Touch yourself," he ordered. "Make sure you're ready for me."

My fingers slid down my stomach, dipping between my thighs as I rolled my thumb over my clit, whimpering at how good it felt.

"Legs wider," he said. "I want to see you. All of you."

Mason liked control. It was in every word he gave me, every heated look. But I was all too happy to oblige, knowing that the reward would be worth it.

So freaking worth it.

"Fuck, you're soaked," he rasped, closing a fist around himself and pumping slowly. "Keep touching yourself. Get yourself right to the edge."

Mason tore open the foil wrapper and sheathed himself before kneeling on the end of the bed. I reached for him, needing him close. Needing him to kiss me and touch me and help me get there.

"Jesus, blondie. Your skin is on fire." He ran a hand from my navel to my throat, collaring me, and I wrapped my arms around his shoulders, sighing as his body fell over mine. He felt so good.

Too good.

He stared at me for another beat, something passing between us. Then he kissed me. Hard and unforgiving, licking his tongue deep into my mouth.

Mason Steele was the storm I never saw coming, but by God, if I didn't mind being swept up in its wreckage.

He slipped a hand between us and grasped his dick, nudging it up against my center, dragging it through my wetness, making me shiver and whimper.

"Ready?" he asked, and I nodded, anticipation bubbling inside me, making my heart gallop in my chest.

"I want you, Mason."

It was silly, but I needed him to know that I wanted this.

Him.

Slowly, he pushed inside me, and a moan slipped out. "Mase, God..." I breathed, so full and stretched.

"Come on, blondie. You can take it." His hand clamped around my hip as he rocked forward another inch, making us both groan. "You feel so fucking good."

I preened at his words, tilting my hips a little to allow him to go deeper, filling me completely. When he was all the way in, he stilled above me, breathing harshly.

"Mase?" I whispered, clenching around him, loving the way he felt inside me.

"I really need to fuck you now." The words were a

barely restrained sound, the column of his throat rippling as he swallowed hard.

"So, what are you waiting for?"

Mason pulled out and slammed back in, making me cry out in sweet agony. "Shit, Harper. You gotta be quiet."

Right. Because I wasn't supposed to be in here with him. *Under* him.

I pushed the unwanted thoughts aside, focusing on every feeling and sensation as Mason fucked me.

It was beautiful watching him unravel. His pinched expression softened into something that looked a lot like euphoria.

He hooked his arm under my leg and spread me open, changing the angle and pace. I could barely breathe; it was so intense, a wave of intense pleasure building inside me. Every stroke hit the spot inside me that made me cry out.

"Shit, you're loud," Mason murmured, kissing me. Swallowing my cries. He was everywhere. Consuming me. Devouring me.

Owning me.

"Mason..." I whispered, my body trembling as the wave crashed. Splintering me apart at the seams.

"That's it, blondie. Come all over my cock," he growled, fucking me in slow, shallow strokes.

Another shudder tore through me as I tried to catch my breath. But Mason didn't let up, flipping us so that I was on top of him.

"Ride me," he drawled, hands framing my waist as I sank down on him slowly.

"It's deeper," I said, wincing as he hit my cervix.

"Too much?" A flash of concern lit up his eyes, and that one look made me melt.

"No, I can take it."

"Yeah, you can." A lazy smirk tugged at his mouth, but it quickly melted away when I circled my hips. A groan of approval hummed through his chest, his hands tightening on my waist. "Do that again."

It was my turn to smirk.

I began moving, up and down, round and round, reveling in the way he watched me: awe and sheer lust simmering in his frosty gaze.

"Fuck, Harper," he groaned as I ground myself against him.

This was fun.

The kind of fun a girl could get used to.

"Blondie?" Mason stared up at me, brows pinched, eyes crinkled.

I didn't want him to see the cracks in my veneer, so I leaned down and brushed my lips over his, distracting him, and reminding us both that this was one night.

An exorcism.

A chance for him to fuck me out of his system— and hopefully mine.

Until he said seven little words that utterly ruined me.

ON THIN ICE   189

"Fuck, a guy could get used to this."

My eyes fluttered open, my body screaming out in protest. God, muscles I didn't even know I had ached.

Gingerly, I rolled onto my side and found the culprit for the weary state. Mason slept deeply, one hand shoved under his pillow, the other rested on his washboard abs.

A bolt of lust shot through me as I remembered how thoroughly he'd fucked me last night.

It had been intense. Nothing like I'd ever experienced before. I didn't want to get carried away with myself because what was the point? But after, when we'd been lying there breathless and sated, something had passed between us.

A moment.

A silent wish.

But Mason hadn't acknowledged it—or the seven little words he'd uttered when he was buried deep inside me—and for once in my life, I reined in the urge to spill everything I was feeling.

And I was feeling a lot.

He'd made it clear it was only one night, and I'd promised him.

A promise I intended to keep.

No matter how much it hurt.

I watched him for another second, listening to the gentle rise and fall of his chest. He was so beautiful it hurt to look at him. The bitter sting of regret swarmed my chest as I quietly slipped out of bed and got dressed.

Something told me Mason Steele wouldn't appreciate waking up with his latest conquest still hanging around. And I had enough self-preservation not to want to be on the receiving end of his wrath again.

"Bye, Mason," I whispered, wishing things were different.

Wishing I was the kind of girl guys like him wanted to keep around. The type of girl who could play it cool and not spill all her feelings and scare the guy away before he had a chance to see beyond my flaws.

Then I slipped out of his room as if I'd never been there.

CHAPTER 13

MASON

I REACHED for the warm body beside me, my dick stirring to life at the prospect of another tumble between the sheets with Harper before the rest of the house woke up. But my hand met a cold, empty space.

"The fuck?" My eyes snapped open as realization settled into me.

She was gone.

Harper was gone.

And she hadn't even stuck around to say thanks for the ride.

Rolling onto my back, I threw an arm over my face and let out a frustrated groan. Last night was supposed to be an exorcism, but now I was pissed and horny.

I hadn't expected her to run out on me. But then, I

hadn't expected her to blow my mind quite the way she had, either.

Holy shit.

The sex had been incredible. We'd spent half the night going at it, finding new ways to make each other come apart.

I'd thought—

Fuck, what was I saying? This was a good thing. Harper was gone, and it saved us any awkward good mornings or goodbyes.

I should have been thanking her, so why did I feel so fucking annoyed?

My cell vibrated, and I grabbed it off the nightstand, hardly surprised to see my brother's name.

SB: Are you awake, Mase?

MB: Yeah, buddy, I'm awake.

SB: Why did Dad leave us?

Shit. It was too early for this. I ran a hand down my face, trying to figure out how to play this one.

Dad was a sore spot for Scottie. He worshiped our old man. Put him on a pedestal he didn't deserve. Mom and I were partly to blame for that. We'd wanted to protect him from the truth—that Samuel Steele was a worthless piece of shit who didn't deserve his son's adoration.

Deciding this warranted a conversation instead of a text, I called him.

"Hey, bud, how're things?"

"Okay, I guess," he said flatly.

"What's wrong?"

"I heard Fenton saying some things at recess the other day."

Fenton Jones was a mouthy little shit that I'd rather Scottie didn't hang around with, but friendships were a difficult thing for him to navigate, and it wasn't like he had a line of kids wanting the privilege of being his friend.

"What things?"

"He said his dad saw Dad out with another woman and kid."

Fuck.

"Said that they went to the new skate park across town. Mase..." He was quiet for a second, and then, "Did Dad leave because he's got a new family now?"

Anger flared inside me. No child deserved the shit my old man had pulled, but it felt ten times worse, given Scottie's situation. He didn't understand the nuances of relationships. He didn't understand that Samuel Steele was a coward who didn't deserve even an ounce of Scottie's attention. But he was still his father. His blood. His DNA.

Scottie understood *that,* and it was all that mattered to him.

"Mase?" he whispered. "You can tell me the truth. I can handle it."

Jesus. What the fuck was I supposed to say? He was growing up too fast. Maturing in his own Scottie-way. But it was a risk I was unwilling to take because I would always protect him, no matter what.

"Come on, buddy. You know Dad loves you. Sometimes people fall out of love, and it's better for everyone if they aren't together anymore. It wasn't about you. It was about Mom and Dad."

"So he didn't replace me?"

I wanted to drive over there and lay into my old man and ask him how the fuck he slept at night, knowing that my baby brother was having all these self-doubts and confusing feelings.

"I haven't spoken to him in a while, bud. I don't know who the woman and kid are. But it sounds like he might have a new girlfriend, and that's okay."

"Does that mean Mom's getting a new boyfriend? Will we get a new brother or sister? I'm not sharing my room. I'm not—"

"Okay, buddy, slow down. Take a breath. I don't think Mom is getting a new boyfriend. But one day, she might. And if she does, she'll always talk to you about it first because Mom loves you, Scottie. She loves you so damn much, just like me."

"I love you too, you know," he said. "I know I'm not always good at showing it, but I do. You're my best friend, Mason brother."

"You're my best friend, too, Scottie."

"You didn't say it." His voice turned quiet, and my chest tightened.

"You're my best friend, too, Scottie brother."

"Have you seen Harper?"

"What?"

"Harper? You go to college together, right? Did you see her? Did she look pretty? What was she wearing?"

Yeah, I saw her. Guilt slammed into me. If Scottie ever found out I railed the fuck out of her, he'd probably never forgive me.

"I... shit, it's early for this, kid."

"I know, but I have to wait until Wednesday to see her again. Can you send me a photo—"

"Hold up, bud. That is not okay. You can't take photos of someone and send them to other people. We don't do that."

He went quiet, tension stretching over the line.

"I'm not scolding you, buddy. I'm just telling you—"

"It's not appropriate, yeah, I know." He released a long sigh full of frustration and pre-teen angst. "I wish I was more like you, Mase. I hate that I don't understand stuff and get stuff wrong all the time. It sucks hairy donkey balls."

"Scottie, come on!"

Damn, this kid was going to send me to an early grave. Especially if Mom caught him saying this shit.

"What? You say it all the time."

"I…" He had me there. "How about try not saying it where Mom might overhear, yeah? And never in school. Or at the center. Or around any figures of authority."

"Fine," he huffed. "I'll only say it around you."

"I can live with that." I smiled.

"Ugh. It's school soon. I hate school."

"I know you do. But school is important, and you're good at it, Scottie."

"I'm good at math," he corrected. "I hate English and all that other stuff."

I chuckled, wishing I was there to noogie him. "You've got this. Mom and I are right behind you. And a new week means…"

"I get to see Harper again."

Well, shit. Nothing like being axed for the girl you were balls deep inside last night.

Not that I could *ever* tell my kid brother that.

"Listen, how about I make you a deal. You have a good week at school. Show up and try your best, and I'll see about bringing you to the rink to watch the team practice."

"Seriously? I can come to Ellet Arena?"

"Sure, if I get the green light from Coach. But you've got to try and keep things together for Mom, okay?"

"Okay, I'll try. But sometimes, I can't help it, Mase."

"Yeah, I know, kid. I know. Listen, I need to go, but I'll talk to you soon, okay?"

"Yeah. Mason?"

"Yeah, bud?"

"I love you."

"Love you, too, Scottie brother."

He hung up, and I let out a steady breath. I didn't want to bring up this thing with Dad to Mom; it was just another thing for her to worry about, but I couldn't do nothing.

So I pulled up his number and sent him a text.

> Mase: We need to talk.

I was almost surprised when his name flashed up thirty seconds later.

> Dad: Free now if you want to call?

I hit call and waited.

"Mason, Son."

"You're a real piece of work. You know that, right?"

"What's this all about?" He went straight on the defensive.

"One of Scottie's friends saw you with your new lady friend and her kid. He had—"

"Shit, he knows."

"Yeah, Dad. He knows. Had all these questions about whether you'd found a new family."

"Mason, I didn't mean for him to find out like this.

It isn't serious. Claire's a friend. We hang out sometimes. It's not—"

"I don't give a fuck what you do with your personal life, but when I have to field questions from Scottie about whether the reason you left is because of your new family, it's a problem."

"I'll fix it. I'll talk to him. You know I would never intentionally hurt him." Bitter laughter crawled up my throat, and he choked out, "M-Mason?"

But I wasn't looking to play his games or pander to his guilt.

"I don't give a fuck who the woman and kid are. All I care about is the boy you abandoned. Fix it."

"I will. I'll try and see him as soon as possible, okay? I didn't—"

"Save it for someone who cares," I sneered, hanging up.

Fuck him and his fucking excuses.

Samuel Steele was a lying, cowardly piece of shit, and I was all too happy to cut him out of my life. But it wasn't so simple where Scottie was concerned.

Feeling tense, I decided to shower first, then go in search of coffee and something to eat. With what little sleep I had, it was going to be a long fucking day.

Worth it, though.

My lips twitched as I let the memories flood in. It was dangerous to go there, to remember last night. But it instantly quelled some of the anger inside me. The memory of Harper beneath me, legs wrapped around my waist like a vise, her above me, riding me like a fucking pro. Taking me like she was born to do it.

I shoved *that* last thought out of my head. It was one night. The sex was great. She was great. But that's all it was—a chance to get her out of my system.

Now I could move on with my life and forget all about my weird fixation with Harper Dixon.

"Morning," I said, joining a few of the guys in the kitchen.

There was always someone hanging around. It was one of the perks or downsides of living in a frat house. I hadn't pledged—not many of the lower classmen did these days—but the house's history was tied to Sigma Delta Pi.

"What happened to you last night?" Ward asked as he hoovered up his cereal.

"I bailed around midnight, I think."

"Lightweight," he muttered.

"Were you alone?" Leon added with a look I didn't like.

"Yeah, why?"

"Because Heller saw a blonde slipping out early this morning. And we can't work out whose room she came from."

"Sure as shit wasn't mine." The lie rolled off my tongue.

"Told ya," Ward said.

"Well, it wasn't me or you, Heller or Mac. We saw Tipper and Johnson come down with their bunnies."

"Who does that leave?"

"Seriously?" I asked.

"What?" Leon shrugged. "Heller said she was hot."

Everything went still inside me. "He saw her?"

"Only from behind. Said she had a really tight ass."

Jealousy surged inside me.

Fuck.

I did not need this shit.

"I guess it could have been Adams."

"Nah," I said.

"He might be an asshole on and off the ice, but the bunnies seem to dig him."

"Twenty dollars says it wasn't Adams."

They both looked at me with confused expressions. Just then, the guy in question came swaggering into the kitchen.

"Mornin'."

"Adams," Ward said for the three of us.

The guy was an ass. Arrogant. Smug. And not nearly as good on the ice as he believed. But Coach didn't play favorites, and Abel Adams had earned his ticket to LU like the rest of us.

"Enjoy the party?" he asked.

"Yeah, man. It was a fucking riot. What about you?"

"Oh yeah, the bunnies were on form. Had me a little fun with Daphne *and* Velma."

"So you didn't have a blonde over?"

"Blonde?"

"Yeah, Heller said he saw a bunny escaping early this morning. Petite blonde in a Lakers t-shirt."

Why did the idea of Harper sneaking out in my clothes send a direct signal to my dick?

"We've been trying to work out who she was with, but we're running out of options."

Abel's expression clouded for a second, and then a big grin cracked over his face. "Oh shit, Heller saw her?"

"So it was you?"

"Come on now, guys." He smirked. "You know I never kiss and tell."

I snorted at that. Shameless fucking liar. But I didn't call him out on his bullshit. I couldn't. Not without outing myself.

So I kept silent, imagining all the ways I would make it hurt if he ever tried to lay so much as a finger on Harper.

Again, with the possessiveness, Steele. She's not yours, remember.

Still, I didn't like the idea of him anywhere near her. She was Aurora's best friend, and Adams had already earned himself a black eye courtesy of Noah for talking shit about his girl.

"Nice," Leon said, holding a fist out for Abel to

bump.

"All I'm going to say is Energizer Bunny." He waggled his brows suggestively.

Fucking asshole.

Not that he was wrong about Harper. He was pretty damn accurate. But he was lying through his teeth about being anywhere near her.

Shit. It was only the morning after, and I already had the serious urge to lay some kind of claim on her.

Which was not part of the plan, and definitely not my usual MO.

"You good, Mase?" Ward asked. "You look kinda pale."

"He wishes," Abel laughed. "Isn't that right, Mase?"

I stood, my stool scraping across the tile. "Go fuck yourself, asshole. I'm out."

I stalked out of there before I did something stupid.

Something I couldn't take back.

Something I knew I would regret. Because I wasn't that guy, I didn't catch feelings or any of that shit. It was just a bad case of post-sex confusion. Her pussy had tricked me into this weird state of possessiveness. That's all it was.

When the memories wore off, so would she.

I was already counting down the minutes.

"Here he is," Coach Dixon said when I entered the locker room later that day. "The man of the hour."

Noah threw me a bemused look, and I discreetly flipped him off.

"You looked good out there, kid. Strong. How'd it feel getting the winning goal?"

"I..." Shit. The goal had felt good, sure, but this, being surrounded by my teammates while James 'The Real Deal' Dixon sang my praises, was all kinds of fucking awkward.

Add in the fact I'd been buried deep in his daughter last night, and the whole thing was like some bad trip. Harper was the last thing I wanted to think about. Especially now there was a chance I would run into her around campus.

"You're too fucking modest, son," Coach Dixon chuckled, clapping me on the back as he headed toward the hall leading to the offices.

"Seriously, if we have to put up with this shit all season—"

"Don't," I snapped at Noah.

"I get it. He's looking to relive his glory days through you. But even you've got to admit; it's a little much."

"Look alive, ladies," Coach Tucker boomed. "I want you out on the ice in five. We've got a big weekend ahead of us."

Two home games against local rivalry, the Detroit U Bulldogs, to be precise.

"Heard you and Adams got into it this morning," Aiden said, pulling on his jersey over his pads.

"It was nothing."

"I'll tell you what I told Noah. If he causes problems, you need to come to me with them, so I can handle it. Okay?"

I managed a curt nod because the lying fucker had decided to run with the story about Harper sneaking out of his room this morning.

Of course, no one knew it was Harper. But I did. And I knew she hadn't been anywhere near the cocky asshole.

My fists clenched against my thighs as I forced myself to take a calming breath. So much for digging her out from under my skin. At least some time on the ice would help expel all the excess energy coursing through my veins.

Energy that only seemed to multiply after my tangle in the sheets with Harper.

"Hey, man, you good?" Aiden stared at me expectantly.

"I'm fine." I laced up my skates, grabbed my helmet, and stood. "See you on the ice."

I made my way out to the rink, trying to shake off the lingering memories. Silently telling myself that I did not absolutely fucking care that she'd left the house without so much as a goodbye.

The second I stepped out on the ice, all thoughts went quiet. I fell into a rhythm with my teammates already skating a few warmup laps. I agreed with the guys—the way Coach Dixon homed in on me made me feel all kinds of uncomfortable. But there was also no denying that it had lit a fire under my ass.

Made me imagine *what-if*.

I wanted it.

I wanted to turn pro.

I'd always fucking wanted it, but the weight of responsibility, the crushing guilt I felt every time I spoke to Scottie, whispered that I couldn't have it.

That I couldn't make it work.

But what if I could?

With Coach Dixon's guidance and his interest in my future, maybe I could. After all, he'd done it. He'd turned a teenage dream into a reality.

Harper's face flashed into my mind. Her big blue eyes locked on mine as her pussy clamped around my dick.

I needed to put her out of my head. Focus on the things that mattered. Like school. My family. Hockey.

I needed to remember all the reasons why I *didn't* like her.

But most of all, I needed to remember that her father potentially held the keys to my future in his palm.

If I was going to do this, if I was going to go after hockey, I needed to leave Harper in my rearview mirror.

CHAPTER 14

HARPER

I COULDN'T STOP THINKING about him.

Mason Steele.

Lakers number thirteen.

The cold, indifferent guy who had been pure fire between the sheets.

Being with him had been like nothing I could have ever imagined. Not only did I confirm that the rumors were, in fact, true, but I also learned that he knew exactly what to do with his monster dick.

As I suspected though—and as he'd made perfectly clear before we got naked—it was one night.

He'd wanted to fuck me out of his system, and from the cold shoulder he'd given me yesterday when I ran into him, Noah, and Rory, he'd done just that.

It stung.

Okay, it more than stung.

But what did I really expect? That we would get naked, and he would fall hopelessly in lust with me?

Maybe, just a little.

I silenced the delusional little voice. I knew what I was getting into when I said yes. When I agreed to his terms. Now I had to live with the consequences.

I shouldered the door to the bar and slipped inside, relieved to find the place half empty. Tuesday nights were typically quiet at Millers, and I was looking forward to an easy shift.

"Hey," Janelle said as I approached the counter.

"How're things?"

"Good, thanks. Slow. But good. Chad's in a foul mood, though."

"You'll find Chad's bad moods tend to reflect on how busy this place gets."

She chuckled. "Kalvin's around here somewhere, doing a stock check, I think."

"Got it. I'm going to put my purse in the staff room and log onto the register. See you soon."

Chad grumbled a hello as I passed the service hatch, and I gave him a small wave. It was better to avoid his wrath when the place was empty.

I went into the staff room and stored my purse in the staff locker, then grabbed an apron and double-tied it around my waist. Tips would be slow tonight, but I'd made enough the other weekend to last me a little while.

I was good with money; I had to be.

When I went back out front, I found Kalvin and Janelle chatting at the bar.

"Hey." Kalvin's eyes lit up. "I was hoping you'd be on tonight."

"You were?"

He nodded. "Jill is great, but she's so..."

"Hey, I love Jill," I said.

"Janelle here was just telling me all her problems."

"Kal," she hissed.

"What? We're all one big happy family here, right, Dixie?"

"Something like that. What's up?" I asked her.

"So, I'm seeing this guy..."

"Scandalous." I smirked, and Kal smothered a laugh.

"Ha, ha. We're not really seeing each other as such, but we're—"

"They're fuck buddies." Kal smirked.

"Right. Gotcha." My mind flashed to Mason, but I shoved those thoughts out of my head. We weren't fuck buddies. We weren't even buddies at this point. "Exclusive fuck buddies or—"

"I'm not seeing other people. I barely have time to see him. But I like him. A lot. And I think he likes me."

"So tell him." I shrugged. "What's the worst that could happen?"

"You make it sound so simple."

"It is that simple. I've never understood the whole

play it cool thing. Leaves a lot of room for misunderstanding and a chance for your feelings to get hurt."

"But if he doesn't feel the same…"

"At least you'll know. Will it suck? Sure, for a little while. But wouldn't you rather know now than a few weeks or months down the line?"

"Huh. I didn't think of it like that."

"I can't believe I'm saying this," Kalvin added. "But Harper has a point. Direct and to the point might work."

"I don't know." She gnawed the end of her thumb, blushing. "We've got a good thing going. I don't want to ruin it. But I also kinda want more, you know?"

Didn't we all.

"Maybe build up to it then," I said because she looked all kinds of sad, and I got it.

God, did I get it.

"Build up to… yeah, I like that idea. Maybe I'll see if he wants to hang out this week."

"Is that code for fu—"

"No." Janelle smacked Kalvin's arm. "I mean, hang out. The non-sex variety. Dating in college is hard."

"Pretty sure that's what he said." Kalvin grinned, and it was my turn to smother a laugh.

"Oh my God, stop!"

"Hey, you three," Chad bellowed. "I'm not paying you to stand around and gossip."

"Someone's pissy."

"Someone's having the dollar-sign withdrawals," I said.

"Maybe you should text your hockey friends," Kalvin suggested, and I glowered at him, flipping him off for good measure.

The less the team came around here, the better.

"Hey, question," Kalvin said as we wiped down the counter.

The shift had dragged. Customers had dwindled off to a handful of couples. Chad sent Janelle home an hour ago before he closed the kitchen and followed not long after, leaving Kalvin and me to close up.

"Shoot."

"What do you make of Janelle?"

"She seems nice enough. Why?"

"I think we had a moment."

"A moment?" My brows crinkled. "Did you miss the part where she's trying to turn her FB into her BAE?"

He stared at me like I'd grown a second head, and I murmured, "Fuck buddy into her BAE. Before anyone else."

"Right. Yeah, I know. But it doesn't exactly sound optimistic, and she's so fucking hot. I think we could have some fun together."

"You want to be her FB, too?" I asked a little incredulously.

"I'd date her. Take her out. Romance her." His brows waggled, but it felt insincere. "I'm not that shallow, Dixie."

"Good to know," I chuckled, but it came out a little strained.

"What? Don't give me those big disapproving eyes. It's college. The majority of people don't find their forever love at college. They fuck around."

Okay, he had me there.

More than I liked.

"Are you really telling me you've been here for over two months, and you haven't gotten freaky between the sheets with anyone?" He gave me a pointed look that made me flush all over.

"I..."

"Case in point, my friend. Case in point," he chuckled. "It's human nature. We all crave connection. That addictive high only sex can give you. So long as everyone has their cards on the table and consents, then it's all good."

How many times had I told myself exactly the same thing? And how many times had I still let the wires get mixed up?

Sex and feelings were inextricably linked for most females. Scientific studies proved women received more oxytocin than men after sex. And that feeling accompanying an oxytocin rush was addictive.

The fairer sex was wired differently, and no matter how much we fought against the tide—or simple biology as the case was—it was hard not to fall into that pattern of becoming attached after sex.

Throw in a heap of childhood trauma and abandonment issues, and it was a recipe for disaster.

It didn't matter that I'd crept out of Mason's bed yesterday morning in one of his t-shirts and fled Lakers House before he woke up or that I hadn't tried to text him or reach out since he rocked my world. Deep down, I knew that if he came around looking for a repeat, I'd say yes.

And I hated it.

I hated that I wasn't strong enough. That my father had screwed me up so badly that I'd risk more heartache just to chase that feeling—that chemical rush—for a little while longer.

"Harper?"

I blinked up at Kalvin and forced a smile. "Sorry, long day."

"Anything you want to talk about?"

"No, I'm good. Thanks." I didn't quite meet his inquisitive gaze. "But my advice to Janelle stands. If you like someone, you should just tell them. Life's too short, and there's plenty more fish in the sea."

At least, that's what I kept telling myself.

The loud knock at my door barely touched the bone-deep fatigue I'd woken with.

"Harper?" Aurora called, and I managed to drag my weary, aching body off the bed and to the door.

"Oh my God," she breathed the second it swung open. "What happened?"

"I got glutened."

"Glutened?"

"Yep."

And I was pissed.

I was careful with what I ate. Careful, to the point that I usually took my own snacks to Millers, but Chad had insisted he'd added something to the menu just for me. Something he'd promised had been cooked and prepared in a safe space.

Careless asshole.

I'd woken in the middle of the night with excruciating cramps and waves of nausea battering my insides. I hadn't vomited, but I hadn't gotten much sleep, which only made the nausea ten times worse.

"Can I get you anything?" Aurora asked, following me inside my dorm room.

"No, I'm loaded up on Isotonix. I just need to ride it out."

"Did you email your professors?"

"Yeah. I'm hoping it wears off fast. I have the group at RCC later."

"Maybe you should call and let them know you won't be there."

"I don't want to miss it."

It was only my second official session with Scottie. He needed routine, and I didn't want to be another person in his life who let him down.

"But if you're sick—"

"I'll be fine by this afternoon," I said defiantly, despite the urge to burrow under my covers and fall into an everlasting slumber.

"Harper..."

"I'll be fine." I waved her off. "I just need to rest."

Once I'd slept off what I could, I would hydrate, load myself up on probiotics, and hope for the best.

It was only for a couple of hours. I could do it. Then I could come home, crawl into bed, and sleep it off some more.

"Are you sure I can't get you anything before I have to head to class?" Rory asked, sympathy bleeding into her expression.

"No, I'll be okay. But thanks for checking in on me."

"Of course. I was worried when you didn't answer my texts."

Leaning over, I grabbed my cell phone off the desk. Sure enough, I had a stream of texts from Rory and a missed call from my mom. "Sorry, I didn't hear them."

"Don't be silly. You're sick. You need to rest. Do you know what it was? That *glutened* you, I mean?"

"Would you believe me if I said my boss's lame attempt at making the bar more Harper-friendly?"

"Your boss did this?" She gasped.

"Well, technically, I did it. He said he wanted me to test a couple of dishes for a new gluten-free range. I stupidly assumed that meant he'd taken extra precautions preparing and cooking the food. But my current physical state would suggest otherwise."

"Were the dishes at least worth it?" A small, uncertain smile tugged at her lips.

"The buttermilk chicken was questionable, but the three-bean chili was so good I thought I'd died and gone to heaven."

"Damn."

"Yeah," I groaned, clutching my stomach as a wave of pain rolled through me.

"Does heat help?"

"Not really."

She checked her phone for the time and frowned. "I should—"

"Go, it's fine. Really. It's nothing I haven't survived a hundred times before."

"I'll text you later."

"Okay. And Rory?"

"Yeah?" She looked back over her shoulder.

"Thank you."

"That's what friends are for."

Her words stayed with me long after the door clicked shut behind her.

I'd never had real girlfriends before. It was nice even if they had all bagged themselves a Lakers hockey player.

Jealousy isn't a good look on you, Harper.

I grabbed the edge of the covers and sank back into the pile of pillows before opening Mom's message.

> Mom: Call me. Mom xo

> Harper: I'm not feeling so good. Rain check?

> Mom: Okay. Call me when you can. Look after yourself. Mom xo

Part of me wanted to tell her she didn't need to end every text with 'Mom xo,' but it would only fall on deaf ears, just like my father's mistreatment of his only child had for all these years.

When I was a little girl, learning how to adapt to my diagnosis, Mom was there. She would comb through ingredient lists, research Harper-friendly foods, and experiment with new recipes. But as I grew older and learned to manage my disease, her interest waned. Or maybe it just was too many years spent listening to my dad's tirades.

One meal won't hurt.

It's just a little stomachache; quit complaining.

Stop making a fuss, Harriet.

Just let her eat the damn pasta.

As my mother, she was supposed to choose me—to fight for me—but Harriet Dixon was weak, and as time went on, she chose him over me.

It was a lonely life, which is why I couldn't wait to come to Lakeshore U.

And now he was here, and I was supposed to just roll over and accept it.

By some small miracle, I managed to make it to the RCC. My insides still felt like a hammer had pounded them, but I was up on two feet, ready for my session with Scottie, and the rest of the kids in the group.

Linda greeted me, casting a concerned eye toward me. "What's wrong?"

"Nothing, I'm fine," I said.

"Harper, if you're sick—"

"Don't worry, it isn't catching," I said. "It's just a flare-up. But I've got it under control, I swear."

"You're sure? Because we can handle things without you today."

"No, I'm here. I can do it."

Just then, the doors swung open, and my name filled the room.

"Harper. Harper," Scottie bellowed.

"Someone's happy to see you," Linda smiled, giving my shoulder a little squeeze. "Any trouble, you let me know."

"Harper."

"Hey, Scottie, how's it going?" I smiled.

"You came back." He looked me up and down. "You didn't die."

"No, buddy. I didn't die. But I'm not feeling so great."

"What's wrong? Do you have the mono? Mom says that's catching. She says—"

"No, I don't have mono." Soft laughter spilled out of me. "Remember I told you that I get sick sometimes when I eat gluten?" He nodded, and I went on, "Well, I got glutened. But I'll be fine. I'm excited about the origami."

"It sounds kind of lame," he murmured.

"No way. Origami is the best."

"Did you see my brother this week?"

"No, I didn't."

He gave me a dismissive nod as I got our station set up.

God, I was a terrible person. But the less Scottie knew about Mason and me, the better.

"He's picking me up today."

Great.

"That's nice."

"I'm sorry Mason shouted at you at the diner the other day. I don't think he wants me to skate."

"He's probably just worried because he knows you're scared and doesn't want you to get upset."

Another nod.

Scottie followed my lead, taking one of the pre-cut shapes and following the folds. He was so damn cute, with all that floppy hair and pensive expression. His eyes were all Mason, but the rest of his features must have been his parents.

"Good job, buddy. That's it. You need to fold right along that crease."

He responded well to my instructions, unlike a kid two tables over, who was giving Greta, one of the other volunteers, a hard time. But Linda had explained that this group wasn't just about fun and downtime. It was about expanding the kids' experiences and exposing them to new things. Some pushback was expected.

Scottie was the perfect student, though. Until he said quietly, "My dad has a new family."

"I... I'm sorry."

"Why are you sorry?" He looked at me with a strange expression.

"It's a figure of speech," I explained. "I just mean, that must be hard for you."

He shrugged. "Mason said that he left because he and my mom didn't love each other anymore. But I think he's lying."

"I'm sure Mason would never do that."

Another shrug, another brush-off.

"He's right about grown-ups," I added. "Sometimes

they fall out of love, and it's better for them to be apart than together. But it doesn't mean they don't love you just as much as they always have."

Scottie didn't reply, though. He focused all his attention on the project—burrowing deeper into the feelings he didn't quite understand.

I didn't push. I just let him know I was there if he needed me, all while trying to ignore the groaning ache in my stomach.

Aurora was right: I shouldn't have come today. My body was in tatters, and I wasn't sure I'd make the drive home. But I was glad I'd made an effort.

Even though I had to tell myself repeatedly, I'd done it for the kid sitting opposite me.

And not his big brother.

CHAPTER 15

MASON

I SPOTTED Harper's car as I pulled into the RCC parking lot.

Fuck. She was here.

Noah had told me she was sick, so I was hoping to avoid running into her. Apparently, she'd been 'glutened.'

Whatever the fuck that meant.

Shouldering the door, I climbed out, prepared to face my fate. At least I didn't have to go in there. They would sign Scottie over to me at the door, so I didn't even have to see her.

Almost three days had passed since I'd woken up alone in bed. Three days for me to get over myself. To get over her.

But it wasn't working.

Jenni had texted me last night, and I'd made up some bullshit excuse. I didn't owe her anything; what we had going wasn't like that. But I didn't want to spend the night with her. I wanted—

No.

Fuck that.

My dick might have wanted to go a second round with Harper, but I didn't want her.

I didn't want—*or need*—anyone.

Shoving all thoughts of her out of my head, I entered the center and made my way down the hall to join the line of parents waiting to get their kids. I couldn't see Scottie, but it looked like they were doing some kind of group activity. Harper sat on a chair outside the circle, her arm wrapped around her stomach. She didn't look so good; her skin was pallid, her expression weary.

Was she still sick?

The thought didn't sit well with me. But it was none of my business.

The group leader stood and clapped her hands, beaming at the kids who stared back at her with a mix of expressions ranging from bored to confused to utterly entranced.

The room became a hive of activity as the kids all grabbed their coats and backpacks and lined up behind the desk at the door. Scottie didn't head for the line, though. He made a beeline for Harper. She got up, but I didn't miss the sharp intake of breath as she moved sluggishly beside him.

Kids and their parents bustled in the hall as I moved up the line, keeping one eye on her and my brother. I could just make out the words, 'I'll be fine' form on her lips, but Scottie looked less than convinced, his brows drawn tight in contemplation.

Of all the people to form an attachment with, it had to be her.

The one girl under my skin.

A girl who had no right to be there.

We were like chalk and cheese.

Oil and water.

Fire and ice.

My mouth twitched at that last one. She'd fucking branded herself onto my soul the other night. There was no other explanation. And I needed to figure out a way to erase her mark, and soon.

"Scottie," the volunteer at the desk called. "Your brother is here."

He glanced over but quickly turned back to Harper. She frowned at whatever he was saying and shook her head.

Jesus. What now?

He fisted his hands at his sides before swinging around and marching over to me. Little brother was agitated, and I knew I needed to get him out of there before things went to shit.

"Hey, bud," I kept my voice light. Easy breezy. "How was group?"

"Okay." He refused to look at me.

"You ready to head home? I thought we could hang out in your room and play a video game or build some Legos."

"Yeah. Whatever." He shrugged, barging past me and storming down the hall.

"Thanks," I said to the volunteer, signing my name on the sign-out form. My gaze flicked to Harper, but she was staring out the window to the hallway beyond.

Shit. What had gone down between them?

But there was no time to ask. Scottie was gone. And he was my priority, always.

The second I turned my back on her, I felt her stare follow. Heated and heavy. Threatening to burn right through the ice around my heart. Right until I walked past the glass window, and I could finally breathe again.

Scottie was in the reception area, waiting. Fidgeting with the straps on his bag as he stared at the floor.

"Want to tell me what that was all about?" I asked him.

"She's sick."

"She can't be that sick if she's here, bud."

I fought the urge to glance back, not that I would be able to see her.

"Come on, let's head out." With my hand on his shoulder, I guided Scottie out of the building and over to my car. "In you go," I said, holding the door open. He looked back over to the building and frowned.

"Come on, bud. Work with me here."

"What if she's really sick?"

"I'm sure she's fine." I closed the door and went around to the driver's side, climbing inside.

"What if it's the cross-tamination? What if she drives home and passes out and has an accident? What—"

"Scottie," I snapped, gripping the wheel. "Breathe, bud. Just take a breath, okay? I'm sure Harper is—"

As if our conversation had summoned her, she exited the building and slowly headed toward her car. My brows furrowed. She was still clutching her stomach, moving at a snail's pace as she practically staggered across the parking lot.

"What the— oh shit." I was out of the car in a second, racing over to her as she slumped against the side of her car.

"You okay there, blondie?" I asked.

"M-Mason?" Her eyelashes fluttered as she peered up at me. But it wasn't surprise on her face; it was sheer exhaustion.

"Fuck," I hissed, reaching for her and helping her stand on two feet.

"Harper, Harper..." Scottie ran over, and I muttered under my breath.

"You need to stay in the car—"

"No. Harper's my friend, too."

"I'm... fine." Harper tried to pull away from me, but she could barely stand.

"Do you need a hospital? A doctor?"

"N-no. I just need... to sleep it off."

In the middle of the parking lot?

Yeah, not going to happen.

"Come on." I slipped my arm around her waist and pulled her toward my car.

"I'm so embarrassed," she murmured, half out of it, as she leaned her head on my shoulder.

It was as if she was drunk. Or high. Or somewhere in between. Is this what a gluten overdose did to a celiac? It seemed a little extreme.

With a little manhandling, I managed to get Harper into the back of my car. Scottie insisted on sliding in beside her.

It didn't seem wholly appropriate, letting my kid brother be her leaning post. But neither did leaving her alone to handle things.

And if I was being entirely honest with myself, I didn't like the idea of anyone else taking care of her.

Fuck.

These possessive thoughts infiltrating my mind were fucking annoying and unwarranted.

She wasn't mine.

She was never going to be mine.

"I'm so sorry," she murmured, her heavy-lidded gaze catching mine in the rearview mirror.

"You can come home with us," Scottie declared. "Right, Mase?"

"I... yeah. You can come sleep it off at ours. I'll drive you back to get your car later."

"Mm-hmm," she murmured, leaning her head against the window.

"Is she gonna be okay, Mase?" Scottie worried his lip between his teeth.

"Yeah, bud. She'll be okay."

At least, I hoped she would.

I was out of my depth.

Lifting my ass off the seat, I dug my cell out of my pocket and pulled up Google.

How to treat being glutened.

Hundreds of hits came straight up, and I opened the first link.

"What are you doing?" Scottie asked, not taking his eyes off Harper's sleeping form.

"We need to make a stop on the way home, okay?"

"Will it make Harper better?"

"I hope so, bud."

Because the sooner she got better, the sooner I could send her on her way.

Harper was still out cold by the time we pulled up outside my house.

"Take everything inside," I said to Scottie. "And I'll get Harper."

My brother grabbed the grocery bag and climbed out of the car, traipsing up to the house. But he hesitated, watching as I got out and went around to the back door, trying to figure out the best way to get Harper out.

I went with brute force, yanking open the door and catching her body before she tumbled out.

"M-Mase?" she murmured.

"Yeah, blondie, it's me. I got you." I managed to slide my arm under her knees and pick her up, saying a silent fucking prayer that none of the neighbors saw me carrying a barely conscious girl into my house.

At least Scottie was present and accounted for. He'd be my witness to my attempt at chivalry—and not kidnap—if the local rumor mill started up.

"Get the door, buddy." I dangled my keys for him, and he snatched them off my finger, jamming them into the door.

"She can sleep in my bed."

Nice try. My lips twitched.

"Let's put her in my room."

"But—"

"I'm going to need you to help me, okay?"

Scottie nodded, his eyes flicking between Harper's lifeless body and the bag still in his hand. He shadowed me down the hall and up the stairs to my room, standing vigil as I laid her down.

Her eyes flickered open, and something inside me tumbled. "This is so embarrassing," she croaked. "Where are we?"

"My house," Scottie piped up.

"You brought me to... wow, okay." She tried to sit up but flopped down in a breathless heap.

"We got you some things." I beckoned Scottie over, and he started unpacking the bag. "Activated charcoal, ginger tea, turmeric capsules, probiotics, and—"

Harper's fingers curled around my arm, my eyes snapping to her. "You did all that... for me?"

"Well, yeah. Dr. Google said—"

"Dr. Google?"

"Yeah, you were practically passed out, and I didn't know what to do, so I went online. Did I get it wrong?"

"No." Harper's soft laughter filled my childhood bedroom. I'd never had a girl in here before, not that I would ever tell her that.

"I just can't believe you, Mason Steele, did that for me."

"Yeah, well, don't let it go to your head. Scottie would never have let me live it down if I'd just left you there."

"Harper." The boy in question stepped forward.

"Hi, buddy. I'm really sorry you had to see me like this."

"Are you going to die?"

"No. *No*! I'll be fine once the symptoms wear off. I promise."

"Hey, bud. Can you go and get Harper a bottle of water out of the refrigerator, please?"

"Yeah, okay."

The second he left the room, Harper turned her weary gaze on me. "I am so sorry. I didn't think—"

"Why'd you do it?"

"Sorry, what?"

"Noah told me you were sick. I didn't expect to see you at the center. If you knew you weren't feeling well, why show up? Why risk it?"

Her expression softened, but she dropped her eyes.

"Harper?"

"I..." She lifted her face again, and I had to force myself to take a breath. Something was happening to me. Something really fucking disarming. "I didn't want to let him down."

She could have said anything—*anything* but that.

"That's admirable... but it was still a stupid thing to do." It came out more of a reprimand than I intended.

"Yeah." A sigh rolled through her. "Can you help me sit up?"

I slid my arms around her and hoisted her up the bed, our faces too close. Harper stared at me, something flashing in her eyes as her gaze dropped to my mouth.

Fuck.

She was in my house. In my bed. Looking every bit as gorgeous as she usually did, despite her pale skin and tired eyes. It wasn't supposed to be like this. Her. Me. *Us.*

A beat passed, the air strained between us.

"Mason, I—"

"Got it." Scottie burst into the room, and I jerked away, standing and cupping the back of my neck.

"What's up?" He frowned, glancing between us.

"Nothing, I'm fine." Harper patted the side of the bed. "Come over here."

He went willingly, perching on the edge of the bed, hanging on her every word.

"Thank you for helping me." She smiled.

"I didn't want you to die."

Jesus. This kid.

"I'm going to be fine. I promise. You and Mason bought the whole pharmacy." Her gaze lifted to mine, full of gratitude and something I didn't want to acknowledge.

"Why don't we go downstairs and get a snack, bud. I'm sure Harper would like a minute to get herself together."

"But I don't want—"

"Scottie," I said firmly.

"Yeah, okay." His shoulders slumped with resignation. "Bye, Harper."

"Bye." She gave him a small wave.

"Take as long as you need," I said, barely making

eye contact. I needed to get out of here, to give myself a minute to think.

"Okay, thanks," she quietly said as I followed Scottie out of the room. But she called after me.

"Mason?"

"Yeah?" I glanced back, struck by a bolt of lightning, when our eyes collided.

"Thanks for doing this."

I gave her a curt nod before walking out of there.

Wondering if I'd made a huge fucking mistake.

"What do you think she's doing up there?" Scottie asked me as he meticulously arranged his hockey card collection out on the kitchen table.

"Sleeping it off, maybe?" I shrugged, eyes flicking to the door.

It had been almost forty minutes since we left her up there. Mom would be home soon, and that was a conversation I didn't want to have. Ever.

I'd never brought a girl home before, so I knew she'd have a field day with this.

"Do you think she's okay? What if she—"

"I'll go check." I shot up out of my chair.

"Don't shout at her."

"What?" My brows knitted.

"Harper. Don't shout at her. Like you did before."

I frowned. "When did I shout at her?"

"At the diner when we had brunch."

"Buddy, I didn't shout."

"You used the tone. I don't like it when you use the tone. Harper probably didn't like it either."

"Bud, come on, I was annoyed."

"At Harper." He looked at me, really looked. As if he was trying to understand, trying to join the dots and connect the wires that got so messed up in his head sometimes.

"She had no right to suggest we take you skating. She doesn't know you like—"

"Hey."

We both whipped our heads around to find Harper standing in the door.

"Hey." I gave her a tight smile. "How are you feeling?"

"Embarrassed, but okay. Thanks again for all the supplies." She held the bag up. "I'll pay you back. I can—"

"No, it's fine."

Tension stretched between us, filling the kitchen with a heaviness that wasn't here before.

"Wanna see my cards?" Scottie asked.

"Is that your collection?"

"It is." He beamed.

"Wow, it's amazing." She came closer, running her eyes over the cards, homing in on one of the cards in a protective cover. "Holy crap, is that a 1979 Wayne

Gretzky Rookie Card?"

"Yeah, it's the best card I have, but it's got a tear. Mom tried to fix it, but you can still see the crease."

"Impressive."

"I've been collecting them since I was a little boy. It's my thing," he said proudly.

"Neat thing." Harper smiled. "Who knows, maybe one day, you'll have a card with Mason's grumpy face on it." Her eyes gazed at mine, the faintest smile on her face.

"It'll happen."

No hesitation, not a flicker of uncertainty. Just a definitive answer as if he knew without a shadow of a doubt that I'd make it. That I'd go all the way.

"Coach Dixon thinks he can do it."

Harper went still, and I wondered whether she realized her hand had curled into a fist at her side.

"I'm sure he does." She glanced away, the temperature dropping to subzero.

What the fuck had happened between them?

I tamped down the urge to ask her about it. *It's none of your business, asshole.*

"Who's your favorite player, Harper?" Scottie stared up at her with big, wide eyes. It wasn't lost on me that it had only taken a pretty girl to bring him out of his shell.

"I'm a Penguins fan. So I'm going to go with Kris Letang or Lemieux." I gawked at her, and she looked over. "What?"

"Nothing." I folded my arms over my chest.

I'd assumed her hockey knowledge was for show. An ode to the fact her father was something of a local legend.

I didn't think—

"Who's your favorite player?" She shot back, some color finally warming her cheeks again.

The same shade of pink she'd flushed when I was deep inside her, fucking into her like I might never get another chance.

Because you won't get another chance.

"Alex Ovechkin, hands down."

"Three times Ted Lindsay Award winner," Scottie started, and I couldn't help but smile.

"Awarded the Hart Memorial Trophy three times." Harper glanced at my brother, and they shared a small, secretive smile.

"Won the Maurice Richard Trophy nine times."

"Don't forget the Conn Smythe Trophy," she added.

Okay. What the fuck was happening right now? I was being tag teamed by my little brother and the girl I was trying—and failing—to get out of my head.

"You know hockey," I said, a little awed.

"Well, yeah." She gave a tiny shrug, her big blue eyes glittering with something.

"Yeah, but I mean, you *know* hockey."

"You do know who my dad is, right?" Harper chuckled, but it sounded all wrong.

"Yeah, but still." It was my turn to shrug.

"She doesn't know more than me, though, right, Mason brother?"

"No, bud. Nobody knows as much as you." I went over to him and ruffled his hair, needing to break the strange tension that had descended over us.

It was too much.

She was too much.

And honestly, I didn't know what the fuck to do with that.

CHAPTER 16

HARPER

"THANKS," I said as Mason drove me back to the RCC. "I know I keep saying it, but you didn't have to do that."

Much to Scottie's chagrin, Mason had asked their neighbor, an older woman with kind eyes and curly gray hair, to watch him until Mrs. Steele got home.

I got the impression he didn't want me there when she returned.

"It was nothing," he said with his dismissive trademark tone.

Things had cooled between us—no trace of the fire that had burned Sunday night. I wanted to ask him about it and see where his head was, but I knew I would only be asking for more heartache, so I swallowed the words.

It wasn't an easy thing to do. Not when I was ignoring my own advice to be honest and upfront.

But despite the rare moments when a temporary truce settled between us, Mason barely tolerated me, and I suspected that if I hadn't ended up volunteering at the RCC, I would never have ended up in his bed.

A truth that was hard enough to admit to myself without hearing him say the words.

"I'm not sure Scottie is ever going to let me hear the end of it though."

"Sorry, I didn't want to cause any trouble."

"It's fine. Although, I'm sure he'll tell Mom all about it the minute she gets home."

A beat passed, and for a second, I thought he might let the silence linger. But he said, "Does that happen often?"

"I'm usually extra vigilant, but my boss wanted me to try some new dishes. I should have known better."

"I didn't realize it could be so debilitating."

"It can be a lot worse than that. I've spent days holed up in the bathroom before. But like I said, I'm pretty good at managing it now."

"There isn't a cure?"

"Nope. Just long-term symptom management. It comes with an increased risk of all kinds of diseases and cancers, so that's something to look forward to." Shock fell over Mason's expression, and I let out a nervous chuckle. "Sorry, it's not exactly a good conversation piece."

"I get it," he said. Only he didn't clarify what exactly he thought he got. And I didn't ask because Mason Steele made me feel off-kilter. He was an enigma, layered and complicated.

I'd never met anyone quite like him before.

It was obvious family was important to him, his biological family and the one he had with the team. But beyond that, I didn't know much about the guy with ice in his gaze and a steel fortress around his heart.

Only, he hadn't been that guy today. He'd helped me. Gone above and beyond to make sure I was okay. I told myself it didn't mean anything, that he only did it to appease Scottie, but it was hard to make myself believe it.

We rode the rest of the way in a thick silence, but I couldn't resist stealing glances at him. Watching him out of the corner of my eye as he focused on the road ahead. I got lost in the strong profile of his face, the way his impressive biceps flexed and contracted under his sweater.

When the RCC finally came into view, I was desperate for some fresh air. But the second he pulled into a parking spot, he twisted around and looked at me.

"You left," he said, catching me off guard.

"I figured you wouldn't want to do the awkward morning-after thing."

He gave me a sharp nod, his expression giving

nothing away. Did he care? Or was he just dead set on torturing me a little more?

"You'll be okay driving back to campus?"

"Yeah, I feel much better."

I didn't, not really. But I wasn't going to embarrass myself any further.

"Okay, well, have a safe journey back."

"Thanks." I grabbed the door handle. "And thanks again for taking care of me."

Another nod.

Another tense beat.

The air shifted, dancing over my skin like a warm breeze, making every inch of my body tingle with awareness. "I should go," I whispered, my heart racing in my chest as Mason watched me.

But I didn't open the door. I couldn't. The heat in his gaze had me pinned in place, burning me from the inside out.

"Fuck," he hissed. "You should go, blondie."

But he reached for me instead.

"I should." I let him pull me in, his fingers sliding along my neck, burying themselves deep into my hair. "I should definitely go."

"We can't..." he breathed, a tortured expression on his gorgeous face.

"I can't stop thinking about the other night." The words spilled out, my admission filling the space between us, making the air thicker. But I didn't care that I'd said the words. I wanted him to know the truth.

He searched my eyes. His expression locked down tight as my heart crashed wildly in my chest while I fought to stay afloat in his stormy gaze.

"Mason, say something…"

He moved closer, dropping his head to mine. Splaying his hand over my jaw, his fingers gently brushed my lips. His touch was almost reverent.

"Mase—"

"Shh," he whispered, ghosting a kiss over my mouth. A featherlight touch I felt all the way down to my soul.

I anchored my arms around his neck, needing more. Needing everything he was willing to give me.

"You need to go," he said again, this time with a pained groan.

We were so close, and yet, not close enough.

"Maybe I don't want to go." I kissed him, making the first move. Stroking my tongue into his mouth.

God, he tasted good. My body practically melted at the feel of him.

"I love kissing you." I smiled against his mouth, completely lost in the sensations swirling inside of me as my lips shaped his. Tasting. Teasing. Taking.

"Harper," he said gruffly, and I smiled harder. Loving how my name sounded rolling off his tongue.

This was happening. It was really happening. Mason wanted me. He wanted me, and it was everything I'd hoped for.

"Harper." It was more insistent now, and my eyelids fluttered open as I made myself focus.

"What's wrong?" I was smiling so hard my cheeks hurt. But this was... it was perfect.

"We can't."

"C-can't?" I crashed down to earth with a resounding thud, my heart sinking into oblivion. "What do you mean? We already—"

"And it was good." He untangled my arms from his neck, shoving me away a little. Leaving me cold. "But... fuck. I didn't—"

"Mason?" My brows knitted as I tried to process what he was saying.

Good. He thought our night together was... good. That wasn't exactly the word I'd have chosen, but he was a guy. They tended to downplay things.

"This can't ever happen again."

"What?" My chest tightened, confusion slamming into me. "I don't understand. You kissed me. You were kissing me."

I hadn't dreamt it. I'd felt it. I'd been right there, kissing him back.

"It was a mistake." He glanced away, and that one small action hurt far more than the confusing words coming out of his mouth.

He couldn't even look at me.

"I see." My voice shook with barely restrained hurt. "And Sunday night? What was that?"

He ran a hand over his face, still refusing to look at me.

"Mason," I snapped, trying to stay calm and keep it together when really, I was breaking apart at his words.

Finally, he gave me his eyes—eyes cooler than the ice on Ellet Arena's rink—and I wish he'd never looked at me.

"It was... a mistake."

A bitter laugh bubbled up my throat. "Wow."

"Look, we had a good time. But that's all it was. You knew that going into it. You're my coach's daughter. It's not—"

"Do not make this about him." Anger spewed inside me like a volcano, my body trembling with frustration and bitter disappointment. "You knew exactly who I was when you took me to your bed."

"And you knew the deal. One night. No promises."

"I did." Damn him. "But I also didn't expect... this."

Because there was something between us. Bubbling. Simmering. Making itself known.

"This was nothing." The words landed like knives, cutting down any hopes I had of getting through to him. "As I said before, it was a mistake."

"You don't want me. You don't want... this?"

"No, I don't."

"Well, then..." I blinked, desperately trying to pull myself together, to rein in the rush of tears clawing their way up my throat.

"Harper, I'm not—"

"Forget it," I said, shifting on the seat and grabbing the door handle again. I needed to escape before I did something foolish like cry in front of him. "You're right. This was a mistake. It won't happen again."

I wouldn't ever give him the chance to hurt me again.

What was that old saying? Fool me once. Shame on you. Fool me twice... yeah, never going to happen.

But he couldn't just let me go. He had to kick me while I was down.

"You won't let this affect your work with Scottie?" he asked.

"Of course, I won't." I shoved the door open and shoved my disbelief down as I pinned him with a scathing look. "Because unlike you, Mason Steele, I'm not an asshole."

I scrambled out of his car, almost tripping over my feet.

But this time, he wasn't there to catch me.

The drive back to Lakeshore was miserable. I'd blasted angry girl rock music into the car, hoping it would help me, but it had barely touched the hurt.

Throw in the waves of stomach cramps that suggested I was going to spend the majority of the night wrapped around the toilet bowl, and suffice it to say. I was in pretty bad shape.

I'd made it back in one piece, though, at least in the physical sense.

My heart was another issue. It felt like it had been cracked wide open. But what did I really expect? It was Mason Steele we were talking about.

He'd made it clear where he stood Sunday night, and I'd still let myself hope. All it had taken was a white-knight routine and a heated almost-kiss in his car, and I'd been a puddle at his feet.

I was done. So freaking done.

With a pained groan, I burst into my dorm room and stripped off my hoodie before grabbing a pillow and my cell phone and marching into the bathroom.

I had two missed calls from Mom and a text from Rory.

> Rory: Oh my God, are you okay?
> Mason told Noah what happened.

He had? Lovely.

> Harper: Mortified. But I'll live. Just got back. If you don't hear from me by lunchtime tomorrow, check in on me.

> Rory: Do you need anything?

> Harper: I'm good, thanks. What did Mason tell Noah?

Rory: Just that you almost passed out outside of the center, so he and Scottie took you back to their house until you felt better. Why? Did something happen?

Harper: Nope. Pretty much happened that way.

Rory: Why do I feel like you're not telling me everything?

Harper: There's nothing to tell. But I am tired and cranky and in for a long night. I'll update you tomorrow. xo

Rory: Okay. But if you need anything, don't hesitate to call me. xo

I wouldn't call, though, just like I wouldn't tell her or anyone else the truth about Mason.

I allowed myself one day to wallow. One day to lick my wounds and eat my feelings.

The bakery that made my favorite gluten-free brownies didn't do same-day delivery, so I had to settle for honey-almond bites. But it didn't matter. My stomach was still sore after Chad's lame-assed attempt at cooking something Harper-friendly.

Rory had texted, checking in earlier, but I'd kept it brief. *I was fine. Feeling better. And yes, I would be back in class tomorrow.*

Mom, on the other hand, was another story. She'd called twice and texted three times. I hadn't wanted to talk to her, but I finally picked up when she called a third time.

"Thank God," she said. "I've been worried."

"Come on, Mom. You know I can deal with a little flare-up."

"I know, but I still worry. You're my baby, Harper. It's my job to worry."

Could have fooled me.

"Are you drinking enough water?" she asked. "You need to—"

"Mom, I'm fine."

"Okay, sorry. I trust you, sweetheart. Have you seen your father yet?"

"Nope."

"Oh." She hesitated. "I thought he might have reached out now he's on campus."

"Really? Because I'm not surprised in the least."

"Harper, that isn't—"

"Mom, come on. I can't remember the last actual conversation I had with him. He didn't even make my leaving dinner."

Mom had booked a nice restaurant downtown, and I'd stupidly humored her.

"He's just—"

"Stop. God, Mom. Just stop." Frustration coated my voice. "He doesn't care. He's never cared. It's time we both accept that. Dad didn't come to LU to try and repair our relationship. He came to reunite with his one true love. Hockey."

"There's still time, sweetheart. I think if the two of you just spent some time together—"

"No, Mom. I'm done. I am so done."

"Harper," she gasped as if somehow, I was in the wrong here.

"I gotta go. My stomach is grumbling."

"Harper, please—"

I hung up. Because I couldn't do it, I couldn't listen to her bullshit for a second longer.

Mom was never going to change, just like he was never going to change.

My parents were and would forever be a lost cause. It was time to accept that and move on.

If only it were that easy.

Pushing all thoughts of my parents down, I opened Instagram and scrolled through the feed. I mostly followed hockey players and sports channels, along with the odd digestive health guru and book blogger. But it wasn't any of their profiles that caught my eye. It was the suggested profiles.

One in particular.

Coach Dixon LU Lakers.

My dad had his own profile.

I shouldn't have looked, but I couldn't help myself, clicking the link and waiting for his posts to load.

Wow. He'd been a coach less than two weeks, and his profile was already filled with reels of him and the team. Every video was like another crack in my already fractured heart.

Him smiling and laughing with Aiden and Coach Tucker. High-fiving Connor and Austin. Clapping the rookies on the back as they glided past him.

But it was the video with him and Mason that sucked all the air from my lungs. Somebody was filming them on the ice together, working through some drills. Mason hung on every word he said, and my father lapped it up. I hadn't seen him look so happy since—

Come to think of it. I couldn't recall a time I'd ever seen him look so happy.

It was like a punch to the gut watching the two of them. I couldn't compete with that—I was foolish to ever think I could.

As I closed the app and clutched my cell to my chest, all I could think was maybe Mason had done me a favor.

I *was* his coach's daughter. And although my dad couldn't care less about me, he would care about one of his players choosing me over hockey.

And I wouldn't survive being cast aside for him— or his beloved game.

CHAPTER 17

MASON

"Looking good, son," Coach Dixon called across the ice as I hit a slap shot.

"You'll be gunning for my record soon," Noah smirked, and I shook my head.

I had no plans to try and outshoot our power forwards, but maybe Coach D was onto something. Going for the shot came easy—easier than I thought it would—and I couldn't deny that perhaps the only thing holding me back all this time was... me.

"Okay, bring it in." Coach Tucker waved his clipboard in the air, and we all piled over to the benches. "You're looking good out there. Strong. Mason, nice slap shot. Maybe Coach Dixon is onto something. Maybe we should be using you more in the attacking zone."

The two of them shared a knowing look. A look that had a strange sensation curling in my stomach.

I'd never been in the spotlight before. It was a strange feeling, one I wasn't wholly used to. During high school, I was good, but I wasn't the star. And I certainly didn't have the support of my old man. He couldn't care less about me and my dreams of going pro. A dream that quickly became nothing more than a fantasy when he up and left us.

But here was Coach Dixon putting all his faith in me because he saw my potential. And now Coach Tucker was suggesting the team use me more. It should have been a fucking dream come true. My shining moment.

It would have been if it wasn't for a twelve-year-old kid back home who I constantly worried about, who deserved stability, support, and a strong sense of family.

Fuck.

Everyone watched me, waiting for me to reply, but all I managed to stammer out was, "Thanks, Coach," hoping it would suffice.

Thankfully Coach Walsh wanted to move on to talk about his progress with our defense because being in the spotlight was not somewhere I felt comfortable.

My mind drifted as he laid out the defensive plan for the upcoming games. Assistant Coach Carson Walsh could have turned pro, but he'd turned to coaching instead. We all knew the story. He'd gotten injured in his senior year and decided to quit. But I had to wonder, after losing his best friend and teammate, Deacon Benson, if he lost a part of himself. He seemed happy enough now, though, trying to keep the team on the straight and narrow, pushing us to be the best players we could be.

Playing hockey and being involved with the sport didn't have to end just because you didn't go pro. He was proof of that. It wasn't something I'd ever considered, but it was food for thought.

The thought settled deep inside of me as I tried to focus on the rest of the pep talk.

By the time Coach Walsh dismissed us, I was more than ready to hit the showers and grab some food from the cafeteria.

"I wonder how Harper is," Noah said in passing. But I didn't miss the sly look he gave me.

I'd had to tell him about yesterday. I couldn't keep it a secret. But I'd given him the PG-13 version—the version that didn't include the kiss and the shit show that followed. If Harper told Rory, that was on her. But I had zero plans of airing our business to anyone.

I'd gone too far. With all of it. Taking her back to my house. Acting like I cared. But things had reached new heights in the parking lot. Harper had that look, the one that screamed commitment.

And I couldn't do it.

I couldn't give in to the connection simmering between us. Because if I did, we'd be skating on thin ice. Waiting for the cracks to splinter wide open and one of us to go under.

I didn't have the time or energy for that.

And she deserved more than a guy who was already pulled in too many different directions.

So I told her it was a mistake.

Told her that *she* was a mistake.

One I wouldn't make again.

The hurt in her eyes had almost gutted me. But it was for the best. It could never work. I wasn't looking for a girlfriend, and she clearly couldn't do the casual thing without catching feelings.

We were a disaster waiting to happen, and I wanted to save her from the wreckage—even if she hated me for it.

"She wasn't in class again," Noah added, drilling holes into the side of my face.

I let out a heavy sigh. "If you've got something to say, Holden, just say it."

"Who, me?" He smirked. "I don't have anything to say."

"You're an ass."

"Takes one to know one."

I tsked, pulling off my jersey. The last thing I needed was Noah running his mouth and it getting back to Coach Dixon that I'd been with his daughter last night.

He came over, getting in my space. "Sorry, I'm just busting your balls."

"Yeah, well, I'd appreciate it if you didn't."

"Mase, come on, I was only joking."

"Joking about what?" Abel asked as he swaggered past. Even his walk made me want to lay him out.

"Fuck off, we weren't talking to you," Noah gritted out.

Bro looked like a fucking idiot half-naked, dick almost hanging out of his hockey pants, but his expression was icy cold.

"Relax, Holden. We're all friends. You got the girl, didn't you? Rory seems like—"

"Don't fucking say her name." He lunged for Abel, but I grabbed him before he could make contact.

"Easy. You don't want Coach to see this."

"Tell him to stay the fuck out of my way then." Noah shouldered past Abel leaving me to deal with the smug fucker.

"Was it something I said?" He grinned.

"Back the fuck off, Adams. He already gave you one black eye. The next time you might not be so lucky."

"Is that a threat?" His eyes narrowed.

I leaned in close and drawled. "That's a fucking promise."

"Yeah, whatever, asshole." He shoved past me.

"We good here?"

I wasn't surprised to find Aiden watching me. Our captain, although he mostly kept to himself, made sure to know what was going on with his team.

"Yeah."

"He's not worth it, you know."

"Come on, Dumfries. The guy's a fucking liability."

"I don't disagree, but he's still on the team. He's still one of us."

"Yeah, whatever." I slung my pads on the bench and sat down, dragging a hand through my hair.

I was pissed. And it had nothing to do with Abel Adams and everything to do with a blonde-haired, blue-eyed pain in my fucking ass.

"You need to get laid." Connor slumped down beside me. "Get rid of some of that tension you're carrying around with you."

"Is that what you do?" I deflected.

"Damn right. Ella is like my own personal physio." His brows waggled suggestively. "You should have taken my advice at the party."

"Nah, she's Coach D's daughter." The lie soured on my tongue. "You never shit where you eat."

"Unless your name's Holden." He held out his hand, and I slapped my palm down on it. "I think a few of us are heading to Millers after here if you want to tag along."

"Don't tell me you're going to start migrating there."

"What's wrong with Millers? The girls like that there are no bunnies, and Harper is working again, so it's a two-birds-one-stone situation."

"I think I'm going to head home and cram in some reading. I can't afford to fall behind."

Connor studied me, his heavy stare digging a little too deeply. "What's going on with you?"

"Nothing. Why?" My brows pinched.

I didn't like outwardly lying to my friends, but it wasn't like I was the care-and-share type, either. I told people things on a strictly need-to-know basis only. And none of my friends needed to know that sometimes I felt like I was fucking drowning. School. The team. Mom. Scottie. Harper.

I shoved that last thought away. She wasn't a part of this. She couldn't be.

If I told them how I really felt, it would make it real, and if it was real, I'd lose another inch of air to the crushing weight of responsibility I felt every second of every day.

"It's okay to let us in, you know," he said quietly, making sure the noise in the locker room drowned out his words. "It doesn't have to be me, Austin, Aiden, or even Noah. But any one of us would gladly listen."

"Do me a favor, Morgan. Save the heart-to-hearts for Noah." I tapped him on the cheek as I got up and grabbed my shower bag.

"One day, Mase." His voice followed me. "One day, you'll understand."

As I stepped under the shower and let the warm water wash away sixty minutes of intense drills, I closed my eyes and let myself pretend.

Pretend that I was more like Connor or Noah or Aiden.

Of course, they all had their own shit to deal with. Who didn't? But they didn't have someone depending on them the way I did—another life in their hands.

Scottie would always need some level of support. Sure, it could have been worse.

Life always could. But I didn't care about what was happening to other people; I cared about my brother, about my mom, and what was happening to them.

But for those few minutes under the spray, I pretended I was just a guy with the whole world ahead of him: a successful hockey career, an understanding girlfriend, and an unconditionally supportive family.

It wasn't my life though.

The likelihood was it never would be.

I didn't go to Millers with the rest of the guys. Instead, I holed up in my room, video-called Scottie so that he could show me his new hockey cards, and then settled down to study.

Noah and Connor were determined to include me though, texting me non-stop. It was easy to ignore the group chat messages, their stupid fucking live-text commentary on their night so far. It wasn't so easy to ignore the video messages. Because I didn't see their goofy antics or hear their tone-deaf rendition of

Nickleback's *Saturday Night's Alright for Fighting*, I only saw her.

Harper.

She was behind the bar again, serving my friends and their girlfriends with the dude that worked there. He made her laugh as they worked side-by-side to serve my asshole friends. But I saw the shadows around her eyes.

Before I knew what I was doing, I'd texted Noah.

> Mase: Should Harper be working? She still looks a bit pale.

> Noah: She's fine. At least, she says she is.

When I didn't reply, he texted again.

> Noah: Want to ask her yourself?

> Mase: Nope. Just didn't want her flaking out again and ruining your night.

> Noah: You know, if I didn't know better, I'd say you're worried about her...

> Mase: Well, she is Rory's best friend and did you or did you not tell me I had to play nice.

Noah: Touché asshole. Tou-fucking-ché. But seriously, she seems okay. Been flirting up a storm with Ward and Leon.

Fuck.

Jealousy snaked through me, only fueled by the video he sent me of the two rookies leaning over the bar to watch as Harper prepared some girly-looking drink.

Noah: She's got a fan club. I think Ward is going to try his luck, unless…

Mase: Unless what?

I played dumb.

Noah: Unless you want me to tell him to back off.

Mase: He's welcome to her.

Noah: If you say so.

Mase: I do. Now quit sending me texts, I'm trying to study.

Noah: All work and no play makes Mason a dull boy.

Mase: Go annoy someone else.

Fuck knows he'd annoyed me enough. Planting a seed of jealousy inside me that showed no signs of stopping. I'd seen Ward in action; he was a hit with the ladies. Harper would probably eat him alive, but that was his problem.

Just then, my cell phone vibrated, and I got ready to tell Noah to fuck right off. But it wasn't Noah. It was a Venmo notification.

> Harper Dixon sent you $25.

A text followed from an unknown number.

> Unknown: I forwarded the money for the stuff you bought me. I hope it covers it. Thanks again for looking after me. H xo

Shit. A stone plunked in my chest.

> Mase: You didn't need to do that.

> Harper: Yeah, Mason, I did.

I didn't reply. What was there to say?

I had to stay away from her. And she was obviously all too happy to let me go.

Harper made me feel things—things I didn't want to feel. Things I had no business feeling. It was a one-way ticket to a whole heap of drama and distraction I didn't need.

The sooner I could forget about her, the better. And I couldn't forget if she kept drawing me into her orbit.

To hammer home my point, I sent her one last message.

> Mase: You should give Ward a chance. He's a good guy.

Before I could talk myself out of it, I hit send. Hoping like fuck, I sounded friendly and supportive and not petty and jealous.

Her reply came two minutes later.

> Harper: Thanks for the advice. Maybe I will. See you around, Steele.

I stared at her words, anger swelling inside me. *It's for the best, Mase. You fucking know that.*

Turning off my phone and removing any temptation I felt to reply and beg her to forgive me, I grabbed my pen and hoped a lesson on supply chain management would help me forget all about Harper Dixon.

The girl I didn't want.

And couldn't have, even if I did.

CHAPTER 18

HARPER

WARD CUTLER WAS CUTE. Dirty blond hair that fell into his eyes, a devilish smile that was impossible to ignore, and that hockey build that made girls get all hot and bothered.

He'd sat at the bar and kept me company most of my shift. But I'd heard the stories about the kind of guy he was. Seen it with my own two eyes.

Like most of the Lakers, he had girls lined up for him wherever he went, and he was all too happy to work his way through them.

I wasn't looking to be his next conquest.

Besides, he was Mason's friend.

Mason might have had no problem with me hooking up with one of his teammates, but I would never do that, even if I told him otherwise.

His text didn't hurt; it made me angry because he was choosing to shut me out when there was obviously something between us.

I had all day to replay how things went down in his car the other night, pick them apart, and try to figure out what had changed. The only conclusion I could come to was that Mason Steele was a coward.

But maybe it was more than that. He had Scottie to worry about. Balancing the team, classes, and his responsibilities back home. He hadn't opened up to me much about things, but anyone could see that he carried a lot on his shoulders.

It was commendable and only made him hotter—way freaking hotter. But I suspected it also made him guarded. Closed off and wary of letting people in.

"You sure you can't come out with us after you get done here?"

"It'll be way past my bedtime." I batted my lashes at Ward, smiling so hard my cheeks hurt. But he was fun to be around. Easy-going and flirty.

Nothing like his moody, broody teammate.

"Another time, then?" He grinned. "I think you and me could have a lot of fun, blondie."

Just like that, my good mood died. Because Mason called me that. Whether he knew it or not, he used that nickname every time he hoped to get a rise out of me.

And for the most part, it worked. So hearing the same nickname roll off Ward's lips felt all wrong.

"Shit, was it something I said?"

He must have noticed my glum expression.

"Not at all," I lied. "I'm just tired."

"I'm surprised Coach D's daughter needs to work to pay her way through college."

"What?" Everything went still inside of me, my fingers digging into the edge of the counter as I gawked at him.

Ward chuckled. Soft. Easy. Either oblivious to the tension humming between us or nervous about it. "I just mean, your old man is ex-NHL. He's a fucking legend around these parts, for fuck's sake. It must have been pretty damn special growing up with him as your dad. I can't even imagine—"

I snapped.

The tether inside me that had been slowly fraying since my father arrived on campus snapped, and I lost it.

"I'm going to stop you right there." My voice trembled with barely restrained anger. "You don't know anything about my father or me."

The blood drained from Ward's face. "Harper, shit. I wasn't—"

"Good. Don't."

"Harp?" Rory chose that moment to wander over to us. "What's wrong?" She glanced between us, concern shining in her eyes. "Ward, what did you do?"

"Do? I didn't—"

"I need some air. I'll be back." I hurried out of

there, crashing through the staff door marked private and practically jogging down the long hall.

God, I couldn't breathe.

Couldn't get air into my lungs quickly enough.

I shouldered the emergency exit and dropped my hands to my thighs, inhaling a ragged breath.

It always came back to him.

My father.

James 'The Real Deal' Dixon.

Ha. The irony.

He'd decided to exclude me from his life, and yet I couldn't escape his shadow if I wanted to.

"Harper?" Kalvin called, and panic flooded me.

I didn't want him to see me like this. Weak. Broken... Hurt.

"Harp—"

"Hey," I sucked in a sharp breath, pasting a smile on my face. "Sorry, I started to feel light-headed."

He gave me a skeptical look. "If the hockey guy upset you, I'll be more than happy to kick him out on his ass."

A nervous laugh bubbled up inside me. "No, no, you don't need to do that. He just hit a nerve. I'm fine, I promise."

"You know, a problem shared is a problem halved."

"If I open that can of worms tonight, I might never be able to put the lid on. But thanks, I appreciate it."

"Anytime. You ready to go back in there?"

"Yeah." I smoothed the hair out of my face and took another deep, calming breath.

"Your friend, the cute one obsessed with literary quote hoodies, seemed worried. Wanted to come back here and check on you herself."

"Rory is good people."

"She can't be that good if she's shacked up with a Laker." His eyes twinkled.

"They're not all the shallow misogynistic players you make them out to be, you know," I said as we went back inside.

"Don't tell me you were actually falling for Ward Cutler's charm."

"How the hell do you know his name?"

"Looked him up, didn't I?" He grinned. "I need to know who's sniffing around my girl."

There was nothing suggestive in his tone, only brotherly affection and protectiveness.

"Thanks, Kal, you're a good guy."

"Tell that to Janelle."

"No luck there yet?"

"I did a bit of groundwork, but she's too hung up on her mystery FB."

"FB, huh?" I chuckled.

"Thing is, I don't want to be her FB. I want to be her BAE." His brows waggled with insinuation.

I shoved him gently, still laughing. But the second we stepped back into the bar, Rory rushed over to me. "Are you okay?"

"I'm fine. Sorry about that." I glanced over her shoulder, looking for Ward. "Where is everyone?"

"The guys are heading to Lakers House for pizza and video games. I wanted to stay and make sure you were okay."

"You didn't need to do that," I said.

"Yeah, I kinda did. Do you think you can take a break for a little while?"

"I can't, it's not—"

"Go," Kal said. "It's quiet now that your buddies left. I can handle the bar, and Kaylee can manage a few tables."

"Are you sure? Chad—"

"Isn't here tonight. So go hang out with your friend."

"Thanks."

I followed Rory to a booth at the back of the room.

"Ward felt awful," she said.

"It wasn't his fault, not really."

"Do you want to talk about it? I know things have been a little weird since your dad started coaching the team, and I've been waiting for you to open up to me..."

"I don't know what to say." I shrugged, avoiding her heavy gaze.

"Harper, come on, this is me. My mom sent me a care package in the form of diet pills and liposuction brochures, for God's sake. I know a thing or two about shitty parents."

"Sorry, of course, you do. I'm not trying to make it a competition."

"Gosh, I don't think that at all. I just want to be here for you the way you were there for me."

"It's just not an easy thing for me to talk about," I admitted.

"Why didn't he tell you about the job?"

"Because he treats me like a stranger."

"I feel like I'm missing something," she said with a sympathetic smile.

"Everyone thinks James Dixon is this local legend. The guy who made it to NHL stardom only to have his dream ripped away early. They don't know the man behind the mask."

No one did except for me and Mom and a few of our neighbors.

"Is he... abusive?" Her face paled, and I shook my head.

"Not in the traditional sense of the word, no."

"But..."

"He wanted a son." The words sliced unhealed wounds open. "And he got me instead."

"I'm not sure I understand."

"Sounds ridiculous, doesn't it?"

Tons of parents experienced some disappointment when they had their hearts set on a certain sex. But once they met their baby and held the little bundle of joy in their arms, those feelings usually dissipated.

"Mom thought she was having a boy," I said. "For

nine months, my father prepared to bring his son into the world, his legacy. And then I popped out and crushed his dreams."

"Harper, I'm sure that's not—"

"He had no interest in raising a girl, Rory." I shrugged. "Still doesn't. You saw how he was at the coffee shop. That wasn't new or unusual. That has been my life for the last eighteen years."

"I don't know what to say. That's… horrible."

"I learned to skate for him, you know. I thought it would bring us closer. It didn't. I have spent my entire life trying to be more like the child he wanted, but he's never going to change. And now he's here, and people are acting like it's the second coming or something. So when Ward started… it hit a nerve."

There was more to it, so much more. But I didn't like talking about it.

I couldn't.

"They don't know, do they?"

"No one does, and I'd really prefer to keep it that way."

The team knew I was their new coach's daughter, and Noah and his friends had picked up on the frosty vibes when they asked me about him. But that was all they were getting.

"God, Harper, I wish you'd have told me sooner," she sighed.

"It wouldn't have changed anything." I picked at a

beer mat, barely able to meet her gaze. The pity I knew would glisten there.

"No, but you're my best friend, Harper. Your pain is my pain. Your anger is my anger. I don't know. Maybe I could have asked Noah to trip him on the ice or something."

"Aurora Hart," I fake-gasped. "I didn't know you had it in you."

Our laughter filled the booth, soothing some of the jagged edges inside me.

"Thank you. I needed this."

She looked at me and gave me a big smile full of understanding and support. "That's what friends are for."

"Yeah." I nodded, feeling a little lighter than I had ten minutes ago. "I'm starting to get that."

Friday, I did something stupid—I promised Aurora I'd attend the Lakers home games against the Bulldogs.

She'd already gotten me a ticket, assuming I would want to go. Since nobody knew about what I was now referring to as 'the incident,' that was how I found myself in front-row seats at Ellet Arena, watching the team warm up on the ice as the visiting team filed into the rink.

"Go Lakers," Dayna yelled, clapping her hands loudly. "Let's go, guys."

"Okay, you. Let's try and rein it in a little. They haven't even faced off yet."

But when Aiden skated right past us, giving her a cocky wink, she turned feral.

I got it. It was hard not to be swept up in the atmosphere, the ripple of anticipation in the air. The announcers led the crowd in a rendition of the Lakers fight song while my heart fluttered wildly in my chest as I watched Mason zip laps around the rink, fooling around with Noah and Ward.

I'd managed to avoid him since Wednesday. After my text thanking him for taking care of me, I decided I was done. But now he was here, just beyond the plexiglass. And he looked so freaking hot. My thighs pressed together to ease the throbbing as memories of our night together flooded my mind.

His head lifted in my direction, and his eyes found mine, and just like that, all notions of ignoring my attraction to him went out of the window.

I couldn't see his expression from behind his helmet, but I could *feel* it everywhere. The intensity. His lingering stare as he whizzed past the glass.

"Okay, that was a little weird," Rory said, and I could feel her eyes drilling holes into me.

Meeting her gaze, I gave a weak smile. "Yeah."

"Harper, what aren't you telling me? Because I'm pretty sure Mason—"

"It doesn't matter." I shook my head, hoping she would leave it.

Thankfully, the announcements started as both teams headed back to their benches for the pre-game pep talk. My father looked like a different man. Laughing and smiling at Coach Tucker as he motivated his players. It was hard to believe it was the same guy I'd grown up with.

He beckoned Mason over, the two of them deep in conversation as players started to move into position. Clapping him on the back, my father let Mason join his teammates.

It hurt. It probably always would. My father had assimilated so easily with the team when he hadn't even bothered to pick up the phone and call me while he was in Lakeshore. But I couldn't let it ruin my college experience.

I wouldn't.

I could support the team from a distance, go about my business around campus, and should our paths ever cross, I could afford him the same attention he'd always afforded me: cool indifference and a boatload of disappointment.

Because his opinion of me and his lifetime of rejection didn't define me. In the same way, Mason's rejection didn't define me.

If only my heart could believe what my head already knew to be true.

The game started, and the crowd went wild as

Aiden won the puck, sending it sliding across the ice to Noah down the right wing. The Bulldogs had some real powerhouse players that checked Noah with such force he went careening into the boards.

"Crap," Rory hissed, clutching my hand.

"It's okay, Lakers," Dayna yelled, cupping her hand around her mouth. "Win it back. Let's go."

A blur of cyan and indigo raced down the defensive zone, trying to block the Bulldog's breakout.

"Go, go," I murmured, watching Connor move to check their attacker. But a Bulldog player came out of nowhere, slamming into him and knocking him backward.

"Oh God," Ella gasped as the rest of the crowd took a collective inhale as Connor went down like a sack of bricks.

"He's okay," Dayna reassured her, "he'll be fine."

But he didn't look fine. He didn't clamber back to his feet and skate it off. He just lay there.

The linesman noticed and signaled to cease play, and the referee rushed over to Connor. Noah was already there, crouched down over his friend.

"Please be okay. God, please be okay." Ella gnawed her thumb as she watched the scene play out. But thankfully, just when it looked like Connor was out for the count, he thumped a glove down on the ice and pulled himself into a sitting position. The crowd cheered wildly for their beloved number twenty-three, the sound reverberating through me.

"See, he's fine." Dayna hugged Ella, the two of them cheering loudly.

He got to his feet and nodded at something the referee said, before skating right up to the plexiglass glass in front of us and pressing his hand against it. Ella laid her hand there, smiling so hard I felt the ache in my own cheeks.

"Fucking love you, kitten," he mouthed.

"Love you too," she replied. "Please don't do that again."

He chuckled before tapping his stick on the glass and skating back to the Lakers bench to be assessed by the medic.

"This game will be the death of me," she murmured.

"Yep. I have a real love-and-hate relationship with it," Rory said, glancing at me. The pity in her eyes making me glance away.

I didn't want to go there.

Not now.

Not here.

So although I stayed quiet, pretending not to hear their conversation over the noise of the crowd, I knew exactly how they felt.

Because hockey to me would always be the thing that brought me endless joy.

And desperate, utter heartache.

CHAPTER 19

MASON

IN THE FINAL minutes of the third period, the score was tied—three to three. After the scare with Connor, the Bulldogs had turned up the heat. Every time our offense went for the breakout, they managed to gain possession. It was a dogfight. Back and forth, back and forth.

There wasn't a single muscle in my body that didn't ping and burn with exertion.

"Take the shot," Coach Dixon bellowed as I looked across the attacking zone for a Lakers jersey. But their defense had Noah and Aiden pinned down.

"Take the goddamn shot," someone yelled.

I couldn't be sure this time if it was Coach D or Coach Tucker. Blood roared between my ears, the ice steady beneath my skates as I rotated my body slightly, leaned my weight forward, pulled back my stick, and took the shot. Just like I'd practiced over and over this week with Coach Dixon.

The puck sailed through the air, and for a second, I thought their goalie had it. But he went down, and the buzzer lit up, our fans going wild.

We'd won.

We'd won, and I'd scored the winning goal.

"Fucking A." Aiden piled on me, slapping me on the back as he celebrated our last-minute win. Then Connor jumped in with Noah and the rookies until I was surrounded by my teammates, whooping right along with them.

"That shot was fucking impressive," Noah said. "I think he's after your job, Cap." He dipped his head toward Aiden.

"If he keeps winning us games like that, he can have it."

"It was a lucky shot," I murmured, not entirely comfortable with their attention.

"Nothing lucky about it. Coach D is right. You've been holding out on us."

We skated toward the benches, and Coach Dixon was the first to congratulate me.

"Good game, son. Damn good game. How does it feel?" He gripped my shoulder, grinning from ear to ear.

"It feels good, Coach."

"Plenty more where that came from by the time I'm

done with you. Listen, son. I put some feelers out and touched base with some old friends from back in the day. A couple of them scout for pro teams now. And look, I'm not making any promises, but I think I could get them down here to take a look at you."

"Whoa, Coach, I don't know what to say." It was a lot, too much to think about while I was riding the high of the win. I could barely think straight, let alone make decisions about the future.

"Yes, you say yes, Mase." His deep laughter rolled through me. "This could be your ticket to the pros, son. Keep putting in the work, keep scoring goals like the one you just did, and teams are going to take notice."

He gave me a proud nod before moving to some of the other guys. I noticed Connor, Noah, and Aiden had made their way over to their girls, the three of them goofing around like idiots.

"Good game." Adams came up beside me.

"What the fuck do you want?"

"What? I can't congratulate you on your lucky shot."

"Nothing lucky about it," I quirked a brow at him.

"Coach D has taken quite the shine to you."

"Jealous, Adams? Because we both know he sure as shit hasn't taken a shine to you."

"Fuck you, asshole. You think you're so fucking slick, coach's new pet. But he's just using you. You'll see."

"The fuck is—" But he was already heading off the ice.

The guys skated over and pulled me into another bone-crushing hug. "Proud of you, Mase." Connor practically squeezed the air out of my lungs.

"Get off me, you big— hey, you good?" I asked, noticing his contorted expression.

"Yeah, I'm fine." He yanked his helmet off and ran a hand through his damp hair. "Nothing a hot shower and some TLC from my girl won't solve. See you in there." He took off, leaving me behind with Aiden and Noah.

"He seem okay to you?"

"He took a big hit," Aiden said. "He'll be okay after a little R and R."

"Come on, hotshot," Noah hooked me around the neck, pulling me in close. "Let's hit the showers so we can get the hell out of here and celebrate in style."

"Nothing crazy," I murmured. "I'm going home tomorrow to pick up Mom and Scottie."

They were coming to watch the second game against Detroit U, but he didn't always travel well with Mom, so I'd arranged to go get them and then booked them into a hotel after the game so they could spend some time in Lakeshore with me.

It was a lot, but I knew it would be worth it to see his face when the puck dropped and the game started.

"Drinks at TPB? We've been neglecting that place," Noah said.

"Are the girls—"

"They have dinner plans. They'll probably join us after."

If Harper turned up with them, I could be long gone before then.

"Why?"

"No reason," I said as we filed off the ice and down the narrow aisle leading to the locker room.

"You sure about that?" he called after me.

I could have ignored him. Could have taken the high road and not fed into his suspicions about Harper and me. But pride got the better of me, and instead, I flipped him off over my shoulder.

His laughter followed me all the way into the locker room.

The Penalty Box was standing room only by the time we arrived. Thankfully, Stu usually kept a couple of tables free for the team, so we managed to grab a seat.

"Get a load of that," Leon whistled through his teeth as he raked his eyes over a group of half-naked bunnies.

"I wonder if Jessica Rabbit will want to soothe my bruises." He smirked, giving the busty redhead another once over.

"Please don't start with the bunny scale shit

tonight. Especially if Rory comes around." Noah cast him a disapproving look.

The bunny scale was some stupid frat boy shit that we all had a bad habit of using now and again. It was locker room talk mostly, but it had gotten personal for Noah when Abel Adams called Rory a chubby bunny, and Noah lost his shit.

"But Rory isn't here right now," Leon argued. "And this place is full to the brim with bunnies ripe for the—"

"Seriously, rookie. Keep it up, and I'll revoke your pass to sit with the cool kids."

"That's your comeback? I love Aurora, bro, but she's turned you fucking soft."

"One day, you'll get it." Noah shrugged, accepting a cold bottle of Heineken from Austin. "Thanks, man."

"Get what?" he asked, sliding onto a seat.

"The fact that since Noah started banging your sis —" Austin pinned him with a look darker than hell itself, and Leon held up his hands. "Fine. Since he started making sweet love to your sister, the guy has turned into a walking, talking vagina."

"What can I say? I'm a changed man. I would choose Rory over you, assholes, every day of the week."

"Right answer," Austin grumbled, clinking his bottle against Noah's.

"You couldn't have picked a chick with a few more single friends to— uh, Holden? Why is your girlfriend here? Didn't you say she had dinner plans?"

We all turned and looked over at the door. Sure enough, Aurora and Ella stood there, and with them was none other than Harper.

There went my plans to enjoy a couple of beers with my friends before heading home to get some sleep.

They made their way over, but I noticed Harper lingered behind.

"Where's Dayna?" Aiden asked.

"She called you a bunch of times. She got a call from her mom."

"Shit?" He shot out of his seat, pulling his cell phone out of his pocket. "Is everything— fuck, my battery is dead. Where is she now?"

"At your place. I think her dad is sick, and her mom is worried."

"I've got to go," he said to no one in particular.

"Keep us updated," Noah said, dragging Rory between his legs. "And if there's anything we can do..."

"Thanks. Hopefully, it's nothing too serious. She'll be devastated if—"

"Go, be with your girl," Connor said.

Aiden dipped his head before hightailing it out of there.

"Shit, I hope Dayna's old man is okay." Noah dropped his chin on Rory's shoulder, sliding his hands under her baggy hoodie.

"I'm going to get a drink," I said to no one in particular.

I needed to be away from Harper.

She hadn't even looked at me, but it was only pissing me off, which was confusing as fuck because it was what I'd wanted.

I managed to work my way to the front of the line at the bar. Stu came straight over. "You good, Mase?"

It would have been easy to ask for something stronger. But we had another game tomorrow, and Coach had a two-beer-and-done rule.

"Just another Heineken, please."

"This one's on me," a voice said from behind me, and I turned to find Coach Dixon standing there.

"Uh, hey, Coach."

"Don't look so alarmed, Mase." He clapped me on the shoulder, taking the stool next to me.

"With all due respect, sir, I'm not used to the coaching staff showing up here."

"I won't tell if you won't." He winked, putting his order in with Stu. "It's only one for the road."

Unease crept up my spine. Pretty sure there were rules on this kind of thing. Did Coach Tucker and Coach Walsh celebrate with us occasionally after a big win? Sure they did. But not in TPB, not like this.

"I just wanted to stop by and see if you'd had any thoughts about my offer. We need to move on this, Mason. Strike while the iron's hot."

"That's really—"

"Dad."

Coach Dixon went still beside me, sheer

annoyance falling over his expression. "One piece of advice, son," he muttered, "never have kids." He gave me a thin smile as he turned to meet Harper's worried gaze. "Harper."

"W-what are you doing here?" Her eyes flicked to mine and back again.

She looked... fuck, she looked gorgeous. Black leggings and a tight black cropped sweater that revealed a slither of stomach. Her hair was braided over one shoulder, but some wavy wisps framed her face. It was really fucking difficult to remember why I couldn't take her home with me and bury myself deep inside her.

Except reason number one was sitting right beside me, looking at his daughter like she was nothing more than an irritating noise in his ear.

"Dad...?" she pleaded when he didn't answer.

"I'll give the two of you some privacy," I said, not wanting front-row seats to whatever father/daughter issues they clearly had going on.

"No need to leave, Mason, son." His hand landed on my shoulder, squeezing. "Harper won't be staying."

Ouch. His words landed like blows, and Harper flinched, hurt filling her expression and dulling the usual sparkle in her eyes.

"Dad, come on, please." She lowered her voice, glancing around the bar. But we were away from the crowd, everything quieter at this end of the bar. "You shouldn't be here; you know that."

"Go back to your friends, Harper. We'll talk about this another time."

He was so dismissive of her, so cold. It made me wonder what had gone down between them.

"Dad—"

But Coach turned his back on her and laid his elbows on the bar. Tears clung to her lashes, but I didn't know what to do. They were clearly on the outs, and I was way out of my territory here.

Her dejected gaze slid to mine, and she looked ready to say something, but a couple of the rookies came over.

"Coach D, we thought that was you," Ward said.

"Just wanted to run something by Mason. Come on, get in here. We should toast the win tonight."

Ward and Leon looked to me, but I shrugged. He was our Coach, for fuck's sake, our elder. It wasn't like we could send him on his way even if the whole thing didn't sit right with me.

"Oh, hey, Harper," Ward said, finally noticing her standing there. "What's—"

She turned around and stormed off, melting into the crowd before I could say anything.

"Okay, that was weird."

"Always been a handful, that one." Coach Dixon blew out a steady breath. "Don't know what I did in a former life to end up with a daughter like that. But the big man upstairs must have really had it in for me."

"She give you a lot of trouble growing up, Coach?"

"Something like that," he murmured, nursing his drink which I noticed was neat liquor.

My eyes flicked back to where Harper had disappeared, a strange feeling going through me.

"The problem with women is they don't know when the hell to stay out of your business," Coach went on. "Honestly, do yourselves a favor and focus on the game. Women are a dime a dozen. But hockey"—he lifted his glass and held it toward us—"hockey will never see you wrong."

Ward arched a brow at me over the top of Coach's head, and I frowned. He wasn't talking any sense. Then as quick as he'd arrived, Coach stood up, drained his drink, and wiped his mouth with the back of his hand.

"I should probably head out," he said. "Leave you guys to enjoy your night. I'll see you tomorrow. Don't stay out too late."

He disappeared into the crowd, and I let out a strained breath.

"Want to tell us what that was all about?" Ward asked as I stared after Coach D, trying to make sense of what had just happened.

"Mase?" Leon added, and I blinked over at both of them.

"Your guess is as good as mine."

"I'm heading out," I said to Austin.

At some point, the team had thinned. My friends had all left with their girls, and the rookies had found their bunny of choice for the night. So Austin and I had kicked back and watched the ESPN highlights while the celebrations went on around us.

He looked up from his phone, and I lifted a brow. "Fallon?"

"Yeah. She wants me to go over."

Fallon was his regular hook-up.

"I sense a but in there..."

"I dunno, man. It feels like it could be something, and honestly, not sure I want it."

"What does she want?"

"Says she wants to keep things simple, but you know what girls are like. They say one thing and mean another."

He wasn't wrong there.

It's why I avoided getting close. Letting myself fall for the old 'I don't want anything serious' line. Because ninety-nine percent of the time, girls always wanted something serious. They just didn't want to risk losing the something casual for the chance of being denied the something serious.

"Good luck with that, bro," I said. "I'm out."

"See you tomorrow." He dipped his head in goodbye, and I made my way across the bar.

It was still busy, and I'd stayed later than I had planned. But after Harper and Coach's weird exchange

—the utter dejection in her eyes—I knew if I went back to the house, I wouldn't be able to sleep.

So I stayed and hung out.

I kept my head down, trying to make it out of the bar without getting accosted by a bunny or fan. I'd almost reached the door when a flash of blonde hair caught my eye.

Surely not.

I strained against the darkness, waiting for another flash of disco lights to give me a better view of the area carved out every weekend as a dance floor.

Harper was on her own, dancing with her eyes closed and arms extended high above her head. Fuck. She looked good, her hips rolling and swaying to the beat. As if she felt me watching, her eyes snapped open, narrowing.

For a second, I thought she might run. Turn around and disappear into the shadows.

But she didn't.

Instead, she began dancing for me, sliding a hand up her chest and brushing her hand along her neck, taking the loose curls framing her face with it.

She was stunning. Utterly fucking stunning, and I couldn't drag my eyes off her. Remembering how good she felt beneath me. How perfect she felt clenched around my dick as I fucked into her.

Shit. Now I was standing there like a creeper with a raging hard-on.

Until a guy stalked up behind her and started

dancing with her, and the lust saturating my veins turned to blind fury.

Don't touch her. Don't fucking touch—

His hands were on her hips, dancing across the smooth expanse of skin as he dragged her body back into his.

I was already moving, storming through the crowd, when Harper slapped his hands away, staggering forward.

Shit. She was drunk. Really drunk if the way she almost tripped was any indicator.

Luckily, I was there to catch her.

"Ohmigod, thanks," she hiccoughed, grinning up at me through hazy eyes. "M-Mason? Nooo. No. No. No."

"You okay there, blondie?"

"I..." Another hiccough and then, "Mason, I don't feel so good."

"I got you." I pulled her into my side, anchoring my arm around her waist.

"I think I drank tooooo much." She waved her hand through the air, and I smothered a laugh.

Harper was a cute drunk.

What the fuck?

Drunk chicks weren't usually my jam. They tended to be annoying as fuck and super clingy. But no matter how much I tried to fight it, there was just something about this girl.

"Hey, man, I can handle her." The asshole who'd

attempted to put his hands on Harper stepped up to us.

I didn't recognize him, but that didn't mean shit. LU was a big campus. I didn't know a lot of students. From the smugness in his eyes, he didn't know me either.

"You need to back the fuck up. She's with me."

"Nah, man. She was dancing with me." He tried to tug her away, but I grabbed his wrist. Hard.

"I said back the fuck up."

His brows drew together, but I saw the flicker of fear in his eyes. "Y-yeah, okay. She's all yours."

"Mason?" Harper curled her fingers into my hoodie, demanding my attention.

"Yeah, blondie?"

Her eyelashes fluttered as she fought against the lull of whatever alcohol was swimming in her bloodstream.

"Can you take me home?"

CHAPTER 20

HARPER

I WAS DRUNK.

White girl wasted.

I don't know what happened. One minute, I'd been standing there, watching my father drink at the bar with Mason, Leon, and Ward, and the next, I'd been drinking shots like they were going out of fashion.

"Go back to your friends, Harper. We'll talk about this another time."

Just like that, he'd dismissed me like a naughty child who'd caught their parent doing something they weren't supposed to be doing. In front of Mason and the rookies, no less.

God, I'd been mortified. And instead of leaving, I'd stayed and decided to get so drunk that all my worries became nothing but forgotten whispers.

So I drank and danced and drank some more. Even after the girls left with Noah and Connor in tow, I'd insisted on staying. Rory hadn't looked too impressed, but I was a big girl. I could take care of myself. Besides, I was in a bar surrounded by hockey players. Someone would keep an eye out for me.

I hadn't expected it to be Mason.

Or maybe, deep down, I'd hoped he would be the one to swoop in and save me.

"Jesus, blondie, how much did you drink tonight?"

"I'll have you knows. I can understand every word out of your pretty mouth," I murmured, slumping against him as he steered me down the sidewalk. "So not enough," I hiccoughed. "But I'm glads it was you."

"Me?"

"Yeah." I peeked up at him, but he was all blurred around the edges. "Who saved me."

"Right place, right time." He shrugged, trying to play it down in that Mason Steele way of his.

"You played a good game tonight. That slapshot was something specials."

"What do you know about my slapshot?"

The second the words were out of his mouth, the air shifted around us. And suddenly, despite the falling temperatures, I felt hot all over. Needy and restless, my skin humming with awareness.

"You're in Hocking Hall, right?"

I nodded. "It's so far, and my legs are tired." I burrowed closer into his side, wrapping my arms around his waist. "Mmm." A contented sigh slipped off my lips.

"Harper," Mason warned.

"But you're so comfy."

He muttered something under his breath but made no move to untangle me from his body.

Thank God.

I wasn't sure I could stand much longer, exhaustion seeping into my bones. Then the world tilted around me as Mason picked me up and cradled me against his chest.

"Hi," I smiled up at him, sliding my arms around his neck.

"You're a fucking liability."

I rolled my eyes at that. He was so grumpy. But his cold exterior didn't fool me. Underneath all that ice and thunder was a good guy. A guy just trying to do right by his family and his team.

"I got drunk. I didn't—"

"You were at a bar, drunk and alone, and you let that asshole put his hands all over you."

"I didn't let him do anything, and for your informations, I told him to go away."

"Informations?" He quirked a brow.

"Yes, that's what I said. Informations."

"You shouldn't have been there alone."

"I wasn't alone. Most of the hockey team was there."

"Harper..."

"Mason..."

"Fuck, woman, you drive me insane."

"The feeling is entirely mutuals."

We reached my dorm, and he lowered me to my feet. "You good?"

"I... I don't feel—"

"Shit, Harper." He caught me again, holding me with one arm while he managed to wrangle my keycard out of my purse and get us inside. "Room number?"

"Two Eleven. Second floors."

"Why do you keep adding an s onto everything?"

"I do nots." My brows furrowed. "Huh, weird."

"Can you make it up the stairs?"

I stared up at him, feeling myself tumble into his icy gaze. When Mason looked at me, it was the strangest sensation, like burning alive and being frozen to death all at the same time.

"Will you be there to catch me if I fall?"

His brows furrowed a little, something flashing in his eyes. "Yeah, I'll be there to catch you, blondie."

I grinned.

He frowned some more.

"Come on, up you go." Mason steadied his hands on my waist as we climbed the stairs to my floor.

I just wanted to get out of these clothes, wash the makeup off my face, brush my teeth, and fall into bed. But given how badly the hall was spinning, I wasn't sure I'd be able to do any of those things.

We reached my door, and Mason leaned around me to open it. "Do you need me to—"

"Don't leaves me," I blurted, clapping a hand over my mouth at how ridiculous I sounded.

His soft laughter rolled over me, cocooning me like a warm squishy blanket. God, I loved it when Mason Steele laughed. It didn't happen often, so being around to witness it always made me feel special.

You're not though, Harper. You're foolish. Silly, foolish—

"Nice room," Mason said, closing the door behind us.

I wanted to run an assessing eye over the state of the place, but since I could barely see, thanks to the dim lighting and the copious amounts of liquor poisoning my bloodstream, I settled for a muffled, "Thanks."

"Want to talk about it?" he asked, and I twisted around to meet his expectant gaze.

"No?"

"No, question mark?" A faint smirk traced his lips. "You're a funny drunk."

"It's all his fault, you knows."

"Whose fault?"

I rolled my eyes. Was he really that clueless?

"Your dad...?"

"He doesn't deserve that title anymore." I smiled sadly. "Hasn't for a really long times."

"What—"

"Oh God." Bile rushed up my throat, and I darted toward the bathroom, almost tripping over my own feet.

"Jesus Christ," Mason muttered, following behind me as I flew into the small en suite and dropped to my knees, heaving. But nothing came up, my stomach groaning.

"What do you need?" he asked, and I held up a finger, my other hand working my hair out of my face. But Mason dropped to his knees behind me, taking my hair in his big hand and holding it for me.

"I think it's a false alarms," I breathed, sitting up to test how I felt.

Everything stayed inside except my dignity. That had gone to hell in a handbasket.

"You sure?"

I nodded, reaching for him. He helped me to my feet, and I inhaled a shuddering breath. "I needs to sleep."

"You need water."

"There's some in the mini-fridge." I swayed on my feet a little, and Mason tsked. "What?"

"You're a mess, blondie. Come on, let's get you into bed."

Now that was something I could get on board with. Falling into his arms, I let him scoop me up and carry me to my bed. He lowered me down, and my breath caught at the intensity in his eyes.

"Mase—"

"I'll get you some water." He detangled me from his body. "You do whatever you need to do."

I was past caring about my bedtime routine. I was crashing, and fast.

Rolling onto my side, I pulled the covers over me and snuggled down. "Do you think you can pull my sneakers off?"

"You're sleeping like that?" He perched against the edge of the desk, watching me with a hint of amusement.

"I'm too sleepy to get undressed or take my makeup off or drink that waters." To prove a point, a yawn crawled up my throat.

"Oh no, you don't. If you don't hydrate, you'll feel ten times worse in the morning." Mason stalked toward me, sitting on the edge of the bed. "Drink." He unscrewed the cap and passed the bottle toward me.

With a pained groan, I managed to sit up enough so that I could wrap my fingers around his wrist and let him feed me the water.

"More." He added when I tried to tug his hand away. "It's not enough."

"You're bossy."

"And you're a pain in my ass."

My lips curved at that.

"What?" He frowned, placing the bottle on the nightstand.

"Nothings."

"Harper..."

"Mason..."

I snuggled back down in the covers.

"You do know you're not in bed, right?"

"As good as." I smiled goofily, my eyelids fluttering closed.

"Fuck's sake," he muttered, stalking off again. When he came back, he'd gotten a t-shirt in his hands. "Okay, blondie, help a guy out." He started dragging the cover-burrito off me.

"No, I'm too comfy. I'm fine. I'm—"

But Mason had me half undressed before I knew what was happening. He fitted the t-shirt over my head and pulled it down my body before pulling my leggings off. His hands remained on my body, his fingertips brushing my thighs. I sucked in a sharp breath, and he startled, snatching his hand away like I'd burned him.

"Okay, if you're all set, I'm going to—"

"Stay." My hand shot out, grabbing him.

"Harper." A beat passed. Tense and heavy. Then he said, "I'm not sure that's a good idea."

"Please, tonight was... really shitty. And you, Mason Steele, you make me smile." He snorted at that, and I frowned. "What?"

"I don't think anyone has ever said that to me before."

"Because they don't see what I see."

"And what do you see, Harper Dixon?"

"I see... things."

"Things?" His mouth quirked as he reached for me, pushing the flyaway hairs from my face. His fingers lingered on my cheek, slipping down to my chin. "You should get some sleep."

"Don't make me beg, please."

"Will you tell me what happened between you and your old man?"

"He's your coach," I said, the words sobering me a little. "It's a conflict of interest."

Mason stood, pulling off his t-shirt.

"W-what are you doing?"

"If we're doing this, we might as well do it properly." He tugged the covers off my body and wriggled them down underneath me. His hand slipped to the belt on his jeans.

"Wait," I said, panic spreading through me like wildfire. "I'm not sleeping with you."

Again.

"Don't worry. I can keep my hands to myself. Besides, I don't fuck drunk chicks," he said gruffly, kicking off his jeans. "Scooch over."

It was a tight squeeze, given my bed was only a single, but Mason felt good pressed up behind me.

"Are you spooning me?" I chuckled, wiggling my butt right in his crotch.

"There's something very wrong with this picture."

"You love it," I teased, feeling a second burst of energy now that he was here.

Now that he was staying.

"For fuck's sake, blondie. Stop doing that." He let out a throaty groan that did all kinds of things to my already turbulent insides. "Okay, enough." His hand went around my waist, slipping under my t-shirt. He splayed his fingers across my skin, and I instantly settled into him.

"Now sleep."

"That feels nice." I purred like a damn house cat.

After my father's blatant rejection in front of Mason and the rookies, I'd felt so embarrassed and hurt that I should have left the bar. But my stubborn streak wouldn't let me. So I'd stayed. I'd pasted on a smile and gone in search of validation in the form of cherry sours and faceless guys.

Stupid, yes.

Necessary, also, yes.

"You're supposed to be going to sleep." Mason huffed.

"Has anyone ever told you you're grumpy?"

"All the damn time." His warm breath fanned my shoulder. It felt good. Too good. Sending a lick of heat through me to places that definitely didn't need waking up right about now.

"Sleep," he ordered.

I got comfortable, stretching and shifting until I was cocooned in Mason's warmth. My eyes shuttered as I yawned again. "My father isn't who you think he is," I murmured. "He's nothing but a big phony."

"Shh, go to sleep," Mason said, sliding his hand up

my stomach, the tips of his fingers brushing precariously close to the underside of my boobs. A violent shiver ran down my spine, and I pressed my lips together, trapping a small whimper.

It felt good.

He felt good.

But he wasn't here for that.

"Mase?" I asked after a couple of tense seconds.

"Yeah?"

"You really hurt me, you know." It came out half-whisper, half-yawn. "I know I'm not supposed to tell you, but that's not who I am. I wear my heart on my sleeve and believe in being upfront and honest with someone. And you hurt me. You—"

"Harper?"

"Yeah, Mase?"

"Go to sleep."

My heart sank. Even now, in the darkness of the shadows, he couldn't do it. He couldn't admit there was something between us. Not that it changed anything; it didn't.

He'd had his shot, and he'd blown it.

We lay there in thick, stifling silence. Even though my body craved sleep, I couldn't drift off. Not with Mason so close, his fingers a featherlight caress over my skin.

In the harsh light of day, I knew I would regret this moment of vulnerability. But I was only human. Being constantly rejected by my father, being treated like his dirty little secret was one thing, but having him here, in my space, and experiencing it was a different kind of torture.

Mason let out a heavy sigh. "You're not going to sleep, are you?"

"What happened to your dad?" I blurted, sober enough that I was aware I was treading on thin ice with him.

"He walked out not long after Scottie got his official autism diagnosis."

"Do you both still see him?"

"Scottie does now and again. Me, not so much."

"I'm sorry." I slid my hands over his, loving how he felt wrapped around me. Even if I knew it was a temporary lapse in judgment on both our parts.

"It is what it is. Scottie has Mom and me. I'll never let that kid down."

"No, you won't."

"What about you and your dad? What aren't you telling me?"

Nothing. Everything.

I let out a weary sigh. "It's complicated."

"The two of you aren't close?"

"That's... the understatement of the century."

"I'm sorry."

"Me too."

"Fuck, Harper, I..."

Say it, I silently begged. *Just say it.*

But all I got was a muffled, "I'm sorry."

Tears filled my eyes, an overwhelming sense of sadness settling in my chest. There was something between us—there was—but Mason was too chickenshit to admit it.

I wasn't enough for my father, and clearly, I wasn't enough for Mason to take a leap of faith, either.

Even if he was here, even if I felt his torment, the possessive way he held me, it wasn't enough.

I closed my eyes and willed sleep to find me. Because I knew when I woke up in the morning, Mason would be gone.

And I would go back to hating him.

My eyes fluttered open, the heavy pounding in my head as grating as the brass band at my old high school.

Dear God, how much had I drunk last night?

Lots and lots of shots, Harper.

Ugh.

Rolling onto my back, I groaned with pain. I couldn't even remember getting back to the building. How cliché.

Sad, dejected girl gets wasted and makes bad life choices.

Sitting up, I pushed the hair from my eyes and scanned the nightstand for my cell phone.

> Harper: Question. Did I leave the bar with you last night?

> Rory: You don't remember?

> Harper: Uh, no.

> Rory: You were pretty drunk. I tried to get you to come with us, but you wanted to stay. Austin said he'd keep an eye on you.

> Harper: Austin. Right.

> Rory: Harper, is everything okay? Did something happen?

> Harper: No, no. Everything is fine just a little hazy.

My eyes landed on my desk, and I frowned. There was a coffee cup and a small paper bag.

"What the—" I shoved off the covers and climbed out of bed, breathing past the nausea rolling through me.

As I drew closer, I realized it was an iced coffee from the campus coffee shop. And there was a note.

My heart ratcheted as I plucked the note off the desk.

Thought you might need this. The barista reassured me the brownies were gluten-free.
P.S. Keep the t-shirt. It looks good on you.
                                    Mase

Mason.

I glanced down and realized I was wearing the t-shirt I'd borrowed from his room that morning I snuck out after the party. But how—

Hazy images filled my head. His scowl as he approached me at the bar. His strong arms lifting me off my unsteady feet. His warm muscular body enveloping mine, his steady breath fanning the back of my neck.

Dear God, Mason had brought me home, practically carried me up to my room, undressed me, and then spent the night.

Because you begged him to stay.

Embarrassment welled inside me, but it quickly softened into something else as I eyed the little paper bag. Mason didn't only spend the night; he snuck out this morning to get me coffee.

Mason Steele got me hangover snacks and left me two Advil.

I didn't want to read too much into it, but I couldn't imagine he ran around campus doing that for many people.

Don't do it, Harper. Don't run away with yourself.

Mason had made his feelings on there ever being anything more between us perfectly clear. I had to respect that.

So I drank the coffee, swallowed the Advil, ate the gluten-free brownies, and allowed myself to text Mason a simple, safe reply.

Harper: Thank you. xo

CHAPTER 21

MASON

I READ HER REPLY AGAIN.

Short and sweet and to the point.

So why did it leave a bitter taste in my mouth?

Shit. I hadn't wanted to leave her this morning. To sneak out without waking her. But I'd made a promise to my brother, one I couldn't break. So I'd managed to untangle Harper from my body, since she'd slept most of the night wrapped around me like a koala, and got out undetected.

I'd even managed to bring her some hangover supplies from Roast 'n' Go.

She'd looked so fucking peaceful, her golden hair spread out around her like a halo. Just the sight of her lying there in her small dorm-issued bed made my heart race in my chest like I'd done twenty laps around the rink.

"Mase, earth to Mason brother." I almost jumped out of my skin when Scottie leaned over and nudged my arm with his controller. "You're not paying attention."

"Ow, what the hell, bud?" I glared at him.

"You've been staring at your phone for the last seventy-two seconds. Who is it—"

"No one." I shoved my cell in my pocket and grabbed my controller. "Are we doing this, or what?"

"I was doing it," he huffed. "You were the one not paying any attention."

"Team stuff," I lied. Because apparently, that's who the fuck I was now. Lying to my brother. Lying to Harper.

Lying to myself.

"Prepare to lick ice." He smirked as the puck dropped, and he gained possession, deke-ing around two of my D-men.

"Lick ice is not a—" I didn't bother finishing my sentence because it would only go in one ear and out the other. "Not so fast, buddy." My goalie saved the shot with his glove and quickly dropped the puck, swiping it to one of his teammates.

"Big hairy balls," Scottie muttered, trying to get ahead of his players. But it was useless. My center was already in the attacking zone, ready to make the shot.

"And that"—I hit the button, a smug expression

coming over me as I watched the puck sail past my brother's goalie—"is how you do it."

"Mase, no fair," he grumbled. "I had you. I had—"

"Unlucky kid." Dropping the controller on the coffee table, I leaned over and ruffled his hair.

"Mase, don't do that. I'm not a kid anymore."

Okay, that was new.

"Scottie, you're twelve."

"Thirteen in fourteen days. That means I'm almost a teenager. You can't call me a kid when I'm a teenager."

"You're seven years younger than me, kid. I'll call you what I want."

He glowered at me, and I couldn't help but chuckle. If it was anyone else, my teasing might have upset him, but I knew my little brother well enough to know when I could push, and when I couldn't.

"Jackass," he muttered under his breath.

"Don't let Mom—"

"Catch me saying that. Yeah, I know."

"How was school yesterday?" I changed the subject.

"Brianne kissed Kallen Nelson. He isn't a weirdo like me."

"Quit talking like that. You're not a weirdo. You're spec—"

"Ugh. Please don't call me special. That's almost as bad as saying autism is my superpower," he mimicked.

"Well, I think it makes you pretty awesome."

"You have to say that because you're my brother."

He stared at the floor, running his hands back and forth over his sweatpants.

"What's going on in that head of yours, bud?"

"Mase, do you think I'll ever get a girlfriend?"

"Sure, when you're much, much older."

"But Brianne's right. I do and say weird things all the time. I can't help it. Thoughts pop into my head and just come out. And everything I usually say is only the truth anyway."

"I know, bud. I know. But we've talked about this. Sometimes, it's hard for people to hear the truth. And there's a time and a place for brutal honesty."

"It's better to be honest than to lie, though." He peeked up at me. "Right?"

Fuck. It was moments like these when I wished I had a handbook to help me deal with Scottie's questions and rigid thinking.

"In theory, yes."

"You know that makes no sense."

"It's hard to explain. I don't want to confuse you over something that doesn't really matter."

"The truth always matters. If you don't tell the truth, you can get into trouble. Mrs. Ecclestein says the truth might hurt for a little while, but a lie can hurt forever."

Smart woman. I ran a hand down my face, checking the time on my cell phone.

"Mom will be back soon, and we can head out. Are you excited about watching the game?"

He nodded. "Will Harper be there?"

"I'm not sure."

"But she's okay, right? She isn't still sick after—"

"No, she isn't still sick. You know that."

Because he'd asked me every time we texted or talked this week.

"One day, when I'm older, I'm going to meet a girl like Harper. She's kind and funny, and she cares about what I think about stuff. You know, since I can't date her, you should date her. Then I'd get to be friends with her after she stops working at the group. Maybe we could hang out and—"

"I don't think that's going to work out, buddy."

"Why." He frowned. "Don't you think she's pretty?"

Jesus. He was really going there after I'd spent the night in her bed.

"Yeah, she's pretty, but she's not my type."

"What is your type? She's pretty. She can skate. She loves hockey and knows all the best players. She can—"

"Come on, buddy, cut me some slack. I've got a big game tonight."

He grabbed his fiddle toy off the table and started twisting it into a complex shape, and I knew we were almost done with this conversation.

"It's okay, Mase," he said without looking up. "If you're worried Harper doesn't like you, I'll tell her she should give you a chance. I'll tell her you're the best. Then we can keep her. Then she won't leave us."

Fuck.

"Scottie, I'm not sure—"

"No, don't worry. I've got this, Mason brother." He looked at me with the kind of sheer determination I'd only seen him wear when he got hyper-focused on something. "I'm going to help you win the girl."

And the worst thing was, I believed him.

"Mase, Mason brother." Scottie waved excitedly from behind the plexiglass as we warmed up. Ellet Arena was slowly filling up, but Coach had agreed we could go out on the ice a little earlier.

I skated past him and Mom, tapping my stick against the glass. The look of wonder on his face was worth the agonizing ride to Lakeshore with them.

He'd told her all about Harper. Gone so far as to throw me under the bus too. But I'd stood firm and told her what I'd told her the day I'd brought Harper back to the house; there was nothing to tell.

Harper was a friend. That's *all* she would ever be.

The lie would have been easier to believe if she hadn't looked at me with *that* look. That soft, knowing expression that screamed, 'You might not realize it now, Son, but one day you will.'

So Scottie had gone on and on about Harper this

and Harper that, and Mom had sat quietly chuckling, casting me furtive glances the entire way.

Not my idea of fun.

"Little bro looks excited," Noah came up beside me as we did another lap of honor to get the fans hyped.

"Yeah, wouldn't shut up the entire ride here."

"They get checked into the hotel, okay?"

"Yeah, and we're all set for tomorrow. Coach said we can bring him down for a little behind-the-scenes tour."

"Count me in."

"Thanks, man. Appreciate it."

"Fuck," Noah choked out, and I glanced up to see what had caught his eye, smirking when I spotted Rory wearing his jersey.

"Still not over that sight, huh?"

"Don't think I'll ever be over it. She's it for me, Mase. Sounds crazy, doesn't it? But I love the fuck out of that girl."

"I'm happy for you. I am." My chest tightened with something I refused to acknowledge.

Thankfully, Coach Tucker called us in to the players' benches to give us another pep talk. "We made the win look easy last night, but that does not mean we can be complacent. Detroit is a strong team, and don't for a second doubt they'll come out tonight looking to remind you of that."

"Coach Tucker is right," Coach Dixon whipped off his ball cap and ran a hand through his salt and pepper hair. He looked a bit tired, dark shadows circling his eyes.

I hadn't said anything about seeing him in TPB last night, and neither had Leon or Ward, but the strange interaction hung between the four of us like a bad smell.

Ward cast me a sideways look, but I remained focused on our coaching staff.

"They'll be hungry for it, so keep your eyes up and watch their center. Give him too much space, and he'll run circles around you."

"We had him pinned last night," Connor pointed out.

"Most of the time. They still managed to get three across the line. Don't let it be three too many."

Something drew Coach D's attention across the ice, his expression darkening. I glanced over my shoulder to find Harper squeezing into the row behind my brother and Mom. She sat down next to Rory, and Scottie instantly twisted around to talk to her.

"Someone looks happy to see her," Noah whispered, and I scowled at him, not bothering to ask if he meant Coach Dixon or my brother.

"Mason, son. Just keep doing what we've been practicing. The rest of you guys remember to use him. He's the secret weapon that could take you all the way this year."

A couple of the guys snickered, shooting me

bemused looks. I kept my head down, uncomfortable with the constant attention he aimed in my direction.

Especially after the bar last night.

"Okay, warm up. And be ready," Coach Tucker ended the pep talk, and we all hit the ice, running a few basic drills while we waited for the Bulldogs.

"He acting a bit strange to you?" Ward skated in close, dipping his head toward the coaches.

"None of my business," I said, and I meant it.

We all knew Coach had been given a place on campus to stay, but beyond that, what he did in his spare time was nothing to do with the rest of the team or me. Yet, I couldn't shake the way he'd acted toward Harper, the dejection in her voice as she talked about him.

That was why I kept my circle close. Because then I didn't have to worry about other people's shit.

My gaze flicked toward the family and friends section, and I shook my head. Scottie had somehow wormed his way between Harper and Rory, the three of them deep in conversation.

"Cute kid," Ward said, noticing.

"Wait until he busts your balls about your performance tonight. You won't be calling him cute then."

"Good thing I plan on putting in a stellar performance then."

"Cocky asshole," I muttered, circling him as I cut across the ice to intercept a puck from Aiden.

"You good?" he asked, and I frowned.

"Why wouldn't I be?"

"You seemed a little distracted in the locker room earlier."

"I'm fine."

"Good to know. Make me look good out there." He winked, gliding off down the ice.

I steered clear of the coaches, waiting for the Bulldogs to finish their pep talk and move into position.

A ripple of excitement went through the arena. Hockey was a bit like a tidal wave gaining momentum. Every week, the fans, the players, and the coaching staff knew it was one step closer to the end goal.

We'd made it last season, but, in the end, we hadn't been good enough. No one wanted a repeat of that this season. We wanted to win—to bring home the trophy.

It had never felt that important to me before, but then, I'd never let myself believe that hockey could be a part of my future. I still struggled with that concept. But having Coach Dixon push and encourage me had got me thinking.

There was a kid in the stands who needed me, though. Who needed people in his life that wouldn't walk away.

As I hovered on the left wing, waiting for the puck to drop, I couldn't help but look over where my family sat—the two most important people in the world to me. Having them here was everything. But Harper's face came veering into the picture. Her infectious smile and bewitching eyes. Every time she pinned those baby blues in my direction, a bolt of lightning went through me.

I'd hated it at first, but I didn't mind so much now. In fact, I kind of liked it.

No one had ever looked at me like she did. Come to think of it; no one knew me the way she did because I didn't share those parts of myself with other people.

When my father walked out, and I became the man of the house at the tender age of twelve—the age Scottie was now—something inside me changed. Maybe even before that, when I'd truly understood all the ways that Scottie was different and what that might mean for his future.

I became his protector. But in order to protect him, I had to protect myself, and the easiest way to do that was to keep people out.

To put up walls so high no one could ever climb over them.

Harper was different. Something told me that given half the chance, she would scale those walls in a heartbeat. And maybe part of me had expected her to. To keep pushing, to keep chipping away at my defenses.

Instead, she'd backed off. Acted like everything that had gone down between us meant nothing.

It didn't mean nothing, but I didn't know if it could mean something, either.

The truth was, I was fucking confused.

And if last night was anything to go on, I couldn't be trusted around her.

Because if she kept pushing—if fate kept pushing us together—one day, I might just snap.

"Oh, sweetheart." Mom pulled me into her arms. "That was... I'm just so proud of you." She held me at arm's length, looking me right in the eye.

"No tears, Mom. I'm begging you," I chuckled, but it was strained against the lump in my throat.

"Two goals, sweetie. That's—"

"It should have been at least four," Scottie wedged himself between us, wrapping his arms around my waist. "Hi, Mason brother."

"Hey, bud. Did you enjoy the game?"

"Yes, Harper, let me sit with her and Aura."

"Aurora, buddy. Her name is—"

"Aura, yeah. That's what I said."

Mom smothered a laugh. "She's such a lovely girl," she mouthed. "And so good with him."

"Harper is a... good friend."

"Friend, of course." Her eyes twinkled with things I did not need to see twinkling in my mother's eyes.

I pulled her into a one-armed hug, pressing a kiss to her hair. "Don't get any ideas, okay?"

"Wouldn't dream of it." Her lips tugged into a telling smile.

"Hey, Mrs. Steele," Noah sauntered over and pulled her into a hug. "It's good to see you again."

"Noah, that was some fancy work out there tonight."

"See, Mase? Your mom likes my fancy work." He flashed me a shit-eating grin. "She might even say my fancy work is better than your fancy work."

"Now, now, Mason will always be my number one."

"And rightly so." His expression dropped a little as he watched her fuss over me.

"Mom, come on. You can't treat me like a kid here." I glanced around the arena parking lot. Most of the guys had moved on already, but a few lingered, talking to the bunnies who made a habit of hanging around.

"What's up, kid?" Noah held out his fist to Scottie, and I watched with trepidation as he navigated the social cue.

"You don't have—" He surprised the shit out of me by fist-bumping Noah back.

"Nice game, number eleven, Noah Holden. Two goals and two assists."

"Nice stats." Noah winked. "How do you feel about pizza?"

"I don't eat cheese."

"Shit, my bad. Fries? Hot dogs? My treat."

"Can Harper and Aura come?"

Noah slid his amused gaze to mine, and said, "I

don't know. What do you think, Mase? Can Rory and Harper come?"

"I think that would be lovely," Mom added a little too smugly.

"Please, Mase. It's my special trip, and I want Harper and Aura to come."

"Fine, they can come." I pinned Noah with an irritated look. The last thing I wanted was to spend more time with Harper. Letting my brother grow more attached. Letting Mom get all kinds of notions in her head.

Fuck my life.

But then the girls appeared, and Harper's baby blues found me, and I knew it wasn't Mom and Scottie I needed to worry about.

It was me.

Because it was getting really fucking hard to keep telling myself that I didn't want her.

CHAPTER 22

HARPER

"What's wrong?" Rory asked as we followed everyone into the restaurant.

"I don't know, is it weird I'm here? It feels a bit weird."

"Scottie really wanted you to come." Her eyes searched mine. "He's a sweet kid."

"He is." I glanced over at the Steele brothers, that silly flutter in my heart reminding me that I wasn't only here for Scottie.

Damn him.

Mason was under my skin. He kept pushing me away and then reeling me back, and I was trying so hard not to let myself get caught up in the small acts of kindness he'd shown me.

But it was hard.

And part of me was so desperate to believe that it was all leading somewhere. Because no matter how much he hurt me or pushed me away, I was a romantic at heart—a girl waiting for her happy ending.

After all, I deserved one, didn't I?

After everything my father had put me through, I deserved someone who would put me first. Someone who loved me for me, and in spite of everything I wasn't.

I wasn't sure Mason was that person. But I'd still never felt this way about a guy before. Which only made me wonder if coming out with him and his family was a bad idea.

Especially, when I was trying not to be that girl.

"Harper, you'd tell me right? If there was any—"

"Shortcake." Noah appeared, hooking his arm around Rory's neck and dropping a kiss on her head. "Let's go. I'm starving."

She gave me an apologetic smile and let her boyfriend tug her toward the plush leather booth the server had picked out for us.

"This looks lovely," Mrs. Steele said, her eyes finding mine as I slid in beside Rory. "I'm so glad you could all join us."

Scottie had been so keen to introduce us at the arena, and she hadn't made it awkward at all. But the way she looked at me made me a little uncomfortable. Like she could see right past my façade.

"The pleasure sure is ours, Mrs. Steele."

"Noah, I've known you going on a year. For the love of God, please call me Melinda."

"Well, Melinda, dinner is my treat. So you and little man pick whatever you want."

"You do know I'm almost a teenager, Noah Holden?" Scottie stated in that deadpan way of his.

"Mase might have mentioned it. What do you want for your birthday?"

"Dad is going to get me a brand-new PlayStation."

Mrs. Steele's expression guttered at the mention of their father.

"Mom wanted to buy it for me, but we can't afford it. Dad said he owed me one for being an asshole."

"Scottie, bud, that's not—"

"Sorry, Mom." Scottie dropped his head, but she leaned in, whispering something to him. He nodded, his fidgeting becoming increasingly marked.

"Hey, Scottie," I said, hoping my plan to distract him—and lessen the pressure—would work. "What was your favorite part of the game?"

He looked up, his brows furrowing a little as he considered my question. "When the goalie came out of the crease and saved Helinksi's slapshot. The chances of saving a shot that fast and that on target are virtually impossible. But he did it."

"Because Austin is a fu—" Noah caught himself. "Austin is the main man."

"Mom says fuck isn't appropriate language for an almost-teenager." Scottie gave a small half-shrug as if he hadn't just dropped the f-bomb in the middle of one of Lakeshore's more upmarket restaurants.

"Mom said it isn't appropriate for anyone, especially not in the middle of dinner."

"Sorry," he grumbled.

"Relax, kid." Noah smothered a laugh. "Rory gives me hell all the time for saying inappropriate things."

"I bet she does," Mason grumbled beneath his breath, his gaze snagging mine. He smiled, and I smiled back, unsure of what game we were playing.

He confused me. More than any guy I'd ever tried to get to know. It was disconcerting to feel so unsure of myself. But I'd promised myself I wouldn't push either.

A promise I intended on keeping.

No matter how much I wanted to say to hell with it and throw my chips in... again.

Why did I have to be like this? So willing to risk my heart over and over for a shot at something real? I mean, I knew why. It was all his fault.

James Dixon. The man. The myth. The legend. And the bitter, bitter disappointment.

People didn't know him the way I did. They only knew his legacy. The mark he'd almost made on pro hockey. They didn't *know*.

But I did.

I'd lived it for the last eighteen years.

"Glad to know Austin was your favorite tonight," Mason said, ruffling his brother's hair.

"Mase!" Scottie batted his hand away. "Don't do that."

"Relax, bud. I'm just messing with you. What looks good to eat?" He slid an arm along the back of the booth, studying the menu in Scottie's hand.

"I want pancakes."

"I'm not sure they do pancakes here. What about a plain hot dog and fries?"

"Pancakes," Scottie said.

"Come on, bud. That's not going to be possible right now. But tomorrow morning, I'll take you for pancakes."

"You promise?"

"I promise."

"Can Harper come?"

Everyone swung their gazes to me, and I wanted the leather banquette to swallow me whole.

"I... Actually, I have plans in the morning."

"What plans?" Scottie asked, earning him a disapproving look from his big brother.

"If Harper says she has plans, that's her business, bud."

"But I'll see you on Wednesday at the center," I added, hoping it would pacify him.

"What are you going to eat, Harper? What about the cross-tamination."

"Cross-tamination?" Mrs. Steele asked.

"Cross-contamination, I'm celiac."

"Sorry, of course. Mason told me he had to take care of you."

"Mom..." He grumbled.

She pressed her lips together into a small, knowing smile. Noah cleared his throat, glancing between us, confused. He and Rory only knew half of the story, and I really wanted to keep it that way.

"Something you two want to fess up?"

"Don't start," Mason warned.

"Did you get sick again?" Scottie asked. "Because you know I read up about celiac disease, and did you know that people with celiac disease are twice as likely to develop coronary artery disease and four times as likely to develop small bowel cancers."

Mason let out a weary sigh. "Not appropriate, buddy."

"What?" Scottie frowned. "I'm only reciting scientific facts. There's also a twelve percent chance of developing unexplained infertility. A twenty-six percent chance of—"

"Okay, we get it." Mason was sterner this time, giving his little brother a silent look that spoke volumes.

"Sweetie, why don't you apologize to Harper. I'm sure—"

"Oh no, Mrs. Steele. Scottie doesn't need to apologize. I'm impressed he did such thorough research." I gave the kid a warm smile. "What else did you learn?"

"Celiac disease is a condition where your immune system attacks your own tissues when you eat gluten. It stops you from taking in nutrients and is usually treated with a gluten-free diet. Even just a crumb of gluten is enough to trigger the auto-immune response in some people."

"You might be good on the ice, Mase, but little bro is going places with that brain of his." Noah winked at Scottie, who sat up a little straighter.

"I am smarter than him." A faint grin traced his mouth.

"Damn straight." Noah held out his fist, and for a second, Scottie gawked at it. But then he curled his hand and bumped it against Noah's.

"Oh, it's like that, huh? The two of you ganging up on me?"

"Scottie knows I'm the coolest."

"No fu— freaking way." Mason chuckled. "I am way cooler. Tell him, Scottie.

"Harper's the coolest. She can skate, and she knows hockey, and she has nice—"

"Scottie," Mason rushed out, and Scottie frowned.

"Hair," he muttered. "She has nice hair."

Relief passed over Mason, and it was my turn to frown. "What am I missing?" I glanced between the brothers.

"Nothing," Scottie said, looking up at Mason, who remained looking at me.

"Nothing," he gave me the faintest smirk.

And I knew, without a shadow of a doubt, there was more to the story than they were willing to share with me.

"Gosh, he just loves being with his big brother," Mrs. Steele said as we watched the guys teach Scottie how to play pool. Although, he seemed to be doing a pretty good job without their instruction.

"He misses Mason a lot?" Rory asked, and Mrs. Steele nodded, sadness creeping into her expression.

"So much. But Mason deserves this." She looked over at him with a wistful expression. "He deserves to chase his dreams."

"It can't be easy, raising him by yourself."

"It's not. But he's my boy, and I wouldn't change him for the world."

"He's such an intelligent young man," I said.

"He's quite taken with you, Harper. I've heard all about your sessions together at the center."

"He's a good kid."

"He is." She glanced back at her sons. "I just wish I knew what the future held for him. Especially if Mason decides to enter the draft."

"You think he won't?"

"I think my son would move home in a heartbeat if I let him."

Her words didn't surprise me. Mason clearly carried the weight of the world on his shoulders. That weight mostly being a ninety-pound twelve-year-old who adored his older brother. But it seemed unfair for him to pay for the sins of his father.

"I hear your father and Mason have been working quite closely together," Melinda said.

"Apparently, so," I replied a little coolly.

Of course, it made sense that Mason had talked to his mom about a local legend like Coach Dixon working with the team. I just hadn't anticipated how much it would hurt to hear the words.

"Hopefully, he can help Mason make some big decisions."

"I'm sure he will." I gave her a tight smile before excusing myself to the restrooms.

What was I doing here? Clinging onto some foolish notion that maybe Mason would, what? Choose me over my father and his chance to go all the way?

My life wasn't a fairy tale. He wasn't going to burst into the restroom, kick down the stall door, and profess his undying love for me.

"You've got to stop doing this," I whispered to myself.

But was it so bad to crave a connection? To want to feel that rush of endorphins when you kissed a guy or fell into bed with him?

Sex was a double-edged sword for girls like me, though. I'd tried the casual thing. Over and over, I'd told myself it would be different, and that I wouldn't catch feelings.

Nobody kept getting hurt but me though.

Time and time again, I let myself believe—*hope*—things might be different. But time and time again, my desire to be loved made me undesirable.

Mason was different, though. For the first time, I found myself building walls. Protecting myself. Because deep down, I knew he had the one thing none of those guys before him had.

The power to break my heart.

Why him?

Why did he have to be different?

Annoyed with myself, I washed my hands and headed back into the bar. Only to be met with a solid wall of muscle.

"Going somewhere, blondie?" Mason smirked, reaching out and snagging a curl between his fingers.

"Oh, hey." I smiled. Bright and breezy, completely at odds with the tumultuous storm raging inside me.

"We're heading out. Scottie is tired, and it's getting late."

"Of course. I'll go and say goodbye." I went to move around him, but he stepped into my path. "Mase, come on," I chuckled, looking up at him with mild exasperation.

But the intensity in his gaze knocked all the air from my lungs. "M-Mase?" I croaked, suffocating in the heat in his eyes.

The air crackled, setting the fine hairs along my arms and the back of my neck on end.

"Sorry about my brother tonight," he said. "You know he doesn't mean—"

"I know, and there really is no apology needed."

Disappointment welled inside me. For a second, I'd thought he was going to say something else. But who was I kidding?

He'd invited me here for Scottie.

Nothing else.

I was finishing up in my small en suite bathroom when there was a soft knock at the door. For a moment, I thought it might be Rory. She and Noah had made sure I got back okay before heading to her apartment.

But when I crossed the room and checked the peephole, my heart ratcheted. The door swung open, and I sucked in a shuddering breath at the sight of Mason standing there.

"What are you doing here?" My fingers curled around the edge of the door, my heart crashing violently in my chest.

It was late, late enough that the girls on my floor were either still out partying or locked away in their rooms, so the hall was quiet. Almost silent. No disguise for the violent thud of my heart.

"I... honestly..." He dragged a hand through his hair, his eyes burning with hesitation and bad intentions. "I don't know."

"You said we were a mistake."

That's it, Harper. Be strong. Don't make it easy on him.

"I know. Fuck, I know. But you're everywhere I look. It's like I can't escape you."

Escape me?

He wanted to escape me?

My heart tumbled into my stomach.

"I tried to get out of the dinner, but Scottie—"

"I'm glad you came."

"You are?" I frowned.

"Yeah, blondie. I am. You're great with Scottie, and I think you won my mom over too."

But did I win you over? I bit back the words, reining myself in despite how unnatural it felt. It wasn't too much to confess your feelings to someone—to lay it all on the line—was it?

"Did they get settled at the hotel, okay?"

"Yeah, he crashed within minutes."

"He really enjoyed watching you play, Mason. His live commentary was pretty awesome too." I smiled.

"He's a good kid. But I worry about what life will be like for him."

"With you looking out for him, he'll be okay."

"But I won't always be there."

Mason got this distant, pained look, his torment bleeding into the space between us. I hadn't even invited him inside, and yet, this moment felt intimate. Private. Like we were in our own little bubble where nothing could touch us.

Before I could answer, though, he said, "Anyway, I didn't come to get all deep, sorry."

"So why did you come?"

"Two reasons. One, you didn't get dessert." He pulled out a little paper bag from behind his back. "They're gluten-free."

"Mase..." Emotion rose up inside me. It was the sweetest thing anyone had ever done for me.

"And two," he went on. "I wanted to ask you to come by the rink tomorrow morning. We're giving Scottie a behind-the-scenes tour. I'm sure he'd appreciate a friendly face."

"You want me to come to the rink... for Scottie?"

"Yeah." The intensity in his eyes was at odds with his words.

"I... will my dad be there?"

A strange expression washed over him. "It's not an official team thing, so I don't see why he would be. My mom will be there too. I bet she'd love to spend more time with you."

His mixed signals were giving me whiplash. But I was too scared to ask what it all meant in case he was genuinely trying to be my friend and nothing more.

"I'll see what I can do."

He nodded, his eyes searching mine for answers I didn't know the questions to.

"Is that everything or—"

Mason pulled me into his arms, holding me tight. "I just... fuck, Harper. I'm not good at this."

"What do you want, Mason?" I gazed up at him, surprised I could get my words out, given how light-headed I felt.

"I... I don't know. All I know is when you're pissed at me, things feel wrong. I've never done this before."

"This?" I arched a brow because I wasn't going to let him get off that easily.

"Yeah, blondie. This." His mouth twitched.

"I'm not sure I understand. You might need to break it down for me."

"This. Chase a girl. I don't have time for all that. Not with the team and Scottie and—"

"I get it, Mason." I slid my hands up his chest, curling my fingers into his hoodie. "You don't know how to let someone in."

His Adam's apple bobbed against his throat as he swallowed roughly. For a second, I thought he might kiss me, but instead, he pressed his lips to my forehead. Soft and lingering, he inhaled a shaky breath and whispered, "You should tell me to turn around and walk away, Harper. I'm no good for you."

"I've never been very good at making the right choices." I looped my arms around his shoulders and touched my head to his. "There's something here, Mason."

"I know." Uncertainty coasted across his

expression. "It fucking terrifies me. I don't want to hurt you. I—"

I kissed him. Slipped my hand around the back of his neck and kissed him, trying to pour everything I refused to say into every stroke of my tongue and press of my lips.

I wanted Mason to choose me. To take a risk on me. But I wasn't going to beg. Not this time. Not when everything inside me was screaming that this thing between us was real and had the potential to be something more.

Something permanent.

Mason had to figure it out on his own terms what he wanted.

And what he was willing to sacrifice to have it.

CHAPTER 23

MASON

"I REALLY APPRECIATE THIS, COACH," I said as he let Mom and Scottie into the media room.

"Family is important, son. Your brother could be the next big thing in hockey."

"I'm not so sure about that, sir. He loves the game, but he has a big fear of the ice."

"Maybe he just needs lots of exposure."

"Yeah, maybe." My gaze went to Harper, who was deep in discussion with Scottie and Mom over by the trophy cabinet.

"And Miss Dixon, do I need to be worried there?"

"She's a good friend, sir."

"A friend," he muttered. "I've heard that one too many times in my lifetime. Just a word of warning, Mason, son. She's Coach Dixon's daughter. I don't know all that's gone on between them, but something doesn't quite add up. That said, he's still my assistant coach, and you're still my player. I can't afford to have the two of you butting heads this season."

"Won't happen, Coach. You have my word."

"Good." He clapped me on the shoulder. "You're a good kid, Mason. But it's time to work out what you want from life, son."

His parting words sank into me, weighing heavily on my chest.

Everyone kept saying I needed to work out what I wanted like it was that simple. Like I only had myself to think about.

"Mase! Mason brother, look at this." Scottie pointed at something in the trophy cabinet, and I went to join the three of them.

"What did you find?" I asked.

"It's the Frozen Four trophy."

"Pretty neat, huh?"

He nodded, fixated on the trophy behind the glass.

Harper caught my eye and smiled. We hadn't talked about last night; we hadn't talked much at all.

After I'd left her dorm room, I'd gone back to the house and lay awake mentally trying to come up with a list of reasons I couldn't go after her. But the problem was, the more time I spent with her, the shorter that list got until there was only one name left.

Coach Dixon.

He couldn't stop me from dating his daughter, but

he could make life pretty damn difficult for me. Maybe for her too, given that I sensed deep issues already existed between them.

"He's so happy," Harper said as we wandered back out into the hall, ready for the unofficial practice part of Scottie's tour.

Noah and a couple of the guys had agreed to come in and give him and Mom a little demo.

"Yeah. I was talking to Coach, and it sounds like he's interested in making this a regular thing for the kids at the center."

"Really?" Her eyes lit up. "They would love that."

"You think?"

She nodded. "Kids like Scottie and the other kids at the center just want to feel included, Mason. They all have hopes and dreams too. Sports, especially physical games like hockey, can really help with development and focus. Jet will be stoked for the opportunity to work with the team."

Her excitement radiated around her like the sun, and I couldn't help but gravitate toward her.

"Mason," she breathed, eyes wide with surprise as she stared up at me. And I realized I'd backed her up against the wall.

"Shit." I rubbed the back of my neck awkwardly.

I couldn't take my eyes off her lips, the urge to kiss her overwhelming the fuck out of me.

Harper's soft laughter hit me dead in the chest. "We should probably stop whatever this is."

"Uh, yeah, okay," I stuttered.

But then the familiar cadence of my brother's voice filled the hall, and he and Mom appeared.

"Hey, bud, you okay?"

"What were you two doing out here?"

"Nothing," I said.

He studied us. "What—"

"Come on, Scottie. You can sit with your mom and me while Mason goes and gets ready."

"See you out on the ice?" I said, and he nodded.

"Break a leg." The little fucker chuckled.

"Scottie," Mom chided him as the three took off down the hall.

"You've been holding out on me," a voice said, and I whirled around to find Noah watching me.

"I have no idea what you're talking about."

"I think you do. I think"—his amused gaze flicked down the hall to where Harper and my family had disappeared—"you're banging her."

"I'm not... exactly."

Fuck.

"I knew it." He flashed me a smug grin. "I fucking knew—"

"Keep your voice down, okay?" I ran a hand down my face. "It's complicated."

"Holy shit. You like her. You actually like her. Do you have any idea how long I've been waiting for this moment? The moment I got to say 'I told you so.'"

"I'm not doing this." I barged past him toward the locker rooms.

"Whoa, whoa, whoa." He grabbed my arm and caught up to me. "Talk to me, Mase. What's going on?"

"She's in my fucking head," I admitted. "And I don't know how to get her out."

"Do you want to get her out?" He gave me a serious look. One that said I needed to tread carefully. But he knew now. I couldn't exactly erase that little tidbit of information.

"I... fuck. I don't know, okay? This wasn't supposed to happen. I don't have time for a—" I caught myself, but it was too late. Noah's expression morphed into one of smug amusement.

"You *really* like her."

"Oh, you can stop now. Forget I even mentioned it." I moved ahead of him, a strange mix of irritation and relief coursing through me.

On the one hand, it felt good to talk to him about it. If anyone knew how it felt to lose sight of the plan, it was Noah. But I still didn't know what my plan was. It was different for me. Any decisions I made directly affected my mom and Scottie.

If I chose to pursue things with Harper, that had implications.

Maybe even consequences.

"Mase, come on, bro. I'm just busting your balls. If you like her, it doesn't have to be that complicated," he said as we slipped into the locker room.

"What's complicated?" Connor looked up, and I gawked at him.

"What the fuck is this?" I ran my eyes over my teammates. I'd expected a handful of them, not half the fucking team.

"Called in a few favors, didn't I?" Noah grinned. "Our biggest fan deserves a proper show."

"I... shit, thanks. You guys didn't have to give up your Sunday morning to do this."

"We're a team," Connor stood, pulling on his pads. "A family. We wanted to help out. Besides, Leon and Ward could do with the extra practice."

"Hey, I'll skate circles around you, asshole," Leon called from across the room.

"Okay, how are we doing this?" Aiden came over. "A little four-on-four?"

"Happy to take your direction," I said. "I appreciate you being here."

"Wouldn't have missed it." He held out his glove, and I bumped it with my fist.

"Thanks."

I swallowed over the lump in my throat. I didn't get close to many people. But as I looked around the locker room, I realized Connor was right.

These guys weren't only my teammates.

They were family.

And I was a fucking lucky guy to have them in my corner.

"I'm coming for you, hotshot," Connor taunted as he skated toward me. I spotted Noah in my periphery, but Ward had him pinned down.

"Take the shot, Mason brother," Scottie bellowed. "Take the—"

Connor checked me hard, and I went down like a sack of bricks, the air whooshing from my lungs. "You hesitated," he said, looming over me. "There's no time to hesitate. Unless you were distracted by a certain—"

"Do not finish that sentence," I growled, letting him pull me to my skates.

Regaining my balance, he handed me my stick with a smug chuckle. "Coach D's daughter has you all tied up in knots still, doesn't she."

"I'm not doing this." I skated off, but his laughter followed me.

"But it's so much fun."

I flipped him off over my shoulder, frowning when I noticed Mom sitting on her own. "Timeout," I called to my friends, heading over to her.

"Where's Scottie and Harper?"

"Oh, they just went to—"

A commotion over by the door leading to the locker rooms caught my attention, and the ground nearly went out from under me as I watched Harper help Scottie teeter along on his skates.

"What the hell is she doing?" I bit out.

"Mason," Mom soothed, "it was his idea."

"What?" I gawked at her because, surely she had it wrong. Scottie was terrified of the ice. He'd had more than one meltdown in the past over it.

"This is a good thing, sweetheart," she said. "He wants so desperately to share this with you."

"Mom, come on. You know what will happen if—"

"We can't always protect him from experiencing life, Mase. He's almost a teenager. He wants to do normal things. And you know how much he loves hockey. Harper is a good influence on him."

"I know, I just—"

"Mason, Mason brother, look at me." His voice was a mix of anxious excitement, and everyone stopped to watch Harper guide Scottie all the way to the edge of the rink.

"Surprise." She peeked up at me, hesitation glittering in her eyes because we'd already had this argument. And I'd told her—I'd fucking told her not to push.

"Scottie thought he might join you and the guys on the ice for a little bit."

"I'm scared, Mason brother. Really scared. But Harper said you'll help me."

"Of course, I will, bud." Emotion balled in my throat, making it really fucking hard to talk. "I won't let you fall. And if you do, I'll help you right back up."

"Promise?" He stared at me with young, vulnerable eyes. But there was a flicker of determination there too.

"I've got you." I held out my hand, and he took it, letting me gently coax him onto the ice. He started stimming as the sensation pushed him out of his comfort zone, a soft clicking noise to help self-regulate his nervous system.

"Harper, you're coming, right?"

"I'm right here, buddy." She skated up beside us. "Wow, Scottie, you're doing so good."

"Look who came to join us," I said casually as my friends approached.

"Hey, Scottie," Connor came forward. "I don't know if you remember—"

"Connor Morgan. Number twenty-three. Shutdown defenseman with one of the best records in Lakers history."

"Good to see you again, kid." He chuckled.

"Mason brother, please tell your friends I am almost a teenager."

"You heard the man," I said around a smile, pride swelling inside me.

Scottie kept his eyes ahead, refusing to look down at his feet. "Think I'm ready for a game?" he deadpanned, and the guys all laughed.

"Little bro's got jokes," Leon said. "Hey, Scottie, want to try shooting the puck? Austin likes to think he's the man, but I bet you can get a goal or two past him."

My brother looked to me, and I said, "It's your call, buddy. We can try a few shots or you and Harper can watch me, and the guys try and put one past Austin."

"I... I want a go," he said, but I felt his hesitation.

"Why don't we do a few warmup shots first. Get a feel for it?"

"Yeah, okay."

"You've got this, Scottie." Harper nudged him gently, a total pro on her skates.

It was like the two of them were old friends. The way he already trusted her. It had irritated me at first. Everything about her had. But now, I only felt gratitude for the way Harper was with him. It was such a rare thing to meet someone who could immediately look past the meltdowns and stimming and his deadpan sense of humor to see the amazing boy beneath all that.

The two of us helped Scottie skate over to one of the nets. Austin moved away, offering his stick to my brother. "It's all yours," he said.

"Wow." Awe wasn't typically an emotion Scottie displayed, but Austin had clearly floored him.

"Ready?" I asked, and he nodded. "Okay, let's start with a wrist shot. You're going to want to put your dominant hand on the top of the stick and your non-dominant hand about halfway down the shaft. Holding your stick like this will help give you proper control and power."

I demonstrated for him, encouraging him to follow my lead. When he was holding his stick correctly, I moved on to the next part.

"Next, we need to be in the correct stance. You want to bend your knees with your body positioned at a forty-five-degree angle in relation to the net.

"Then, for the wrist shot, you want to—"

"I think I've got it," Scottie said, eyeing the net. Sweeping the puck forward, he transferred his weight, rotated his body, and took the shot.

"Holy shit," Noah whooped. "Little bro is coming after your spot on the team."

A faint grin traced my brother's face.

"Where did you learn to do that?" I asked, and he shrugged. "Just because I'm afraid of the ice doesn't mean I don't pay attention."

Shit, he was right.

Of course, he was right.

"We're going to start training," I said. "Whenever I get home, you and I are going down to the rink."

"For real? You'll train with me?"

"Hell yeah, I will."

Scottie threw his arms around my stomach and almost sent us both flying, but I managed to right myself, clutching him tightly to my chest. My eyes found Harper, and she smiled.

"Thank you," I mouthed.

She gave me a small, understanding nod.

"This is the best day ever," Scottie announced. "Now all we need is for Harper to agree to go out with you, and both our dreams will come true."

Harper smothered a laugh as my gaze bounced between her and my loose-lipped brother.

"What's that you say, Scottie?" Noah smirked. "Big bro wants to take Harper out on a date?"

"Holden," I hissed, aware of Harper watching and listening less than five feet away.

"I think Mason wants to kiss her. He's always looking at her mouth."

Fuck.

"Sounds like it," Noah agreed, amusement dancing in his eyes.

He was loving every second of this, and I was dying on the inside. But Scottie was so damn happy and relaxed. I didn't want to ruin things.

Even if Harper was right there and able to hear everything.

"You sly, sly dog. No wonder she blew me off the other night." Ward whispered as he circled Scottie and me. "Want to go a little one-on-one?" He crouched down to meet my brother's eye level but didn't get too all up in his space.

Their patience and effort with him were more than I could have ever have asked for.

"Can I, Mason?"

"Sure, just take it easy, okay."

Scottie glided across the ice with Ward to where Aiden and Leon were.

"He can skate," I said as Harper joined me, slightly awed.

"Looks like he can do a whole lot more than just skate," she said.

"You knew." I peered down at her. "You knew this was a good idea, but I didn't want to hear it."

"Mason, it doesn't mat—"

"Yeah, it does. I was an asshole."

"You just wanted to protect him."

Yeah, and maybe myself.

I didn't like change. I liked control and order. It was the only way I'd managed to be the guy my mom and brother needed while allowing myself to come here to LU.

But Harper was a flash of color in my black-and-white world. A ray of sunshine peeking through the thunderclouds that circled overhead, and I was starting to crave her light, her warmth, the inherent goodness inside her.

She had me tied up in knots, and nothing made sense anymore.

But seeing Scottie come to life on the ice, seeing his rare smile, and the way Harper watched him with bursting pride, made sense.

And scared the absolute fuck out of me.

"Mason?" My name was a breathy sigh on her lips, and fuck, if it didn't do things to me.

"Yeah, blondie?"

"Thanks for inviting me today. I really—"

"Coach D," someone yelled. "Didn't expect to see you here."

I swung around just in time to see Harper's dad approaching Mom.

Fuck.

Harper went still beside me. "I thought you said he wasn't coming?" Her voice shook with anger and something that sounded a lot like betrayal.

"I swear to God, I had no idea he would be here."

"Mase, Mason brother." Ward helped Scottie skate over to us. "It's James 'The Real Deal' Dixon. He's here. He was one of the best of his time."

"I know. Pretty amazing, right?" I winced at how conceited it sounded.

"Mason, son, get over here. I heard we had a special visitor today and wanted to come down and meet him."

Shit. He still hadn't spotted Harper.

"I'm sorry," I whispered to her as she stood rigid beside me.

"It's fine. You should go."

"But—"

"This is Scottie's morning. Go." She tipped her head toward the other end of the arena, where Mom and her father were deep in conversation.

I didn't want to leave her. I wanted to demand the

truth about whatever had happened between them. But Scottie was tugging my jersey.

"Mason, go," she said with exasperation, her expression a mask of cool indifference.

I didn't like it, not being able to tell what she was thinking. She was usually so open. Her heart on her sleeve for all to see.

But right now, she felt closed off.

Distant.

But I had a twelve-year-old kid to think about.

The team and my future to think about.

So I gave her a small nod, took my brother's hand, and skated away from her.

And toward her father.

CHAPTER 24

HARPER

I WAS AN IDIOT.

How many times was I going to give Mason the power to hurt me?

It wasn't his fault, not this time, not really. But my stupid, foolish heart didn't get the memo as I skated off the rink and slipped away before my father could spot me.

That was one conversation I wanted to avoid for eternity.

He was Mason's coach—the man who held his future in the palm of his hand. Of course, Mason would choose him. He had his mom and Scottie to think about. His family.

I couldn't compete with that.

After quickly changing out of the skates I'd

borrowed from the team's extra stock, I headed out. But instead of going back to the dorm, I headed to Roast 'n' Go for a much-needed chai tea and tasty Harper-friendly pick-me-up.

When I entered the coffee shop, I was surprised to see a familiar face. Janelle, sitting alone, waved at me as I joined the line.

"Want anything?" I mouthed, and she shook her head.

Once I was loaded up on tasty goodness, I made a beeline for her table.

"Hey," she said as I approached.

"Can I?"

"Sure." She collected up some of her things to give me room. "Busy weekend?"

"I watched the Lakers games."

"Did they win?"

"Both games."

"I'm not a huge fan. I'm too busy to keep up with their games."

"Pre-med, right?"

"Yeah, third year. And it is kicking my ass. You're a first-year English major?"

I nodded. "I am."

"Enjoy it while you can. Some days, I feel like I'm drowning."

"Did you talk to your *friend*?" My lips curved.

"Not yet. We keep missing each other. But I think I'm going to take your advice and lay my cards out.

Life's too short, and I feel like I'm missing out on so many of the little things, you know?"

Did I ever.

"Well, if it doesn't work out, rumor has it there's a certain tall, dark, and handsome bartender who would love to get to know you a little better."

Her eyes almost bugged as she filled in the blanks. "Kal?"

"Don't tell him I told you," I chuckled. "He'll never forgive me. But I figured it couldn't hurt. It's always good to have options."

"I did pick up on some vibes from him. But I noticed he's quite flirty with most of the staff."

"Oh, you're not wrong there. Kal is a real charmer." I sipped on my tea, hardly surprised that I already felt better, being away from the arena.

Away from him.

"So why haven't the two of you ever hooked up?" Janelle asked, and I shrugged.

"He's like the big brother I never had. It would be weird. Besides, I tend to have a type."

"Ooh, do tell."

"Athletic. Emotionally unavailable. You know the type," I said.

"Too well."

We shared a smile, the type of smile that bonded girls over their endless experience with guys who would never commit.

"You know, in freshman year, I told myself I

wouldn't do it. That I wouldn't spend my college experience chasing commitment. But it's—"

"Hard?" I whispered.

"Yeah. I don't mind the casual thing. But after a while, it gets kind of lonely."

"We should do this more often," I said. "It sounds like we have a lot in common."

"I have a double-shift at the medical center later. And I'm picking up Jill's shifts at Millers all week. But soon?"

"Sure. Just let me know when you're free next."

I broke off a chunk of brownie and popped it into my mouth, enjoying the sweet, chocolatey explosion on my tongue. It wasn't as good as my favorite mail-order bakery, but it was still pretty darn good.

Until I remembered Mason had bought me these exact brownies, and the sweetness turned bitter.

"Is everything okay?" Janelle asked, and I smiled weakly over the lump in my throat.

"Yeah, fine."

Maybe if I kept telling myself the same lie over and over, eventually, it would come true.

I hung out for the rest of the day in my dorm room, avoiding life. But unable to avoid the elephant in the room.

I, Harper Rose Dixon, had let myself fall for Mason Steele.

Despite every warning and alarm bell and gut intuition, I had fallen head over heels in *something* with him.

It wasn't love. I knew that. But it was more complicated than lust. Because when you peeled back the layers of the Lakers brooding left-winger, when you got a glimpse of the guy underneath that cool icy exterior, you were left with a good man. A man who only wanted to do right by his family.

By his brother.

Watching them together, the way Mason protected and encouraged and guided Scottie told me enough about the guy beneath the hockey jersey.

And it was enough to steal a part of my heart.

I let out a weary sigh, trying desperately to ignore the ache in my chest. He hadn't reached out after I fled the arena, but then, I hadn't really expected him to. He had to drive his mom and Scottie back to Pittsburgh. For all I knew, my father had taken them out. Showing off his protégé and making a fuss of his family.

The thought made my stomach churn.

My cell vibrated, and I hoped to see his name, disappointment crashing over me when it wasn't.

> Aurora: Hey, Noah told me what happened. Are you okay?

Harper: What exactly did he tell you?

Aurora: That your dad showed up and you took off. I'm surprised you were there in the first place...

Harper: Really?

Aurora: No, but I was waiting for you to tell me.

Harper: I think I made a stupid mistake, Rory.

My cell started ringing, and I hit answer. "Hey," I said.

"You like him, don't you?"

"I... yeah," I confessed. "I tried so hard not to fall for him, Rory. But I did. And now everything is a mess."

"Oh, Harper. Why didn't you tell me?"

"Because I knew you'd tell me it was a bad idea. I knew you'd tell me that Mason Steele isn't the kind of guy who gets close to anyone."

"Babe, come on. I'm the girl who fell in love with Noah Holden. Noah freaking Holden. If you had told me two months ago that I'd be here, I would have laughed at you.

"There is always an exception to the rule, Harper. Maybe you're Mason's."

"I'm not," I said quietly, the words breaking some secret part of me.

"But Noah said there was some serious tension between the two of you."

"There is, but it doesn't mean he's going to act on it."

"So you two haven't..."

"You know we have." I let out a weary sigh.

"The Halloween party?"

"Yep."

"Harper! I'm so mad you didn't tell me. But I get it." She hesitated. "It isn't easy admitting you're falling for a Laker."

"I kept telling myself I wouldn't do it. That I wouldn't let myself get carried away..."

"You know, a wise girl once told me, 'We are all fools in love.'"

I had said that because, like me, Aurora was a huge fan of Austen.

"Well Charlotte Lucas had it right. I am a huge fool."

"No, you're not," Aurora chuckled softly. "Opening your heart to someone isn't a bad thing, Harper. It's that special part of us that makes us human."

"He's the first guy I... no, it doesn't matter."

"Go on, you can tell me."

"He's the first guy I ever spent the night with."

Twice.

I'd had hookups, sure, and I'd had first dates that

led to one-night stands. But I'd never stayed the night or fallen asleep with a guy. Sometimes it was my decision, sometimes, it was theirs, but it always felt like a big deal. Like once the morning rolled around, and the sun came up, they would see between the cracks of my easy, breezy, I-can-do-casual-sex façade.

"You were a virgin? But I thought—"

"No, I don't mean sex, Rory," I tsked. "I mean, like sleeping over. Waking up together."

And then it hit me. We hadn't gotten to that part. Not really. Because I'd left the first time it happened, and he was gone the second time.

"Ah, I see."

"I'm an idiot."

"You're not. You're just—"

A knock at my door startled me.

"Someone's here," I said, clambering off my bed, half-expecting to see Natalie or one of the girls from my floor.

I didn't expect to find Mason standing at my door for the second time in less than twenty-four hours.

"Harper?" Rory said, reminding me she was at the other end of the line.

"I need to go. I'll call you later."

"Is everything okay?"

"I'm not sure."

I hung up before opening the door.

"Hey," Mason said, looking a little sheepish. "Can I come in?"

"You want to—"

He took a step forward, right to the threshold of my door. "Invite me in, blondie."

"I... Would you like to come in?"

His mouth twitched as I stepped aside and let him enter. "What are you doing here?" I closed the door and leaned back against it, wary and cautious.

"I didn't like how we ended things this morning."

"Oh."

"Look, I know it's none of my business, but if we're going..." He trailed off, glancing down at the light gray carpet as he ran a hand over his head and down the back of his neck.

"If we're going to what?" I asked, blood roaring between my ears, my heart beating wildly in my chest.

Mason looked up, staring at me with those cool, assessing eyes of his, my skin vibrating with awareness. He strode toward me, not stopping until we were almost chest-to-chest. His hand went to the door above my head, and I cracked my neck to look at him.

"Mase—"

He curved his hand around my neck as his mouth crashed down on mine, stealing the breath from my lungs and erasing the questions on the tip of my tongue.

He tasted like mint and licorice, the clean, slightly bitter taste my new favorite flavor.

"Fuck," he breathed, kissing me harder, shaping my mouth with his. His tongue teased mine, licking into my mouth before he trailed hot wet kisses down my jaw.

"Mason..." I twisted my fingers into his hoodie, pulling him closer.

Needing him so much closer.

He pressed me into the door, pinning me there with his hips. "Never gonna get enough of this," he murmured, his hand splaying around my throat as he controlled the kiss.

But then he broke away, and I whimpered, trying to lean back in. A wicked smirk tugged at his mouth as he gazed down at me. "So fucking responsive."

"Stop teasing me," I pouted, hardly able to believe this was happening.

"We should probably talk." He blew out a steady breath, and I wondered if he was as breathless as me.

Breathless and completely overwhelmed.

"Or we could talk after..."

"Want to go somewhere with me?"

"You want to go somewhere, *now*?" My brows furrowed because we'd gone from zero to sixty and back down to zero again.

"Yeah." Mason's expression softened, and he reached out, tucking my hair behind my ear. "What do you say, blondie? Go out with me?"

The last thing I wanted was to leave this room and face reality. Out there, too many things were against us. In here, it was safe. It was easy to pretend.

"It'll just be the two of us," he said as if he could hear my thoughts.

"Where do you want to go?"

"Will you trust me if I say it's a surprise?"

God, there were so many things I wanted to say. But Mason was here, and he wanted to take me somewhere to talk after giving me one of the best kisses of my life.

How could I do the sensible thing and say no?

The answer was I couldn't.

My heart was his the second I opened the door.

I just hoped this time he didn't leave it in pieces.

"You're quiet," Mason said as we drove to wherever it was he was taking me.

I had an idea as we'd headed out of Lakeshore and taken the highway toward Rushton. But I didn't want to voice my suspicions in case I was wrong.

"Just thinking," I said, smiling over at him.

"Anything you want to share?"

"Did Scottie enjoy his time at the arena this morning?" I chose a safe topic.

"He did. Talked about it the entire ride home."

"Something tells me you'll have a hard time keeping him off the ice now."

"I still can't believe you did that for him."

"It was nothing." I shrugged.

"No, Harper, it wasn't." Something passed over Mason's expression as he watched me out of the corner of his eye. "Any guesses where we're going yet?"

The ice rink came into view in the distance, and I sat a little straighter. "I thought you said we'd be alone."

"We will, don't worry. I called in a favor."

"You... I don't know what to say to that."

"I'm sure you'll find a way to thank me." Mason smirked, sending a bolt of lust through me.

God, when he was like this—all flirty and cute, it was hard to remember why I needed to keep a level head around him.

He pulled into the small parking lot and cut the engine. The ride had been tense. Not awkward, but that anticipatory kind of silence where you didn't know what to say or do. Because you knew one word or look or touch could change everything.

"Why did you bring me here, Mason?" I asked, trying to get a read on his thoughts.

"Come on," he said, climbing out of his car. He came around and opened the passenger door, and I got out. But he didn't let me go. Instead, he pinned me to the side of his car and toyed with my hair.

"What?" I asked.

"Scottie is going to be so fucking happy when I tell him you said yes."

"Said yes?"

"You're telling me you didn't hear him this

morning, at the arena?" His brow lifted with mild amusement.

"I may have heard something, but I didn't think he was serious."

"You do know Scottie, right? Cute kid. Tells it like it is. Interprets everything literally. Has a really twisted sense of humor, apparently."

"So when he said you're always looking at my mouth..."

"He pays attention."

I sucked in a sharp breath, aware of every part of Mason pressed up against every part of me. He was all hard muscle and raw power, and he felt so good.

It was the best kind of foreplay. The anticipation and build up. Not that I'd ever gotten this far with a guy before. But with Mason, it was different. There had been little moments all leading to this point.

"Come on." He hooked his fingers into my jean belt loops and kissed my forehead. "We should head inside."

I wanted to argue, to demand a proper kiss, but I was too stunned to formulate words. Let alone try and take control.

Mason took my hand and tugged me toward the familiar building. "We've got the ice to ourselves."

"Okay..."

"I want you to show me some more of your moves."

"I can do that."

He glanced down at me intently. "I want you to show me everything."

"I... I don't follow."

"I think you do," he said, yanking the door open and motioning for me to go on ahead. My heart was a band of wild horses galloping in my chest as we headed for the counter.

"Mason," the heavy-set man said. "Good to see you.

"We all set?"

"Place is all yours. Feel free to grab your skates. The rest is all taken care of."

The rest?

A trickle of unease went down my spine. "What did he mean, the rest?"

"You'll see. Come on."

In less than five minutes, we had our skates on and were heading for the rink. The blast of cold air as we went through the doors was a welcome reprieve from the heat simmering inside me.

It was strange being here when the place was empty. I was used to an audience. Fresh-faced kids and their parents oohing and ahhing as I whipped around the rink.

Mason let me go on ahead, and I did a couple of circles before I realized he'd stopped at the boards.

"Aren't you skating?" I frowned.

"I am. But I want to watch you first. Show me what you've got, blondie."

"Seriously, you want to watch me skate?"

He nodded, his eyes dark and stormy.

"Fine." With a little shrug, I pumped my legs and took off at lightning speed, laughter bubbling in my chest as I glided around the rink, arms out by my sides. Steadying my weight as I changed height. Up and down. Round and round.

Skating brought me so much joy. Eddied every bad thought out of my head. But having Mason's hungry gaze on me while I skated was a whole new experience.

Butterflies soared into my stomach as I passed him, his dark eyes tracking my every move. Eventually, I slowed down, catching my breath. My cheeks were cold, and my lungs burned, but I'd never felt more alive.

"So, what did you think?"

Mason reached for me, pulling the hem of my hoodie until we were chest to chest. His arm went around my waist, holding me there.

"You're good, blondie. Really fucking good."

"I love skating."

"It shows." He swallowed. "But can you do it with a stick in your hand?"

"W-what?"

"You play."

"No, I don't." I tried to pull away from him, but he held firm.

"I looked you up, Harper. I know."

"Y-you... oh my God." I squeezed my eyes tight, trying my hardest not to let the tears fall.

He'd Googled me.

Mason Steele had Googled me and discovered my biggest secret.

"Hey, hey." He slid his hand along my jaw and gently coaxed my face back to his. "I had this feeling there was more to it. You're a great skater, Harper, and you love hockey. It seemed the next logical step."

"I can't believe you Googled me." I gazed up at him with disbelief.

"Cleveland Suburban Hockey League rising star. Impressive."

"You'd think," I murmured. Because what should have been my crowning moment was tainted by yet another crushing disappointment.

It was also the day I realized nothing I did or achieved would ever be enough for my father.

CHAPTER 25

MASON

SHE WAS PERFECT.

That's all I could think of as I watched her skate laps around the rink with the confidence of someone who loved the ice.

Who *knew* the ice.

Of course, I already knew her secret. Had discovered it after I'd taken Mom and Scottie home and sat in my car, desperate to text her and explain.

I hadn't invited Coach Dixon. Hadn't even mentioned it to him. So when he'd showed up, singing my praises to Mom, it had thrown a wrench in my plans.

Harper had hightailed it out of there before I could even weigh my options. And it had pissed me off. Not her reaction. But her father's. The way he was so downright dismissive of her. I didn't like it.

But I couldn't bulldoze either of them for answers. So I'd found myself digging for dirt on the internet.

There's something I never thought I'd say.

The air crackled around us, a live wire ready to catch fire. We were doing this. Me. Her.

Truth was, we'd been doing it for a little while now. I'd just been too fucking stubborn to see it for what it was.

It didn't matter that there had been no kissing or touching or any of that stuff. Being around Harper was an experience all by itself. She made my heart race, and my palms sweat. She made me laugh and smile and feel good.

She gave me hope.

Fuck, she made me believe that there were good people in the world. People who would accept and love Scottie for who he was.

She did that.

"Talk to me," I urged her. Because I needed her to explain it to me. I needed to know her truth.

"I don't even know where I would start. It's a conflict of interest, remember?" She gave me a sad, defeated smile.

But fuck that.

This moment had nothing to do with her old man. It was about her. About us.

About the way I felt every time she walked into a room, and those baby blues found me.

I grabbed the back of her neck and pulled her closer, getting right up in her space. "It's just you and me here, Harper. You don't have to tell me anything you're not ready to share. But I didn't bring you here on a whim, okay? I brought you here because I... I like you.

"I, Mason Steele, like *you*, Harper Dixon. And I want to know you, babe. The good, the bad, and the ugly."

"Even if it ruins your opinion of one of your childhood idols?"

"Even then."

"Can we sit?" she asked, and I nodded.

We hopped off the rink and moved over to one of the benches.

"My dad always wanted a son." She peeked up at me, uncertainty shining in her baby blues. "But he got me instead. I tried to be the child he wanted. I learned to skate. Joined the local pee wee hockey team. Worked harder than any other kid there just to get him to notice me, to be proud. But nothing I did made a difference."

Her pain was palpable, bleeding into the air around us. I hated it, fucking hated that she'd been made to feel that way. I'd witnessed the same thing with my own dad when it became apparent Scottie wasn't like other kids his age: the withdrawal, the rejection, the crushing disappointment.

No kid should ever have to experience that at the hands of their own parents. Their blood. It made me fucking livid.

"I think it only made him angrier that I was good. Better than some of the boys on the team. The coach wanted me to attend some training camps to give me more experience, but the signup fee was expensive. He wouldn't pay. My father wouldn't pay, and that's when I knew." Silent tears rolled down her cheeks. "That's when I knew nothing I ever did would be good enough. Add in the fact I had celiac disease, and I was just the burden he never asked for."

"The fuck?" I gawked at her because how could she be talking about the same man who had rolled up to the team with a smile on his face and hunger in his eyes?

Coach Dixon loved hockey. He loved coaching the team. Working with the players. It was his life. You could see that in every interaction he had. So what Harper was saying and what I'd witnessed didn't add up.

It didn't make sense, and yet, I'd seen the shadow in his eyes, sensed that there was more to the story.

I'd figured he was just a man chasing a dream that had slipped through his fingers. But it was more than that.

So much more.

And it all centered around this girl.

"James Dixon is a local hero." Her expression dropped. "But he's always been the villain of my story."

"Fuck him," I said, hooking my arm around her neck and pulling her into my side.

My need to protect Harper was almost as strong as my innate need to protect Scottie.

"Mason, he's your coach," she chuckled, but it was strained. "Pretty sure you can't say that about your coach."

I nudged her back a little so I could look at her. "That's not how things work in my world, Harper. If you want respect, you earn it."

And her old man had lost every shred of respect I had for him the second she confessed.

You didn't turn your back on your kid. No matter what.

"I'm sorry I ruined things."

"What?" My brows pinched, disbelief coursing through me that she felt the need to apologize for things beyond her control. "You didn't ruin anything," I said. "I knew something was off, but I was too chickenshit to do anything about it sooner."

"And what are you doing about it now?" A flicker of a smile ghosted her lips.

Fuck, this girl.

This tenacious, kind, fucking amazing girl.

"Didn't I make it pretty obvious? I don't share the

rink with just anyone, you know." I leaned closer, touching my head to hers.

"Mase." Her breath hitched.

"Hey, I got you, babe. I got you."

"For real?"

"Yeah, for real, blondie." I brushed my thumb along her tear-stained cheek, anger bubbling inside me.

But she was right. It was a conflict of interest. Wanting her while working under Coach Dixon was always going to be a problem. But now that I knew the truth, it was more nuanced than that. Mostly because I wanted to barge into his office and ask him what the fuck his problem was.

"I thought..."

"What?" I pushed. "Tell me what you're thinking."

"I thought you'd chosen him over me. I know it's silly, but I thought—"

I kissed her. Softer this time, sliding my mouth over her lips and swallowing her whimpers. Harper looped her arms around my neck, anchoring us together. It was hard to believe that I'd almost talked myself out of this, her.

I'd been so set on keeping her at arm's length, denying myself the connection between us, that I didn't see what was right in front of me.

Connor and Noah were right.

Fuck, they were right.

"You, Harper. I choose you."

She blinked up at me, her long black lashes brushing my cheeks. "Y-you do?"

"Yeah, blondie, I do. I wouldn't be here if I didn't."

"But my dad... I don't want to ruin anything for you."

"You won't. Come here." I wrapped her into my arms again, loving the way she felt pressed up against me.

"Can I ask you something?" I inquired.

"Anything."

"When he turned up at TPB, you said something to him. You said, 'You shouldn't be here.' What did you mean?"

I had my suspicions, but I needed to hear her say it.

Indecision flickered in her eyes, and I really fucking hoped it was because she didn't know if she could trust me with the truth, and not because she wanted to protect her old man.

"My father is an alcoholic." She got up, pacing in front of the boards. "Has been most of my life. He cycles through sobriety and relapses more than a yo-yo."

"Shit, Harper, I'm sorry."

"So that's not what you suspected?" She arched a brow.

"I'd be lying if I said the thought hadn't crossed my mind. But it doesn't change the fact it sucks."

"Yeah." She let out a weary sigh. "It hasn't been easy on me or Mom, Mom mostly. But she says she took vows to love him through thick and thin… so here we are."

She tried to glance away, but I refused to let her. Going to her, I gently gripped her chin between my fingers. "You deserve better."

"Yeah, but I'll never know better." She gave me a sad smile that hit me dead in the chest. "I'm such a cliché."

"What do you mean?"

"What did you think of me when you first met me, Mason?"

Her question threw me for a loop, and I hesitated over my reply.

"It's okay," she added. "You can tell me."

"I thought you were just another bunny, using your father's name to get close to the team. But that's not who you are."

"No, it isn't. But I am too much. I get that. When you've had to fight your entire life for even the smallest scraps of attention from a parent, I think you either default to shutting everyone out or trying to pull everyone in.

"I know I do the latter. I crave attention and validation. Even though, deep down, I know I need to love myself before I can expect anyone else to love me. Classic daddy issues."

"That's not—"

"Yeah, it is." Harper's expression guttered. "I've tried so much to be less, but I always end up right back at square one. This is who I am, Mason. I'm not perfect by any stretch of the imagination, but I wear my heart on my sleeve, I'm honest, and I'm a good person. I—"

"Stop," I said, hating to hear her talk about herself like that. I got it—her father's rejection had deeply affected her. Molded and shaped her.

A lot of things made sense now, but I still couldn't move past the part where her old man had practically disowned her.

"I'm a mess." Strangled laughter spilled from her lips. "Sorry, I didn't mean to offload like that."

"Shh." I brushed my thumb against her bottom lip, chasing it with my mouth. "I wanted to know. I want to know everything about you."

"You don't have time for a relationship." She reminded me.

"You make time for the things that are important to you." I gazed at her, really looked at her, and I couldn't deny the truth any longer.

I wanted her.

I wanted Harper, and not only in my bed. I wanted her by my side and in my life.

"Why did you bring me to the ice rink, Mason?"

"Because I knew if I didn't get you out of your dorm room, I'd end up buried deep inside you again, and I wanted us to talk first. I wanted to be really clear that this means something to me." I brushed the hair from her eyes, my thumb lingering on the pillow of her mouth. "You mean something to me, Harper."

"So why aren't you kissing me?"

A smile curled on my lips as I closed the distance between us, hovering my mouth over hers. I'd kissed her already, but this felt different. It was a promise to everything I'd just confessed. But it felt nothing but right as our mouths crashed, our tongues slicking together.

"Fuck," I hissed, my body burning with need. I grabbed her ass, pushing us into the boards, needing to be closer.

Needing to be—

"Slow down, hotshot," she chuckled, running her fingers through my hair and down the back of my neck. "We have time."

"Time, yeah..." My lips pursed as I tried to get a hold of myself.

"Come skate with me." Harper took my hand, tugging gently, but I held firm, still not over the kiss.

Her.

Everything that had transpired between us.

"Mason." It came out soft and pleading, her megawatt smile fisting my heart.

I'd spent so fucking long keeping people at arm's length. But I wanted to pull her in. Gravitate around her warmth.

"Fine," she huffed when I still made no effort to move. "But if you let me go, you've got to catch me."

I pulled away, smirking as her hand fell to her side.

"Oh, it's like that, huh?"

"Better run, blondie," I said. "Because once I catch you, I'm never letting go."

I hadn't had this much fun in a long time. After I chased Harper around the rink and finally pulled her into my arms, we played a little one-on-one. She was good, not good enough to get past me, but there had been something sexy as fuck watching her wield a hockey stick.

"What now?" she asked as we changed out of our skates.

"That depends on you, I guess." I looked up and found myself drowning in her baby blues.

"Me?"

"Yeah, I can give you a ride back to the dorm, say good night, and see you tomorrow. Or... I can stay over."

"You want to stay over?"

"Only if you want me to." It would fucking kill me to take her home and not get invited up, but I'd accept my fate because I was the one who needed to grovel here.

"I want you to stay over." She smiled, but then her expression dropped. "But what about if somebody sees us?"

"Then they see." I shrugged. "You're not my dirty

little secret, Harper. I want this. I want you." I curled my fist into her hoodie and yanked her across the bench to me.

"Mase!"

"Come here." Lifting her, I slid her onto my lap so she was straddling my thighs. "Hi." I grinned.

"Hi." Harper looped her arms around the back of my neck. "You know, a girl could get used to this."

"What's that?"

"Being at the center of your attention."

"Something tells me when Scottie finds out about this, he'll stake some weird claim on you too."

"That's... I'm not really sure what to say to that."

Laughter rumbled in my chest. "You know, he told me he was going to help me win you over."

"You didn't need his help. You did it all by yourself." Harper kissed me, a gentle brush of her lips across mine. But it wasn't enough. I needed more. So much more.

Cupping the back of her neck, I deepened the kiss, taking what I wanted—what I needed.

She opened for me, whimpering as my tongue plunged into her mouth, licking with fervor.

"I have thought about nothing but how you felt underneath me. So tight and wet."

"God, Mason," she breathed, a shudder going through her.

"You took me so fucking perfectly." I touched my head to hers, inhaling a sharp breath.

I wanted her again so fucking much. But not here, not like this.

"Come on, let's get out of here," I said.

"Tease," she chuckled, clambering off my lap.

Harper turned away from me, but I stood abruptly, hooking her around the waist, dropping my mouth to her ear. "Tease, you say?"

"Mm-hmm."

I ran my hand down her body, loving how she shivered under my touch. My fingers slipped under her indigo Lakers hoodie, toying with the waistband of her jeans.

"Mase, we shouldn't..."

"Shouldn't what?" I rasped, so fucking hard for her.

"Someone might— ah," Harper moaned as I shoved my hand inside and cupped her pussy.

"You're so wet for me, babe."

"I... Mason!" She tried to press her thighs together, but I sucked on the soft skin beneath her ear.

"Let me make you feel good."

"H-here?" She choked out, and I nodded, dipping two fingers inside her damp panties. She smothered another moan as I pressed them inside her, curling deep.

"Fuck, I didn't think this through." I held Harper's body tight to mine as I worked her, rolling my thumb over her clit in small, tight circles.

I'd never fooled around in public like this. But I

had the wildest fantasy of laying her out on one of the benches and worshiping every inch of her body.

Harper made me weak. And until recently, I'd always assumed that in itself was a weakness. But I realized now it didn't have to be.

Harper understood what Scottie and my mom meant to me. She understood that I couldn't just walk away from them.

She got it in ways no one else did. And yeah, maybe that was because I didn't let people in. But Harper had found a way past my defenses, and I didn't hate it.

In fact, it made me feel ten feet tall that she wanted me and everything that came with wanting me.

"Mason, don't stop." Harper wrapped an arm around the back of my neck, her body trembling as I kept plunging my fingers in and out, curling them deeper as my thumb teased her clit.

"Yes, dear God, yes," she cried, trying to bury her face in my arm, but I grabbed her chin and smashed my mouth down on hers, swallowing her moans.

Our kiss was clumsy, all teeth and tongue and sweet desperation as I tried to get her off before someone did discover us.

"I really need you to come, blondie," I whispered against her mouth.

"Touch my boobs," she urged.

"Y-yeah." I smirked because I had zero problems taking orders from her. Slipping my hand under her hoodie, I found her braless, her small, perky tits the perfect handful. "Like this?" I asked, massaging gently.

"Harder."

I squeezed harder, brushing my thumb over her nipple, and her entire body went off like a rocket.

"Yes, yes, God, yes," she breathed, melting against me as the force of her orgasm hit.

Fuck, she was sexy like this.

Confident and all too willing to tell me what she needed to get off.

"Good?" I asked, and she nodded, all limp and heavy in my arms.

"So good. But I can't believe we just did that." Craning her neck, she peeked up at me, and I grinned.

Because this girl.

This fucking girl...

"Believe it," I said, kissing her nose. "Because that was just the beginning."

CHAPTER 26

HARPER

"Okay, so how are we doing this?" I asked as Mason pulled into a parking spot outside my dorm building.

"Doing what?" He frowned.

"You know, like should I go in first, then ten minutes later, you can come in and pretend to be a delivery guy or something. Do you have a ball cap you can wear—"

"You want me to pretend to be...?"

"A delivery guy." I nodded, realizing how ridiculous I sounded.

But the truth was, I was nervous.

Mason had laid it all out for me. He wanted this.

Me.

And it was all I'd wanted... but never actually expected because I didn't get the guy.

I didn't.

"Yeah, not going to happen." Mason shouldered the door and climbed out of his car, coming around to my side. He yanked open the door and looked down at me. "Let's go."

"But what if someone's up? What if they—"

Mason reached in and lifted me out of the seat onto my feet. "We're not doing that."

"Doing what?"

"Playing games. Hiding this. Pretending..." He hooked his arm around my back and pulled me close. My hand went to his chest as I gazed up at him, still a little dumbstruck that this was happening.

"In case I didn't make it clear enough back at the rink when my fingers were deep inside you. You're mine, Harper. I don't give a fuck who knows it."

"I..."

All I could do was nod.

Mason chuckled, dropping a kiss on my head before pushing the door shut behind me and locking the car. Hand in hand, we walked toward my building. It was late, and the place seeped in darkness, but that didn't mean there weren't prying eyes everywhere.

When we reached the door, I glanced up at Mason, and he cocked a brow. "So just to confirm. We're really doing this?" I asked.

"Open the door, Harper."

"Bossy." I rolled my eyes playfully despite the butterflies fluttering wildly in my stomach.

He made me nervous because this was all so new. And if Natalie got wind of things...

I didn't even want to think about that.

But he was right. I had nothing to hide.

Inhaling a steady breath, I opened the door, and we slipped inside. Mason kept his fingers tucked in the belt loop of my jeans. It was so intimate and cute. I couldn't help but swoon.

Who knew Mason Steele could be such a sweetheart.

"I'm on the—"

"Second floor," he said. "I remember."

"I never properly thanked you for the hangover supplies, did I?"

"It's okay. You can thank me later." I heard the smirk in his voice but didn't glance back at him because I was pretty sure my cheeks were on fire.

My heart careened against my chest as we climbed the stairs, the tension unbearably thick.

The first time I was with Mason, it was finite. One night to quell the attraction between us. This time was different.

This time, I wouldn't have to worry about waking up beside him or sneaking out before he woke up because he was choosing to be here. With me.

My heart did another violent little flip in my chest, and I stalled. Mason stepped up to me, wrapping his arm around my waist and dipping his head to my ear. "Why'd you stop?"

"No reason."

"I get it," he said. "You're nervous."

"I am n—"

"It's okay, babe. I am too."

"You." I twisted around to look at him. "Mason Steele, nervous?"

His eyes simmered with lust and other things I couldn't even process as he gazed down at me. "Got a lot to lose this time."

It was a quiet, definitive statement. One that settled deep inside my chest.

He pressed a kiss to my head and nudged me forward. "If we don't want an audience, we should probably go to your room."

"Y-yeah," I stuttered because the way he looked at me made me melt into a puddle.

Relief sank into me when we reached my door without being spotted. There was tomorrow morning to deal with, but I didn't want to think about that. Not yet. Not with his hand underneath my hoodie, stroking my skin.

I couldn't think straight, high on his touch. The fact was he was here, and he'd chosen me.

I knew it wouldn't be that straightforward. He was my father's protégé, his star player. James Dixon wouldn't just give that up. But Mason said it didn't matter. He said he'd handle it. And I trusted him.

We went into my room, and Mason closed the door. "Come here," he said.

I went willingly, falling into his arms. He leaned down, brushing his mouth over mine. My fingers slipped under his hoodie, needing him closer, needing to feel his warm, smooth skin. All that shredded muscle.

"Fuck, Harper," he hissed as I dragged my fingernails down his abs.

"You feel so good," I said.

"I'll feel even better when you're naked and underneath me."

"What are you waiting for, hotshot?"

"Mase, call me Mase," he said, stripping me out of my clothes. Kissing me every time he got close. The slope of my neck, my shoulder, the curve of my breasts.

Mason licked and kissed and sucked his way down my body until he was on his knees before me, staring up at me with raw hunger in his eyes. "These need to come off." He tapped my foot, and I lifted my leg, letting him slip off my boots. Right first, then left. Then his hand slid up my legs, resting on the waistband of my jeans.

"You look good down there." I fought a smile, my stomach curling with heat.

"Not as good as you'll look on your knees for me. I've dreamed about it, you know."

"You have not."

He nodded. "After that night in TPB when you tried to befriend me."

"You mean the night you told me one of your teammates would pity fuck me?"

The blood drained from his face as his fingers dug into my hip a little. "Harper, I—"

"It doesn't matter. What's done is done. I'm a big girl, Mason. I can make my own choices. And I choose you."

"I was an asshole." He leaned in, pressing a kiss to my hip bone. "But I've never done this before, and the thought that you might have some kind of power over me... it freaked me the fuck out."

I ran a hand through his hair. "It's okay."

"It's not. But I'm going to make it up to you."

Slowly, he peeled my jeans down my legs, the rush of cool air making me shiver.

"You're so fucking beautiful, Harper."

He helped me step out of my jeans and worked his way back up my body, trailing his fingertips over my skin until his hand pressed against the side of my neck.

"Get on the bed," he said, voice thick with need.

I did as he instructed, propping myself on one elbow to watch him strip out of his own clothes. My breath caught as his body came into view. All that defined muscle and smooth, tan skin.

"Like what you see?" he chuckled, brushing a hand down his stomach all the way to his black boxer briefs. The impressive bulge there. Mason grasped himself, squeezing hard, hissing at the contact. "Do you have any idea how hard you get me?"

"Show me," I said.

A faint smirk traced his mouth as he pushed his briefs over his hips and kicked them off before fisting his monster dick and pumping slowly.

"That is incredibly hot."

"Not as hot as watching it slide in and out of your pussy."

"Mason!" I gasped, gushing at his words.

I was so turned on, desperate to feel him. To touch him. But the anticipation was a rush like no other. Watching his eyes flare with desire as he ran his gaze over every inch of my skin while jerking himself.

"Spread your legs," he demanded, and my knees fell open. "Touch yourself." My hand slid down my stomach. My fingers toying with my clit.

Mason came to the end of the bed. He dropped to his knees on the mattress and leaned over me. Running his crown through my wetness.

"Ah, that feels... God..." He nudged my clit, stealing my breath. "Mason," I begged, arching into him as he teased me. Dipping lower, positioning himself right there, giving me just the tip.

"Stop teasing me," I whined, needy and restless as I writhed beneath him.

"Did I say you could stop touching yourself?" he gritted out, still jerking himself.

"You're not playing fair."

"I want you desperate for me," he smirked, and I glowered at him.

Laughter rumbled in his chest, but he slid in a little too far, and it turned into a strangled groan as I squeezed around him.

"Fuck, Harper. Condom."

"No... no, no," I said as he went to pull away. "I'm on birth control."

"I'm clean. I get tested regularly."

"Then fuck me already." I pulled him down on top of me, locking my legs around his waist.

"Needy little thing."

"You love it," I sassed.

"Yeah." He hooked his arm under my thigh and spread me open, slowly pushing into me. "I do."

"Yes... God, yes." I lifted my hips slightly to let him go deeper, breathing through the slight sting as my body stretched for him.

"You good?"

"So good."

"Jesus, Harper... your pussy has me in a vise."

"That's not me. It's your monster dick."

"Please don't keep calling it that. I'm trying to fuck my girlfriend, and you're ruining the mood." He rocked forward, making me cry out in pleasure. But his words rang out in my head.

"Hold up." I grabbed his face. "What did you just say?"

"I'm trying to fuck you?"

"No, you used a very specific word."

"You're not seriously going to freak out on me while I'm inside you."

"Mason." I swatted his chest. "You can't just drop the G-word on me and not give me any warning. I didn't know. I didn't—"

"Stop"—he covered my mouth with his hand —"talking and let me make you feel good. We can do the talking thing after."

I nodded; my words drowned out by his palm.

Mason rolled his hips again, creating a delicious friction.

"After, right." My breath caught as he hit the end of me, sending sparks of pleasure zipping through me. "God, you're so good at this. We should do it more often."

"Harper, I swear to God." He stared down at me. "Stop fucking talking."

"Sorry, I... God, yeah, like that."

Mason picked up the pace, driving into me over and over, his hands all over my body, his mouth paying particular attention to my boobs. Which I freaking loved.

"I love your tits," he rasped, tonguing my nipple before closing his mouth around it and sucking.

"Oh, God," I cried. "I'm coming."

"Jesus, you go off like a rocket, don't you?" He smirked before kissing me through the waves of pleasure crashing over me. Mason sat back on his haunches. "Flip over, on hands and knees."

"I'm not—"

"Trust me," he said, softening something inside of me.

Because I did trust him, he'd given me no reason not to.

I got into position, shuddering, when he ran his hand from my nape to the bottom of my spine before curling his fingers around my hip and sinking inside me.

"Fuuuuck," he groaned, leaning over me a little. He gathered my hair in his hand and wrapped it around his fist before slowly pulling out and pushing back in. Letting me catch my breath at the new overwhelming sensations.

"It's so deep."

"You feel incredible. I wish you could see yourself like this, Harper. Fucking made for me."

His words lit me up inside as I began to unravel again.

"I need to go harder. You feel too fucking good." He rode me faster, his pelvis slamming against my ass. My room filled with the sounds of sex. The sounds of us as we both raced toward a release.

"Shit, I'm not going to last," he groaned. "You're too tight." His hand slipped around my hip, dipping to find my clit. "Come for me again, blondie. Come all over my cock."

He pinched my clit, and I shattered. Pretty sure my

soul departed my body for a second as I cried out his name, over and over like a prayer to the gods.

"Fuck, Harper." Mason came hard before rolling off to the side and pulling me down with him.

We lay there quietly. Watching each other.

"Say something," I whispered, suddenly feeling stripped bare before this complicated guy.

"I don't know what to say. That was…"

"Yeah." I swallowed over the lump in my throat. "I should probably go clean up," I said, desperately needing to lighten the heavy tension that had descended over us.

"Wait a second." Mason hooked his arm around me, refusing to let me go. "What's wrong?"

"Nothing."

"Harper…"

"I've never done this before," I admitted, my chest constricting with the truth.

"And you think I have?" He reached for my face, brushing the hair from my eyes and tucking it behind my ear. "We're in this together, okay?"

"Okay."

"Now get over here." He pulled me flush against his body, kissing me deeply. "You are—"

His cell phone started vibrating, and he let out a heavy groan. "It could be Scottie. Sometimes he needs me…"

"Of course. Do your thing. I'll go clean up." I gave him a soft kiss before slipping out of bed, a little awkwardly given the fact we hadn't used any protection.

Another first

But it felt right.

Everything about Mason did.

God, I really hoped I wasn't rushing in headfirst. But he'd said we were in this together.

I quickly cleaned up in the bathroom and went back to him. "Is he okay?"

"What?" He was busy texting on his phone.

"Scottie?" I asked, a little confused.

"False alarm. It's just the group chat." He threw his cell on the nightstand and tapped the bed. "Get back over here."

"Group chat, huh?" I smiled, climbing back into bed with him. "And does the group chat know where you are?"

"Nope." He pulled me down, wrapping me into his arms. "And let's keep it that way for a little bit."

"What?" I eased back to look at him, a sinking sensation going through me.

Was he already having second thoughts?

"I thought you said we weren't going to hide?"

"We're not hiding." He brushed his nose alongside mine, stealing a kiss. "We're just giving ourselves some time. I need to talk to your dad."

"But—"

"I know your relationship is complicated, but he's still my coach. I owe the team that much."

"Oh, okay." That made sense.

But it still felt like he was backtracking a little.

"Hey, come on. It isn't forever. I'll talk to him at practice tomorrow, and we can go from there. I probably need to talk to Scottie, too."

"Mason... are you having second thoughts?"

"What? No. No, Harper." He drew me close, kissing my forehead. "You're my girl."

His girl. I liked the sound of that.

Silence settled over us, and, for as much as I hated it, I couldn't shake the feeling that something had changed.

But it was Mason. He wasn't out to hurt me. He wanted me.

He'd *chosen* me.

Everything would be fine.

I just had to believe it.

CHAPTER 27

MASON

I'd fucked up.

Everything had been going great. Harper was amazing. The sex... was off the fucking charts. Holding her in my arms and just being with her... everything I never knew I needed.

And then Jenni texted me, and I lied.

I hadn't meant to, but when Harper asked how Scottie was, I'd panicked.

She didn't know about Jenni because there was nothing to know. We weren't in a relationship. I hadn't seen her in weeks. But still, the second I saw her text asking if I wanted to get together soon, guilt had punched me dead in the stomach. She deserved to know the truth, but it was not a conversation I wanted to have while I was lying in bed with the girl who had knocked me on my ass and stolen a piece of my fucking heart while she was at it.

I watched Harper sleep, mesmerized by the gentle rise and fall of her chest as she lay on her back, her head inclined toward me, her slender fingers wrapped around my thigh.

It was a little after seven, but I'd been awake for hours, my body well-accustomed to early starts. But I didn't want to wake her. She looked too peaceful.

I'd always thought Aiden and Connor, and more recently Noah, had been talking shit when they said being with their girlfriends was the best kind of therapy after a tough game, but I got it now. I could watch Harper sleep all day long and never grow tired. She was so fucking beautiful.

And she's all mine.

My cell vibrated, and she stirred. "Hmm, what time is it?"

"Still early." I reached back for my phone. "Go back to sleep."

She murmured something as she burrowed closer to me, and I glided a hand down her back, loving how soft and warm she felt. But she was out cold again, so I opened up my cell phone. I wasn't surprised to see Scottie's name. He usually texted me as soon as he woke up.

> SB: So... did she say yes yet? Or do I need to help you get the girl still?

> MB: I love you bud but I am capable of getting my own girlfriend.

> SB: Harper's your girlfriend?

> MB: Would that be okay?

> SB: I think so. I like Harper a lot. Are you going to get married? Can I be your best man? We could get a dog and it could be the ring bearer. I've always wanted a dog. A small one like a wiener or Pomeranian. Not a big one. They scare me.

Laughter rumbled in my chest, and it hit me that nothing about anything my brother had just said scared me.

I glanced at the sleeping girl beside me, and my heart slammed against my rib cage like a freight train. It was hard to believe how quickly I'd fallen under her spell. But here I was. So fucking gone for her.

"Tell Scottie I said good morning," she murmured.

"He's twelve. I am not telling him that."

Harper's eyes fluttered open, and she smiled up at me. "Pretty sure you knew what sex was at twelve."

"At twelve, my favorite pastime was jerkin' the gherkin."

"Oh my God." She exploded with laughter, clutching the pillow tightly. "You did not just say that."

"What?" I tried to keep a straight face. "It's true."

"Not so hard to believe Scottie will be having those same urges then."

"No. No fucking way. He's still a kid."

"He's almost thirteen."

"It's different. He doesn't understand—"

"Mase, he's still a teenage boy. His body will get it even if he doesn't quite understand it."

Shit. She was right.

"He's growing up," I said, but it was laced with trepidation. Life wasn't going to be easy for him. Friendships. Relationships. The big scary world. But Harper was right. It was happening whether I liked it or not.

"Yeah, he is. And he's so lucky to have a big brother to talk to." She rolled onto her stomach and laid her hand on my chest, sending a lick of heat through me. "Especially one who cares so much about him."

"Still, not sure he needs to know that I spent all night between your thighs."

"It wasn't *all* night." A coy smile tugged at her lips.

"Are you saying you weren't satisfied? Because we can fix that."

"Hold that thought." She leaned up and pressed a kiss to my mouth. "I need to pee."

Harper clambered off the bed and disappeared into her small en suite. But the second I heard the tap run, an idea came over me.

Getting up, I headed for the door and knocked.

"I'll be out in a minute," she called.

"Actually," I said, slipping inside. "I think we should probably stay right here."

"Mason, what—"

I leaned around her and reached into the shower, turning the water on. It would be a tight squeeze, but it didn't really matter, given that I intended on being deep inside her in the next two minutes.

"Shirt off," I said, tugging the hem of my t-shirt, the one she'd borrowed that first night we were together.

"I want you wearing this every night." I clutched the t-shirt in my hand. "Unless you're naked. Either will do."

"I'm not sure we'll both fit," she said, eyeing the shower cubicle.

"We'll fit," I said, pushing my boxers down my hips and kicking them off. Harper did the same with her underwear until we were both naked.

"Now what?" Anticipation glittered in her eyes as I stalked forward, sliding my hands under the backs of her thighs and picking her up.

Harper squealed, wrapping her legs around my waist, and I carried her into the shower, pressing her back against the cold tiles. "Mmm," she purred, wiggling against my morning wood. "A girl could get used to this kind of wake-up call."

"Good." I kissed her, sucking her bottom lip into my mouth and biting gently. "Because I plan on waking you up like this a lot."

"Mason?"

"Yeah, blondie?"

"Less talking." She grinned, grabbing onto my shoulders for more leverage as she fitted our bodies together, and slowly sank down on my aching dick. "And more fucking."

Now there was a plan I could get on board with.

"So spill," Noah said as we changed after practice.

I'd been all set to talk to Coach Dixon and set the record straight about Harper, but he never showed. Coach Tucker didn't seem too concerned, but it had me wondering what was going on after Harper confided in me about his history of alcohol abuse.

I didn't say anything, though. It didn't seem like my place. And I was still figuring out how to navigate the fact I was seeing the assistant coach's daughter.

"What?"

"Don't give me that," he rolled his eyes. "Either you saw Jenni last night, or you and Harper—"

"Keep your voice down," I hissed, glancing around the locker room. But it had already thinned out; most of the guys were gone for the day.

"I'm going with option B."

"You're an asshole."

"And you're boning Coach D's daughter."

"Holden, I swear to fucking God..."

"Relax, no one is listening. Besides, if they were, they know better than to run off and tell Coach."

"I'd planned on talking to him today, but he isn't here."

"Yeah, what's up with that? Coach Tucker almost seemed too laid-back about it."

"Who knows." I shrugged, hoping he'd drop it.

"So, you and Harper. Is it a bit of fun or—" I shot him a harsh look, and he grinned. "Well, holy shit. My boy went and caught feelings."

"Fuck off. It's new." *Really fucking new.* "And we're not going to make a big deal about it yet."

"What, why not? Rory and I tried to keep it a secret, and you saw how that worked out for us."

"A) Mine and Harper's situation is not the same. B) Her father is our coach, or had you forgotten that tidbit of information? And C) I need to break it off with Jenni before we go public."

"What do you mean you need to break it off with Jenni? I didn't realize there was anything to break off." He gawked at me like I'd grown a second head.

"There isn't. But she still deserves to know we're done."

"Fucking hell, she's already made you soft."

"Who, Jenni?" I frowned.

"No, Harper, you idiot."

"Look, I'm just trying to do the right thing here. Make sure that no one can mess this up before it's even gotten started."

"I get it," Noah said. "But let me ask you one thing. Does she know?"

"No, that's why I need to tell her."

"Not Jenni, asshole." He rolled his eyes. "Harper. Does Harper know about Jenni?"

"There's nothing to know." My brows pinched as I rubbed the back of my neck, feeling really fucking tense all of a sudden.

"You're either a really clueless idiot, Mase, or you're a really fucking clueless idiot. You can't start a relationship by lying to your girl."

"I'm not lying. There's nothing to tell."

"I know you're not that fucking stupid."

"Look, if I tell her about Jenni, it might freak her out. And things are good, Holden. Really fucking good. I don't want to ruin that."

"At the end of the day, it's your call," he said. "But I'm going to go on record and say I think this is a bad idea."

He didn't know what he was talking about. Which was fucking ironic since he had a similar situation with his regular hook-up before he and Rory went official.

"It'll be fine," I said, nixing the seed of doubt he'd planted.

"I hope so, hotshot." He smirked. "For your sake."

Harper: Mom hasn't heard from him.
He does this sometimes when he's
fallen off the wagon.

Mason: Shit, okay. Coach Tucker
didn't seem too concerned but if he
doesn't show in the morning, I'll talk
to him.

Harper: Okay...

Mason: Are you okay?

Harper: I'd rather my father wasn't an
alcoholic and neglectful bastard but
here we are.

Mason: I'm sorry. I'll make you feel
better later.

Harper: Oh yeah, and how do you
intend on doing that?

Mason: I can think of a few ways.

Guilt snaked through me as I glanced up just in time to
see Jenni enter the bar. We had a place on the edge of
town we hung out at sometimes, so it made sense to
meet her here.

Mason: I gotta go. But I'll text later.

> Harper: Okay. I'm meeting some
> friends now but I'm free tonight. xo

Jenni's face lit up when she spotted me, and I felt like a giant asshole. I guess since Harper, I saw things in a whole new light because Jenni was looking at me the way Harper looked at me.

Fuck.

"Hey." She slipped her purse off her shoulder and slid into the booth. "It's good to see you."

I nodded, unsure of what to say.

"How have you been?"

"Good, thanks." I kept it light. Casual. "Busy with the team and my brother."

"Of course." She smiled. "How is he?"

"He's okay, thanks for asking."

"You know, Mason, I'm glad you texted asking to meet. I've been hoping to—"

The door swung open, and a group of girls filed inside, laughing and joking. But one laugh stood out among the rest.

Harper found me almost immediately, her whole face lighting up. But I saw the second she realized I wasn't alone, the light in her eyes guttering out, replaced with confusion.

"Shit," I muttered under my breath.

"Mason, what's wrong?" Jenni turned right as Harper reached us. "Harper?" she said.

"Janelle?"

"Janelle?" I frowned. Who the fuck was Janelle? "Hold up. You two know each other?"

"Janelle works at Millers. What are you doing here?" Harper pinned me with a desperate look.

"It's not what you think."

"Mason?" Jenni said, her gaze swinging to mine.

"Uh, this isn't how I'd planned to do this." Shit. I rubbed a hand over my jaw, trying to figure out what to say.

This... this was why I avoided relationships. Because they got messy. Because people got hurt. And the way Harper was looking at me, with pain in her eyes, was something I never wanted to put there.

Before I could talk myself out of the giant fucking hole I'd dug, Harper said, "Wait a minute... oh my God." She clapped a hand over her mouth, shaking her head. "Mason... he's... he's your fuck buddy."

Jenni nodded. "Yeah. We've been seeing each other on and off for months."

"The fuck?" I barked. "That's not—"

"I am such an idiot," Harper stepped back, all the color drained from her face.

"It's not what you think," I said, panic rising inside of me. This was not supposed to happen. They were not supposed to know each other. Not that it mattered, not really. Not if everyone understood the truth. But from the betrayal etched onto Harper's expression, it was clear she didn't.

Her mind had gone straight to the worst-case scenario.

Fuck.

"Harper, that's not—"

"He texted me earlier to meet. I was about to go for it before you showed up," Jenni said. "How do you two know each other again?"

"We..."

"We're together," I blurted, instantly regretting it from the way the temperature cooled around us. Two angry women glared at me like I was the devil incarnate.

"Together?" Jenni repeated, and I nodded, risking a glance at Harper.

But she was still. Her expression was a mask of hurt and confusion.

"So let me get this straight," Jenni turned her attention to my girlfriend. At least, I really fucking hoped she was still my girl after this shit show. "All this time, you were giving me advice on how to tell Mason that I wanted more, and you were—"

"I didn't know your secret guy was Mason." Harper paled. "You never told me that. I am so sorry."

"Natalie was right about you," Jenni sneered. "You are a desperate whore."

"N-Natalie?" Harper choked out. "You two—"

"We have mutual friends, yeah. She's told me all about your revolving door of guys. But I like to make up my own opinion of someone before I cast judgment."

"Revolving door? What are you talking about? That's not... She said that? Natalie said that?" Jenni nodded with disgust, and Harper flinched. "And now you think I'm a... a whore?" Her voice shook with hurt.

"If the cap fits." Jenni folded her arms over her chest and scowled at Harper.

"Yeah. No," I snapped. "If you think I'm just going to sit here while you attack Harper, you can leave. If you should be blaming anyone, it's me. I went after her knowing you and I were involved."

Harper sucked in a sharp breath, and I instantly regretted my choice of words. But this clusterfuck was the last thing I was expecting when I turned up here. And I wasn't good at... at this.

"Harper, that's not... we hooked up occasionally. Past tense."

"Great." Jenni shot up. "That's really great. I came here today to lay my cards out on the table, to tell you that I wanted more, and you came to tell me that you're seeing her? You two are welcome to each other," she threw her hands up, "I'm done. I'm so freaking done."

Jenni stormed out of the place, but the tension remained.

"Harper, I—"

"Don't," she said on a shaky breath. "All this time, and I never imagined she was talking about you."

"I don't know how the fuck this happened." I

dragged a hand through my hair. "I came here to tell her it was done. Over. Not that we even had anything. It was just sex. The occasional hook-up. I swear, that's all it was."

"Not to Janelle. Jenni." She shook her head. "Whatever the hell her name is. Why didn't you tell me about her?"

"Because in my head, there was nothing to tell. I didn't make any promises to her. We weren't exclusive. We were friends—"

"With benefits." Her expression faltered. "Is that all I am to you?"

"The fuck?" I jerked back, shocked she would even ask that. "No, and you know it."

"Do I? What's to stop you from doing exactly the same thing to me?"

"Because I... I care about you. Come on, Harper. This is getting blown way out of proportion."

"Was that who you were texting this morning?"
Shit.

"I... yeah. But she texted me. I swear, I never—"

"I need to go."

"What? Why?" I grabbed her hand. She couldn't leave. Not without hashing this out. "We need to talk about this. I don't want Jenni, Harper. I want you. I was here for you."

"I... I can't do this right now. I need some time to think."

"You need time..." I scoffed. "Yeah, whatever. You

408   L A COTTON

know, this is exactly why I don't do relationships. Too much fucking drama."

She flinched at my cruel words, but I was pissed. Pissed she wouldn't hear me out. Pissed Jenni had spewed all that shit about Harper being a whore.

Pissed that I was now imagining her—my fucking girlfriend—with a line of other guys.

"I'm glad to know where you stand on things." She gave me a sad, defeated smile before walking away from me without so much as a second look.

CHAPTER 28

HARPER

MASON WAS Janelle's fuck buddy.

It would have almost been funny if it didn't hurt so much.

Walking into that bar and seeing them sitting there had only reinforced every doubt and insecurity I'd ever had about myself.

They had been together. More than a few times if Janelle's account had been true.

Mason and Janelle.

Is that the kind of girl he typically went for? Smart. Quiet. Kept to herself.

Discreet.

She hadn't blabbed to us that she was seeing a Laker. Hadn't even hinted at it.

I didn't expect Mason to be a saint. He was a

hockey player, for Christ's sake. Sex was par for the course. And I wasn't exactly the Virgin Mary either. It wasn't even about the sex, not really. It was knowing he had someone he turned to. All this time, I thought we were developing this connection, that I was special.

That I was his exception to the rule.

And now I just felt stupid and insignificant.

I didn't go back to my dorm. I couldn't. Not after she dropped the Natalie-bomb. So I'd asked Rory to take me back to her place.

"I'm sorry I ruined our plans," I said, another wave of embarrassment rolling through me at the fact that she, Ella, Jordan, and her girlfriend Noelle had witnessed everything.

"You have nothing to apologize for. Come on," she said, unlocking her apartment. "Let's see what Harper-friendly comfort food I can find."

"Thank you." I followed her inside.

"You know, and this is just my unsolicited opinion; maybe you should have stuck around to hear him out."

"I was just so embarrassed, Rory. Not to mention hurt. We spent this amazing night together. He dropped the G-word, and then I discover he's secretly breaking things off with his fuck buddy, hoping I won't find out. It doesn't exactly make me feel like a priority."

"You're right, and I get it. I do. But it's Mason we're talking about. He's... not like the other guys."

"What do you mean?"

"He carries a lot on his shoulders. He isn't used to

considering anyone else's feelings. He probably thought he was doing you a favor by not telling you about Janelle."

"Well, that's just stupid."

"Have you had the talk?" She gave me a pointed look.

"The talk?"

"Yeah, the ex-talk. The body count talk?"

"No. I'm not sure I ever want to have that talk."

"Yeah, I told Noah I didn't either. I don't need to know his entire sexual history. Do you know why? Because it doesn't matter to me. I love him. All parts of him. Even the ones I wish were a little less active."

"I gave her dating advice, Rory. I was basically telling her how to get the guy. My guy."

Her mouth tipped with mild amusement. "But you didn't know it was Mason. That isn't your fault."

"No, it's his."

"Harper, come on, this isn't a reason to throw away what you guys have."

I'd told her everything on the walk here. She knew how I felt about him, that I was falling hard and fast for number thirteen.

"I don't want to throw it away. I just want—"

A loud bang on Rory's door startled me. "Rory, what did you do?" I hissed.

"Nothing, I didn't... Fine, I told Noah we were coming here."

"Aurora!"

"What? I didn't think he'd go tattling to Mason."

"Harper, open up. I know you're in there."

Another bang.

Another hammer to my heart.

"Don't worry. I'll deal with this." Rory went to the door and cracked it open an inch. "You need to leave; she isn't ready—"

"Not going to happen," Mason said. I couldn't see him, but I could feel him—his desperation.

Rory was right. Things had gotten blown way out of proportion. But I was hurt. I needed time to lick my wounds and figure out what—

"Come on, blondie. I know you're in there," he called. "I'm not leaving until you see me."

"Mason, this isn't—"

"It's okay," I said, approaching Rory. "I'll talk to him."

"You're sure?"

I nodded, switching places with her. "What do you want, Mason?"

His eyes were an arctic storm, freezing me from the inside out. "We're not doing this."

"What?"

"We're not letting some insignificant bullshit get in the way of this."

"I'd hardly call the fact you've been seeing Janelle—"

"How many times do I have to say it? I wasn't seeing her. It wasn't like that. And I didn't tell you because it didn't come up. Because whenever I'm with you, the only thing I'm thinking about is how much I want to kiss you.

"It's you, Harper. It's only ever been you. Did I handle the Jenni stuff wrong? Yeah. But I've never done this. I'm going to mess up, babe. I'm going to get it wrong. But talk to me. Hear me out. Don't fucking run from me just because you're pissed or hurt or embarrassed."

"I just feel so stupid, Mason."

His hand snapped out, grabbing my sweater, and he tugged me forward. "You're not stupid. You're fucking perfect." He gazed down at me. "Perfect for me. And you're all I want."

Mason kissed the end of my nose. "Jenni was way off base saying all that shit to you. Who the fuck is Natalie anyway?"

"She lives in my dorm. She's had it out for me since I moved in."

"Yeah, that's not going to fly with me. I'll talk to her."

"No, Mason. I would never ask you—"

"You're not asking me. I'm telling you. If she says another bad word about you, she's done."

"You're a little bit scary when you're pissed."

"I'm not pissed, Harper. Well, I am. But that's not the half of it. Watching you walk out of that bar fucking terrified me. I thought I'd lost you. I thought—"

"I'm sorry." I leaned up, laying my palm on his cheek. "I panicked. I guess I'm waiting for the other shoe to drop."

"What do you mean?"

"This. Us. I still can't quite believe it's real."

"It's real, Harper." Mason looped his arms around my waist, holding me tight. "I'm sorry I didn't tell you about Jenni."

"I'm sorry I ran."

"See." His mouth twitched. "That wasn't so hard, was it?" He kissed me soft and slow, letting his tongue slide lazily against mine.

"Mason," I whimpered.

"Don't leave me again, blondie. I need you, okay? I really fucking need you."

"Uh, guys," a little voice called, and I glanced over my shoulder to find Rory peeking around the door. "Not that I'm not happy for you both, because I am. Yay." She smiled. "But can you maybe move this inside? I love this building and don't want to be evicted because my friends are getting freaky in the hallway."

"Rory, we're not getting freaky," I laughed, burying my face in Mason's chest because everything that had happened at the bar seemed so silly in the face of this. The fact he'd chased me down to set things straight.

"Yet," he rasped in my ear, sending a shiver through me.

"Put the girl down, Steele, and get inside," Rory ordered. "Noah is on his way over with supplies?"

"Supplies?" I asked.

"Yeah. Apparently, he wants to, and I quote, 'celebrate another Laker switching to the dark side.'"

"Asshole," Mason muttered, ushering me into Rory's apartment.

"Do you two need a minute?" she asked. "I can go hide in my room and put on some loud music."

"I think we can keep our hands to ourselves." I fought a smile.

"Speak for yourself." Mason wrapped his arms around me from behind, dropping his chin to my shoulder. "I'm desperate to be inside you," he whispered.

But not quiet enough, apparently because Rory turned bright red and stuttered, "And that's my cue to disappear."

"No, wait," I called after her. "He's joking. It's a joke."

"Pretty sure I'm not joking, blondie." Mason kissed my neck.

"Behave!" I scolded. "Noah is coming over."

"So? I've spent weeks watching him and Rory dry-humping at every turn. Payback is a bitch."

"Oh my God, what is wrong with you?" I wriggled out of his hold. "Go sit and cool off, horndog. I'm going to help Rory get us some drinks."

Rory chuckled, giving me a little shake of her head. "Welcome to my world," she said as I reached her. "Everything good?"

"I think so." I glanced back at Mason, who had made himself comfortable on her couch.

"I'm so happy for you. And him. Definitely him." Aurora smiled. "You're a good influence on him."

"I'm not sure about that." I dipped my head, feeling a little insecure still.

"Harper, he's crazy about you. Surely, you know that?"

"I... I feel it, yeah. When it's just the two of us. Or we're with Scottie. It feels like we're a team, you know?"

"I do."

"It's just when we go out there." I tipped my head to the door. "Out there is kind of scary."

"Being scared only means that you care. That you have something worth losing. You know, you taught me that." She reached for my hand, squeezing gently. "The Janelle/Jenni thing was just a big misunderstanding. One he didn't handle very well, sure. But it doesn't define the start of your relationship unless you let it."

"You're right. Of course, you're right." I looked over at Mason again and his head snapped up. Something passed between us as he smiled at me.

"You've got it bad, haven't you?" Rory chuckled.

"So bad."

"Loving a Laker isn't easy," she said quietly. "But it's worth every second of doubt, I promise."

I didn't correct her and tell her that I didn't love

Mason. Not yet. Because the truth was, it wouldn't take much to hand over my heart.

I was halfway there already.

"No way, no fucking way." Noah slammed his hand down on the table with fake outrage. "I did not do that."

"Swear to God, Rory," Mason laughed, his hand toying with my hair as we sat in the booth at Zest. "He was a fucking mess."

The second Noah had turned up at Rory's apartment, he'd announced we were going out—the four of us.

A double date.

I'd been hesitant at first, especially after what happened with Janelle. But the three of them talked me into it, and I was glad because it had been nothing but fun.

Noah didn't give me a chance to get all up in my head as he entertained us with stories from his freshman year. How he and Mason had struck up a quick friendship. But for every embarrassing story Noah had about Mason, Mason had one right back.

"Ahh, the joys of dating an athlete." She gazed at Noah, clearly unaffected by Mason's attempt to one-up him. "You know, I have a funny story about Noah," she said.

"Shortcake"—his eyes went wide—"don't you dare—"

"Do tell," I chuckled, inching closer to Mason. He leaned in, brushing his lips over my cheek.

"It was when I was still staying with the guys. He came home one night wasted and thought it would be a good idea to come and see me. Then he spent half the night puking in my bathroom."

"It was not half the night." Noah poked her in the ribs, and she trapped a squeal with her hand. "It worked though, didn't it?"

"What worked?"

"Got her to let me spend the night in her bed so she could keep an eye on me."

"Fucking pussy," Mason muttered, shaking his head. But when his gaze snagged on mine, his expression softened, and I wondered if he was remembering the night he'd looked after me.

"This is nice," I said. "Thanks for making me come."

"I'm just happy Mase pulled his head out of his ass." Noah tipped his bottle in our direction. "She's good for you."

"Yeah"—Mason gazed down at me—"she is."

"But are we going to address the elephant in the room?"

"Holden..."

"Coach D—"

"I'll tell him as soon as he's back at practice."

"Maybe I should talk to him?" I suggested. I didn't want things to go south for Mason because of me. Because my father resented and blamed me.

"No," Mason said. "I said I'll handle it, and I will."

"Okay."

Just then, a group of rowdy people entered the bar, and a familiar voice made me look over at the door.

"Noah, what did you do?" Rory directed her accusatory gaze at him.

"I... may have mentioned to Connor that we were here." He shrugged, mouthing to me, "Sorry."

"It's fine. I guess they'll all know soon enough."

"Relax," Mason said, squeezing the back of my neck. "They're my friends. Our friends."

"I know. It's just a lot all at once."

I'd barely had time to get my head around everything, and now we were about to out ourselves to half the team.

"Lovers," Connor strolled up to the booth, shoving his way to the end on Noah and Rory's side. "Isn't this cozy."

"Don't be an ass, Con," Rory said.

"Sorry, Rory, baby. I'm only busting Mase's balls. I see you two figured your shit out."

"Don't start," Mason murmured.

"Relax, I'm happy for you. Even if she's way out of

your league." Connor winked at me, pulling Ella down onto his knee.

"Hi, guys," Dayna said. "Sorry to gate-crash. Noah said—"

"It's fine," Mason replied, dragging me further along the banquette so we could let her and Aiden sit down.

"So you two are what exactly?" Aiden asked.

"What do you think they are, Cap?" Noah tsked. "Joined the dark side, didn't he?"

"About fucking time, too," Connor added, fist-bumping Noah.

"You guys are so weird." Ella rolled her eyes.

"How are things with your Dad?" I asked Dayna.

"He's feeling a lot better, thanks. Thankfully, it was nothing serious."

"That's good."

"Our numbers are growing," Ella said. "This is a good thing. Soon we'll outnumber the bunnies."

"Kitten, you'll never outnumber the bunnies," Connor scoffed. "Two disappear, and another four pop up."

"There's plenty of guys left to go around," Noah said, earning himself an elbow to the ribs from Rory. "Come on, shortcake, I didn't mean—"

"Quit while you're ahead, bro." Connor smirked.

"What are you doing this weekend, Harper? We're trying to talk Rory into girls' night. While the guys are away, the girls will play."

"Are you trying to give me a heart attack?" Noah rubbed his temples.

"Relax, we won't do anything too crazy." Ella grinned. "It'll be fun. Please come, and then Rory will come."

"I'm up for girls' night," I said.

"Yay." Ella clapped. "I've invited Jordan and Noelle too. I'm thinking drinks and dancing. Maybe a strip cl—"

"Okay, kitten. Enough of that." Connor slapped his hand over her mouth. "Noah and Mason are new to this game. You can't be planting those kinds of seeds of doubt before a big weekend of games."

"Pretty sure she's joking," Rory said.

"Don't be so sure, Rory, baby. I've seen how wet my girl gets when she watches Magic Mike."

"Connor Morgan!" Ella ripped his hand away. "You did not just say that in front of all our friends."

He shrugged. "We don't keep secrets."

"That's... I... ugh. You're such an asshole at times."

"But I'm your asshole, kitten. And you wouldn't have me any other way." He nuzzled her neck, and she melted against him.

"Please don't maul Ella at the table," Rory said.

"Jealous, shortcake? Because that can—"

"Don't you dare." She held up a hand to Noah.

"If we ever end up like them," I whispered to Mason, "we need to check ourselves."

"So you don't want to sneak to the restrooms and—"

"Mason!" I shrieked, but he was already grinning.

"I'm joking. Unless you want to—"

"Do not finish that sentence."

He pulled me back into his side, dropping his mouth to my ear. "I'm really glad you're here, Harper."

I turned to look at him, instantly falling into the possessiveness in his eyes.

"Me too."

CHAPTER 29

MASON

"Harper." I kissed her shoulder. "I gotta go, or else Coach will—"

"Hmm, what time is it?" She stretched out like a damn house cat, the sheet falling down her body.

A body I'd gotten well acquainted with last night.

Fuck, she was perfect.

And she was mine.

I was a lucky sonofabitch.

"Early. Go back to sleep. I'll see you later." I pressed another kiss to her shoulder before dragging my tired ass out of bed and throwing on my clothes. I needed to stop at the house first and grab my things for practice. It was on the way, so it wasn't a big deal.

Once I was dressed, I slipped out of her dorm room

and made my way downstairs. I didn't expect to run into anyone.

"Sorry, my bad." I went to move around the girl, but she grabbed my arm.

"Mason?"

"Uh, yeah. Do I know you?"

"We've seen each other around. I'm Natalie."

So this was the bitch who had talked shit about Harper to Jenni. Janelle. Whatever the fuck her name was.

"I've been hoping for an introduction—"

"What are you doing?" I knocked her hand off my arm.

"E-excuse me." She reared back.

"Come on. You're smarter than that. You know exactly where I just came from." I waited for her to piece things together.

"Shit," she murmured. "Jenni..."

"If I ever hear you talking shit about Harper again, you can kiss your reputation goodbye."

"You can't threaten me." She stood her ground. "Besides, it's true. She's a wh—"

"Watch it." It was a low menacing growl. "Harper is twice the girl you will ever be. You put people down to make yourself feel better because, really, you're nothing but a sad, insecure girl trying to get ahead in life. Stay away from me, and stay away from Harper. We clear?"

She blanched, tears clinging to her lashes. "I... yes.

Yes, we're clear."

"Good. Harper is a good person," I said as I moved past her. "But I'm not. You'd do well to remember that."

As I walked out of their dorm building, my mouth curved a fraction. Something told me Natalie and her mean girlfriends would no longer be a problem for Harper.

"Mason, son. My office," were the first words I heard when I entered the locker room.

A rumble of speculation went up around me.

"What have you done to piss off Coach this early?" Adams asked, and I flipped him off.

"You think this is about Harper and Coach D?" Noah said quietly, and I shrugged.

"If it is, I'll deal with it."

I'd made my choice—it was her.

The rest would figure itself out. But I did need to talk to Coach sooner rather than later.

I pulled on my jersey and took off barefooted toward Coach's office. Knocking twice, I waited.

"Come in," he called.

"What's up, Coach?"

"Take a seat, son." He motioned to the empty chair. "I'll get straight to it. Did you know Coach Dixon had invited a couple of scouts down to come watch you play?"

"He mentioned it. Why?"

Coach Tucker ran a hand down his face, his expression pensive. "I got a call from the Blue Jackets yesterday to confirm a meeting."

"You didn't know." I deduced.

"No, I didn't. I knew James had taken you under his wing, and I'll be honest, Mason, he made a good case, given how well you've been playing. But something's going on with him, and I can't quite figure out what. I still haven't talked to him yet, but he isn't coming in today again. Texted me this morning."

Shit.

I tapped my foot on the floor, tension radiating inside me. I needed to air my concerns. Tell him what I knew. But it meant breaking Harper's confidence. Something that didn't sit well with me. Not after yesterday.

Not after I'd finally made her mine.

"Mason... tell me where your head's at, son."

"There was an incident," I said.

"I'm listening."

"Friday night, after the game. A few of us hit TPB. Coach D showed up."

"He came to the bar?"

I nodded.

"What happened?"

"He said he wanted to follow up on our conversation about the scouts."

"Did he have anything to drink?"

"One drink. Whiskey, I think. He did buy me and two of the other guys a drink, though."

"Jesus," Coach blew out a steady breath. "You didn't think to come to me with this sooner?"

"I'll be honest, Coach. The entire thing made me feel uncomfortable, but I figured that everyone deserves the benefit of the doubt."

"We have rules about this kind of thing for a reason."

"I know," I said. "I didn't want to cause unnecessary drama. It was one drink, and he didn't hang around."

"Anything else I should know before I decide how to deal with this?"

It was now or never.

Fuck, I really hoped I wasn't about to mess this up.

"I know you and Coach D go way back, but how much did he tell you about his life now?"

"Mason, if there's something you need to tell me, now would be the time, son."

"I have reason to believe Coach Dixon is an alcoholic, sir."

"And how did you come across this information?"

"Because... because I'm seeing his daughter, sir."

"So let me get this straight," Noah said as we waited for the girls to join us in Harper's favorite coffee shop. "Coach D is MIA, possibly passed out in some seedy motel—"

"Seriously." I gawked at him.

"What?" He shrugged, taking a sip of his fancy-ass-looking coffee. "It's like a bad soap opera. I mean, he's okay, though, right? Coach has spoken to him?"

"He's had a text conversation with him. So we know he's alive."

"And you fessed up to Coach about the other night at TPB? Which, by the way, I'm still pissed you didn't tell me about."

"So needy," I teased, and he flipped me off.

"And he organized the meeting with the Blue Jackets without talking to Coach Tucker?"

"Yep."

I still didn't know how to feel about that. It had felt weird having all his attention but finding out he hadn't shared his plans with Coach Tucker only confirmed that something felt off.

Although, it was probably a moot point once he found out I was seeing his daughter.

I dragged a hand down my face, trying to scrub some of the tension away. It had been a strange day.

The guys had given me a ton of shit in practice about Harper. Then Adams and I almost got into it when he made a remark about her I didn't fucking appreciate.

Coach Carson had told me to go cool off, and then Coach Tucker had lost his shit, reminding his team we had a championship to focus on.

"It'll be okay, you know," Noah said. "Everything will work out."

"Yeah."

I just didn't want Harper to be mad at me for telling Coach about her father's addiction.

My leg jostled as I stalked the door, waiting for her to arrive.

"Jesus, Mase. You're going to rub a hole in the carpet," he chuckled. But the joke was lost on me.

When Rory and Harper finally appeared, and she aimed her smile in my direction, the tight coil inside me unraveled a little.

"Hey." Rory flopped down beside Noah while Harper perched on the arm of my chair.

"How was practice?" she asked.

I slid my arm around her waist and lifted her onto my lap. "It was a clusterfuck."

"What? Why?"

"And that's our cue," Noah said. "Let's go find some Harper-friendly snacks, shortcake."

"What? Why?" Rory frowned. "We just got here."

"And now we're going over there." Noah ushered her toward the counter, and I grimaced.

"Mase?"

"So your old man was a no-show again."

"I thought he might be."

"I talked to Coach Tucker..."

"You told him?" She searched my eyes, and I nodded.

"I had to. I should have told him about TPB anyway. So when he asked, I couldn't lie."

"Okay."

"Okay?"

"Yeah, okay." Harper slid her arms around my neck and lowered her face to mine. "I don't owe my father anything, Mason. And honestly, if he is drinking again, I don't think he should be around you or the team."

My brows crinkled as her words sank into me.

She meant it, every word. Because that's who Harper was. Selfless and supportive, she genuinely cared about the team and me.

Jesus, I'd been so fucking wrong about her.

"I'm just sorry he made you promises he'll probably never keep."

"Fuck, Harper," I breathed, closing the distance between us to graze my mouth over hers. "What did I ever do to deserve you?"

"I ask myself that same question every day." She smirked, kissing me once. Twice. Sliding her hand over my jaw and teasing me with her tongue.

"Careful, blondie, or I might get ideas."

"Only the bad kind, I hope?" Mischief twinkled in

her eyes, and I loved it. I fucking loved how easy it was between us.

"Is it safe to return?" Noah, the fucking idiot, grinned at me.

"Yeah. You're good."

"I got some brownies. Mason said you can have these ones." He slung them down on the table, and Harper reached for them, inspecting the bag.

"Thank you."

"How's team morale with my dad MIA?"

"Everyone feels a little restless. Coach isn't giving us much information, and we've gotten used to practicing without him," Noah said. "But we'll still kick ass this weekend."

"The University of Rochester Mavericks, right?"

"Yeah," I said. "It'll be a tough win." They were good, one of the best teams in our conference.

"Nah, we've got this. Told you, Mase, we're going all the way this season. I can feel it in my bones. And you'll sign with Blue Jackets, and everything will work out." He winked, and I wanted to throw something at his head.

"The Blue Jackets are interested?" Harper asked, and I shrugged.

"Your old man reached out. They said their scout would come down and take a look at me."

"Mason, that's a big deal."

"Yeah, but I'm not getting ahead of myself. I still don't even know if I want it."

"You want it," Noah snorted. "We all want it, or we wouldn't be here. It just depends on whether or not you want it enough."

"Noah..." Rory leaned over and ran her hand over his shoulder.

"What? I'm just saying—"

"Yeah, yeah, Holden, we get it." I blew out a frustrated breath. Because he was right. Of course, he was right.

My future wouldn't just happen for me; I had to make choices. Hard choices. Ones I still wasn't ready to make.

I thought I'd been ready, but then Harper had burrowed her way under my skin, and everything had changed again.

"You have time," she whispered, pressing her lips to my cheek.

"Yeah."

But right now, all I really wanted was time with her.

Wednesday night, I drove Harper to her shift at the RCC. She was nervous about seeing my brother now we were official. But I knew she had nothing to be worried about. I'd already talked to Scottie, and he had taken it all in stride. He was more excited that he 'got to keep Harper' than anything.

So I was hardly surprised when the two of them came bounding out of the center together, deep in conversation.

"Hey, buddy, how'd it go?" I asked, pushing off the side of my car to go meet them.

"We made junk art. I made a robot."

"A very cool robot." Harper smiled. "Next week, we're going to paint the models and make a display."

"Sounds fun."

"It was okay." He shrugged, making a beeline for the car.

"Everything okay?" I asked Harper, pulling her into my arms.

"Yeah. He's been fine. What did you get up to?"

"Oh, you know. Sitting in the car, reading up on product management. Riveting stuff, blondie."

"My good little student." She pressed a kiss to my lips.

"I'll gladly be your student. You can teach me all the things." I went in to kiss her again, but my brother shouted, "Stop kissing your girlfriend. It's gross."

Harper buried her face in my chest, murmuring, "Busted."

"He's got to get used to it," I said. "I can't keep my hands off you."

"The feeling is entirely mutual. Maybe we can stop on the ride home for a little late-night-make-out session." She grinned.

"Deal."

"Come on." Harper grabbed my hand and tugged me toward the car.

I hadn't told her, but part of me had been worried that Scottie might be upset about things once he realized I had to make room in my life for Harper too. He was so used to being the sole focus of my attention. Outside of hockey, at least.

Now there was another thing pulling me away from him.

But it wasn't a choice between Scottie and Harper, and I knew that was all down to her.

Harper loved my brother. She accepted him and all his complex layers. And it was one of the reasons I'd started to look at her in a different light. She was patient, understanding, and encouraging. She was exactly the type of support my brother needed to flourish. And the fact he seemed completely taken with her was only the icing on the cake.

We got in the car, and Scottie groaned, "Finally. You made me wait forever."

"Minutes, bud. We made you wait like three minutes. Where to for dinner?" I asked him. "You can choose."

Scottie contemplated my question, his eyes flicking to Harper and back to me. "I really want to go to Sombreros for tacos, but will you be able to eat them, Harper?"

His compassion floored me, and I swallowed over the lump in my throat.

"I'll find something to eat wherever we go, bud. Don't you worry about me."

"I worry," he said. "About Mom, and Mason, and you. You're supposed to worry about the people you care about. Isn't that right, Mason brother?"

"That's right, bud. Tacos good?" I asked Harper, and she nodded.

"You Steele boys are something special, you know," she whispered, dropping her head against the seat to watch me back out of the parking spot.

"Mase?" Scottie piped up.

"Yeah, bud?"

"Fenton Jones said now that you have a girlfriend, you'll have sex. Does that mean you're going to make babies?"

"Jesus," I breathed while Harper tried to contain her laughter. "I'm glad you think this is funny."

"Come on, Mase, it kinda is." She covered her mouth with her fist.

I shook my head with mild amusement, meeting Scottie's gaze in the rearview mirror. "It's a good thing I love you, bud."

"So will you?" he asked.

"Will we what?"

"Have sex and make babies? Because Fenton has a baby sister, and I'm not sure I want one."

"So, what do you think?" I asked Harper as she tucked into her gluten-free taco salad.

"So good," she murmured around a mouthful of food.

"The best," Scottie concurred, meticulously building his taco.

"This was a good call, bud," I said. "Nothing like—fuck." The air sucked clean from my lungs as I watched our father enter the restaurant.

"Mason, what's wr—"

"Dad! Dad's here." Scottie dropped his taco and started flapping his hands. But as Dad spotted him and lifted a hand in a small wave, his expression morphed from excitement into trepidation. "Do you think he's with them?" he asked quietly.

"No, bud. I don't think he's with them." After my last conversation with our old man, he wouldn't dare. But I didn't think he'd show up unannounced either.

Yet here we were.

"I'll go talk to him," I said, ready to tell him to get the fuck out of here. But Harper reached over and laid her hand on my arm.

"Maybe we should ask Scottie what he wants to do. There's plenty of food. We could invite your dad to join us."

"I'm not sure—"

"Can we Mason brother?" Scottie stared up at me.

"Scottie, bud, what if—"

"It's okay," Harper whispered, slipping her hand into mine.

It was too late anyway because Dad reached our table and there was no way in hell Scottie was going to let him go now.

"Hey, buddy. Mason, and... sorry, I don't think we've met. I'm Sam. Samuel Steele."

"Hi Mr. Steele. I'm Harper, Mason's—"

"Girlfriend." Scottie, the little shit, cut in.

"Girlfriend, you say. Got to admit, I didn't see that one coming, Son."

I bristled at the surprise in his voice, as if I owed him anything.

As if he cared.

"How did you know we were here?" I changed the subject.

"Why don't you sit down Mr. Steele," Harper said. "We have room and there's enough food to go around."

His face lit up, but I wasn't surprised. Harper had that effect on people. Sunshine on a cloudy fucking day.

"I wouldn't say no to a taco." Dad slid into the booth next to her. "Your mom told me I might find you here."

"You went to see Mom?" Scottie asked. "Did you tell her about your new girlfriend?"

Dad sucked in a sharp breath, almost choking on it and I smothered a laugh. At least Scottie could inadvertently call him on his bullshit, even if I wouldn't.

Not here.

Not like this.

Clearing his throat, he helped himself to a glass of water and said, "Actually, I was looking for you. I wanted to explain some things..." He looked to me, and I saw the guilt there. But it didn't change anything, not for me.

"Maybe I should give the three of you some privacy," Harper suggested.

"I want you to stay." Scottie beat me to it. Because I wanted her to stay as well.

"It's fine, Harper. Stay, please. I can see my boys obviously trust you."

A hell of a lot more than you, I swallowed the words.

"I-I don't have a new girlfriend, Son. Claire is... a friend."

"Do you have sex with her? Because Fenton Jones said—"

"Scottie." I shook my head.

"Sorry." He shrunk into himself.

Dad winced, glancing around the restaurant to check who might be listening. Even now, even after everything, he couldn't be the man Scottie needed him to be. And I fucking hated it.

"I thought you'd got a new family." It was a quietly

spoken statement. One that ripped a hole through my chest.

"No, Scottie. No. That's not..." Dad looked to me for help, but he was on his own on this one. I'd spent years picking up the pieces after him.

Awkward tension descended over the four of us as Dad frantically tried to dig himself out of the hole he'd created. But he couldn't do it.

Because he was a coward.

"I..."

"Why don't you tell your dad about the junk model you made at the center today?" Harper suggested, and his shoulders sagged with relief.

"I would love to hear about that, Son."

As Scottie launched into an in-depth description of his robot, Harper caught my eye and smiled. Thank fuck she was here because I'm not sure I could have restrained my frustration and anger if she wasn't.

I reached for her hand across the table, and she entwined our fingers together. A silent promise that she was here.

That she wasn't going anywhere.

"Well, that was interesting," I said with a weary sigh as Harper and I lingered by the car, waiting for Dad to say goodbye to Scottie.

"I can see where you get your patience and heart from... your mom." Harper grinned up at me. "I know it's hard for you, but Scottie is happy, and that's all that matters."

"Yeah." I looked over to where he was hanging on Dad's every word, trying to ignore the stab of jealousy I felt. "But what happens when one day he does get the new family? What then?"

"You'll deal with it." Her expression softened. "You'll help Scottie come to terms with it. Because that's who you are, Mase. You put your brother first."

I hooked my arm around her waist and pulled her flush with my body, gazing down at her with so much fucking gratitude. "Right now, I'm not thinking about putting Scottie first. I'm thinking about doing very, very bad things to you."

"Mason!" Her eyes lit up, lust shining there.

"You're amazing, blondie. You didn't have to do any of that back there, but you did."

She looped her hands around the back of my neck and leaned in. "Yeah, well... you Steele brothers are kind of important to me."

"You mean that, don't you?"

"Every word."

"Harper, I—"

"Mase, Mason brother, guess what?" Scottie bounded over to us with Dad in tow, and Harper let go of me, moving to my side. "Dad said he'll buy me some collectors cards. You know the rare ones I've been trying to get. He has a friend who can get them."

"I bet he does."

"Be nice." Harper nudged my ribs. "That's awesome, buddy," she said. "I want to see them all when you get them."

"You like hockey, Harper?" Dad asked.

"I... something like that."

"Harper's dad is James 'the Real Deal' Dixon," Scottie said.

"He is? I... I didn't realize. You must really know your hockey then. No wonder Mason has taken a shine to you."

That awkward tension returned.

"Well, we need to head home," I said, more than ready to end this little family reunion. "Mom is expecting us."

"Of course. Thank you for letting me stay and have dinner with you."

"Anytime, Mr. Steele. It was nice to meet you."

"You too, Harper. Mason, Son." He held out his hand and I stared at it.

"Mason," Harper whispered, giving me another little nudge. I grabbed it and shook it.

"Thank you, Mase, for everything." My brows furrowed at his strange choice of words but before I could ask what he meant, he went to Scottie and crouched down. "And I'll see you soon, okay?"

"Okay, Dad."

"Be good for your mom and brother."

"And Harper," Scottie added, surprising the shit out of me. "She's part of my family too now."

Harper's breath caught and she looked up at me, a hundred questions glittering in her eyes.

I lifted my shoulders in a small shrug and whispered, "He has a point."

"Mason," she let out a nervous laugh.

"Scottie speaks facts, you know that."

"But—"

"No buts, blondie." I leaned down, stealing a kiss, not giving a single fuck that my old man and brother were watching. "The Steele brothers have decided," I whispered. "We want to keep you."

CHAPTER 30

HARPER

My father was still MIA. According to my mom, he hadn't been home, but he had texted her. No doubt it was the usual excuses.

He needed some space.

Needed time to get his head on straight.

He'd come back stronger. Ready to turn things around.

But it was always empty promises.

It wasn't unusual for him to disappear over the years when his demons, his regrets, got too much to bear. But part of me was surprised he was willing to risk his job with the team.

"Oh, Harper, I didn't see you there." Natalie came into the kitchen, making a beeline for the refrigerator.

"I'll be out of your way in a second," I said.

"You don't have to rush off."

444 L A COTTON

I frowned. That was new.

"Look, I'm sorry, okay? I've been a total bitch to you since the beginning of the semester."

"I guess we're doing this," I murmured, leaning back against the counter, staring at her. Waiting. Because if she thought I was going to make this easy on her. She was wrong.

"It's my issue, not yours."

"You don't say. You didn't even give me a chance."

"Fresh start?" Her smile might have been all bright, white teeth and full of apology, but the olive branch felt insincere.

As far as I was concerned, she could keep it. I didn't need her or anyone else's validation.

"To be honest, Natalie." I pushed off the counter and stood tall. "I'm not interested in being friends with someone who will stab me in the back the second I turn around."

"W-what?"

"Enjoy your smoothie," I said, grabbing my bagel and walking out of there feeling lighter than I had in days.

It had hurt when Janelle spewed all that crap at me. But it was about her, not me. She felt betrayed, and attack mode was the best form of defense. I wasn't a whore. And I certainly wasn't going to let the likes of her and Natalie dictate how I felt about myself.

Upstairs in my room, I handed Mason a bottle of water and flopped down beside him on the bed.

"I had an interesting conversation with Natalie just now."

"Oh yeah?" He played dumb.

"Yeah, it was so weird... she tried to apologize."

"Huh, weird."

"I thought so. All these weeks, she could have offered me an olive branch, but she chooses the week you've spent more time here than you have at Lakers House."

"Maybe she's a fan."

"Or maybe," I climbed into his lap, straddling his thighs. "You said something to her?"

"I can't recall anything." He smirked, sliding his hands around my ass. "But I'm glad she got the message."

"Mason!" I swatted his chest. "You can't go around threatening everyone who's ever upset me."

"No?" He flipped us, rolling me beneath him and pinning me against the mattress. "Because it seems like the logical thing to me. Adams gets one more chance before I lay him the fuck out."

"I don't want you getting into trouble over me."

"I protect the things I care about, blondie. Always have. Always will." He leaned down, brushing a teasing kiss over my mouth. "Now, where were we?"

"You were hungry, I believe."

"That's right." He lowered himself down my body, taking my leggings with him. I let my legs fall open, baring myself.

"Fuck, Harper. Are you trying to kill me?" Mason ran a finger down the center of me. "These need to go." Slipping his fingers into the elastic of my panties, he slid them down my hips and wasted no time latching onto my pussy.

"Oh my God, Mase," I cried, jamming my fingers into his hair, holding him right there because, by God, it felt good as he licked me.

"You taste so fucking good." He came up for air, pressing two fingers slowly into me and curling them deep, watching my reaction as he teased me. "Play with your tits," he ordered. "I want to see how many times I can make you come before I fuck you."

A bolt of lust shot through me, tightening everything inside me. His dirty mouth was something else. But I loved that about him.

I was beginning to love a lot of things.

"Tits, babe," he growled, and I pushed my t-shirt up my body and unsnapped the front clasp on my bra, letting my breasts spill out.

I knew exactly how to touch myself to get off, but I liked to put on a show for Mason, rolling and tweaking my nipples while he ate my pussy.

"Yes," I whimpered, sparks of pleasure firing off around my body. "God, yes. I need..."

"I know what you need." Mason pulled his fingers out and speared his tongue inside me, his thumb working my clit.

I went off like a rocket, crying his name over and over.

Mason licked me through the ebbing waves before crawling up my body and kissing me hungrily. "Change of plans," he said. "I need to be inside you now."

"Yes." I slid my hand into the back of his hair, anchoring us together as he lined himself and slowly sank into me.

A groan of approval rumbled in his chest, a sound I would never tire of hearing. Because I did that. I made this broody, closed-off guy fall apart.

And there was no better feeling in the world.

Sunday, I agreed to work the lunchtime shift at Millers, which seemed like a really bad idea after a night of drinks and dancing with the girls.

Janelle had quit. A fact I didn't feel great about, but it wasn't my fault. I didn't even know she existed when Mason and I started fooling around.

The team was traveling back from Minnesota after back-to-back games against the University of Rochester. They'd lost one and drew the other, and part of me wondered if morale was down because of my father's sudden disappearing act.

"It's slow today," Kal said as I placed some empties on the end of the bar.

"Have you talked to Janelle?"

"Hell no. That ship has sailed. I'm team Harper all the way."

"Thanks," I chuckled. "I appreciate it. I hope we get some customers soon, or it's going to be a long—"

"Harper?" Kal said, but I couldn't speak, watching with disbelief as my father wandered into the bar and scanned the room. He found me, and his gaze darkened.

"Friend of yours?" Kal asked.

"Unfortunately. I'll handle this, okay?" I hurried over to him, my heart aching at the unkempt state of him. If I needed any proof that he'd fallen off the wagon again, this was it.

"Dad, what are you doing here?"

"So this is where you work?" He scoffed. "It isn't much."

I forced myself to take a deep breath, trying to usher him to a table in the back of the room. "Why don't you sit, and I'll get you something to drink."

"Whiskey?"

"I was thinking water or soda."

"My money is as good as anyone else's."

"Of course, it is. I just think—"

"You just couldn't keep your nose out of my business, could you?" he sneered, anger simmering in his bloodshot eyes.

"W-what?"

"Don't play dumb with me, girlie. First, your mother decides to grow a pair and tell me it's over. And then Joe tells me he's letting me go. Just like that, he cut me from the coaching staff. All because of you."

Mom had what?

I couldn't process what he was saying. It didn't make any sense. So I focused on the one thing I could.

"Dad, I swear, it wasn't me. I didn't talk to Coach Tucker. I didn't—"

"Lying, little bitch. You couldn't just let me have this could you?"

"Dad!" His words cut me open like jagged glass. No matter how much time passed or how old I got, when he got nasty like this, I was still the small girl desperately wanting her father to love her.

"That's not fair." My voice shook. "All I have ever wanted is for you to notice me."

"Notice you?" He laughed, but it was a brittle sound. "I've spent the last eighteen years trying my damned hardest to forget about you."

"Why? Why would you say that?" Pain lashed my insides. "What is so awful about having a daughter?"

"Because you were supposed to be my boy." He slammed his fist down on the table. "You were supposed to be my legacy. And instead, I got stuck with you."

My heart didn't just break. It shattered. I'd always

known he hated me. But knowing it and hearing him actually say the words were two very different things.

"I think you should leave," I said, voice trembling and tears rolling down my cheeks.

"I'll leave when I'm good and ready. Now get me that drink."

"No."

"No?" His bloodshot eyes fixed on mine. "I had it, Harper. I had it, and then it was gone, but being here, working with the team, that was my shot, and you ruined it. You ruined—"

"Enough."

Mason stepped up behind me, and relief and shame warred inside me as I sagged against him.

He was here. Mason was here, and I was so freaking relieved and so deeply, utterly ashamed.

"Mason, son. What are you doing here?"

"With all due respect, sir, what are you doing?"

"Mase," I grabbed his arm as he stepped around me, putting himself between my father and me.

My father tutted. "Don't be worrying yourself about Harper. She was just about to get me a drink." He tilted his head toward the bar. "What's a guy got to do to get a drink around this place."

"Dad, please, stop..."

"Don't talk to me, you little Judas. I'm telling you, Mason, don't ever trust a woman. They'll only stab you in the back the second you turn around."

"Okay, we're leaving," Mason went to grab my father, but he shoved him off.

"I'm not leaving until she admits she sold me out to Joe."

"It wasn't Harper." Anger vibrated from every inch of Mason.

"What are you saying, kid?"

"I was the one who told Coach Tucker, and I'd do it again in a heartbeat."

"You what?" Dad shot up out of his seat and got right in Mason's face.

"Dad!" I shrieked, lunging for them, but Kal rushed over and grabbed me, pulling me away from them.

"Kal, do something," I begged.

"Your guy can handle himself," he said. "Look."

Sure enough, Mason stood his ground, standing taller than my father by about an inch. But it wasn't his height that gave him the ace card; it was his expression. That arctic gaze that had frozen me to the core on more than one occasion.

Whatever my father saw there made him back off an inch. And another until he slumped down in the booth again. "You sold me out? After everything I've done for you."

"You have a problem, Coach. You need to get some help."

"What do you know about my problems? You've got the world at your feet, and you're too chickenshit to—"

"Okay, James, that's enough."

Coach Tucker and Coach Carson appeared both wearing the same disappointed expressions.

I was too stunned to fight Kal as he still held me tight, and I watched the Lakers coaches haul my father out of the booth and toward the door. But my father couldn't let it go. He had to have the last word.

"She's not worth it, kid," he yelled at Mason.

"Actually, sir, that's where you're wrong." Mason stepped forward. "Harper is a good person. Better than you'll ever be. But don't worry. I'll be all she needs. I'll love her enough that she'll never have to worry about you again."

"Oh my God," I gasped, clapping a hand over my mouth, my heart ready to burst out of my chest. Because had Mason really just said what I thought he had?

"That was pretty fucking epic," Kal whispered. "Especially for a hockey player."

Mason turned slowly, giving my father his back and settling his stormy gaze on mine. Kal let me go with a quiet, "Go get your guy, Dixie."

We moved like magnets, eating up the space between us until Mason was right there.

"Are you okay?" he said, reaching for me.

"I... that was so embarrassing. I can't believe he—"

"Harper, listen to me and listen good. I don't give a fuck what he said or did. I only care about you. So I'll ask you again. Are you okay?"

"Y-yeah, I think so. I... you said you love me."

"Caught that, huh?" His mouth tipped up.

"Is it...?"

"True? What do you think, blondie?"

"I don't know." I went up on my tiptoes and looped my arms around his neck. "Maybe you should say it again. Just so I can be sure."

"I love you, Harper Rose Dixon. I don't know when the fuck it happened, and it caught me by surprise, but it doesn't make it any less true. I love you."

"Thanks. That's really nice of you. But I'm sorry, I'm not sure—"

Mason attacked me, digging his fingers into my sides and tickling me.

"Okay, okay, you got me," I conceded. "I'll say it."

Mason drew me closer, leaning down and touching his head to mine, completely uncaring that we had a small audience of Kal and the few diners seated at their tables.

"Only say it if you mean it," he whispered, a flicker of vulnerability in his eyes.

"I, Harper Rose Dixon, love you, Mason—"

"Matthew."

"Mason Matthew Steele."

"Thank fuck for that." He grinned, and I grinned back.

Because Mason loved me.

The boy with ice around his heart loved the girl with her heart on her sleeve.

And it didn't get much better than that.

"Sweetheart, thank God," Mom rushed out. "I've been worried sick."

"I'm okay," I said, hugging myself tight as I stood outside of the ice rink.

After the disaster at Millers, Mason had sweet-talked Chad into letting me finish my shift early. He agreed, but only if Mason promised to bring the team by once a week.

Mason didn't even hesitate.

He'd whisked me away from Lakeshore and straight to his house in Pittsburgh, where we picked up Scottie and his mom and headed to the rink.

It was exactly what I needed.

I'd called Mom on the ride over but had gotten her voicemail. In some ways, I'd been relieved. I wasn't ready to talk to her about everything. But after five missed calls and two text messages, and a few words of encouragement from Melinda, I finally picked up.

"Harper, I am so, so sorry. I didn't know he would do that. I didn't—"

"Yeah, Mom, you did." A fresh wave of tears rose up inside me. "You just didn't want to believe it."

"Gosh, sweetheart. You're right. I haven't been the mom you deserve. I love you so much, Harper Rose, but he's my husband, and I love him. I think a part of me will always love him, but he's ill, Harper. Your father is ill, and he needs help, and I won't keep picking up his slack."

"So you meant it then? You're really leaving him?"

"I am."

"Why didn't you tell me?"

"Because I didn't know if I could go through with it, and I didn't want you to be disappointed in me."

"It's a little late for that, Mom."

She sucked in a sharp breath. "I deserve that. But love is complicated, sweetheart."

"I met someone," I blurted out. "And he loves me, Mom. He loves *me*."

"Y-you met someone?" Her disbelief spoke volumes. "I didn't know."

"There's a lot you don't know about me."

"I guess there is." Sadness bled into her voice. "But I hope you'll let me fix that, sweetheart. I hope it isn't too late for us."

"I need some time, Mom. To figure some things out."

"Of course, take all the time you need. I'll be right here whenever you're ready."

"Okay."

"And Harper?"

"Yes, Mom?"

"I love you, sweetheart. And I know I haven't always shown it, but I'm proud of you, baby. I'm so, so proud."

We said goodbye and hung up, and oddly, I felt

lighter. Things would take time to heal between us, but part of me knew she was a victim, too. It didn't excuse her taking sides over the years, but I got it. She loved him, and she was right; sometimes, love made you do crazy things.

"Is everything okay?" Melinda asked me as I rejoined her on the bench.

"Yeah, I think so."

She reached over and patted my hand, offering me a warm smile.

"Seriously, bud, have you been practicing on the sly?" Mason gawked after Scottie as he deked around his older brother and took off toward the net with the puck.

"Go, Scottie." Melinda and I clapped, watching Mason get his ass handed to him by a twelve-year-old.

"I hope I'm not speaking out of turn," she said. "But Mason told me some things... about your father, and I just wanted to say that you will always have a place here with us. Even if that son of mine screws things up between you guys. And I'll let you in on a little secret, I'm really hoping he doesn't." Melinda winked. "My boys both see something in you, and it's your heart, Harper. The fact Mason trusts you with Scottie tells me all I need to know, and I'm just so happy you met my boy. Or should I say boys."

"Thank you. That means a lot."

She squeezed my hand again. "You should go out there with them. I know Scottie would love it."

"I don't want to impede on their time together."

"Harper, they love you. Go. I'll be more than happy watching from the sidelines." She gave me a reassuring pat on the hand.

With a small nod, I got up and headed for the ice.

"Harper. Harper's coming on." Scottie headed in my direction, his one-on-one game with Mason all but forgotten.

"Look at you," I said. "You're doing so good out here."

"I'm not scared anymore," he beamed. "Check this out." Scottie whizzed around me in circles, making me a little dizzy.

"Okay, bud. Why don't we let Harper find her balance before wowing her with your skills."

"I've got skills, too, you know," I teased.

"Show me, show me." Scottie took off toward the net, leaving me with Mason.

"Go easy on him. He likes to win," he said.

"So this is strategic losing?" I arched a brow, smothering my laughter. "Because from where I was sitting, it looked a hell of a lot like Scottie was out skating you."

"He's my little brother. Of course I'm going to let him win."

"Right. And me? Will you let me win?"

He closed the gap, lowering his face to mine. "Always."

"Harper, Harper. Come on. I want to show you—"

"He's going to steal you away every time we bring him out here, isn't he?" Mason grumbled, but my heart soared at the fact he was already thinking about next time.

"That's because I'm his favorite."

"No way. I'm his big brother. He idolizes me."

"You really want to put it to the test?"

"Funny." Mason scowled. "I don't mind sharing you on the ice. So long as I get you all to myself off it."

"So you don't want to take him to the arcade after we get done here?" I gave him a coy smile.

"You told him we'd... fine. The arcade. But then this ass is mine." He palmed my butt before pushing off on his skates and whizzing down the ice.

My smile was so wide my cheeks hurt. But this was family. Mason, Scottie, and their mom. The way they laughed and loved together. And now I was a part of that.

"Harper is on my team," Scottie announced the second I reached them.

"Hang on a minute," Mason said. "That's not really fair. Harper's good."

"But she's a girl." Scottie frowned.

"Girls can play hockey. Some can even play better than boys." My eyes flicked to Mason, and he arched a brow.

"Is that so, blondie?"

"Guess we'll find out. Ready, buddy?" I asked Scottie, who nodded eagerly. "Okay, so in a second, you drop the puck in the middle." I faced off against Mason.

"You're going down, blondie."

"Fighting talk for a guy who's about to get his ass handed to him."

Mason smirked. "Bring it on."

"Don't you hurt her, Mason brother," Scottie chimed, and I fought a smile.

"Wouldn't dream of it," Mason mumbled.

"Good. Because she won't marry you if you hurt her, and then she won't be my sister."

Mason looked alarmed for a second, but then his eyes softened. "Yeah, bud. You're right. I promise to be careful with her." His eyes locked on mine, his gaze like a warm caress as he mouthed, "I love you."

"I love you, too," I mouthed back. Aware that we had a small audience but not caring one bit.

"I love you three," Scottie shouted, flapping his hands with excitement, and Mason exploded with laughter, lunging for his brother and ruffling his hair.

This was family.

This was everything I'd ever wanted.

And I was going to hold onto it for as long as I could.

EPILOGUE

MASON

"WE MADE YOU SUGAR COOKIES," Scottie announced the second I stepped into the kitchen.

"I thought something smelled good." I ruffled my brother's hair before squeezing Harper's shoulder and peering over her shoulder. "What are they supposed to be?"

"Hockey stick candy canes." He pointed to half of the oddly shaped cookies. "And these are goalie Santas, obviously."

"Obviously." I stifled a laugh.

"Hey, don't mock the cookies." Harper twisted around to look me in the eye. "We worked hard on these."

"We made a gluten-free batch, too. So Harper won't get the cross-tamination."

"Good thinking, bud. Can I borrow you for a second?" I asked Harper, and she nodded.

"Keep piping the icing like I showed you," she instructed Scottie.

"I got it," he said.

She smiled, following me up and out of the kitchen. "How is he?" she asked.

"Pissed."

"Yeah, I know that, Mase. But *how* is he? What is his mental state like?"

"He's still getting his head around it all. But you know Connor, he'll bounce back."

"I still can't believe he could be out for the rest of the season."

In our last game before the winter break, Connor took a nasty hit and tore his MCL. They were currently going back and forth on whether to operate or not.

I wanted to believe he could make it back to the team before the season ended, but if he ended up having the surgery, it would be a longshot. And if he didn't, he could do more damage.

"I'm sure Ella is keeping him distracted. They just need to make a decision so he can get into physical therapy and work toward getting better."

Harper wrapped her arms around my waist and gazed up at me. "He must be devastated."

"He isn't thrilled. But he's putting on a brave face. I told him we'd go see him once the festivities are over."

"I'd like that." She went up on her toes and kissed me.

"Hmm." I banded my arm tighter, pulling her closer. "Don't tease me. Especially not while we have Scottie and your mom to babysit." My hands skated down to her ass, grabbing a handful.

"Now who's teasing?" She quirked a brow, and I dove in for another kiss, swallowing her little whimpers as my tongue slicked into her mouth.

"Mase," she murmured, pressing her body against mine. I couldn't resist grabbing her thigh and hitching her leg around me, so I could grind against her and—

"I'm home," Mom called from the other end of the house, and I let out a frustrated sigh, dropping my head to Harper's shoulder.

"Later, hotshot," she chuckled, tapping my chest.

"You say that now. Wait until Scottie decides to join us for a midnight analysis of the Lakers' chances this season."

"We both know you're going all the way." She cupped my face, her big blue eyes locking on mine. "I love you."

"I love you too."

So fucking much that sometimes I didn't know what to do with all the emotions inside me.

We'd spent the last few weeks easing into our relationship. I stayed over at Harper's more than I stayed at Lakers House. We'd study or watch a movie, or I hung out at Millers when she worked a late shift.

Then I walked her back to Hocking Hall where I'd spend time learning all the ways to make her come undone. We spent a lot of time with Scottie too.

It was important to me that he knew I hadn't replaced him—that Harper loved him almost as much as I did. Especially since things between him and Dad were a little strained after Claire did in fact get promoted to girlfriend. It hadn't come as a shock to me, but Scottie was having a hard time adjusting. More and more, he chose spending time with us over Dad, but I wasn't ever going to force him into a situation where he was uncomfortable. So the three of us went to the rink or played video games, or I watched whatever their latest harebrained idea was. Anything to make him happy.

Until Connor got injured, life was pretty fucking fantastic. The team was on a near-perfect winning streak. I'd been invited to practice with the Blue Jackets in the new year. Harper and her mom were slowly rebuilding their strained relationship. And Scottie had made two new friends at the RCC. Friends who understood what it was to be different.

Watching them together—the girl I loved and the boy I'd do anything to protect—was one of my favorite things, even if I occasionally got a little jealous.

Harper and Scottie had a special bond. He trusted her. And most importantly, I trusted *her* with him.

"Harper," Scottie called, a hint of impatience in his voice, and I smiled.

"What?" Harper asked.

"I'm beginning to think you're right."

"Right?"

"He loves you more than me."

"Not possible." She nudged my shoulder as we walked back into the kitchen. "You're his idol."

We found Scottie in the kitchen with Mom and Harper's mom, Harriet.

"Told you they were kissing," Scottie deadpanned, hyper-focused on piping a Lakers-themed pattern on the cookies.

"We weren't—"

"Harper's lips are all puffy." Scottie tipped his head as if to say, 'You know I'm right.'

Mom and Harriet both smothered a chuckle.

"We thought we might take Scottie to the holiday market in town tonight," she said.

"Mason and Harper will come with us?" he said.

"Actually, bud. I was kind of hoping to take Harper out tonight. Just the two of us."

His eyes lifted to mine, and I braced myself for the inevitable fallout. Scottie had been glued to us since we got here a few days ago, and we'd had a lot of fun together. But I needed some time with my girl.

Alone time.

"Where will you go?" he asked.

"It's a surprise. But we'll tell you all about it tomorrow."

"Mase..." Harper started, but I squeezed her hand.

"I could come. I bet Harper wants me to—"

"The market will be fun," Mom said. "And I know Harriet is looking forward to spending some time with you."

"I was hoping you could show me all the best spots," she said with a warm smile.

Scottie looked to me again. "Fine."

"Thanks, buddy. We'll make it up to you."

"I know." He gave me a small dismissive shrug and went back to his sugar cookies.

"A date, huh?" Harper whispered. "What should I wear?"

"Doesn't matter," I replied, wrapping her into my arms while the women helped Scottie start to clean up. "Because I'll only be stripping you out of them the first chance I get."

HARPER

"It's so beautiful out here," I said, pulling the blanket up around my chest. Mason tucked me closer into his side, dropping a kiss on my head.

"I thought you'd like it."

"It's perfect."

The little restaurant was a small rustic place set on the edge of the Allegheny River. The owners had set up a huge fire pit out back with a view of the small outside skating rink they had erected for the holidays.

We'd finished dinner and came outside to enjoy the atmosphere.

It was perfect.

He was perfect.

Mason Steele. My boyfriend.

Mine.

There were days when I still couldn't believe it.

"Do you want to skate?" Mason asked me.

"Maybe later."

I was more than content just sitting here, taking it all in.

He checked his cell phone again, and I frowned. "Expecting a call?"

"I..."

"Mason?" I twisted around to look at him a little closer.

"So I might have—"

"Mind if we join you?"

"Rory?" My head whipped around. "What are you doing here?"

"Surprise," she beamed.

"Hey, Dixie, looking good."

"I thought I told you not to call me that." I glowered at Noah.

He, Connor, and the rest of the guys thought it was hilarious to adopt Chad's nickname for me. I, on the other hand, didn't feel so great about it.

"Oh, come on, you love it." He grinned, holding out his hand to Mason. "You're looking good too, bro."

"Fucking idiot," Mason tsked, and we all laughed.

"I still don't get it. You're here. I thought you were staying in Lakeshore."

"We are." Rory and Noah sat down on the double bench beside us. "But we thought we'd come surprise you."

"Mom invited them to spend a few nights," Mason said. "But I wanted to surprise you."

"As an early Christmas present, we've booked you girls into a spa for the day," Noah added. "While Mase and I take little bro skating."

"That's... thank you." I kissed Mason, soft and lingering. Noah cleared his throat, a smug smile plastered on his face.

Mason flipped him off, demanding one more kiss.

"Sorry," I said, cheeks burning. "We get carried away sometimes."

"I know that feeling." Aurora flashed me a small, knowing smile.

"Have you talked to Ella?" I asked her, and her expression dropped.

"She's holding it together for Connor. But I know she's crushed. It's his dream. All he's ever wanted, and now—"

"Positive thoughts only, shortcake." Noah wrapped his arm around Rory, and she laid her head on his shoulder. "If anyone can be back on the ice in time for the Frozen Four, it's Con."

"Is it wrong that we're here? Enjoying ourselves while they're—"

"Nope. We're not doing that," Noah added. "Connor will make a full recovery, and we will win the tournament. He'll go on to marry Ella and have a long and happy career with the Flyers."

Rory sucked in a sharp breath, and the three of them shared a sad look.

"What?" I asked, sensing I was missing something.

"He was going to propose," Rory said. "On Christmas morning."

"Oh, my God."

"Picked out the ring and everything," Noah said grimly.

"When he's feeling up to it, we should do something nice for them," I suggested.

"We will. He's one of us. Just because he's out doesn't mean we'll forget about him."

As the three of them discussed the remaining games the Lakers had coming up, my thoughts turned to my dad.

I knew what losing your dream could do to a person. But the guys were right; it wasn't a career-ending injury. Connor could come back from this, and he and Ella would be fine.

There had been no contact from my dad. Not since that night at Millers, where he'd told me exactly what he thought of me. It didn't hurt as much now as it had then. Because I realized family wasn't always the people you shared DNA with—it was the people you chose—the people who chose you right back.

I had Mason, Melinda, and Scottie. I had Mom, although that relationship would take some time to heal. And I had Rory and the girls.

If anything, I pitied my father. He hadn't been able to let go of his dream to see what was right in front of him, and that was his loss because he would never get to know what a good person I was.

"Hey, you okay?" Mason nudged my arm, and I looked up at him, smiling.

"Yeah."

Because I had all that I needed right here.

Mason was my home now.

MASON

"Shh, blondie. You gotta be—"

"Ah," Harper cried, but I swallowed the breathy sounds, plunging my tongue into her mouth as she rode me. Slow and deep, her pussy clenched around my dick like a fucking vise.

She was perfect.

And she was mine.

I would never get enough of this, of her.

"It's too deep," she murmured, trying to drag air into her lungs as her hips rocked in little circles.

"You're saying one thing, but your pussy is saying

another, babe." I spanned my hand around the back of her neck, crushing us together.

"Mase..."

"Quiet, babe." I snapped my hips up, keeping one hand on her waist to control the pace. "You gotta be quiet."

We had a house full of people.

Granted, everyone was supposed to be sleeping after a night of too much food, beer, and skating.

Harper had fallen asleep almost instantly, but I'd woken her up with my mouth on her clit, and my fingers buried deep inside her. I needed some time with my girl. Needed to feel her come apart, hear her cry my name.

I just needed her.

"God, you get me so fucking hot," I praised, licking up her throat and tugging her earlobe between my teeth.

"Mmm." She rocked faster, her eyelids fluttering as she struggled to stay focused.

"Eyes, babe. I need your eyes."

They snapped open, two blue pools I wanted to drown in.

"I love you," I said, voice thick with lust and emotion.

"I love you too. So much."

"Come for me then. Show me," I demanded, slipping a hand between us to massage her tits.

"Mase!" Her head fell back as she came hard, rippling around me.

"Fuck, Harper, I can feel you..."

"I... so good... so, so good." She curved her hand around the back of my neck, anchoring us together as I raced toward my own release, fucking into her like a man possessed.

"You said we had to be quiet."

"Let's hope everyone's asleep then," I gritted out, so close.

So, so cl—

Pleasure barreled down my spine as I filled her up. "Mine," I breathed against her lips.

"Yours."

I'd been so adamant I didn't need the distraction or drama that came with a girlfriend. But Harper had shown me that love didn't make you weak.

It made you strong.

It gave you something worth fighting for.

Something worth living for.

And it gave me a deep sense of peace knowing that whatever came our way in the future, we'd face it...

Together.

BONUS EPILOGUE

HARPER

"Gunner, you've got to pass the puck, kid." Mason ran a hand down his face as he skated over. "If your teammate is open and you find yourself pinned down by the other team pass the puck."

"But I want to score," Gunner said as if it was the simplest thing in the world.

"Don't we all, kid. Don't we all."

"He's good with them," Jet joined me as I watched Mason lean down and try and explain things to Gunner, one of the kids who attended the inclusion group at the RCC.

Over the Christmas break, Jet had invited Coach Tucker and Mason in to talk to him about the possibility of establishing a regular hockey session for the kids. That had been almost two and a half months ago, and it had been a huge success. Mason's patience and understanding coupled with Scottie's newfound enthusiasm for skating had the kids eager to come and give it a try.

"Yeah, he is." I smiled, my heart doing that silly little flip it did whenever I thought about Mason.

"You're good with them too," Jet added.

"Thanks."

"In fact, he might need your help right about now." Laughter rumbled in his chest as Gunner tried to steal the puck off Mason, another one of the kids swooping in to help.

"Oh God," I chuckled, excusing myself.

I headed onto the ice, hardly surprised when Scottie skated straight over. "This always happens." He let out an exasperated breath. "Now we'll never finish the game."

"It's all part of the fun though," I said, gently shoulder checking him.

Scottie didn't look convinced, but he followed me over to Mason and Gunner.

"Hey," I said, trying to keep a safe distance from Mason.

He noticed, frowning. "What are you doing all the way over there?" He came for me, trying to slip his hand around my waist.

"Mason, the kids," I scolded. "And Jet is right over there."

"I can behave."

"Mm-hmm."

"Your brother and his girlfriend are gross," Gunner said to Scottie who nodded.

"It's even worse when they stay over. They make all these noises in the night and—"

"Okay, you two." Mason threw me a horrified look as he ushered the kids toward the rest of the team. "Back to it. I'm determined to get you to nail this play."

I smothered a laugh, mouthing, "I love you."

His expression softened as he mouthed it right back.

I loved him like this, patient and understanding with the kids. He was such a positive role model for them, and there was something incredibly sexy about watching him lead a bunch of eleven- to thirteen-year-olds on the ice.

I was so enamored watching him, I didn't realize everyone was looking at me.

"What?" I asked, cheeks flaming at the sudden attention.

"We're waiting for you," Scottie said.

"Me?" My brows furrowed.

"Yeah, Mase said we can't start without our best player."

"And... I'm your best player?" My eyes flicked to Mason.

"Always, Dixon. Now let's play some hockey."

MASON

"At last." I kissed my way up Harper's neck, licking and sucking the soft skin there, soaking up every whimper and moan she made.

"Mase..." Her laughter wrapped around me. "We should probably slow—"

"Nope. No. We should definitely speed up. You're wearing too many clothes, blondie. I need you naked and under me, now."

"You had me this morning." She slid her hands to my chest and shoved gently.

"And I need you again." I wanted her all the fucking time.

Harper relented, reaching between us so she could pull off her Lakers hoodie. The one I'd gotten her for Christmas with my number on it.

Yeah, I was that guy now. Putting my number on his girl and asking her to wear it as much as possible. But seeing her in it did things to me. Crazy fucking things.

"Mmm, I love your tits." My hand glided up her stomach and over the shell of her bra, squeezing.

"Mase..." she breathed.

"Tell me what you need, blondie."

"You." She grabbed the nape of my neck and smashed our mouths together, kissing me like a girl starved.

I let her take control for a second, let her wrap her tongue around mine and set the pace. My dick strained against my sweats, my blood sizzling in my veins as Harper devoured me.

"Fuck, you get me hot," I rasped against her mouth, sliding my fingers into her hair to take back the reins.

"I need you," she murmured, trying to steal another kiss but I held her just out of reach, studying her face. The deep flush to her cheeks, her swollen, slightly parted lips, her gorgeous blue eyes so full of lust and love and impatience.

Soft laughter rumbled in my chest. "What happened to 'we should probably slow down?'"

"Mase... don't tease me." She pouted, all sex and seduction.

Jesus, she was beautiful. Inside and out. And part of me still couldn't believe that she was mine.

M-Mase?" It was a small, uncertain whisper.

"Fucking love you, Harper Rose Dixon."

"Show me," she said, a flash of vulnerability in her eyes.

She needed this. The intimacy and the validation. And I got it. After what she'd endured at the hands of her father, I got it. A man I'd once respected.

After the truth came out that night at Millers, James had checked himself into rehab. But it was too little too late. He'd lost everything. His wife. His job. His reputation. His last shot at ever getting to know his incredible daughter. But I'd stay true to my words that day—I'd loved her enough for the both of us.

I couldn't drag myself off Harper long enough to

strip us both naked. My lips chased her skin as I pulled off her leggings, my hoodie, my sweats.

"Mason," she whispered, breath hitching as I grasped my dick and ran the crown through her pussy. "Oh my God."

"You're so fucking wet," I rasped, nudging up against her clit, teasing her.

I could make her come undone just like this but there was nothing better than getting her right to the edge then sinking inside her, feeling her pussy flutter and tighten around me.

"Fuck me, I need you to fuck— ah," she cried out as I slammed home, filling her up as deep as I could get.

"Wrap your legs around me," I demanded, pulling out slowly and rocking forward, making us both groan. She felt too fucking good, taking me so perfectly. My hand slid up her stomach and over her tits to collar her throat as I pounded into her, over and over. Relieved that, for once, we didn't have to worry about someone overhearing us.

We had the house to ourselves for a few hours, and the only way I wanted to spend them was deep inside my girl.

"Mason," Harper panted, barely able to catch her breath as pleasure streaked across her expression. "It's so good."

But I knew what would make it even better.

Licking down her throat, I lowered my head to catch her nipple between my teeth.

"God," she cried as I licked and laved. "I'm so close."

"Give it to me then," I urged, desperate to feel her fall apart again.

I teased the small peak, switching from breast to breast as I slowed my pace, grinding my pelvis against her clit.

"Yes... yes... oh God." She came hard, crying my name over and over, giving me exactly what I wanted. "I love you," she breathed, gazing up at me.

"Fucking love you too." I kissed her, chasing my own release. Wanting nothing more than to lose myself in her.

Harper wasn't my escape, she was my home. My safe space.

My sanctuary.

She was the best fucking thing to happen to me, and I would never take that for granted.

Not for a second.

HARPER

"Wow, Noah, the place looks great," I said as we followed him inside his and Rory's newly decorated apartment.

"Doesn't it?" Rory beamed.

Aiden and Dayna were already here.

Mason held out his hand, pulling me in for a quick kiss.

"What was that for?" I asked, a little breathless.

"Just because." He smirked, and my stomach dipped.

"You girls go get comfy," Noah said. "Rory's made a bunch of food." He tilted his head toward the kitchen counter and the small spread there.

"And we have champagne," she added. Noah arched a brow at that, and she rolled her eyes. "We're celebrating. It's allowed."

"Damn right." Aiden came over. "We're going to regionals," he grinned.

"Fine. But no getting drunk," Noah conceded. "Last thing I need is you getting sick."

"You worry too much." Rory leaned up and kissed his cheek. "Come on, Harper." She grabbed my hand. "Let's leave the guys to it. I'll give you the tour."

"Hey," Dayna said as we joined her. "This is nice."

"Right? I love it here." Rory grinned. "I was worried that it might be too soon. But Noah was over at my place all the time, so it made sense. Although I'm not sure Austin will forgive me anytime soon."

"He's still sulking?" I asked, and she grimaced.

"After everything with Connor and then Noah moving out, he's a little sore about things."

"So I'm guessing he didn't tell you yet then?" I asked.

"Tell me what?"

"Me and Mason are moving in."

"What?" Her eyes went wide.

"Yep. We're taking your old room on the third floor. Mason is over living at Lakers House, and I've never really liked it at Hocking Hall, but I couldn't afford anything else."

"So you're going to live with my brother and Connor?"

"They're seniors." I shrugged. "They won't be around forever. And that house is too perfect to let it slip through our fingers. Austin actually approached Mason about it."

"Well, so long as you're happy, that's all that matters." Dayna smiled.

"Thanks, I think it'll be a good move. There's an empty room for Scottie to sleepover so it's kind of perfect."

"It's kind of crazy to think that Connor and Ella have been together the longest and—"

"Dayna," Rory shook her head. "Positive vibes only remember."

"I know. I want to believe they can work through it, but it's been tough on her."

"Tough on both of them," Rory corrected.

"Yeah."

Silence descended over us until Rory let out a small sigh. "Today is supposed to be a celebration," she said. "We can worry about them without letting it dampen your good news and the team's shot at the championship."

"You're right," Dayna said, hopping up. "We need a

little pick-me-up." She went over to the counter to retrieve the bottle of champagne and three glasses.

"Here." She came back, offering each of us one before uncorking the bottle and filling our glasses. "To Rory and Noah, on their new apartment," she said.

"And Harper and Mason on their exciting news," Rory added, and they both looked expectantly at me.

My eyes flicked to the guys, and Mason's eyes found mine.

"To them," I said. "The men who love us."

His mouth curved with recognition and my heart fluttered.

"To loving a Laker." Dayna chuckled. "I'll toast to that."

"Me too." Rory said, and I dragged my eyes off my man, raising my glass to my friends.

"To loving a Laker."

PLAYLIST

In the Stars - Benson Boone

Flowers - Lauren Spencer Smith

Love You From A Distance - Ashley Kutcher

TV - Billie Eilish

Testosterone - Grace Davies

1 step forward, 3 steps back - Olivia Rodrigo

Snow On The Beach - Taylor Swift, Lana Del Ray

Memories - Conan Gray

Control - Zoe Wees

Saturday Night's Alright (for Fighting) - Nickleback

Red Flags - Mimi Webb

Love In The Dark - Adele

If You Ask To Me - Charli D'Amelio

Falling Apart - Michael Schulte

While You're At It - Jessie Murph

Traitor - Olivia Rodrigo

Long & Lost - Florence and the Machine
People - Libianca
While You're At It - Jessie Murph
Your Daughter - Chase McDaniel
Wings - Jonas Brothers

ACKNOWLEDGMENTS

I had so much fun writing Mason and Harper's story (and let's not forget Scottie - that kid is the best). This group of characters are shaping up to be one of my favorites. I hope you're enjoying them as much as I am.

Next up, is Connor and Ella. I hadn't planned to write them a full book but Connor has been very loud throughout the other books. Brace yourself though, because things are about to get rocky... but I promise it'll be worth it.

Once again, thank you to my beta team for being on hand to help me - Jen, Amanda, Carrie, and Jenn - I appreciate your insight and feedback. Special shout to Jen for putting up with all my questions!

To my editor Kate, and proofreaders, Darlene and Athena, thank you for working to my tight deadlines! To all my Promo and ARC Team members, thank you for your continued support. And a special shoutout to my audio producer Kim over at Audibly Addicted for bringing this series to life - I'm so excited to hear grumpy Mason.

And, of course, a huge thank you to all the readers,

bloggers, bookstagrammers, and booktokkers who have supported the series - your continued support means everything.

Until next time...

L A xo

ABOUT THE AUTHOR

Reckless Love. Wild Hearts

USA Today and *Wall Street Journal* bestselling author of over forty mature young adult and new adult novels, L. A. is happiest writing the kind of books she loves to read: addictive stories full of teenage angst, tension, twists, and turns.

Home is a small town in the middle of England where she currently juggles being a full-time writer with being a mother/referee to two little people. In her spare time (and when she's not camped out in front of the laptop), you'll most likely find L. A. immersed in a book, escaping the chaos that is life.

L. A. loves connecting with readers.
The best places to find her are:
www.lacotton.com